Flashman's Waterloo

Robert Brightwell

This book is dedicated to my parents,
David and Sheila Brightwell

Published in 2016 by FeedARead.com Publishing

First Edition

A CIP catalogue record for this title is available from the British
Library.

**Headlines from the French *Moniteur* newspaper covering the
return of Napoleon:**
- 10 March: The Corsican ogre has just landed in Golfe-Juan
- 11 March: The tiger has arrived at Gap
- 12 March: The monster has slept in Grenoble
- 13 March: The tyrant has crossed Lyon
- 18 March: The usurper has been seen sixty leagues from Paris
- 19 March: Bonaparte strides along but he will never enter Paris
- 20 March: Napoleon will be tomorrow below our city walls
- 21 March: The Emperor has reached Fontainebleau
- 22 March: His Imperial and Royal Majesty entered yesterday his
castle of Tuileries among his lawful subjects

Introduction

This sixth packet of memoirs from the notorious Georgian rogue, Thomas Flashman, covers the extraordinary events that culminated in a battle just south of Brussels, near a place called Waterloo.

The first six months of 1815 were a pivotal time in European history. As a result, countless books have been written by men who were there and by those who studied it afterwards. But despite this wealth of material, there are still many unanswered questions including:

- Why did the man who promised to bring Napoleon back in an iron cage, instead join his old commander?
- Why was Wellington so convinced that the French would not attack when they did?
- Why was the French emperor ill during the height of the battle, leaving its management to the hot-headed Marshal Ney?
- What possessed Ney to launch a huge and disastrous cavalry charge in the middle of the battle?
- Why did the British Head of Intelligence always walk with a limp after the conflict?

The answer to all these questions in full or in part, can be summed up in one word: Flashman.

This extraordinary tale is aligned with other historical accounts of the Waterloo campaign and reveals how Flashman's attempt to embrace the quiet diplomatic life backfires spectacularly. The memoir provides a unique insight into how Napoleon returned to power, the treachery and intrigues around his hundred day rule and how ultimately he was robbed of victory. It includes the return of old friends and enemies from both sides of the conflict and is a fitting climax to Thomas Flashman's Napoleonic adventures. As always, if you have not read them already, the adventures of Thomas' nephew in the later Victorian era, edited by George MacDonald Fraser, are strongly recommended.

Robert Brightwell

"Are you sure we should be doing this, sir?" asked old Jasper as I pushed the creaking door open.

"Oh yes, it is a little treat I have promised myself for a long time."

"But they will hear us in the big house, sir. I don't think her ladyship will be happy."

"Nonsense man, it is three in the morning; they will all be asleep. Now put your fiddle down and light some of these candles so that we can see what we are doing." I held up my lantern to shine its beam across the little chapel. There were eight short pews down either side of the aisle and a small stone altar at the far end, but it was not these I was interested in. I walked down one side using the light to read the memorials on the wall to the local worthies.

After six years abroad, the last two living mostly in wooden lodges, it was strangely comforting to be back within the solid stone walls I had known in my childhood. I knew many of the families whose names were carved into the stone slabs and just a mile away was another chapel where my own ancestors resided. As the light grew in the little church so did a feeling of unease about what I was planning to do, but I pushed it aside and looked down at the tombstones set in the floor for my quarry.

"Here it is, sir," called Jasper from the other side of the church. I grinned in delight as I saw the new crisply carved tomb that he was pointing to. It was chest high, cut in local limestone and capped with a large brass plaque.

"It was good of him to keep the top nice and flat, that will make things much easier," I crowed as I strolled across. One of the heavy oak pews had been shortened to make room for this fresh edifice, which made some useful steps up to its surface. In a moment I was standing on it and staring down at the polished inscription glinting in the light from the lantern at my feet. The name *Lord Augustus Berkeley* was followed by a nauseating description of the peer's virtues, which bore no similarity to the permanently bad-tempered, overbearing, vicious and spiteful villain I remembered.

"Noble and charitable my arse," I scoffed staring down at it. I didn't recall any charity when I was forced to flee to India back in '02 to avoid his lordship's heavies. Admittedly he had just discovered I had bedded both of his daughters in a single night, but that was not entirely my fault. We had been in Paris then, but his henchmen had pursued me all the way to London, where they doubtless had orders to break my skull and drop my body in a weighted sack from a bridge over the Thames. I had promised myself then, as I was forced to sail away on the Indiaman to the other side of the world, that one day I would come back and dance on his grave. Now that promise was about to be fulfilled. "Go on Jasper, get your fiddle and strike up a jig."

As the old family retainer moved to the back of the chapel to retrieve his instrument, still grumbling to himself that no good would come of the night's work, I reflected that this was not quite how I had expected my homecoming to begin. My ship from Canada had landed three days before. My friend Campbell and I had caught the stage from Portsmouth to London but then found I had missed the mail coach north. Too impatient to wait for the next one, I had hired a horse and come on alone.

Despite changing my mount halfway, it had still taken me two days and it was well past nightfall when I reached the Flashman family estate. I had ridden the last few miles almost from memory as I could see little of where I was going, but eventually the hooves crunched up the gravel drive I had known so well. However, my plans for a jubilant homecoming had to be postponed; when Jasper had finally opened the front door to my persistent knocking, he told me that it was well past midnight and my father was a-bed having taken a sleeping draught for his gout.

"I will come back and see him in the morning, then," I told Jasper. "Now I want to go and see my son and find out what kind of welcome I can expect from my wife. Are they both well, do you know?" As readers of my earlier adventures will recall, I had only discovered my son's existence recently and had not spoken to my wife in six years.

"It will be too late for that now, sir," the old servant had cautioned. "They will be a-bed too. You had best spend the night here and see everyone in the morning." He had been right of course but I had been in no mood for sleeping, which had led to our current nocturnal adventure.

The first few notes scratched from Jasper's violin and while there was little room to dance, I started to shuffle my feet over the waste of brass that was Berkeley's eulogy.

"See, you old bastard," I shouted down at him. "I am still here and if there is any justice you will be in the fiery pit. Huh, you said I had no breeding but now you are just a breeding ground for worms, while here I am dancing over your rotten corpse, how do you like that?"

I think I must have been exhausted and part out of my mind as I had hardly slept in three days. Suddenly the whole situation seemed ridiculous and I just stood and roared with laughter. Jasper stopped playing and stared at me in astonishment as I shouted at him in delight, "I have only gone and bloody survived. Everything they threw at me and yet still I have made it back." God, there had been a lot too since I had last been in that chapel; I had faced countless columns of French infantry, Polish lancers, Spanish partisans, vengeful dwarfs, angry fathers and husbands, republican plotters, secret police and more recently, American soldiers, sailors and Iroquois warriors.

Despite all their efforts to kill me, in various colourful ways, I had made it back with nothing more than a few scars to show for their trouble. Now, at last, the future promised peace and tranquillity. The war in America was winding down; Napoleon had abdicated from the throne of France and was ruling his new kingdom, the little island of Elba. Europe was at peace at last. Nothing it seemed could disturb a well-earned period of rest and relaxation for one Major Thomas Flashman, soon to be retired on half pay and determined never to stand on a battlefield again.

In fact, I had not only survived, but if I played my cards right I could live a prosperous and comfortable life. My wife, Louisa, was now a wealthy woman, having inherited Berkeley's estate, while the reason our marriage had failed lay mouldering beneath my feet. But a lot can happen in six years, and I had no idea how my wife felt about her husband after her father had done his best to poison her against me.

6

Campbell had told me that a man called Lamb had been with her when he had last seen her in London. Jasper had also confirmed that this Lamb character had been spending a lot of time on the estate recently. Indeed, just before he died, Berkeley had been making enquiries at Horseguards, the headquarters of the army, to see if they would confirm me as dead so that Louisa could re-marry. Fortunately the wheels of officialdom work slowly. Horseguards wrote to Wellington, my former commander in Spain and his letter advising that I was in all probability dead, arrived only just after my letter from Canada confirming I was still very much with the living.

I had no idea if Louisa wanted to re-marry or if that was her father's idea. Campbell had confided that she must have had some feelings for me as she had asked him if there was any hope for my survival at their last meeting. Back then he had thought me dead too and she had cried when he told her that almost certainly I had been killed. Well I would just have to be especially endearing, give her time to get used to me being around again and rely on the old Flashy charm. What girl could resist that? I found that out a few seconds later.

"What on earth do you think you are doing dancing on my father's tomb?" The sharp female voice cracked through the chapel like a whip. As I whirled round I saw a woman in a hooded cloak walking towards me while another elderly servant looked nervously around the door behind her, holding a blunderbuss gun across his chest.

"Thomas!" She stopped in her tracks when she recognised me. As her head tilted up the candles showed me her face for the first time in six years and by God she was still a stunner. Sight of her took my breath away for an instant. She looked exactly the same as the girl I had married on an Indiaman ship ten years before, when we had both been twenty-three. My, a lot of water had passed under the bridge since then.

While I looked in wonder at her beauty, her eyes abruptly blazed with anger. "So this is the first thing you wanted to do when you got home, is it? No thought to see me or your son, just to dance over my father's body and taunt him in his grave?"

"No, no," I protested. I cast around for an excuse and saw one trying to sidle out of the chapel holding a fiddle. "He told me you would be asleep," I cried pointing an accusing finger at Jasper. The old man dutifully cringed from the look of scorn Louisa gave him before she whirled back to me.

"Don't try and tell me that dancing on my father's tomb was Jasper's idea as well," she raged as I started to climb down onto the stone floor.

As soon as I was on the ground I turned to face her, giving her what I hoped was my best winning smile and holding out my arms in welcome. "Come here, my darling, your husband is home."

She came all right. I barely had a chance to glimpse in the gloom of the church her right hand before it slapped me hard around the face. "Husband," she shouted scornfully. "I came halfway around the world to find you in India, but then you row with my father and never send me a single letter, not one in six years until you hear that I am rich."

Well that was just too much. "Damn you," I roared. "I don't care about your money; I have six years' rent from my London house untouched. I came because I wanted to see you and my son. And anyway," I added indignantly, "I did write, I must have written you a hundred letters. But your father, *the noble and charitable lord*, according to his inscription, burned them as they arrived and told me to stop writing as my correspondence would never be delivered." In truth I had written no more than a dozen letters before Berkeley responded, but my protestations took the wind out of her sails. She looked reproachfully at her father's tomb and evidently did not need convincing he was capable of such an act.

She continued in a softer tone, "Surely you realised that I would not have minded you waking me at any time of the night. I have had a man staying at the coaching inn at Rugby with horses for you ever since I got the news you were alive and coming home."

I had been on the back foot at the start of our conversation, but now I sensed I had the upper hand and I was determined to keep it. So I drew myself up a little and tried to look pompously stuffed as I responded, "I heard you have been spending a lot of time with a fellow called Lamb, I did not want to arrive unexpectedly and cause a scene."

"Charles and I are just good friends…"

"Charles Lamb… You don't mean old Spanker who used to be in Byron's crowd?" She coloured at that and I crowed in delight as I realised who my rival for her affections was. He was a timid fellow who had been in Byron's circle of friends years ago, when I had been trying to make some gelt selling them forged antiquities. I had heard in one of the fashionable brothels in town, that instead of rogering the girl, he got his jollies by spanking her instead. You can rest assured that I spread that story around so that he soon had his new nickname.

"So has he tanned your arse too?" I asked vindictively, and as her colour deepened I saw that he probably had. But unless you were a Haymarket whore, Charles Lamb was lamb by name and lamb by nature. He was notorious for avoiding any kind of conflict. I could just imagine that he was now terrified of coming across me. "Wait a minute, though," I queried as old memories came back to me. "Didn't he marry one of those girls who liked to dress up as a page boy to please Byron?"

"Yes," Louisa admitted irritably, "but there was a scandal and they are getting a divorce." I didn't know it then, but found out a few days later that it was a capital scandal too. It was the talk of London during 1813, not that gossip ever made it to Canada. Lady Caroline Lamb had become obsessed with Byron and had been having an affair with him before and during her marriage. But she had to compete with others for Byron's attention, including Spanker's own mother, who was another notorious society trollop. When Byron spurned Caroline Lamb she confronted him and made a tremendous scene which culminated in her trying to cut her own wrists with a broken champagne glass. Georgian society was infamously liberal, but it had its limits and that was going too far. A mistress had to know her place, especially if she was also someone else's wife! Caroline Lamb had been bustled away to Ireland, leaving Spanker to find amusement elsewhere.

He had been a junior minister in government and the son, at least legally as most doubted his paternity, of Lord Melbourne. As the

9

injured party in a divorce, I could imagine that Louisa's father would see him as a suitably noble marriage prospect. Berkeley was desperate for his daughter to shed her union to a disreputable but conveniently missing husband. Yes, it was a wedding that would have tidied up several loose ends, but now I had gone and ruined everything by re-appearing.

I had expected Louisa to look embarrassed or ashamed, but not a bit of it. Her chin rose and a shrewdly calculating look crossed her face. "If we are going to talk of gossip and rumour, we could talk about a story Lady Jersey told me of you and a Spanish woman in Seville Cathedral."

That shocked me, I can tell you. I knew that the story of Agustina and I had been the talk of the army in Spain after a spiteful priest tried to ruin my reputation, but I had no idea that the tale had reached England. "Whatever you heard is an outrageous lie," I blustered before she held up a hand to stop me.

"Thomas, let us both leave the past where it belongs." She came forward then, smiling at me, and put her arm through mine. "Come, husband, let me take you home."

Chapter 2

I awoke next morning in what must have been the lord's old bedroom in the centre of the house, with his naked daughter sleeping beside me. It gave me no small pleasure that the old bastard would be spinning in his grave if his ghost could see me. Everything he had, apart from his title, which went to a nephew, was now Louisa's – and as her husband, it was now mine too. It was not the money that was important, but the place in society. Despite my attempts to shirk every danger across several continents and campaigns, I had emerged with much credit. I was considered by many, including Wellington, as something of a hero and a man who had accomplished many challenging missions. But heroes were ten a penny now the war was over, with many already put on half pay. Instead my elevation from third son of a local landowner to having my own country estate, meant that I should have been able to live comfortably for the rest of my days. On top of that I had a son, my own flesh and blood, whose existence I had hitherto been unaware of.

I remember lying there that morning and being completely confident that I had seen the last of my army days. At last a life of pleasure and comfort was spread out before me, without the slightest hint of bayonet charges, murderous savages or the various other homicidal lunatics that I seemed to attract. For once I do not think it was naiveté on my part, for only one man could have possibly foreseen the extraordinary chain of events that were to come and he was sitting quietly on an island in the Mediterranean at the time. And even he could not have predicted the critical role that I was to play in the dramas ahead.

I saw my son for the first time that morning; he was named Thomas after me. A hatchet-faced harridan of a governess brought him to me while I was having breakfast. As I gazed at him in wonder, I was uncomfortably aware that I had no idea about dealing with children. I had not had much to do with them since I had been one myself. The boy looked as though he had been scrubbed to within an inch of his life. His cheeks positively glowed under carefully combed hair as he stared curiously at me in what were probably his best clothes.

"I am pleased to meet you, Papa," he intoned and then blow me if the little squirt did not give a bow in greeting. I roared with laughter at the stiff formality, causing the lad to step back a pace nervously while staring at his mother for a clue as to my amusement.

"Don't worry, lad," I said getting up and ruffling his blonde locks. "We will spend some time together this afternoon." I thought back to how my friend, the Iroquois warrior Black Eagle, had planned to spend time with his son when I had left him a couple of months previously. "I know, I will take you hunting."

The boy shrank back in alarm while the two women in the room reacted as though I had suggested an afternoon of hard liquor and cockfighting in the stews of London.

The governess got in first, puffing herself up like an outraged bullfrog. "Sir, the boy has lessons all afternoon."

"Well he will be missing them today, then, won't he?" I retorted. "I have not seen my son for six years; it will not matter if he misses some algebra. It is a waste of time anyway."

"But Thomas, your son is only just learning to ride," intervened Louisa more soothingly, "and there are no hunts organised for this afternoon."

"Don't you worry about that," I said grinning. "Leave that to me and I'll wager that we will bring home a nice fat buck for dinner, won't we, lad?" I said grinning encouragingly at him, but the boy appeared apprehensive at the prospect. He glanced appealing up at his governess as though he would prefer an afternoon of Latin verbs to a jaunt out with his father. Could this really be my son, I wondered; he had certainly not got his bookishness from me. The boy had his mother's green eyes and fair hair and I struggled to see a sign he had any Flashman blood at all. "Dress him in green and brown," I said curtly to the sour-faced governess as she started to lead the boy away. The last thing I needed was him being presented in a red jacket and white breeches for a traditional fox hunt.

After breakfast Louisa busied herself with her estate manager, making no effort to involve me in the running of my new home and lands. I did not mind as I wanted to ride back to the Flashman property and see my father. I thought he would tell me what had really been going on while I was away. I was shocked when I stepped into his study for he seemed to have aged at least a dozen years in the six I had been away.

"Why the devil did you not write to me before?" he scolded after he had heard my adventures.

"I couldn't while I was hiding in Paris and in Canada there are no mail coaches - the weather brings the whole country to a virtual standstill during parts of the year. But the governor general said he would include my arrival in one of his reports."

"Well if he did, someone supressed it. Old Berkeley spent the last year of his life trying to get you formally declared dead so that he could arrange for that Lamb fellow to marry Louisa."

"The bastard," I said with feeling. Then I decided to broach the subject that was uppermost in my mind. "Do you think Louisa still has feelings for Lamb?" I enquired as casually as I could. "How much time did he spend with her?"

The old man shot me a piercing glare. "You should know better than me what her feelings are towards you." He grinned then and added, "But I don't think you need to worry about that rascal. He could not get back to London fast enough when he learned that you were alive. He was well aware of your reputation."

"My reputation?" I asked puzzled. "What do you mean?"

"Good grief, boy, the papers have been full of your exploits while you have been away. Did you not lead a charge with some Spanish general at Talavera and then don a French uniform to discover that the French were planning to trap the British army? There was also the tale of you riding disguised as a Polish lancer in the midst of the French invasion force for Portugal. Then after you had been wounded at Albuera, we heard you were one of the first to fight your way into the fortress of Badajoz." He laughed and slapped his knee in delight, "Lamb knows that you must have killed countless men and I can only imagine the tricks you learned with those savages in Canada. He was terrified you would come after him when you discovered he had been dallying with your wife."

13

I sat back in my chair, stunned for a moment. While all those tales my father had heard were true, and there were more besides, not one of those actions was intentional. More often than not, I was screaming in fright at the time. I could not help but laugh out loud at the absurdity of the situation.

My father beamed at me and then leant forward and gripped my shoulder. "I have not had much chance to say this to you until now, but I am proud of you, son, right proud. I'll be honest and say that you have taken to soldiering a lot better than I thought you would. I did not think you had it in you as a boy."

"Oh you would have been surprised if you had seen me in Spain," I said nonchalantly. But by the devil, he would have been appalled after reading the papers, if he had seen the bowel-loosening moments of fear that had occasioned those tales. "But I am home now," I assured him. "And I have no intention of going abroad again," I added, with what later proved to be unfounded optimism.

He gave me the news then of my brothers and their families and how my investments had fared while I had been away. Then content that I was at least solvent, I returned to the Berkeley estate.

Thomas Junior was waiting for me in a green tweed suit and so I decided to change into the old buckskins I had brought back with me from Canada. Both the lad and Louisa looked bemused as I stood at the top of the stairs bedecked in tasselled suede, with my old tomahawk stuck in my belt and a borrowed musket under my arm.

"You can't go out dressed like that, you will be the talk of the village," exclaimed Louisa.

"Nonsense, they can prattle about what they want, but now my son and I are going hunting, aren't we, Thomas?" The boy looked a little uncertain on that point but dutifully followed his father out of the house and off towards the woods. I tried to engage him in conversation, but it was heavy going. He did not seem to have any friends among the village boys and compared to my childhood with two brothers, his life seemed very dull. The only time he appeared at all animated was when he told me about the book he was reading. I could not help but doubt his parentage again; perhaps there were

14

others before Lamb that my father was not aware of. I knew all too well that Louisa's sister had whelped a kid with a coachman on the estate. If you have read my earlier memoirs you will know how that incident nearly got me killed. I wondered if Louisa had pleasured herself with the servants while I had been away. She was a passionate woman and it was hard to believe that Lamb had been her only lover.

The lad and I strolled across the fields and entered the woods at the edge of the estate. I knew there were deer in those trees as I had seen many while riding along the track that led through the middle of them. We left the path and started to stalk silently through the woodland. I had eventually got quite good at this in Canada and I tried to teach my son what my friend Black Eagle had taught me. The boy soon moved silently beside me, but whether that was my tutoring or the fact he was not heavy enough to break most of the twigs, it was hard to say.

Eventually I spotted some deer tracks and we crouched down to move even more stealthily through the trees.

"There," I whispered, pointing. "Look, can you see that deer track in the mud? And look beyond it, a wet hoof print on that leaf. It has not yet dried out so the animal must be close." I learned these tricks when I was in North America, I explained to him. "We hunted deer, buffalo and even bears over there." To my disappointment, the boy was singularly unimpressed with my hunting experience. He looked with puzzlement at the tracks I was clearly pleased to find and then stared into the trees over my shoulder. "I think the deer must be close," I whispered and then to encourage any sort of response from him I added, "What do you think?"

He looked at me with guileless innocence and then pointed past my shoulder, "It is over there," he whispered.

I whirled round and strike me if he wasn't right: a big six-pointed buck not more than a hundred and twenty yards off, gnawing at some tree bark. Feeling something of a fool at my unnecessary tracking, I slowly brought the musket up to fire while whispering for the boy to stay behind me. As the gun butt nestled into my shoulder I moved partly behind a nearby tree to hide from the animal and rested the barrel against the trunk to steady it. I squinted to line the muzzle up

15

with the chest of the deer and then raised the gun slightly to take account of the range. With my old hunting gun in Canada I would have been confident of at least a hit, but I had never fired this weapon before and they all had their peculiarities of aim. I took a breath to steady myself and slowly squeezed the trigger.

I just had time to glimpse a new chunk of wood fly off the tree trunk near the animal's head before the musket smoke obscured my view of the animal darting off into the trees. The forest was still ringing with the loud report of the gun when I turned round, cursing loudly at the miss, to discover my son was no longer there.

"Where are you, boy?" I shouted as I looked around. He had been standing right behind me a moment before, but now there was no sign of him. Then I saw a polished boot protruding from behind a nearby tree. "What are you doing hiding?" I demanded.

Slowly the boy edged sheepishly out. He looked anxiously at me with wide eyes and then stared down at the still smoking gun in my hand. "Why were you hiding?" I repeated more calmly.

"I don't like the sound of gunfire, it frightens me," he whispered.

You might have been disgusted by such craven timidity but I wasn't. In fact I beamed in delight at the boy, for here, at last, was conclusive proof: he was clearly a Flashman after all.

Chapter 3

Louisa and I settled down into a routine of sorts. She made it very clear that she did not want my help in running the estate, which she had done for years on behalf of her father. I could have insisted but it would not have helped rebuild our somewhat fragile reunion. Instead I was left to amuse myself, but in no doubt that everything I did would doubtless reach the ears of Louisa through some estate worker.

For years I had sat in army camps, ridden on campaigns and quivered with fear on battlefields, all the while dreaming of a more peaceful life on a country estate. But now I had such an existence I soon became hellishly bored. There was nothing to do except hunt and that soon became tedious. All the local farmers wanted to talk about was the weather, the size of the harvest or some freak two-headed calf that had apparently been delivered stillborn from a cow near Coventry. And if you tried to ignore them, why, the impertinent devils would just knuckle their brows and step out in front of you, forcing you to stop. Then they insisted on enquiring about my health, how pleased I must be that the war was over and whether I had ever seen a two-headed cow in Spain!

I suggested that a trip back to London might be necessary, but Louisa got upset at the thought that I was tired of her already. In truth her company was the highlight of the day or should I say night. But I could not keep her between the sheets beyond mid-morning as the servants kept trying to bustle in on some errand such as bringing us breakfast or feeding the fire. You could hear the silly maids giggling outside the door and whispering about whether we had fornicated ourselves to exhaustion or if we were likely to be awake. One even questioned my stamina in the saddle, the cheeky bitch.

Eventually, sensing my growing irritation with this bucolic life, Louisa suggested a party to welcome me home, with all of the local quality invited. I grudgingly agreed that this was a good idea, but then she had to ruin it by insisting that Lamb be asked to come too. That was going too far and I swore I would sooner push an egg in a bottle than agree to that. I was not having the cuckolding little wretch

17

anywhere near Louisa again if I could help it. But she told me that he had been writing to her, terrified that I would come to town and call him out for a duel or murder him in the night. She said that I had to make peace with him as he had been a good friend to her when she had thought me dead.

"I'll bet he was," I retorted, but then there were tears from her and I found myself agreeing to let him come. Oh I had thought of calling him out, too; I could probably have beaten him easily with swords or pistols and no one would have blamed me for killing the odious little villain. But there was always the chance that he could get off a lucky shot. Having had a ball pass through my innards once, it was not an experience that I wanted to risk repeating.

So a month after my return I found myself standing in the ballroom of Berkeley Hall getting my fist pumped by all the nearby gentry and kissing their shrill wives and watching as they piled in to eat and drink their fill and more at my expense. At least there was less talk of two-headed cows; most of the conversation centred on the Congress of Vienna. Now Napoleon was beaten, the allied powers and representatives of the new French king were meeting there to discuss how the continent of Europe would be divided up between them. Naturally after the euphoria of victory had died away, suspicions had grown between the allies. People were in full cry that the Russians were getting too much and that it was dangerous to let those sausage-eating Prussians get too powerful. Most were completely bemused at what that treacherous bastard Talleyrand was doing at the congress at all representing the French king, given that previously he had been Napoleon's foreign minister. One thing all present were agreed on, though, was that with all those damned foreigners involved, good old John Bull would not see his fair share.

I had just endured listening to some local archdeacon railing at the treachery of the French – he had quite splenetic views for a man of the cloth that involved hanging most of them – when Louisa pushed through the press of people around me. I saw following her the pale face of Charles Lamb. I also became uncomfortably aware that many faces in the room were turning to watch the encounter. Given the

18

efficiency of the gossips, I'll wager that everyone there had heard the story of Lamb and Louisa getting together and their shock at my resurrection from the dead. Conversation in the room gradually stilled as Louisa stood before me. In a loud voice she said, "Thomas, I would like to present you to Charles Lamb." She then gave me a warning glare and murmured "Remember you promised to be polite, you gave me your word."

Lamb hesitantly held out his paw and said with an obviously forced grin, "Hullo Flash, it is good to see you again." You could have heard a pin drop as I looked down at the proffered hand. I would not have been surprised if some local squire was running a book on whether I would simply chuck him out or brain him with the fire poker first. But with Louisa watching I had little choice but to swallow down my natural inclinations and grip his fist with a smile as forced as his own.

"You are welcome, Lamb," I replied stiffly.

There was a collective sigh of disappointment from the masses, many of whom turned back to their own conversations when they saw no sport in the offing.

"That is good," said Louisa, somewhat triumphantly. "I will leave you two to talk of old times," she said shooting me another stern glance before she swept away to attend to some old countess who was waving to attract her attention. A stricken look crossed Lamb's face as he watched his protector move off. He had been a stuck-up bastard with me in the past, but now the boot was on the other foot and it was time for me to pay him back.

"Flash, I really am most dreadfully sorry, you know."

Checking we were not being overheard any more, I gave him my nastiest smile and replied, "It is Major Flashman to you, Spanker."

Lamb wrung his hands together and looked even more anguished. "I swear we thought you were dead. Berkeley promised as much. He said he knew of people who had seen your corpse and that the confirmation was just a formality." He looked for some show of understanding but I just glared silently at him, enjoying his discomfort. "You have probably heard of my troubles with Caroline," he continued

19

miserably. "Louisa was mourning you and we just fell to comforting each other somehow."

"Don't you dare mention my wife's name," I snarled at him. I decided it was time to play on his fears. "Have you any idea how many men I have killed, with pistols, swords, cannon and even my own bare hands?" He blanched as I added, "Dozens, and not one of them has done me the disservice you have."

"Please, Flash, I mean Major Flashman. You can call me out if you wish, you have that right. But I implore you to remember that I am as much a victim here as you. I was misled as to your vitality..."

"You certainly were," I sneered. "I have spent the last two years with the Iroquois warriors in Canada. Do you know what they would do with someone like you?" Without waiting for a reply I continued, "They would kill and scalp the devil." He started to go green at the thought and so I added maliciously "Have you ever heard a scalp torn from a skull? It makes a nasty tearing and sucking sound. You never forget it once you have heard it." I thought he would throw up then and wondered if I had gone too far. I had wanted to scare him enough to keep away, but not to do anything desperate. "Stay this evening," I allowed, "but after that I do not want to see you anywhere near this house or Louisa – is that understood?"

"Oh yes, Flash," and he sagged with relief before correcting himself, "I mean Major Flashman. And I promise that you can count on my discretion."

He went off then for a fortifying glass of brandy and I did the same, not for the first time that evening. I knew he would not bother me again and if you think I had been harsh on him, well consider this. In the intervening years he has been cited in two divorce cases as a lover; in one the husband had tried to blackmail him. He has also taken a number of young homeless girls into his house ostensibly as an act of charity. It was no coincidence that they were all pretty wenches and, according to rumour, he used to inspect their quarters in his nightshirt every evening and find some excuse to pull one of them over his knee for at least a spanking. Has this harmed his reputation? Of course not. He is Lord Melbourne now and until recently was the prime minister.

He was the first prime minister for our new queen. It was the talk of society that while young Vicky looked up at him as a father figure, he had rather more carnal designs on her, despite being forty years her senior. King Spanky, now there is a thought! Fortunately, before he could act on this ambition, his government fell and he was replaced.

I forgot about the rogue as I tried to enjoy myself that evening. I fell in with my brothers who were determined to help me drink the house dry. It felt like I had a quart of brandy on board when one of them suggested that I demonstrate for them the tomahawk throwing that I had just been telling them about. In no time a maid was prevailed upon to fetch the weapon from my study. The closed door to the hall was selected as the target from twenty feet, with a cross drawn on it with some billiard chalk to aim at. Soon wagers were being made amongst those near me as to whether I could hit the thing. I was quietly confident; we had aimed at the end of a tree trunk in Canada. Any warrior who could not hit a door at that distance would have been laughed out of camp.

Once my brothers had completed their bets, I hefted the handle of the familiar weapon in my hand for a moment and let fly… Then a lot of things happened all at once.

First I noticed that the door was starting to open as some fool chose this moment to enter. You might have expected me to be worried by this development, but I wasn't. I don't know if you have ever thrown a tomahawk, or a knife for that matter. If you have you know that you can feel if the throw is true as soon as the weapon has left your hand. I knew instantly the axe's shaft left my fingertips that my throw was very wrong indeed. It had been at least three months since I had last hurled my tomahawk and I was clearly out of practice. Being tight on brandy did not help either. The steel blade of the weapon glinted in the candlelight as it whirled across the room directly towards three men standing talking to the left of the door. Foxed with drink though I was, I remember gasping in horror. This was Leicestershire rather than London, but even so, braining one of your guests was still considered something of a social *faux pas*. Before I could utter a cry of warning the blade brushed the hair of the nearest man with his back to me and

21

then buried itself deep in the oak panelling of the wall just beyond him. I saw the fellow reach up and feel his head and then stiffen as he noticed the still vibrating shaft of the axe stuck in the wall.

My brothers were hooting with mirth. The man turned to glare at them. I had already recognised the back of his head and it would be a cold day in hell before I apologised to its owner. Charles Lamb stared at me with a look of shock, still holding the back of his head, and then gazed back at the axe in disbelief.

As usual, I felt my natural ebullience rise at surviving another moment of crisis, in this case, fuelled by a generous dose of spirits. "It's all right, Spanker, I missed you," I bawled at him across the room. I gestured to the grinning men around me, "These fellows had just wagered me a guinea that I could not scalp you from here." There was more laughter at that, which slowly spread across the room as people recounted what had just happened to those who had missed it. This was the type of revenge they had been disappointed not to see when Lamb and I had shaken hands. One boozy fellow staggered across to me and, slapping me on the back, slurred, "Bided your time to catch the swine unawares, eh?" He beamed at me with unfocused eyes while his breath smelt like the fumes from a distillery. "I'll wager you could trim off a mosquito's eyebrows at twenty paces with your little axe what?"

"You can depend on it, sir," I boasted although I swore inwardly that there was more chance of another two-headed cow being born than me giving a second demonstration. As others came up to congratulate me on my marksmanship, I looked back at Lamb, who was surveying the growing mirth with a look of disgust. Then without uttering a word he strode out of the now open door. I was feeling well pleased with myself, at least until I noticed one face that was not laughing. It was clear that everyone in that room, and especially Louisa, believed that Flashy the feared soldier and temporary Iroquois warrior, had put that tomahawk exactly where he had intended.

Chapter 4

Things were a bit frosty between us for a day or two. Louisa was convinced I had broken my word to be pleasant to Lamb and I was not going to admit that I had been aiming at the door; not that she would have believed me if I had. We argued and I had just decided that it was time for me to return to London for a spell, when a messenger arrived carrying a letter for me from the French embassy in Paris. It was from Wellington and, compared to his normal brusque notes, it was positively cordial. He congratulated me on my survival, apologised for his earlier confirmation of my probable death and rounded off by offering me a job on his staff.

"What is it?" asked Louisa, hearing me snort in derision as I reached the end of the missive.

"It's from Wellington offering me a job on his staff. He must be mad if he thinks I will accept. Being one of his staff officers has nearly got me killed more times than I can remember." I had tossed the letter down on the table and was starting to get up when Louisa surprised me by suggesting that I should accept. "What on earth do you mean?" I demanded. "Are you hoping I will get killed so you can go back to your old friends?"

"No of course not, but the war is over and Wellington is not in the army any more."

"Not in the army? Why the devil is he in France, then?" Wellington had been a soldier for all the time that I had known him. I could not imagine what else the man who had defeated every army France had sent at him could be doing in Paris.

"He is the British ambassador to France," said Louisa grinning. "So you see this is not an army job at all, but a diplomatic one."

"They have sent Wellington as the British ambassador to France?" I repeated in disbelief that the British government could be that tactless.

"Yes, and according to Lady Melbourne, he is quite enjoying himself. He has already slept with two of Napoleon's mistresses and taken as his embassy a mansion that used to belong to Napoleon's sister."

I forgot our row and burst out laughing. For all his starch I knew Wellington for a randy devil; in fact he had once made a play for Louisa when we were in India.

"So why don't you consider the job," Louisa persisted. "You know you are bored here in the country."

"But it is in Paris. I have been there twice before and neither visit ended well." I still harboured dark memories of being there just two years previously, when I had been reluctantly recruited into a plot to overthrow Napoleon and had been forced to escape with the secret police on my heels.

"But it is different now," Louisa continued. "The war is over and the government is already laying up ships and dismissing regiments to cut its costs. Your reputation as a soldier will soon be forgotten as people turn their attention back to trade and getting rich. This is a great opportunity for you to start a new career. You will be a person of influence and diplomats always get a lion's share of honours and titles. You could have a British knighthood to go with your Spanish one, maybe even a peerage."

For a brief moment I was seduced by the thought of *Lord Flashman*, but then my natural cynicism came to the fore again. I have heard such speeches a dozen times from Wellington, Wickham, who had been in charge of Britain's spies, and countless others. The bastards all look you in the eye and assure you that the simple task that they are asking you to perform will be perfectly safe. The next thing you know, your bowels are churning in terror as you are forced to flee from one nightmare situation to the next. Well I was not falling for it again. I was home and safe and that was where I was going to stay. Not only that, I had the perfect excuse to stay out of harm's way. "Never mind honours," I insisted, "I have been away from my family long enough." I gave Louisa what I thought was my most winning smile as I played my trump card. "You said yourself that I have not spent much time with you and the boy and you are right. We need to spend time together as a family."

To my surprise Louisa just beamed in delight. "Oh but we will, darling. Because when you go to Paris we will be coming too."

So it was that two weeks later, despite my very best endeavours, I found myself with Louisa, little Thomas, the harridan of a governess, two maids and a valet, climbing up the gangplank of some squalid little packet ship to stand on the soil of France once more. It had been a miserable, choppy crossing and I took some satisfaction from the sickly pallor of our party as they climbed gratefully up onto solid ground. The trip from Dover had only taken a few hours and we had shared the meagre first class accommodation with a family of émigrés returning to France. The man was a loud and obnoxious Frenchman, who claimed to be a noble and was very prickly over his status. I can't remember his title but I called him the Comte de Grenouille or 'Count of Frogs' behind his back to amuse my son. The comte insisted on his party sitting at the head of the dining table on either side of the bemused captain for the luncheon that was served. I was happy to let him for the food on those ships is always as appetising as a pig's swill bucket. We had brought our own. I tucked into a game pie while watching the poor countess trying to spoon a green soup into a face that was verging on the same colour.

"She was telling me her parents were both guillotined during the Revolution," Louisa recounted while we ate. "She is terrified of going back, but her husband is determined to reclaim the family estate." I had read that the new French government had decided against restoring lands to their pre-revolutionary owners, but it appeared the good comte was not going to give up his inheritance so easily.

"Those lands have been in my family for three hundred years," he had told me as we waited to embark. "I will be damned if I will leave them in the hands of those treacherous villains, damned do ye hear, sir." With that, he led his brood up the gangplank before us and started shouting at nearby harbour officials as though he was there to reclaim the whole country as his birth right, not just his estate. They shook their heads wearily and largely ignored the fool. They had probably seen this kind of performance many times before over recent weeks.

Once it was clear I could not escape this trip, I had been reading up on French affairs. Following Napoleon's forced abdication, the brother of the king guillotined during the Revolution had been installed as

King Louis XVIII. By all accounts he was an unappealing, grotesquely fat man, who made our own lard-arsed prince regent look like an emaciated urchin in comparison. After years of war, the country was bankrupt and certainly in no position to compensate the swarms of returning nobles like the comte for their lost estates. Nor could the new king risk the resentment of the French middle classes by confiscating property bought legally from the government of the last twenty years. No, I reflected, in all probability the comte would indeed be damned, although he would not go quietly.

He was still raging as I led our party past him towards the customs sheds, beside which carriages for hire could be seen waiting for business. I looked about me and saw that while it had been over ten years since I had last been in the port of Calais, it was very different. Before, during the Peace of Amiens in '02, the place had been swarming with uniforms; soldiers, sailors, port officials, all had official dress, often with sashes of red, white and blue. Now the white royalist ensign flapped forlornly from a flagpole, with just three gold *fleur de lys* embroidered on it to show that it was not the town's sign of surrender. The few officials that could be seen were now mostly in civilian clothes and at first I thought that they would not bother to check our papers at all. But at length one did shamble over to intercept us and examine the invitation from Wellington that served as our passport. The official's eyes widened in surprise as he recognised the signature at the bottom of the document. Our ambassador might have been a former enemy, but he was clearly respected and soon two carriages and a cart for our party were whistled up, while our luggage was being hoisted onto the jetty from the packet ship.

I have always found that an easy manner and a few coins is the best way to oil bureaucracy and in ten minutes, with the help of half a dozen porters, we were all loaded up and ready to go. At the same time, the good comte was learning the hard way that things had changed a lot since his childhood in his mother country. His title carried little weight and harbour masters did not cower like some feudal serf on his family estate. Mules could learn a trick or two from French officials when it comes to stubbornness and intractability. The

26

man in charge was just then insisting to the comte that it was necessary to search all of their baggage for contraband. They were clearly just getting their revenge for his tirades as Christ knows what you would want to smuggle *into* France. All the good stuff such as brandy and silks comes *out* of the country. I guessed that once they got the noble's luggage open they would rob the poor fool of all the valuables they could lay their hands on. Judging from his apoplectic reaction to their demands, the good comte realised the same. It was turning out to be a fine homecoming for him. For devilment I could not help but lean out of the carriage window as the wheels rattled past the scene and wish him a happy return to his estates. He absolutely dashed his hat to the ground and stamped on it in frustration as a reply.

It took two days to reach Paris and in that time my fear over being on French soil again completely disappeared. The differences we had seen in the port were only exaggerated further in the countryside. The land we crossed had been invaded the previous year by Russian, Prussian and Austrian armies, who had driven back Bonaparte's French defenders, while the British army had driven up into the south-west of the country from Spain. Wherever we went the people had a weary, beaten look about them. Many businesses in towns had closed – some looked to have been looted, perhaps by the foreign armies – and in the markets we saw there was little food to be had.

In towns where we stopped to change the horses or stay the night, the populace generally treated us with surly indifference. The exception was the old soldiers. In each village we visited there would invariably be a table outside a café where a group of crippled men would be gathered sitting in the last of the autumn sunshine. The old army greatcoats they had on did nothing to hide the empty sleeves or trouser legs of these wounded old war horses. As a soldier, albeit a reluctant one, myself, I knew how close I had come to sharing their fate, or worse. So I always made a point of going over to them and buying a bottle or a loaf to share. More often than not we fell into talking about old times even though we had been on different sides.

I met a few who had fought in battles against me while I had been in Spain, but the majority had been wounded in the 1812 campaign in

Russia. I thought I had known cold in Canada, but there I had at least been wrapped up in furs. The stories they told of that awful retreat literally chilled the blood. It had been a struggle for them just to stay alive with few winter clothes or supplies and swarms of Cossack cavalry picking off the stragglers and harrying the rear-guard every step of the way.

I remember they told one tale of when the army was trapped up against a huge river with Russian armies coming up behind for the kill. All seemed lost until some Dutch engineers plunged into the water with wood and ropes. Despite the ice floes they managed to build two rickety bridges that saved the bulk of the army – although the freezing water killed most of the engineers. Berezina I think they called the place and those that had been there had a sad haunted look on their faces as they told the tale. When I congratulated them on their capital escape they did not look any happier. They explained that they had been forced to pull down the bridges after they had crossed to stop the Russians from using them and that many civilian camp followers and wounded stragglers had been trapped without hope on the Russian side when they did so.

I could not begin to imagine the horror of that scene as those still to cross realised what was happening. I had thought the French soldiers in Spain had suffered with the partisans, but I was swiftly realising that they were the lucky ones compared to those who went to Russia. Three quarters of a million men from all over the French empire had started the campaign but only a fifth came back. Now, despite all their sacrifices, everything that they had fought for was being swept away. They were scornful of their new king, who apparently needed help to climb into a carriage, never mind ride a horse. He had never commanded an army and according to them had surrounded himself with courtiers who were determined to return the country back to the days before the Revolution.

"Before we were led by men of destiny," grumbled one old corporal. "Now we are led by profiteers and lickspittles." He actually used a rather coarser French word for toady than 'lickspittle' but you get his meaning.

28

He was not wrong about the profiteers either. Previously when I had been in France the price of goods for an English tourist was double that for a French citizen. But now, when that Englishman arrived with a party in two coaches and a wagon for luggage, the cost of food and wine rose to extortionate levels. But the price of vittles did nothing to dampen my spirits for the French fervour for revolution had clearly been quelled. This meant that a posting in Paris for a while would be a safe one for Flashy. Already my mind had begun to turn to the delights of a diplomatic career; embassy receptions aplenty, perhaps invitations to the French court, a soft bed to sleep in every night and not the slightest whiff of gun smoke.

The sight of the British embassy when we finally reached Paris only heightened my expectations. It was a magnificent mansion with familiar red-coated guards at the front and spacious grounds to the rear. While Louisa took the carriages off to one of the more fashionable hotels, I entered the embassy and was soon climbing a sweeping staircase towards Wellington. From now on thinks I, my only exertions are likely to be bowing, hat raising and ordering flunkeys to fetch me things.

Chapter 5

"I want you to join the French army." Wellington said the words in the same casual tone he had just used to offer me a scone and for a moment they did not register at all. When they did, though, I choked on my half-swallowed mouthful of food, while my hand twitched allowing my saucer to slip from my fingers and shatter on the floor around my feet.

"What?" was all I managed to gasp. Surely I had misheard, but there was no mistaking the smug look on our ambassador's face as he took delight in surprising me with his proposal. I had met him just fifteen minutes previously, which had been spent pleasantly enough discussing old times and catching up on news. Then without any prior warning, he dumbfounded me with that demand. The astonishment must have surely shown in my face as he started to explain.

"You are the perfect man for the job; you have disguised yourself among the French before. That is the reason I wanted you on my staff."

"But…but… Why?" I stammered still trying to take in this shocking turn of events.

"Oh you cannot have failed to notice on your way here that good King Louis is not exactly popular. Many of the royalists are frustrated with him because he is not helping them get their estates back. Meanwhile, everybody else is suspicious of him because they are worried he might give in to pressure from the royalists and try to do precisely that. Some agitators are even talking about a return of feudal rights."

"You surely do not think that there will be another revolution, do you?" I asked. I had a sudden image of myself in a tumbril cart with a load of bewigged and powdered courtiers being dragged to a new guillotine in front of a howling mob. I nearly brought my scone back up at the thought and hastily put my cup down before that joined the shattered crockery at my feet.

"No, no, I don't think there will be any storming of the barricades again anytime soon," soothed Wellington, who was oblivious to my rising sense of panic. "But there are rumours of a coup being planned to replace Louis with his royal cousin the Duc d'Orleans." He gave a slight sniff of contempt as though he considered Orleans a very inferior candidate for monarch before continuing. "He is of royal blood but his father, the old duke, was a supporter of the Revolution, so he would be more acceptable to the republicans." Wellington gave a snort of disgust before adding, "Not that his support did the old duke any good, he was guillotined with the rest."

"But I thought that we supported Louis on the throne. He is the legitimate monarch. Surely we want him to stay?"

"Of course we want Louis to stay. He was the next in line for the throne and from the British point of view," Wellington grinned wolfishly, "he is completely useless. His rule will ensure that France remains weak and pliable. But Orleans has also made it known that he would be a friend to Britain. If the French people unite behind him then there is no appetite in London to go to war again to keep Louis on the throne."

"What about our allies?" I asked. "Surely they have a view as well."

"The Russians suggested Orleans as king in the first place and Prussia will go along with it. The Austrians wanted Bonaparte's son as king but that was because the lad is also the Austrian emperor's grandson, but no one else will go along with that."

"But I still do not understand what this has to do with me joining the French army."

"It is simple; the coup cannot happen without the support of the French army. Everyone is either trying to judge which side will come out on top or attempting to keep favour with both sides. They tell us whatever they think we want to hear. I need someone I can trust to mix amongst their officers and tell me what people are *really* thinking. We will lose face if we are still supporting Louis when he is overthrown. But the British government does not want to abandon the legitimate monarch unless it really has to."

For a moment I was relieved to hear that he had nothing more dangerous planned than my loafing around the officers' mess listening

31

to gossip. I had half feared that he expected me to fight my way into the palace and kidnap Orleans to get him out of the way. But then I realised that there was still a huge range of practical obstacles to Wellington's plan. "But I can't just go up to a recruiting office and ask to be let into the army. They're laying off soldiers like everyone else. I would also need to be an officer, and a senior one at that, to be in a position to hear what side their generals are planning to support."

"Oh don't worry about that." Wellington airily brushed my objection aside. "I have some oily little official in the French War Ministry who is keen to show on which side his bread is buttered. He will add you to the army lists as an officer."

Good God he is serious, I thought, and I felt a familiar tightening around my chest as the fear began to grow. For the more I thought about this ridiculous proposal the more dangerous it seemed. If some strange officer had turned up in Wellington's headquarters in the peninsula and started asking questions, he would soon stand out like a goose in a bear pit. Men who were planning to overthrow a king would be on their guard and doubly cautious. If they had the slightest suspicion that I was a traitor, then it would not be long before the body of an unknown French officer was dropped into the Seine with a livid slash across his throat. How in heaven's name, I wondered, was I staring down the muzzle of death again when I was just minutes into my new diplomatic career in a time of peace? Then, perhaps because I had been out of the army for a few months and had relaxed too much during the intervening period, I blurted out what I really thought about the scheme.

"But dammit, I could get killed."

I watched as Wellington's eyes widened in surprise. In the fraction of the second that it took me to realise that I had actually given this opinion aloud, I experienced a new moment of horror. It was unthinkable for an officer on Wellington's staff to admit he was a coward. But it was too late now. I cast desperately for something to add that would help me retrieve the situation. "I have my wife and son with me. I let them come because I thought this would be a safe posting. Now you talk of me joining the ranks of our enemies and heaven knows where that could end."

The cold bastard just smiled at me in response. He had so successfully suppressed any feelings of fear himself in battle, that I doubt he felt the sensation at all any more. I am certain that it did not cross his mind for a moment that I might be afraid. He had seen me emerge apparently relaxed from far tougher assignments. Instead, he assumed that my concern was for my family. "Do not worry, Thomas," he said making his rare use of my first name. I will make sure that Louisa and your son come to no harm." As you can imagine, I did not find that at all reassuring. I did not want the lascivious devil anywhere near Louisa if I could help it. My suspicion of the way his mind was working was confirmed by his next statement. "Of course we cannot have you appearing at any official functions as a British officer with your family, while you are also masquerading as a French officer elsewhere. The risk of discovery would be too great. But I would be honoured to act as escort to your good lady if circumstance allows."

I'll bet you would, I thought. Land Flashy in the soup again to leave the way for you to have a clear run at the poor fool's wife. Doubtless he had heard of her affair with Lamb and fancied his chances at another successful seduction. The way he had been ploughing his way through Napoleon's mistresses and the crème de la crème of French society beauties, it was a wonder he had the energy. He certainly did not waste time on a lengthy courtship. Rumour had it that he favoured a swift frontal assault, an escalade up their stockings and if he had not hauled down their colours by the end of the evening, he soon moved on to another fortress which looked more likely to breach. Well my family might be 'safe' from physical if not moral harm, but the same certainly could not be said for me. I cast around for another excuse to get me out of this hellish situation, but the duke was already countering my next objection before I had uttered a word.

"Now if you are worried that you might find yourself in the ranks of men opposing British interests, then fear not. We will have you out long before that happens. You won't have to face your old comrades on the field of battle." It was more my new comrades down a dark alley that I was worried about, but Wellington continued blithely on. "No, I just need you to judge if the army will support a coup and when the coup is likely to happen. Then the British government will need to decide whether to continue to support our fat friend or change horses to the Orleans mount." He stood and came around the table indicating that our interview was coming to an end. "As you can see it is a vitally important role you will play and I cannot think of a safer pair of hands to place my trust in."

'Christ, here we go again,' I thought as he grasped my hand and even patted me on the shoulder in a comradely fashion. I wondered if I could somehow arrange an army posting in some far-flung barracks, well out of the way of the plotting, but once again the cunning peer was ahead of me.

"Make an appointment to see the undersecretary at the War Ministry tomorrow," he told me. "That is the cove who is trying to curry favour with us and I will let him know you are coming. He will make sure that you are ideally placed to hear what is happening."

A few minutes later and I was back out on the street in front of the embassy cursing my confounded luck. I could have shrieked at the heavens in frustration. I had only been back from Canada a few weeks and now here I was again with mortal danger breathing down the back of my neck like an amorous mistress. I cursed Wellington for his ridiculous confidence in my skill and his inability to see me for the coward that I was. I damned Louisa for talking me into this trip and I swore against the useless fat French king. They all seem to have conspired together to ruin my life once more.

I was in a foul mood when I got back to my hotel and told Louisa of my new appointment. To my annoyance, she saw at once the great responsibility on my shoulders and the trust that Wellington had placed in me.

"But Thomas you will be advising the government on one of the most important issues of the day. If things go well you are bound to be given honours and recognition, it is an excellent start to your diplomatic career."

"That is if I survive it," I muttered.

"Oh, of course, you will. This is nothing to what you have done before."

It was then that I realised that Louisa was as much fooled by my reputation as anyone else. There was no one that I could share my true feelings with, and I don't think I ever felt more alone than at that moment. I could hardly bawl out my real thoughts on the matter, not with Thomas junior looking up at me from across the room. Instead I suggested we go out, I had a sudden urge to get very drunk, but Louisa would not hear of it.

"No, you cannot be seen out with us now, you don't know who we might meet that could come across you again when you are in disguise."

Thus instead of even just one night enjoying the delights of Paris with my family, I found myself trapped in our rooms with a plate of cold meats and a bottle of brandy for company. So much for the diplomatic life!

Chapter 6

The next day I found myself trudging morosely through the streets of Paris in an inconspicuous brown suit of clothes to the French War Ministry. I had awoken that morning thick-headed from the brandy, but feeling more resilient about my new orders. I had to join the French army, but I would do all I could to stay anonymous within its ranks. If I did not draw attention to myself then there should be no danger. As long as those blasted frogs got on with their coup without delay, well I could be home by Christmas and it would take wild horses to drag me out of the country after that! In the meantime, I would just feed Wellington lines about private meetings with sentries guarding every entrance or conspirators stopping their conversations whenever I walked by. That would give him the impression that I was diligently digging for intrigue. The British government would have to make their own choice on which royal horse to back without my help.

To make sure that I did not slip up with any silly mistake, I read some briefing papers that Wellington had ordered sent round to my hotel. I also pored over several back copies of the *Moniteur* news sheet for more timely gossip, as that was the sort of thing that would be talked about in the mess. I was astonished to discover that virtually all of Napoleon's old generals and marshals were now loyally serving the new king. While their emperor might have brought them up through the ranks to unimaginable riches and honours, these commanders had not hesitated to drop him like a hot brick when it was clear he would have to abdicate. The war minister was none other than Marshal Soult, the man whose French army had nearly trapped us at Talavera and who had fought a long campaign with Wellington across Spain.

I found the ministry building without difficulty as I had been there once before nearly three years ago. It had been when that incompetent fool Grant and I had been hiding out in Paris. I had been arrested, ironically enough, while disguised as a French army officer. If you have read my previous memoirs, you will know that some treacherous swine called Henri Clarke, who was the war minister then, had tried to use me as an informer on a plot to overthrow Napoleon. Instead of stopping the plotters, Clarke had intended to use the half-baked scheme to round on his enemies in government.

Well, the ministry looked a little different from those days. Instead of the tricolour flag flying from the flagpole at the top of the building, it was now the white royalist flag. The sentries on either side of the gate also now sported white cockades in their shako helmets rather than the old red, white and blue ones that they had all worn in the old days. But they showed no interest in me as I strolled nonchalantly between them and into the courtyard beyond. There I found a full company of grenadier guardsmen, in their blue uniforms, drawn up in four ruler-straight ranks. They were huge fellows, their height exaggerated by tall bearskin helmets. Judging from the bushy grey moustaches that adorned most of them, I suspected that they were probably from the Old Guard, the elite veterans drawn from the Imperial Guard. They were all staring fixedly to their front while ahead of them a young man barely out of his teens, wearing a white coat, harangued them about presenting arms to all members of the royal family.

"It really won't do," he insisted. "The Duchess of Angoulême was ignored twice yesterday. All those of the royal blood must be properly saluted."

At first I thought the young man was some eager courtier, but then I realised that he had a sword at his hip and an epaulette on his shoulder and that his white coat was a royalist officer's uniform. He finished his tirade by drawing his sword and with an unusual flourish of the blade he shouted, "*Vive le Roi!*" and stared expectantly at his men for a response. I thought back to all those times I had seen men like these shout their loyalty to their emperor. The roar of, *Vive l'Empereur!* from their marching columns had always sent a shiver of fear down my spine. It was clear that many of them were struggling with this new allegiance. There was a moment's hesitation and then around half of them shouted, no, snarled would be a more accurate description, "*Vive le Roi*," in return. You could almost smell the hostility in the air as the old soldiers glared with barely disguised contempt at the young man capering before them. I think he must have sensed it too, for he had the

37

good sense to march swiftly away before he tried their patience further.

If he was their company commander then I would not have bet a single farthing on him surviving his first engagement with an enemy. For if there was ever an officer who was destined to get a ball in the back from one of his own men, it was that young man. I gave a wry grin of amusement before I rapidly remembered that I was about to become an officer in this army myself. I walked past their ranks as I headed to the main entrance to the ministry. I glanced back at them as I passed and even in this city courtyard they were an intimidating sight. There was an implacable confidence to them as though whatever madness the world indulged in, they would do what they thought was right anyway. If they were former members of Napoleon's Old Guard I knew that these specially selected veterans had never retreated or been beaten in battle. The emperor had often kept them in reserve, which led to them being cynically called 'the immortals' by other more expendable parts of the army. But at a key moment in a battle when he released them, they never let him down. Well, judging from their faces that morning, I had a strong suspicion that the Duchess of Angoulême was still going to be ignored.

Once inside the ministry I announced myself at the desk as a visitor for the undersecretary and prepared for a wait. Pen-pushing clerks invariably like to make you stand around to show their own importance. I wandered over to a noticeboard which the last time I had been here had carried a 'Wanted' notice for Grant and myself. This time most of the board was covered with announcements about the disbanding of regiments. Where units were being retained they were also being renamed. I remember the former first regiment of cuirassiers were now the Cuirassiers du Roi, while the third regiment now carried the title of the Dauphin, the heir to the throne. If there was a tenth regiment it was probably now named for the royal pot washer. Heaven help them if they try to rename the soldiers outside for the Duchess of Angoulême, I thought. I saw a few more young officers in the royalist white coats, but most were in the traditional blue and judging from scars and decorations, they were the more experienced

38

men. I had just found an interesting notice detailing the different ranks of royalty and nobility and which ones should have arms presented to and which should be merely saluted, when I sensed someone standing at my side.

"The undersecretary will see you now, sir," the flunkey announced and led the way towards a grand staircase. We were soon in a wide corridor, which I vaguely remembered from my previous visit. Back then I had been terrified, fearing execution or torture and I knew that at the end of the passage was the huge office of the minister himself. I noticed that there were now blank spaces on the walls where pictures had hung before and some busts of famous generals had been removed from the wall alcoves. I guessed that these had been depicting heroes and battles of the previous regime that were now deemed unacceptable – which made Marshal Soult's accession to the role of minister even more remarkable. I was feeling quite relaxed when I was shown into the office of the undersecretary, which made the shock of discovery all the greater.

For a moment we both stared at each other in astonishment. If the flunkey announced me I do not recall it, in fact I cannot even remember him leaving the room, but he must have done as when we did start talking we were alone.

"It is you...Moreau," the undersecretary gasped. I think words must have failed me at that point for he then rummaged about on his desk to find the note from Wellington. "You are using the name Flashman with the English duke?"

"No, no, I am Flashman, Moreau was a false name I used before… But how on earth can you be here?" For there in front of me was none other than my old nemesis, Henri Clarke, who had been Napoleon's minister for seven years and one of his most trusted aides. This was the man who had ruthlessly and cynically put down plots against the emperor by republicans and probably royalists as well. Yet now here he was, still a senior man under the king in his old ministry.

"You are truly British?" asked Clarke and then he roared with laughter. "My God and I had you in my office before and let you go. I learned afterwards that you were with that spy Grant, but when my

39

men came to arrest you they found you had run." He laughed again and added, "By the saints, I could so easily have caught you both."

I was getting my wind back now. Thinking back to that time, I remembered the wife of a Bonapartist general who had provided us with shelter and who had later shared her bed with me. "What about Madame Trebuchet, did you have her dragged to the guillotine?"

"No," said Clarke still smiling. "Her friends protected her, but I managed to get most of those I wanted to stand before a firing squad."

"But I still don't understand. How are you here? The royalists must know who you are and what you have done."

"Of course," said Clarke genially. "But like Soult and countless others, they need us to run the country. You must have met some of the royalists; they have no idea of government. And anyway," he added, "I was one of those that persuaded Bonaparte to abdicate so they owe me for that. The king has graciously confirmed me as a peer of France and now I serve a new master."

He looked as smug a bastard as I have ever met as he calmly boasted of abandoning friends and embracing former enemies to maintain his honours and station. Oh, I don't deny that I would do the same in those circumstances, but I do draw the line at framing innocent rivals in plots to get them executed. I still remembered how he had terrified me when we had met before and I looked about the room, thinking of a way to prick his pride. "But your office is not as large as the one you had before. How does it feel to watch someone else do your old job?"

"It is merely a temporary situation, I assure you." Clarke's eyes glittered dangerously and I remembered, too late, that I needed this man's help. A word from him in the wrong ear could again see me in yet more peril. He gave me a cold calculating smile before continuing and I guessed that he at least had not forgotten where the balance of power lay in this interview. "So, Major Flashman, why is the British ambassador so keen to have you recruited into the French army?"

I was not sure what Wellington had told him and I thought the little he knew the better. So I just shrugged and replied, "Well, you know, just to keep an eye on things. You can't be too careful."

He laughed again. "Do you take me for a fool? Surely you know me better than that. I can tell you exactly what your mission is and if you want I can even tell you how it will end."

I had an uncomfortable feeling that he knew far more about what was about to happen than I did and so I gestured for him to continue, "Please do."

"Wellington asks for you to be given a posting on the staff where you can judge the mood of the French army. It is obvious that he is trying to assess the level of support for the Duc d'Orleans as an alternative monarch." He paused before adding, "Ah, I see from your face that I am right."

"So what level of support is there for the good Duc d'Orleans?"

"You will find out for yourself, but I will tell you that most of the army hate Louis and what he stands for. They resent the changes to regimental names and traditions, they don't like seeing their comrades disbanded and most of all they feel that their dead from recent years have died for nothing. But the question that Wellington should be asking is would the army act alone to replace Louis."

"And would they?" I prompted. He wanted to show off his knowledge and so I might as well make use of it.

"No. Louis has been cleverer than you think. He has given all the top marshals their honours and titles to tie them into the new regime." He gestured around his office. "As you have been so astonished to notice, even I have kept my peerage and have been given a role in his administration. Most of us, having abandoned an emperor, feel it would be distasteful to abandon a king as well."

"So the army will stay loyal, then," I confirmed. This was turning out to be much easier than I thought. With no plot, there was little risk and I could tool around a French army mess for a couple of weeks and then go back to Wellington with the news. I should have known that frog politics is never that simple.

"No," stated Clarke, making me look up sharply. "I have suggested that the army will not act alone, but it is busy sending out agents to see if others will join in an attempt to overthrow Louis. Just this morning a well-known general sat where you are now asking for my opinion of the likely support for the Duc d'Orleans as king."

I sank back in my chair with resignation as I belatedly realised that I was about to enter a complicated web of intrigue and conspiracy. "So what did you tell this general?" I asked.

"As you know over the last year this country has been invaded by you British, the Austrians, the Russians and the Prussians. Above all the people want peace and prosperity and no more invaders plundering their farms and their property. The allies have all approved and supported Louis' claim to the throne and so, for now, the people will not want to disturb the peace." He paused then but I was sure that there was more to come.

"So what would change their minds?" I prompted.

Clarke grinned. "I see you are learning that things are not straightforward. They will change their minds if their prosperity is threatened, particularly if the king starts to revoke sale agreements made during the time of the republic to return lands to nobles."

"Which is exactly what the émigrés are pressing for," I offered.

"But not just the émigrés. Some of those who secretly want Orleans as king are pressing for it as well. They know it is their best chance of uniting the country against Louis. In case you are wondering, I am one of those who is urging the king not to cancel the land sales."

What Clarke said made sense although whether his final statement was true was anyone's guess. I suspected he told everyone that he was on their side and in the end would do what was right for him alone. In fact, most of the senior government and army people were probably doing the same – all trying to judge which side would come out on top – and my presence showed that the British government was no different. "What a mess," I concluded with feeling.

"I wish you luck with your enquiries, Major Flashman," said Clarke smiling again. "And now to your recruitment. Will you be using your old French name again in the French army? Will it be Major Moreau?"

"Yes I suppose so, no wait, I think Colonel Moreau sounds better."

"A promotion," said Clarke amused. "Now why would I agree to that?"

"I am sure you would not want stories of our previous meeting getting out," I suggested. "For example details of how you let a pair of British spies escape and suggestions that not everyone you executed was guilty."

"My ruthlessness will hardly be news for many," said Clarke reaching for a form and dipping his pen in an inkwell. "But I will agree to your request, Colonel Moreau to show that I am willing to offer your ambassador, the duke, every assistance. I am sure he will remember me if things turn out to his advantage. Now, where should I place you so that you will be in the heart of things?"

He looked up then and was amused at the consternation that must have been showing in my face. For I was not at all sure that I wanted to be at the heart of things. With everyone scheming and plotting against each other, it would be impossible to know who to trust. A garrison posting in some country town now had far more appeal. As if guessing my thoughts, Clarke watched me like a cat playing with a mouse. He stopped writing and steepled his fingers as though considering various diabolical alternatives. Just when I thought I could stand it no longer he announced, "There is a vacancy on Marshal Ney's staff. He commands more respect than any other general among the men. If there is to be a plot they will certainly want him on board."

For a moment I felt relief, for I knew of Ney. I had even seen him once in Spain when he had ridden past me while I was disguised as a Polish lancer. He was by reputation more of a fighting man than a politician. He led his men by example, in the front ranks facing the enemy, and I had read that he had commanded the rear-guard on the awful retreat from Moscow. As a result, he had earned the epithet *the bravest of the brave*. Then I realised that while he might be one of the more straightforward soldiers amongst the general staff, if there was any fighting he would be bound to be in the thick of it. Well, I would just have to make sure that I had slid out from his command before then.

Chapter 7

When I called at the military outfitters later that day to be measured
for my new uniform the tailor nervously offered me two different bolts
of cloth, one white and one blue. I did not hesitate to choose the blue
one. No conspirator would share an opinion with an officer in royalist
white. I had a letter of appointment in my pocket with the seal of the
War Ministry while Clarke was writing to Ney to announce that the
vacancy on his staff had been filled.

I was in no rush to start my new duties and had to wait two days for
my uniform to be completed. I spent part of that time studying the
military record of my new commanding officer so I would not give
myself away. I had seen him just before the battle of Busaco when he
had been part of the French army invading Portugal, but that was the
only battle we had shared. I had witnessed first-hand what the French
had experienced campaigning in Spain and as long as no one pressed
me for too much detail then I imagined I should be able to get by. I
had been badly wounded at Albuera, with the scars to prove it, and I
could always claim that I had missed a key event due to my injury.

Politics is a dirty business and in Paris then officials seemed to have
more faces than a whole box of dice. No one was expecting the event
that did befall France a few months later but there was a general
feeling that change was in the air. Everyone was hedging their bets and
none more so than the journalists and editors of the main news sheets.
While they contained fawning accounts of affairs at court and fulsome
praise of the king, the writers were also careful to include detailed
accounts of the visits by the Duc d'Orleans to regimental barracks,
hospitals and also inflammatory speeches from various aristocratic
agitators calling for the return of their property. On top of that, there
were reports of a royalist officer found floating face down in the Seine
downstream of Paris, with the more scandalous papers in full cry at his
apparent murder. Meanwhile, an émigré was in court accused of
burning down his former home with some of the occupants still
trapped inside when he was refused the right to reclaim his old
property.

Oh yes, the political cauldron of Paris was well on the boil back then, and about to be tossed into the stew was your humble obedient servant. I read every news sheet with a mounting sense of agitation. But unlike my previous adventures, instead of being able to hide out in some funk hole, I was expected to return back to my hotel each evening for tea and muffins with my family. Louisa was blithely unconcerned at any risk, which compared to my earlier exploits on various battlefields, did seem insignificant. But I had the recent memory of very real danger when involved in plots in Paris. I knew a stranger asking too many questions in the wrong place was asking for a blade between the ribs. But I could not show fear especially in front of my son. He was now asking me for bloodthirsty tales of all my previous battles and gazing at me in wide-eyed wonder as I made most of them up.

Everything was a bit unreal back then, but I was brought back down to earth the day after my new uniform arrived, when a message was delivered to my hotel from Clarke. It advised that Michel Ney, Marshal of France, Prince of Moscow and Duc d'Elchingen had invited his newest staff officer to join him in a ride along the Champ du Mars at dawn the following morning.

The Champ du Mars was a huge park in Paris just by the military school. Few people promenaded there early on a cold October morning and so it was a good place to exercise a horse as well as get the measure of a new subordinate. I was up promptly the next day donning the unfamiliar blue cloth coat and staring at my candlelit reflection in a mirror. It looked like some costume I was about to wear on a stage, and I supposed that in a way that was exactly what I was about to do. There were just a few night soil carts and early tradespeople on the streets as I rode slowly towards the park. The meeting point was a statue of the Roman God Mars. I knew precisely where it was as I had taken little Thomas there the previous afternoon to reconnoitre the area after receiving the message. There had been troops of soldiers parading down the wide paths then, with a royalist officer encouraging the sparse crowd to shout *"Vive le Roi!"* as they went past. There was only a desultory cheer; more noise was made by a band of grubby urchins who ran alongside the soldiers mocking the monarch's wide girth by yelling, "*Vive le dumpling!*" instead.

I arrived early; it did not do to keep a marshal of France waiting. The statue stood in a little recess in the trees lining the main thoroughfare through the park. There was an early morning mist, but as far as I could see the path was deserted in both directions. I dismounted and tied the reins to the railing surrounding the ancient god of war, who glared angrily back at my impertinence. It was only when I stepped out in the centre of the path that it occurred to me that if someone intended me ill, then this would be an ideal place for an ambush. I immediately tried to dismiss the unwelcome thought.

While some might find me irritating, surely Ney would not have me assassinated without meeting me first – I had given him no cause for concern. I tried to reassure myself that it was perfectly normal for the marshal to ride out in the park first thing in the morning. I knew he was a cavalryman, having started out as a humble trooper in a royal hussar regiment. The Revolution had given him the opportunity to demonstrate his courage and leadership abilities and he was made a general within twelve years of joining the army. He probably rode every day for exercise and now when the park was empty would be the ideal time. No, I reassured myself, everything I had read about him indicated that he was not the sort of man to have someone killed without good cause. No sooner was the thought in my head than I heard a twig snap in the trees across the path from the statue.

I tensed and without consciously thinking about it, my hand dropped down to the hilt of my sword. I cursed myself for not bringing any pistols, but I could hardly turn up to a meeting with a French marshal as his new staff officer with a brace of barkers stuffed into my belt. I was supposed to be a French officer, safe and secure in the French capital, for heaven's sake. I took a deep breath to steady myself and stared once more up and down the path. Still no one was in view. There had to be lots of wild animals in the woods – that was surely what I had heard. I could hardly flee down the path to encounter the marshal known as *the bravest of the brave* and admit that I had been scared away by a clumsy rabbit! No, I had to stand firm.

I reminded myself again that Ney was not known for treachery, but then I remembered who had arranged this meeting. Clarke would stab his own grandmother in the back if he thought he would benefit. I only had his word that Ney wanted to meet here; he could easily have sold me out to the Orleanist faction within the army. Then I heard more twigs break in the trees ahead, this time three or four clear snaps of wood in quick succession. You don't get to be a poltroon of my experience without a strong sense for self-preservation. Instinctively I knew that the branches had been broken deliberately to attract my attention. I felt a prickle of fear shoot up my back as I knew with certainty that someone was coming up behind me. I imagined a muzzle being pointed at my exposed back and knew that I had to at least put them off their aim before I bolted into the trees. Years of reacting in blind terror stood me in good stead now as I started to move. I twisted fast and low to my right while whipping my sword from its scabbard and slashing the tip forward, towards the chest of the figure I saw from the corner of my eye standing just three yards behind me.

I'll say this for the man; he had nerves of steel, for he did not even flinch as the blade lunged towards him. Marshal Ney must have realised that I did not have the reach to touch him and he just stared impassively down at me, while surprise, shock and recognition chased each other across my face.

"Marshal, I am sorry," I stammered, only just remembering to speak in French. I started to straighten up. "I thought it was an ambush… Oh..." For only then did I notice the cocked pistol pointing at me from the marshal's rock steady hand.

Ney ignored my protestations and called out over my shoulder, "Are there more of them?"

"No sir," came a voice from where the twigs had been broken. "He has come alone."

Ney gave a grunt of acknowledgement and then turned his attention back to me. "Colonel, unless you plan to use that blade of yours, I suggest you put it away."

I did as he suggested; I was not going to use the weapon against two men who would both be well armed. I was not sure what was happening and fear still prickled up my spine, but I thought some righteous indignation was well overdue. "With respect, sir, what the devil is going on? I came here at your invitation to join your staff, not to be held at gunpoint."

"I always find it prudent to deal cautiously with Clarke's creatures, especially when nobody seems to know them. You are Clarke's creature, are you not?"

"He appointed me to this posting, yes," I admitted before launching into my carefully planned cover story. "But I have spent most of my career in Spain. I fought at Talavera, Busaco and Albuera, where I was badly wounded." Which was all true as far as it went. I could even describe the battles if he had pressed me.

But Ney simply nodded as though accepting my statement as true. His pistol though had not moved an inch since I had first seen him. "But now you plan to spy on me for Clarke and report to him who I see and what I say?"

He obviously knew Clarke well and would not believe that I had been appointed without some ulterior motive. I racked my brains for some explanation that would serve. If Ney hated Clarke as much as I did, he was likely to shoot his agent out of hand. The best lies are always those closest to the truth. Looking at Ney standing all proud and erect, with a glare of grim determination in his eye, I realised exactly how I could gammon him. "No sir, I plan to spy on you for the British, for Wellington himself."

"What?" For the first time his pistol wavered in his grip and I knew my suspicion was right. Show me any successful general and while they want respect from fellow commanders on their own side, they yearn even more for recognition of their achievements from enemy leaders they respect. I knew for example that Wellington burned with an inner frustration every time someone mentioned the fact that while he had beaten half a dozen French marshals he had never faced Bonaparte. I had guessed that a French marshal would, in turn, be gratified to have the respect of the great British general.

"Wellington has heard how you earned your title of *the bravest of the brave* and he knows you command great respect with the French

48

soldiery." I larded on the compliments before I continued. "He wants to know what you think about the Duc d'Orleans, but as the British formally support King Louis, he could not simply ask you. Clarke offered to find out and that is why he put me on your staff."

Ney nodded slowly as he considered this. I could tell he was pleased, though; his chest appeared to puff up another inch as he slowly un-cocked the pistol and dropped it into his pocket. I glanced over my shoulder and saw Ney's companion, another army officer, emerging from the trees behind me and walk towards us. He had a short-barrelled carbine musket held easily in one hand.

"Sir," I urged. "If we could talk privately it would be better for your reputation and my own."

"De Briqueville," called Ney. "Collect our horses and that of Colonel Moreau. I wish to talk to the colonel alone." He turned and started to walk up the main path through the park and I fell in step beside him. "Do you report personally to Wellington as well as Clarke?"

"Yes sir. My wife has some English family, which is the reason Wellington trusts me."

Ney grunted his acknowledgement and continued walking while he considered his response. We must have gone at least twenty paces before we spoke again. "I don't care what you tell Clarke, but tell Wellington this: Marshal Ney will do whatever is in the best interests of France. And when Ney decides he can no longer serve someone he will look that person in the eye to tell him. I was the one who told the emperor that there was no choice but for him to abdicate. If necessary I will look the king in the eye and tell him the same." He stopped and turned to me. "And tell them that Marshal Ney does not involve himself in plots and intrigues."

"I will, sir," I replied as we resumed walking. While his answer sounded emphatic, I realised that it still did not tell me whether he positively supported the king's claim to the throne or if he was just waiting for events to unfold. I decided to try a different tack. "You said you will do what is right for France, but from what I have heard, the royalists are worried about your loyalty. Could you do something to reassure them?" I had thought that this was a cunning move on my part. If I could persuade the most influential soldier in the French army to speak up in support for the monarch the British government backed, then surely this would take some of the wind from the Orleanist sails. But before I could imagine the rewards I might receive for this diplomatic coup, Ney gave a snort of derision.

"I have sworn an oath of allegiance, what more do they want?"

"Perhaps a public show of support while attending court?"

Ney turned to me, his eyes blazing with sudden anger. "Those arrogant courtiers might fear me because they know I command the respect of the soldiers, but they do not understand what the name Ney stands for. They sneer at us behind our backs. Do you have any idea how many times my wife has come home from the court in tears? That bitch Angoulême refuses to recognise any titles given by the emperor and many others follow suit. She refers to my wife as Madame Ney instead of the Princess of Moscow or Duchess of Elchingen. If she had a longer memory she might remember that my wife's mother protected her mother, the old queen, from the mob during the Revolution."

"How did she do that?" I asked, curious.

"She was a waiting woman to the old queen and fiercely loyal. When they stormed Versailles she stood on a balcony blocking their way and buying the family time to make their escape. Later, after the old queen was guillotined, my mother in law lost her wits and killed herself jumping from a window. Now her daughter faces scorn from that same queen's family." His voice was calmer as he added, "My wife has always had some sympathy with the royal house, which makes their rejection of her all the more hurtful. As for me, I will support them because I want peace for France." We walked in silence for a while after that; Ney was gazing at the ground ahead and appeared lost in thought. I did not want to interrupt him. From what he had told me, it was clear that he would not support the Orleanists and that was valuable information which Wellington would want to know. Abruptly he looked up again and asked, "Were you on the hill at Busaco? That was a bloody business."

"I was," I confirmed. But I did not think it would be politic to mention that I was reluctantly leading a charge of Connaught Rangers down the slope, rather than being part of a French column marching up it.

"It was folly to attack where we did. If Massena had spent as much time on his horse as he did on his mistress, we would have beaten the British then once and for all."

I remembered the tales about Massena's mistress from my time riding in disguise with the French. She was no stranger to costume either, as during the rare times Massena was on horseback she used to go with him in the uniform of a hussar. To show that I had actually been there, I thought I would repeat some of the gossip I had heard from the soldiers. "Was the girl very pretty? I heard tales that you had to give reports of the British positions through their bedroom door."

Ney barked with laughter. "Yes I did once and I think she nearly killed him. But being fucked to death is not a bad way to go, eh." He slapped me on the back and I was reminded that while he might be a prince and a duke now, he had started out as a common cavalry trooper. "Spain was a tough business; we should have left it alone."

"But not as tough as Russia?" I prompted.

"No Russia was worse." He stared into the middle distance then, his mind clearly casting itself back to that unspeakable horror. Then in almost a whisper he added, "I took a division of thirty-five thousand men into Russia. I had two hundred men left at the end, but their balls were attached with wire."

I had thought that the suffering I had seen the French endure at Torres Vedras was bad but I could not imagine surviving the retreat in Russia. From what I had heard Ney had been wherever the fighting was toughest. Often when everyone else had despaired, he was the one who had rallied the men and got them going again. It was easy to respect a general like Ney and I was suddenly glad that the war was over.

We reached a crossroads in the paths and Ney looked over his shoulder to see that de Briqueville was bringing the horses. "Well, Colonel, tell Wellington what I told you and I wish you well."

"But I am supposed to stay on your staff." I had realised as we were talking that being on Ney's staff would probably be the safest place for me. He knew a little of my real mission and I thought would keep this knowledge to himself as he was not involved with the plotters. On top of that, anyone would think twice about harming one of his men and incurring his wrath.

Ney laughed, "Well you can if you wish, not that it will do you much good. Tomorrow I leave for my country estate at Coudreaux and I don't plan to come back to Paris until the spring." De Briqueville had ridden up and passed me the reins to my horse while staring at me curiously. Ney swung lightly up into his saddle and called over his shoulder, "Don't forget what I told you," before spurring his horse off down the path.

Chapter 8

That meeting with Ney was in October 1814 and I will spare you the detail of the next four months, as in truth not a lot happened. In fact it was one of the softest billets I have ever had serving my country – which lulled me into a completely false sense of security and left me woefully unprepared for the horrors to come.

Wellington was delighted with my news from the marshal. He felt sure that the Orleanists would not move without Ney's approval. So I was to remain on his staff and keep my eyes open for any attempts to contact him as well as for any other gossip among officers in the War Ministry. So there I was, free to enjoy the delights of Paris and with very little to do. At the end of each day I retired to one of the best hotels in the capital, a warm bed and a willing wife. We spent a few weeks away from the city on jaunts to explore other places, with me officially following up leads that came to nothing. The weather was cold that winter and I would dress up warmly in civilian clothes with my hat well down. Even if I had met someone who knew me as Colonel Moreau, they would have been hard pressed to recognise me. So we did all the tourist things, often with young Thomas along, and I was forced to agree that the diplomatic life might be for me after all.

When I was in uniform I found that being able to say that I was on Marshal Ney's staff instantly earned me respect and access to anywhere I wanted to go. De Briqueville was cautious of me at first. He was the one that had asked around about me for Ney and not surprisingly had found no one who had heard of me. But his marshal had accepted me onto the staff and that was good enough for him. He was fiercely loyal to our mutual commander and one evening he told me why.

He had been an officer of Ney's on the retreat from Moscow when the five thousand men of the rear-guard had been cut off from the main force by a Russian army of eighty thousand. They had all thought that they were lost, but after a diversionary attack, Ney set off in the last direction anyone expected: back to Moscow. They only went a few miles but in a snowstorm they evaded Russian cavalry who were searching for them on other roads. Then Ney led them along a stream which he correctly guessed flowed into the Dnieper River. He wanted the big river between him and the Russians before he moved west again but the ice was perilously thin. They had waited until night to cross in the hope that the drop in temperature would make the ice a fraction thicker. Then the men had started to cross, well spread out, one at a time. While the ice had rumbled and sometimes cracked, most had got across without incident and fires were lit on the far bank to guide those across where the ice seemed thickest. There was no question of bringing across the heavy cannon, but they had dozens of carts containing the wounded. With all the men on foot across, Ney ordered an attempt be made at bringing one of the lighter carts of wounded over the ice.

One can only imagine the thoughts of the wounded on that cart. If they stayed behind they would freeze to death or be murdered by roving Cossacks. But if the cart went through a hole in the ice they would be swept away by the current and drown. De Briqueville, it turned out, was the mad Hector who had volunteered to drive this first cart over the ice.

"God," he told me, "you should have heard the noise the ice made as we started across. Bangs like musket shots while the poor devils wailed in terror in the cart behind me. A maze of little cracks spread out from the wheels and the horses started to panic, but I drove them on as the ice held. The further we went out the worse the noise got, but I thought we still had a chance. When we got to the middle I realised that we were surrounded by cracks and then the piece of ice we were on started to move. Before I could do anything it was tipping."

He absolutely shuddered, either at the imagined cold or at the memory before continuing. "I just managed to throw myself clear as the cart plunged through the ice. The men inside were screaming as it dragged them and the horses down under the ice after it. For a moment I was in open water and by the saints, the cold cut into me like lance points. The current pulled at me but I managed to grab hold of a jagged edge of ice around the hole we had fallen through. My fingers were already frozen and the flow of the river was strong. I thought I was lost and then I heard a voice calling my name and telling me to hold on. It was the marshal. He had crawled out on the ice to save me. He grabbed my wrist and somehow he hauled me out of the water. Some others came to help but the marshal waved them away, not wanting more weight on the ice. Then he dragged me all the way to the bank himself."

I sat back and looked on Ney with even greater respect after that. I could not imagine any British general doing the same. Oh, I have seen Wellington ride into danger many times and lead his men bravely from the front. But to so abandon his precious dignity and crawl out on his belly to rescue one of his men? No, I could not see it. He would look on with regret as you slipped under the ice and he would write a touching letter to your people expressing his sympathy, but nothing would get him crawling anywhere.

De Briqueville never actually said it, but there was an unspoken understanding between us that he was Ney's man to the end. I was welcome to join him while I was doing the marshal no harm, but if he sensed I was doing the marshal a disservice I had better watch my back. He was still wary of me as an agent of Clarke and knowing that slippery bastard you could not blame him for that. He asked me plenty of questions about my own service and while I could talk about battles I had been at, I always had to start evading answers when he talked of other officers and general camp life. Thank God he had never served in Spain or I would have been truly lost. He was still suspicious of me until I had the most extraordinary stroke of luck. We were sitting together in a large café in the centre of Paris when I saw a man I knew.

"Isn't that Major Lagarde?" I asked pointing to a tall grey-haired officer who had just walked in. Even in a room half full of soldiers, his ramrod straight bearing stood out as a man who age had clearly not bent.

"It is Colonel Lagarde now, do know him?" asked de Briqueville. He was clearly intrigued to find at last another French officer who might know me.

"Yes, we served together in Spain." Lagarde had commanded the escort taking Grant from Spain to Bayonne in France. I had joined his men disguised as Lieutenant Moreau to rescue Grant. Lagarde and the other officers in the group had been most uncomfortable about taking a man who had surrendered honourably towards their capital, where they knew torture awaited him. So they had delivered him to the city square in Bayonne as they were ordered, but as Clarke's agents were not there to collect the prisoner, they simply abandoned his cart to give him a chance to escape. I had known that Clarke's agents would probably not be there as messages had been intercepted by the partisans and delivered to Wellington. But still the fool Grant would not escape as he had given his word not to until he had reached Paris. You can read about that affair in my earlier memoirs. For now, I just thanked my stars that I had kept the same French name I had used before.

"Then you must introduce yourself to him," insisted de Briqueville, getting up and clearly suspecting that I did not know Lagarde at all. But he needn't have worried for the man himself saw us staring at him and quickly beamed in recognition.

"Moreau, by Satan's beard what fool made you a colonel? Congratulations, my friend, I am pleased to see you have lived long enough to see the peace, such as this humiliating fiasco is." He turned to de Briqueville and added, "You want to watch this mad lunatic, he keeps disappearing on you when you least expect it. If he is not charging alone into a partisan attack, he slips away when he is safe in France." I started at that for he was obviously referring to when I left his company to try and rescue Grant. But Lagarde must have seen the consternation cross my face and held up a hand to forestall any explanation. "To protect your honour let's not discuss that here. I can guess where you went and even if your entreaties to get the stubborn fool to run were as ineffectual as my own, well I respect you for trying." He laughed before adding, "Now let me buy you both a drink and this time, Moreau, I am going to insist that you stay here to finish it."

So we spent most of the afternoon in that café talking about old times and past battles and if half my tales were from my imagination, no one seemed to notice. De Briqueville certainly accepted that I was a genuine French officer after that meeting, for he made a point of shaking my hand as we parted, which he had never done before.

It should have been an idyllic sojourn, the kind of posting that I had long dreamed about. But as the weeks passed and the end of the year approached, I began to have something new in common with my French comrades: Wellington as an enemy. The man was behaving like a debauched satyr, chasing after every society woman who gave him a second glance – and there were plenty of those for, as Louisa kept pointing out, he was a good-looking man. He got even worse when it was announced that he would be leaving Paris early in the New Year to be Britain's negotiator at the Congress of Vienna. He made a special point of pursuing any woman rumoured to have slept with the emperor; he might not have beaten Napoleon in battle but he was determined to beat him in bed. If the man cut a notch in his embassy bedpost for every conquest, then he appeared determined to whittle it down to a stump before he left.

Normally I would not have given a tinker's curse who he slept with. Indeed, I would have raised my hat in salute at what a fine example he was setting for his more junior colleagues. But when such a lecherous roué seems to set his sights on your own wife, well that is just too much. To make matters worse Louisa did not seem that unwilling an object of his desire. She had been out riding with him twice, but assured me that the British ambassador had behaved in an entirely respectable manner.

"I don't know what you are worrying about, we spent the entire afternoon in the saddle," she told me trying to allay my concerns.

But while I could not admit it, I had pimped my own Spanish cousin to Wellington in the past; I knew all too well what his afternoon ride often entailed. "That is *exactly* what I am worrying about," I snarled resentfully. Louisa looked puzzled for a moment until she took my inference and then she stormed from the room.

Perhaps we had been living closely in that hotel for just too long, although I had done my best to take her out to enjoy the delights of Paris. We had attended embassy functions when no French military guests were expected as an English couple. But we had also attended shows, exhibitions and all sorts of other events as a French officer and his English companion. Things came to a head with the embassy Christmas ball; it was to be one of the biggest events in the embassy social calendar. As I half expected, Wellington refused to let me attend as numerous French officers would be present along with many others who knew me as a British officer. I could see his point – I could hardly maintain my cover in those circumstances – but then he had the audacity to invite Louisa to the ball as his special companion. Well, that was the thick end of enough and no error. I put my foot down and absolutely, emphatically and categorically refused to let her attend. Not that it did me any good as she went anyway!

I would have stopped her leaving but I had been out that night with de Briqueville and some other French officers. I had staggered back to the hotel after midnight, tight on cognac, expecting to find Louisa there asleep, but there was no sign of her. I stared at the empty bed in disbelief for a moment. Where the deuce was she? For a moment my fuddled brain refused to believe that she could have so blatantly defied me. She knew what Wellington was like almost as well as I. But dammit she had always had a soft spot for him and knowing that there would be no lasting attachment, perhaps she fancied getting her muttons elsewhere for a change. For all I knew, Wellington's conquests had formed a Paris club and you were considered outré in society now if you had not been bedded by him. I stepped into her dressing room to find her favourite jewels were missing from the box and I could not see a blue silk ball gown on the rail that she had just had made. The maid left to watch little Thomas was a poor liar, an excellent attribute in staff, that. For she tearfully insisted that she had no idea where the mistress had gone but let slip that Louisa had told her I would probably be out with the boys all night.

Well, now I knew exactly where she was and with a mounting sense of outrage I strode angrily down the street towards the British embassy. If it was not already too late, I was determined to recover my lawfully wedded before our trusty ambassador had cocked his randy leg over her. But when I got there, they absolutely refused to let me in, because I did not have an invitation, dammit. Some flunkey hustled me out of sight of the crowd while I railed, threatened and demanded they produce my wife forthwith. I might as well have shouted at the wind to stop blowing for all the good it did. In the end, two burly soldiers bodily ejected me from the back entrance of the embassy, out of sight of the other guests and then for good measure escorted me back to the hotel. To make sure I stayed there, they stationed themselves at the front and back entrances of the building.

I paced up and down our hotel suite in a rage, but the more I considered the situation the more I realised how impotent I was. For even if Wellington and Louisa were playing the two-backed game, they would both deny it. I had no proof and if I made any rash accusations there would be one hell of a scandal. Wellington would probably call me out and I would ruin the reputation of my own wife as well as what credit I held in military and diplomatic circles. No, the more I thought about it, there was little choice but to grit my teeth and give them the benefit of the doubt. It was not the first time I had shared a woman with Wellington; in India I had unwittingly stolen his mistress. As far as I could see, the only positive in the situation was that even if they had slept together, His Majesty's Britannic ambassador was likely to move swiftly on to the next conquest.

Louisa finally returned at eight o'clock the following morning. You can be sure I watched her reaction closely, but while she was surprised to see me she showed not the slightest trace of guilt. Her hair and make-up were still perfect, too perfect for someone who had spent most of the night dancing as she claimed. She explained that Wellington had sent a man and a carriage for her and had insisted she join him. The equerry had orders that if she was in the hotel alone he was not come back without her.

"But I am your husband and I forbade it," I exploded angrily.

She did not look the slightest bit perturbed but just kissed me on the cheek. "Don't be silly, when did that matter," she said gaily as she walked off to get changed. "And anyway," she called over her shoulder, "I could not ignore the command of the ambassador."

"But you cannot have been dancing until now," I persisted. "What have you been doing?"

59

Still cheerfully ignoring any suggestion of impropriety she replied, "Oh we danced until the small hours and then played cards and games. It was such jolly fun and then the embassy gave us breakfast before we left." She yawned loudly. "I am going to bed now, darling; I will speak to you later." With that, she closed the door and left me at a loss for words.

I never did get to the bottom of what happened that night, although given the parties involved I have my suspicions. If Wellington had left me with a cuckold's horns well he did the same to half of Paris that summer. In the cold light of morning, I decided that it would be best to simply let the matter lie. I had no proof of wrongdoing and even if I had, making a fuss was unlikely to end well for me. It was not as if I had been a model husband throughout my marriage. No, I had at last found a relatively safe occupation; I had a beautiful wife and family, a splendid house and a fortune, I would have been mad to rock the boat.

Little did I know that a few hundred miles to the south several boats were being prepared that would do more than rock my world; they would capsize it.

Chapter 9

Now you might be surprised that we have got this far into my account culminating in the battle of Waterloo, with barely a mention of Napoleon. But you would not have been if you had walked the streets of Paris that winter, for Bonaparte was very much yesterday's man. Many remembered his empire with pride, but they also recalled that their former emperor was the individual who had united all the European powers against them. They had seen their country invaded and humiliated. Those allies were even then sitting in Vienna picking over the remains of their empire, deciding on their borders, the size of their army and navy as well as any reparations that must be paid.

Despite what some claimed afterwards, no one was thinking of Napoleon then. He was safe ruling his much reduced kingdom, the island of Elba, and most felt he had been fairly treated. The Prussians had wanted to hang him, but the other allies would not consider that. Rulers of nations are never keen on killing one of their own; you never know when revolution can strike again.

So while an emperor considered his destiny, a fat king sat seemingly safe on his reinforced throne and a skittish Duc d'Orleans dithered endlessly over whether he wanted to make a bid for the crown at all. Wellington left Paris at the end of January to join the discussions in Vienna while your correspondent chose this moment to take his family for a trip to the Loire. We stayed with friends of de Briqueville, glad to have a change from city life. Louisa and I had by unspoken agreement decided not to mention the embassy party again and we had a merry time. There was hunting with hounds, ice skating and the cook at the small chateau we stayed in was a master of his craft. Rarely have I been more happy and relaxed on active service, which as I have learned from long experience is often a portent of doom and disaster.

The break in the country had convinced us both that it was high time that we returned to England. A carriage took us back to Paris at the end of February and I arranged an interview with the new ambassador at the beginning of March. Britain's latest representative in Paris was called Stuart, a career diplomat who was handpicked by

Wellington himself. At thirty-six, he was only three years older than me, but had the look of greasy ambition all over him. It was not just his expensively cut clothes or condescending manner that signalled his different approach; even the furniture of his office gave him more airs and graces than the man who had conquered Spain and invaded half of France. Instead of the large dining table that Wellington used for meetings with his papers spread over it, Stuart sat behind an ornate Louis XIV-style desk that decorously proclaimed the opulence and power of his position.

Well, he did not intimidate me, for all of his gilt mouldings did not hide the fact that he was the new boy in town. It was his weakness which I could exploit to get him to do what I wanted. The Paris embassy was a top post and he would be determined not to make a muff of it. So he asked for my news and I told him what I knew of the Orleanists and the latest trivial gossip from the War Ministry, while he expressed his pleasure at having such a well-placed man.

"I am more than happy to continue in this role," I lied to him, "but I fear that the longer I stay the more likely I am to be revealed as a foreign agent."

"Lord Wellington was most complimentary about your abilities, Major Flashman," assured the pompous ass. "In fact he urged me to pay close attention to the information you provided. I would be most reluctant to disturb an arrangement that his lordship valued so highly."

"I am gratified to hear his lordship appreciated my humble efforts, sir," I fawned at him. "But if we are not careful all will be undone. I have been followed several times now and I know that enquiries have been made of French soldiers who have served in Spain to see if anyone knew me. It is only a matter of time before I am revealed as false and they may well discover that I am employed by this embassy."

"I see," said Stuart nodding. "But surely we are entitled to gather intelligence."

"Of course, Ambassador, but we have suborned a French ministry official to falsely give me a king's commission in their army. I am not sure if you have met Clarke the under-secretary, but he will not hesitate to create mischief over this if there is an advantage in it for him."

"You mean he cannot be trusted?" asked Stuart starting to sound concerned.

"Trusted," I laughed. "I would not trust him further than I could spit a hedgehog. He would sell out his own mother for advancement. If he was challenged over why he appointed me he would probably claim he was blackmailed by the British embassy to exonerate himself and point the blame in our direction."

"Good God," exclaimed Stuart.

"Yes," I agreed, warming to my theme. "I could easily imagine that he might even claim that I was the link between the British embassy and the Orleanists and instead of simply monitoring their plotting, we were in league with them and encouraging the overthrow of the king. You can imagine how well that news would go down not only in the French court but also in London. There would be one hell of a scandal." The colour was starting to drain from Stuart's face now showing that he was indeed imagining along those lines and considering the consequences for him. "Perhaps," I continued, "it would be better for me to return quietly to London. Then the Orleanists will have no reason to continue their investigations to reveal my true identity."

"Yes, quite true," agreed Stuart. "That does sound sensible, Major Flashman. I am much obliged to you for your sound judgement and advice. Lord Wellington was surely right to recommend your experience in these matters."

I barely hid a smile of delight; he was easier to manipulate than my six-year-old son. In a moment he was up and pumping my hand and assuring me that he would look to my departure as a matter of urgency. I went back to the hotel feeling well pleased with myself and assured Louisa that thanks to my diligent management of our novice ambassador, we would be on our way home within the week.

So two days later as I sat finishing lunch, I was not entirely surprised to receive an urgent summons to report to the War Ministry. I assumed that it was to do with my prompt dismissal from the frog army and even wondered if there was any sale value to my French colonelcy as there would have been in the British army. It was I remember Sunday the 5th of March. I was mildly surprised that they had called me in on a Sunday, when normally few people were in the building. But perhaps Clarke had chosen the time so that there would not be people there to ask questions as files were surreptitiously removed and records destroyed. Whatever the reason, I was unconcerned as I strolled along to the ministry building. For despite what I had told Stuart, no one had been asking questions about me at all and I felt quite secure in my role. On announcing myself at the desk, an attendant was called and soon I was being shown upstairs to that now familiar corridor where the minister and other senior officials had their offices. A surprising number of officials were working, which seemed deuced odd. I peered in one room as we passed and saw two generals locked in a heated discussion and being very furtive about it. They slammed the door in my face when they saw me watching them and for the first time I felt a prickle of alarm. Was Orleans finally making a move? I wondered. Surely not, I would have heard something, but then I had been away for the last two weeks in the Loire. Oh God, if a plot broke out just after I had confidently assured the ambassador that all was calm, well it would be the certain end of my diplomatic career and no error.

I turned to go into Clarke's office, he would tell me what was happening, or at least as much of it that served his purposes. But to my surprise, the attendant pulled me back and continued to guide me along the corridor. I realised that we were heading towards the minister's room at the end. That settled it. Something was up, for the minister of war would not involve himself in the dismissal of a lowly colonel. Which raised the rather more pertinent matter: Why the hell did he want to see me?

"Colonel Moreau, Minister," announced the attendant before hastily withdrawing behind me. An angry babble of voices abruptly stopped as I stepped into the room. I don't think I had seen so much gold braid in one place ever before. For sitting around a large table, were two marshals of France and another four senior generals. They were all

64

encrusted with bullion and sitting as stiff as waxworks. I gathered I had walked in on a disagreement and I quickly scanned the faces for ones I knew. General Souham was there and his eyebrows rose in surprise as he recognised me. We had once shared a carriage from Bayonne. Two others had their backs to me and did not look round at the interruption as they whispered amongst themselves. But one of the marshals got up and strode in my direction. I did not need the life-size portrait behind the desk to tell me that this was Soult, the minister of war himself.

"You are Ney's staff officer?" he demanded.

"Yes sir," I responded, feeling increasingly bewildered at events as he grabbed my shoulder and steered me back towards the door I had just entered.

"I want you to ride to Ney." He was virtually whispering so that those behind him could not hear. "Go now. Do not stop to talk to anyone and when you have him bring him straight back here. Do you understand?" I started to reply but he interrupted me, "Tell Ney it is a matter of the utmost importance. Do not let him delay a moment." With that, he was pulling the door open and absolutely pushing me out of it. "Now go, man, go." I stepped back into the passageway more confused than ever as to what was happening. But when I looked over my shoulder Soult was still glaring at me from the doorway and waving his hand to indicate that I should be moving faster. "Go, man," he repeated. "Ride like your life depended on it. France is relying on you."

Well with a cry like that from a French minister of state, I could hardly saunter along. There was nothing for it but to reach down and grab my sword so that it did not get between my legs and break into a run down the corridor back in the direction I had come from, with several startled faces staring after me from the side rooms.

Well it was clear something was afoot and if France was depending on Flashy then things were in a far more parlous state than anyone can imagine. One thing was for certain: I was under no suspicion or I would never have been sent on what was evidently an important mission. Whatever it was, it needed Ney to succeed and the only thing

I could think of was an Orleanist coup. But that would have been carefully planned and if I were a judge, whatever had happened had caught those generals unawares. They were not calmly plotting; they had been caught out by something. My coward's instinct picked up something else in the minister's office: fear. Whatever was going on was frightening some of them, and generals and marshals of their experience do not scare easily.

It was a two hour ride to Ney's country house at Coudreaux, east of Paris. At least it was if you knew where you were going. By the time I had got a horse and ridden outside the city it was mid-afternoon. I had to ask for directions three times before I found myself trotting down the gravel drive and by then it was dusk. I had considered a myriad of plots and schemes that could have been underway while I rode, although I never contemplated what had happened as that would have been too ridiculous. I had also wondered what would serve Britain's cause. Perhaps things would be better for the allies if Ney stayed at home. But without knowing what was afoot it was hard to judge and Ney seemed a steadying influence. He had said he would do what was best for France and a peaceful and stable France was in Britain's best interests.

I rapped on the front door and it was pulled open by a footman who had the bearing of an old soldier written all over him. Mind you, he can't have been a lucky trooper for as he stood back and invited me to enter I saw that he had lost his right arm and his left leg ended in a wooden peg. Seeing that I was an army colonel he was already saluting with his remaining arm as he enquired, "Good evening, sir, is the marshal expecting you?"

As I stepped into the house I saw a young boy standing at the bottom of the stairs. He was about the same age as my Thomas, but dressed in a perfect miniature of a French lieutenant's uniform. He was throwing me a salute as well, aping the mannerisms of the old trooper now closing the door. The boy must have been one of Ney's sons and so I brought myself smartly to attention and returned his salute with a grin and a wink as I replied to the doorman. "No, but I must see the marshal urgently."

But before the old retainer had had the chance to make a move, a door to my right opened. Ney himself strolled out wearing some patched britches and what looked like a thick woollen smock over an old shirt.

"Michel," he called to the boy, "I thought I told you to go to bed... Colonel Moreau, what on earth are you doing here?" The marshal did not look pleased to see me and waved again at the boy, who scampered away up the stairs.

"Who is it?" a woman's voice came from the room Ney had just left.

"It is one of my staff officers," replied Ney over his shoulder before adding, "he will not be staying long."

"Nonsense," called out the woman. "You cannot send him back to Paris now, it is dark. He must join us for dinner."

Ney growled a noise over his shoulder that could just be taken for assent. Then he turned back to me. "Well, what is it? Has Clarke sent you to check up on me? You should know better than to disturb me with my family."

"My apologies, sir, but I come from Marshal Soult. He has asked me to bring you to him straight away, about a matter of the utmost importance."

"So what is going on? Surely you know."

"I'm sorry, sir, I don't. But something is happening. There were a lot of senior officers in the War Ministry for a Sunday. Soult was very clear that I should ride straight to you and bring you directly back to him without talking to anyone else on the way."

Ney gave another growl of annoyance. "It will be those bloody Orleanists getting them excited again. Soult never can resist playing politics, the damn fool."

"I am not so sure, sir. There were several generals in Soult's office, including Souham, and they looked scared rather than excited. Are we going to leave now, Marshal? Should you explain to your wife?"

"You have not met my wife, have you?" asked Ney with a grin. "No, we will leave in the morning and there is no need to tell her anything of this. I have just been summoned to an urgent staff meeting, do you understand?"

I agreed and was shown into the drawing room to meet his wife. From his comment I had expected a formidable woman, but she was most welcoming, giving me a seat by the fire to get warm after my ride and chattering gaily about her family. The marshal, though, was lost in thought and did not join the conversation. He slumped down in a chair on the other side of the hearth and stared moodily into the flames. At one point he looked up and asked, "Who else was in Soult's office when you were there?"

"They were all senior officers but I only recognised Souham," I told him. I am sure his wife missed nothing as she kept glancing across at him with a look of concern, but she left her husband with his thoughts and continued to prattle on to me.

The next morning the one-armed valet woke me just before dawn to advise that the marshal would be leaving as soon as it was light. I met Ney in the hall a short while later, he was still dressed in civilian clothes.

"Well let's get going and find out what this nonsense is about," he said briskly. "I am calling at my Paris house for my uniform. I am also seeing my attorney there, he should know if any plots are afoot. I am not walking into a meeting with Soult unprepared." In a few minutes we were mounted up and riding hard back to the city. With hardly anybody on the roads it seemed like no time at all before we were back in the capital. I looked anxiously about, but there was no sign of any insurrection. No barricades, no smoke from fires. If anything it was too quiet, with few people on the move for the start of the week. Our horses were soon trotting up the cobbles of the Rue de Bourbon where Ney had his town house. The marshal went to get changed while I waited in the salon eating a boiled egg and a bread roll, which was all the breakfast the elderly housekeeper could provide at short notice. Her husband had been sent off to fetch the attorney and no sooner was Ney back downstairs than the man was hammering at the door for admittance.

The little lawyer was bursting with excitement as he was shown into the room, "What extraordinary news, Marshal."

"What news?" asked the marshal impatiently. "Do you know what is going on? For my aide doesn't," he added gesturing at me.

"You don't know? Why Bonaparte has landed near Cannes to retake the country. The king's brother is already heading south to arrest him. It is all in the *Moniteur* this morning."

There was a stifled sound of someone half choking on boiled egg before Ney gasped out "What!" and sank down on a chair. There were those afterwards who swore that Ney was in league with Bonaparte from the start, but I for one can confirm that he wasn't. The man looked as stunned as a beaten prize-fighter. He wasn't the only one, as I thought it could not possibly be true. Bonaparte had been beaten and humiliated, forced to abdicate and driven to obscurity. It had to be a false rumour, but no, for the little lawyer was waving a copy of a newspaper in front of Ney's face to show him.

"But that is madness," the marshal murmured as he read. "He has no army and no support. The bloody fool, why couldn't he have stayed where he was? He could have lived with respect and honour, but now this..."

He looked distraught. The emperor's departure from his little kingdom of Elba seemed the ultimate folly. It was doomed to failure. As the little lawyer pointed out in the report from the *Moniteur*, already his advance party had been arrested in Antibes and he had been forced to flee into the hills to escape the wrath of the loyal populace of the Provence region. It was absurd to think that the allies would ever accept Bonaparte back on the throne of France.

"He must be stopped," said Ney decisively and then he looked at me. "It is time that we met Soult."

Chapter 10

I tried to look grim as we rode to the ministry, but I could not share the marshal's grief. While I have been present at many historic moments, you often did not appreciate their importance at the time. Usually you are simply struggling to survive. Here was one momentous event that I was right at the heart of. For there was no doubt that this would be a time that people would talk of for years to come. I had met Bonaparte once before in '02, when he was at the height of his power. He had stood astride my time like Caesar or Alexander, dominating Europe and influencing the whole world. And like Caesar, he seemed oblivious of the fact that his time had come to an end.

Now as a British agent I would have a ringside seat at his downfall. I would be able to spy on what would be a national tragedy for France, as it brought down its Corsican demon once and for all. I did not need to go to the embassy for instructions, for I knew that they would want me to stick to Ney like a hungry limpet. What a diplomatic coup it would be for me. Why, I would be famous, the man who was there at the end of Napoleon, a modern day Brutus. That was, of course, assuming that some angry frog mob had not lynched the bastard before we got there. No, he had nearly a thousand men with him; it would be down to a stalwart regiment or two to stop him. Ney leading his men forward, with Flashy encouraging them on – from the rear, if I had anything to do with it. It would be a capital victory and if I did not end up with a British knighthood, well there would be no justice.

Now that we understood what was going on, the near empty streets made more sense. It was as though the whole city had woken up to the news and was now holding its breath to see what would happen next. There were no public shows of support for either the former emperor or the king. The few people we saw were just scurrying about their business. A number recognised Ney riding in his marshal's uniform. Most now avoided his eye and hurried away, but a few watched him with suspicion, no doubt wondering where his loyalties now stood.

We rode in silence for a while and then Ney looked at me curiously. "Do you not have to report what is happening to Clarke or the

British?" It was the first time he had mentioned my link with the British embassy since the day we first met. It unsettled me for I had begun to convince myself that I had been accepted as a French officer. But Ney only knew that I reported to the embassy; he had no cause to suspect that I was, in fact, a former British officer.

"No sir, I imagine that they are reading the papers as well as us." Then for sauce I gestured to a baker who was hurrying into his shop as we approached. "Do you think they are wondering if you will declare for the king or the emperor?"

He stiffened at that and growled, "They should know that I will always declare for France."

If the streets were nearly empty, the War Ministry was not. It resembled a kicked ants' nest as officers and attendants hurried about with orders and maps and occasionally shouted to each other about the whereabouts of units and their commanders. Bonaparte might only have landed from Elba with the five hundred men of his Old Guard and a similar number of cavalry that he was allowed to keep, but no one could accuse the War Ministry of not taking the threat seriously. As Ney swept through the throng I saw people nudging each other and pointing in his direction. He was a rare visitor and if anything his presence served to highlight the importance of the situation. Soult welcomed us into his office, appearing tired and dishevelled as though he had been in the room ever since I had last seen him.

"It is good to see you," he said to Ney, shaking him warmly by the hand. Then the minister turned to me and indicated I should take a seat, gesturing to a chair in front of his desk. "I need to speak to the marshal in private," he told me.

There was a small balcony in Soult's office overlooking the city and the minister led Ney onto it, shutting the glass doors behind them. For a moment the two old campaigners, in their best dress uniforms stood silently staring out over the capital and its people that they had fought so long for. Then I saw Soult start to talk in urgent tones. This was one conversation I wanted to listen in on. The window next to the balcony was open a few inches and I moved swiftly towards it. Crouching down on the window seat, I put my ear to the gap and was

71

just in time to hear Ney say, "If that is what you think you must do. But you know he must be stopped and it would be better if one of us did it."

"I agree," said Soult wearily. "You are right, it has to be done. The Duc de Berry is planning to ride south to Besançon. I'll not see that royal popinjay claim the credit for capturing him. The sixth military division covers the area, but he will have no idea how to organise it. I will give you command. The men will be more confident with you in charge and you can make sure that the matter is handled properly."

"The duke is better than most of them," grumbled Ney. "He has at least seen a battle, if only from amongst the staff. But I agree, the men will have more confidence in me and we need to finish this quickly." He paused for a moment or two before adding, "I will leave as soon as I have seen the king."

"The king," replied Soult sounding surprised. "What do you want to see him for? He is ill and not seeing anyone at the moment." There was another pause and then Soult continued, "I think my news unsettled him. He probably thinks we are all suspect now."

"Yes," agreed Ney, "and that is why I must see him." They started to wish each other good luck then and I realised that they were about to come back in. I sprang away from the window to lounge back in my original chair, picking up a magazine to pretend I had been reading it all along. They took a few moments longer to emerge from the balcony than I expected and I spent the time studying this extraordinary publication. It was a cross between a court journal and one of our sporting papers. The front page carried a feature on what the well-dressed royalist should wear when hunting on his reclaimed estate. So help me it absolutely recommended a powdered wig for hunting, as though the last thirty years had not existed.

Ney came in alone, leaving Soult still with his thoughts on the balcony. I sprang up like the attentive staff officer, but Ney barely noticed. "We are going to the Tuileries Palace," he murmured as he strode towards the door.

The royal court was just a short walk away, but as Soult had predicted, seeing the king was not going to prove easy. He was rarely

72

seen in public and in all my time in Paris my only visions of him had been in very unflattering cartoons which gave him the dimensions of a plum pudding. There was also a famous portrait which had been exhibited, showing him picking up a bare-breasted female figure that was meant to represent a fallen France. I remembered the painting well as it appeared to me that instead of picking the girl up he was reaching down to fondle her right tit.

This being my first visit to the palace, I hoped that I might finally get the chance to meet the royal dumpling, but it seemed not to be. After waiting for over an hour, while watching Ney pace up and down in an anteroom, he sent me away to try to find de Briqueville. I spent three hours searching all of his favourite haunts, even checking on a general's daughter that I knew he had been tupping on the side, but there was no sign of him. I returned to the palace to find Ney still pacing in the anteroom.

"Are you still waiting, sir?" I found myself blurting out the obvious.

He ignored my question. "Did you find de Briqueville?"

"No sir, he is not at home or at any of his usual places."

"Mmm, General Dupré mentioned that he had been paying court to his youngest daughter. The blackguard wanted me to warn de Briqueville off as not good enough for his precious Persephone." Ney grunted in amusement before adding, "This from a man who started out as a butcher's boy. You don't think he could be with her, do you?"

"I *know* he is not, sir," I replied looking the marshal in the eye.

"Very good. Well I have told them that I am not leaving until I have seen the king and so you had better get comfortable, it might be a while yet."

We waited an hour together with me stretched out on a bench seat reading some periodicals about court life that had been left on a table for visitors. Ney spent most of this time pacing slowly up and down the room, lost in thought. Twice flunkeys came in and whispered to him about delays. They were trying to get us to return the next day, but I saw the marshal vigorously shaking his head at the suggestion. Eventually some bewigged steward in a coat dripping in gold braid arrived to show us into the royal presence. We entered an audience

73

chamber, but there was no sign of the king. At one end was a curious pyramid of cloth with a few courtiers loitering nearby and there were several other groups of the nobility gathered in huddles around the room talking among themselves. It was certainly a grand place with gilt decoration everywhere you looked and silk *fleur de lys*, the royal symbol, sewn every few feet on the carpet. I expected our steward to lead us through this chamber to another smaller room to meet the king, but instead he guided us to the cloth pyramid.

I have seen some astonishing sights in my time, but that one stays long in the memory for it was so unexpected. There we were, striding across that grand hall and then the steward was gesturing for us to stop and I was vaguely aware of Ney starting to bow. I was still gazing around for sight of the king when some movement caught my eye. I realised with a start that there was a head at the pinnacle of the pyramid. It was a huge fat head with flabby jowls under the chin and dark, pig-like eyes that were staring at me with curiosity. I still did not quite understand what I was seeing until a fat bejewelled hand appeared through a fold in the middle of the cloth and at last the penny dropped.

The king was sitting on a large throne raised up on steps several feet above the floor. What I had taken as a triangle of cloth was a long cloak that had been artfully draped around the monarch to disguise his immense girth. But as he now moved I caught a glimpse of the vast bulk underneath. Rarely can fabric and fastenings have been put under greater strain. The silver buttons on his waistcoat could have had one of our eyes out if he had sneezed. I saw now that the painting I had seen of him fondling the tit of Madame France had been a monstrous flattery. Indeed, what I had taken as cruel cartoons in the news sheets could actually have underestimated the reality of the situation.

I must have been staring open-mouthed in astonishment. I was brought back to the present by a kick in the ankle from Ney as he hissed, "Moreau, bow, you fool." I hastily did as commanded. Ney raised himself from his bow. Muttering under his breath to me, "Stay here," he started to walk towards the king. "I apologise for my aide," I heard him say. "He was quite overawed to be in the presence of your majesty and forgot his manners."

"That is quite all right, my friend." The king's voice was high and quavering for a man-mountain of flesh. I could not hear what was said between them after that as they conversed in low voices. But staring around the hall, I saw that I was not the only one paying an interest. Several of the other groups of courtiers were watching the encounter with some drifting towards the throne, no doubt to eavesdrop on what was being said.

As I stood upright again I noticed the steward nearby watching me with intense disapproval, but I was too curious to care. "Can he walk?" I whispered. "He must weigh, what, two hundred kilogrammes? Surely his legs cannot support the weight?"

The steward puffed up in indignation. "Of course His Majesty can walk," he whispered at me. I must have shown some disbelief in my face for he added, "His Majesty suffers badly from gout, which is why he sometimes travels in a chair on wheels, but I can assure you he can walk when he needs to."

There was a small crowd of courtiers in front of the king now listening to his conversation with Ney and I crept forward a few paces myself. The king's reedy voice could be heard asking Ney to, "Do all you can to stop more bloodshed and strife for our country. It has long deserved a period of peace. I know you are a marshal I can rely on."

Ney was conscious of the audience around him and he spoke loudly for them all to hear. "Sire you can count on me to act most energetically against the invader. I hope soon to bring him back in an iron cage." With that, he took another deep bow and turned, striding towards me and the door beyond.

I just remembered to take a bow myself before turning. As I did so I heard the king exclaiming to those still near him, "Iron cage? I did not ask that of him. Oh, oh..." He was quite agitated at the thought, but I heard no more as I followed the marshal from the room.

Chapter 11

From the title of this packet of memoirs, you will no doubt have guessed where this account will end. Now, I have had an event-filled career and seen many battles and sights in my time from the capture of the Gamo, Assaye to Badajoz, I have stood on the ramparts of the Alamo, faced scalping Iroquois, run from Zulu impis and seen unspeakable horrors in the African jungle. But whenever I talk of my life there is normally only one incident that everyone wants to know about – especially when they discover my unique perspective on it. 'Waterloo!' they will exclaim all misty-eyed. Then some old dodderer will inevitably start marshalling the cutlery and showing me where those that mattered went wrong, but you will see that for yourself presently. It was a bloody and brutal business and it did change the world, but the really astonishing thing was not the battle, but the time that led up to it. How one man almost singlehandedly recaptured a country that had previously rejected him and then came deuced close to beating the combined might of the rest of Europe.

That is why I started this account where I did; it would have been wrong to just write of the days of the battle itself. For to do that, would deprive of you seeing what a truly exceptional achievement it was. It was an extraordinary time that involved the giants of my era performing incredible feats, things I would not have thought possible. If there had been any justice Napoleon would have won at Waterloo and you may be surprised to learn that the unwilling instrument of injustice was, in a large part, your correspondent. But I am getting ahead of myself now, for we must go back to when his venture looked doomed to founder at the outset.

Louisa was in bed by the time I got back to our hotel that night, but I woke her up to give her my news. She was impressed that I was to be so close to a key moment in history and agreed with me that it could set the seal on the start of my diplomatic career. We celebrated my good fortune by rattling each other in fine style – little did I realise that it would be the last time I was to enjoy that pleasure for many months.

I set off in fine fettle for Ney's town house the next morning to start our journey south. On the way, I picked up the latest news sheet. The reports were all five days old as it took time for information to reach Paris, but it looked like Bonaparte's rebellion would be over before we got there. The paper was full of reports from across Provence of his party being hunted by royalist forces. It appeared that he was hiding out in the nearby mountains like some renegade. Given the delay in news, he might already have been killed and captured or could even be being dragged in chains to Paris by some other ambitious commander.

"They would have to kill every one of his guard first," said Ney when I mentioned this to him later. "General Cambronne took the cream of the Old Guard to Elba with him; they will not die easily." He gave a heavy sigh before adding, "I would rather you be right but I fear that there will be work to do when we get there." He gave me a sidelong glance before gesturing at the paper and asking, "Have you seen the piece on page three?"

I pulled the paper back out of my pocket and there, hidden away in the corner of the page, was a small article I had previously overlooked. Marshal Soult had resigned as minister of war. No reason was given but I guessed that he wanted no further part in operations to capture his old commander. Now the conversation I had overheard on the balcony made more sense as did the king's assertion that Ney was a marshal he could rely on.

"Can you guess who has replaced him?" asked Ney with a wry grin. When I looked puzzled he added, "It is your old friend Clarke, back to do the same job under the king that he did under the emperor. I doubt he will have the same reluctance to capture our old master."

It took nearly three days of hard riding to reach Besançon and thinking back, there was still no cause for any alarm. We questioned couriers travelling in the opposite direction and very few had any news. As far as anyone knew, Bonaparte and his little band of men were still roaming around in the Jura Mountains, while royalist troops were being gathered to round them up. Some men we met knew the mountains well and assured us that at that time of the year, early March, the main passes would be blocked; there was no question of him dragging guns or wagons through them. At most, some single-file tracks might be passable, but with ice and deep snow, they would be treacherous for any not familiar with them.

I was delighted. Rounding up any bedraggled survivors that might emerge from that barren terrain would be easy work. We would be back in Paris with Bonaparte in chains by the end of the month. In fact, in some ways I was even a bit disappointed with the emperor, for he evidently had not learned from his earlier mistakes. His Old Guard might be brave and loyal, but nothing destroys an army's morale like days tramping bollock-deep in snow, whether it be on the Russian steppe or in the French mountains. Trust me; you don't want frostbite in your nether regions.

We reached Besançon on the 10th of March, I was cold and stiff from so long in the saddle. But the marshal was eager for news and the information we quickly gathered soon dispelled any hopes I had for a relaxing hot bath. The problem with heading towards an unfolding event in those days was that you caught up with the news. A courier from the south might take five days to reach Paris, but only two or three to reach Besançon. So after no real news since we left the capital, rapidly we received a handful of reports and none of them good.

General Bourmont, the local commander, had welcomed us to the army depot and wasted no time in showing us up to his office so that we could talk in private. Bonaparte and his little army had emerged from the mountains near the town of Gap. They had covered a distance of some two hundred miles over mountainous winter terrain in just seven days. It was an extraordinary feat which had caught the royalist forces completely on the back foot. Many of them were still patrolling areas around the coast. The fifth regiment was hurriedly sent to intercept him and finally made contact just south of Grenoble. What happened there has passed into legend.

The fifth regiment was arrayed across the road in a double line with orders to stop the emperor at all costs. The five hundred men curved their line onto the hills on either side of the route so that they could all fire down on anyone approaching up the road. They must have seen Napoleon's scouts appear at the end of the valley and then the emperor

78

himself on horseback with the neatly drilled lines of his Old Guard marching behind in column. They showed no concern at the men waiting for them, marching with muskets resting on shoulders. As they got closer Napoleon's marching band struck up the *Marseillaise* – a tune that had been banned under the Bourbons and which represented the Revolution and the old empire like no other. There must have been a stirring in the waiting ranks then but they stood firm and silent, watching the column come on.

When they were just three hundred yards off, Napoleon called a halt to his men and boots slammed into the gravel as they stood to attention and the band fell to silence. You must have been able to hear a pin drop in the valley as Napoleon slowly dismounted and started to walk alone towards the waiting regiment. I later spoke to one of those soldiers and he described the scene. Bonaparte paced calmly towards them with his hands clasped behind his back. He looked up at the men flanking the road and gave a slow nod of approval as he moved on. He only stopped when he was a hundred yards short of the centre of the line – well within the range of every gun. The officers of the fifth stayed silent, unsure what to do. This was the man who had led them to conquer Europe. Could they really just shoot him down like a wild dog? As they hesitated, it was the emperor who called out loudly, so that all around him could hear.

"Soldiers, do you recognise me?" he shouted and as he did so he brought his hands forward and held open his coat. "If there is one among you that wishes to kill your emperor then here I am."

At that moment one twitching trigger finger could have stopped the venture in its tracks, but none of the soldiers wanted to make that first move. My informant told me that they had talked about what they would do as they waited for the emperor to arrive. Some still felt a sense of loyalty towards him, but others feared that if he was allowed to proceed then France would fall into a bitter civil war and chaos.

"Forty-five senior men of the government in Paris have called me from Elba," the emperor continued. "And my return is supported by three of the main powers of Europe. Already the king has left the capital. Now, my soldiers, will you stand in my way?"

It was all misleading bosh, of course, but they did not know that. Calling them *his* soldiers reminded them of the glory he had led them to in the past. Their emperor was now promising them peace, prosperity and above all pride in their nation and a return to their status as the respected guardians of France.

"*Vive l'Empereur!*" It was not clear who shouted it first but in a second the cry was taken up all along the ranks and guns were raised or dropped and men rushed forward to acclaim their new commander-in-chief.

With that moment of bluff and effrontery, Bonaparte had increased the men he had under arms without spilling a drop of French blood and for him, things just got better. As word of his proclamations spread, he was enthusiastically welcomed into Grenoble by its citizens. Thereafter, two more locally based regiments went over to him.

He promised people whatever they wanted: peace and prosperity to merchants; security of tenure to those fearing that their land would be reclaimed by aristocrats and a return of *la gloire* to his soldiers. He may well have promised the mayor a new town clock and a night with the empress for all I know, for he was as much a politician as he was a general.

And if you say to yourself, well, the French were fools to believe him, just think back to when you last stood before a politician's hustings. I will wager a penny to a sovereign that the rogue promised that he would work to reduce your taxes and yet not cut any government spending that you value. He probably claimed he would improve government efficiency as though the idea occurred to him in his tub that morning and no one else had ever considered it. Yet still we vote for them and forget their broken pledges at the next election.

Napoleon was no worse and, many would argue, better, as at least he had delivered on many of his promises in the past – certainly enough for people to give him the benefit of the doubt this time. He had brought France order from the chaos of the Revolution, a legal system that they still use today, new roads and bridges, scientific institutes. I am sure someone told me that he had spent more on setting up schools across France than he had spent on the army. I doubt that is true, but if it is, it is only because he never fed his armies outside France and left them to live off the land. He had ruled France for fourteen years and was not known for dishonesty. He did lie, of course. He won every election he stood in, but winning was not enough for him and so votes were rigged to give him overwhelming majorities. He also routinely lied in his despatches about his battles, only reporting a fraction of his casualties and greatly exaggerating the losses of his enemies. But people either did not know or did not care for they knew he had popular support and they enjoyed reading about the great victories of their soldiers.

This trust was brought home to me that morning in Besançon when Bourmont, the old general who had told us this tale, turned to us and asked if any of Bonaparte's claims were true. I was so astonished that I forgot myself and replied without deferring to Ney.

"Of course they are not true!" I exploded. "The British government has nearly bankrupted itself to get rid of Bonaparte, why on earth would they want him back?"

Bourmont looked surprised at my intervention, but Ney smoothed things over. "My aide has recently been a liaison officer with the British. Now, when did he make these claims?"

"It was on the 7th, three days ago, sir," replied Bourmont.

"Well we both met the king three days ago in Paris and he had no intention of leaving," said Ney calmly. "It is just some of his usual boasting. Do we know where Bonaparte is now or where he is heading and how many troops he has?"

Bourmont looked slightly reassured at that. "He is heading for Lyon, sir, the Comte d'Artois commands there. I have sent all available troops to support the comte. They should arrive in time to help with the defence of the city. We don't know how many men the emp… I mean General Bonaparte has now, but I would guess at a few thousand."

"Where is the Duc de Berry? Isn't he is supposed to be in command here?"

"I believe he is still in Paris, sir," said Bourmont awkwardly, refusing to meet Ney's eye.

I felt the hair start to rise on the back of my neck. I have had the misfortune to be in more than my fair share of military disasters; just two years previously I had watched in Canada as the British General Procter threw away every military advantage. There had been confused leadership and a skilled and determined enemy then and this was all starting to smell familiar. Instead of a coup for my diplomatic career, I was now sensing an imminent catastrophe. Bonaparte was famous for using speed and surprise to win victories and he had done so again. He had crossed the mountains far quicker than anyone imagined possible and now was plunging through the soft underbelly of France towards its second city. Instead of rounding up a small band of exhausted soldiers and a rejected emperor, the royalists were struggling to get their troops in the right place, while their commander had not yet stirred his royal rump from the palace!

The royalists should have expected something like this and I realised with a sinking feeling that so should I. Ney's next words did not make me feel any more comfortable.

"Well I am not going to do any good here. I will write to d'Artois and ask to be employed in the vanguard of the army, where my presence will hopefully carry some weight. Have we no troops here at all, then?"

"Just five hundred," answered Bourmont shifting uncomfortably. "I have not sent them on as they are not reliable. They are calm in the barracks, but word of General Bonaparte's proclamations has spread like wildfire. They have already shouted support for his return and many have removed the white cockade from their uniforms. I don't doubt that they would throw in their lot with him if given the chance."

"Perhaps I should ride to Paris," I suggested tentatively, hoping for a way to slide out. "I could inform them of the urgency of the situation and suggest that the Duc de Berry bring as many reinforcements as quickly as possible." Once I was away, wild horses would not drag me south again until the situation was firmly under control. But the marshal was not going to let me escape that easily.

"I suspect," replied Ney grimly, "that there are already plenty of people riding to Paris with news. No, let's wait until I get a reply from Lyon, then we will decide what to do."

Bourmont put us up in the officers' quarters while we waited for a response to Ney's message. There was no immediate danger, but my grim sense of foreboding was not lifting. Despite his use of the relatively lowly title of comte, d'Artois was the king's younger brother and not very humble at all. In fact, he was one of the most strident royalists and had been pressing his brother to repeal many republican laws and return land to the nobility. He had a high-handed attitude to anything republican and was probably the last man you would want to lead an army whose loyalty was wavering. The Duc de Berry was his son and if the man had any sense he would know the effect that his father's attitude would have on the populace. It probably explained his tardiness in leaving Paris.

I took a turn about the town. There was a tension that you could almost touch. The streets were mostly deserted and when you did come across someone, they rarely looked you in the eye. Perhaps it was my uniform that frightened people for several scurried inside buildings and slammed doors shut as I approached. Whether that was because they thought I was for the emperor or the king it was hard to say.

Chapter 12

We thought we would get an answer to Ney's enquiry late the next day at the earliest and I was happy to stay in Besançon until then. It was still some hundred miles away from Lyon and for the moment the place was quiet. However, we did not have to wait that long. I had just settled myself into the officers' mess after my walk around the town, when there was the clatter of steel-shod wheels and hooves in the courtyard outside. I have seen some strange harbingers of doom in my time, from jealous Spanish dwarfs to painted tribal chiefs wearing nothing but a loincloth, but rarely have I seen one so luxuriously appointed. The polished sides of the well-sprung carriage still gleamed under a coating of dust from the journey. You could make out armorial crests painted on the doors while the liveried driver and flunkies sitting on the back box announced that the occupant was a man of status. Any lingering doubt on that point was also assuaged by the escort troop of hussars who gathered a respectful distance away in the corner of the courtyard. At first I thought it must be the Comte d'Artois and wondered what the hell he was doing this far back from the front. But Bourmont told me that the crest belonged to the Duc de Maillé, who was chief of the comte's household.

I watched expectantly for his lordship to emerge and Bourmont busied himself arranging refreshments for our noble visitor, but the duke had other ideas. One of the footmen on the back box scrambled down and after taking some instruction through the carriage window, hurried to our headquarters building. So it was that five minutes later a stony-faced Marshal Michel Ney, Prince of Moscow and Duke of Elchingen was seen striding towards the carriage window to attend on the occupant like some tavern pot boy. Bourmont and I followed in his wake, but a gloved hand appearing at the carriage window pointing at Ney and then at the ground by the carriage door showed that only he was required. The marshal gave a barely suppressed growl of fury at this fresh indignity and continued forward. I meanwhile decided that it might be timely to use my rank to interrogate the young captain commanding the escort to find out what the hell was going on.

The carriage and its escort clattered out of the square a few moments later. If I had been feeling merely disquiet before, then I was now in a growing state of funk for the news from the escort commander was far worse than I had feared. The royalist cause seemed determined to wrestle a catastrophic defeat from the grasp of victory.

I walked back to where Ney was explaining to Bourmont what he had been told. "He says that the Comte d'Artois has been betrayed and that he has decided to abandon Lyon and fall back on Paris." Ney gave a bark of laughter before adding, "He had no orders for us and just told me to do what I could to stop Bonaparte's advance."

"But…but…" Poor Bourmont was struggling to comprehend what had happened and given the circumstances you could hardly blame him. "But Lyon is the second biggest city in France," he exclaimed at last. "The comte must have had more men than the emperor to defend it, not to mention the city walls and the guns on them. For heaven's sake Bonaparte has no artillery at all. He could have just shut the city gates and waited for reinforcements to lift a siege."

"He had to leave," I interrupted them, "because the good comte had so antagonised both his own soldiers and the people of Lyon, that they were ready to open the gates of the city to the emperor as soon as he appeared."

"That cannot be," protested Bourmont. "Lyon is well known as being a stronghold of the royalist cause."

"Well, it is not any more," I told him. "Posters supporting the royalist cause were being torn down as soon as they were put up, according to the officer commanding the escort. And in their place were proclamations like this." I held out a paper that the officer had given me. Ney unfolded it and held it so Bourmont could read over his shoulder as well.

Frenchmen, in my exile your complaints and desires have reached me.
You have asked for the government of your choice – the only legitimate one.
I have crossed the sea and I am here to resume my rights, which are yours.
Victory, swift and triumphant lies before us.
The eagle with the nation's colours will fly from village spire to village spire,
even to the towers of Notre Dame. Napoleon

"The officer said there were hundreds of proclamations like this around the city," I told them. "The tricolour was being flown from some of the public buildings and he thought that many of the soldiers sent to defend the town would go over to the emperor." What I did not add was that the escort commander had sounded almost wistful as he told me this, as though he quite liked the idea of serving Bonaparte himself.

"My God," gasped Bourmont. "If he takes Lyon he will have most of the south-east. It will be a civil war then."

"The north-east will come out for him too," mused Ney. "He has always had support there. It would be him in the east and us in the west." He abruptly shook his head as though coming out of a reverie before continuing more briskly, "No, there is still time to cut off the head of this snake yet. It is just one man; we cannot let him destroy France. I promised the king I would stop him and so I shall."

"Are we going to join D'Artois?" asked Bourmont.

"No, he is the best recruiting sergeant Bonaparte has. We will collect all the loyal troops in the eastern departments; gather them at Lons-le-Saunier. Bonaparte is moving so quickly he does not have scouts. We will fall on his flank. The soldiers who have followed him will think twice about firing on other Frenchmen serving their lawful sovereign."

I rather thought that soldiers fighting for Ney might think twice about firing on soldiers serving their beloved emperor, but before I could make an objection Bourmont raised a more relevant point. "How many men do you think we can gather? Will we outnumber the emperor's followers, do you think?"

Ney gave a grunt of irritation before replying. "I have been studying the troop returns. I think we should be able to gather six thousand men. Bonaparte might have ten thousand by now, but don't worry I shall settle the accounts with him. We are going to attack the wild beast when and where he least expects it."

He looked at us expectantly and while Bourmont was still ashen-faced at the sudden change of events, he managed to stammer "It... it will be an honour to serve with you, sir."

They both turned to me, but for a moment I was too stunned to speak. I mean of all the wretched luck. Instead of my moment of history rounding up an exhausted and defeated renegade ruler, I had been pitched straight into the heart of what was about to become a civil war. Not only that, it was plain as a pikestaff that I had ended up on the losing side. For despite what Ney claimed, I could not see many soldiers fighting for him against Bonaparte. Ney commanded the highest respect among the troops as one of Napoleon's marshals, but at the end of the day, Napoleon was the emperor. To make matters even worse, I was his bloody aide, expected to be at his side in whatever madness he proposed; and he was not known as the '*bravest of the brave*' for nothing. I had a sudden vision of just the two of us in a cavalry charge against the entire French army and the ground around us boiling in shot and shell. I realised that I was shuddering at the thought.

"Are you all right, Colonel?" asked Bourmont staring at me curiously.

"What… ah… yes… I was wondering if we should not involve the allies in this. I mean the Austrians, British and Prussians could all get armies here quickly and they would have no divided loyalties. They could provide a firm backbone to any resistance…" You can guess who I was about to propose as a messenger in this venture. But I saw that I had blundered by suggesting that there was any lack of backbone in the royalist forces.

"No," stated Ney firmly. "If foreigners set foot in France it will be time for every Frenchman to declare for Bonaparte." He smiled at me then and put his hand on my shoulder. "I know you have the best interests of France at heart, as do I, but we Frenchmen have to do this ourselves."

I came as near as a toucher then to revealing my true identity. Shouting that I was no more French than the Duke of Wellington, who was more Irish than English, but most assuredly not French. However, I was deep in the dark country then and having some people around me who at least thought they were a friend was better than none. I also took comfort in some other news that the commander of the escort had given me. Napoleon had apparently declared that he was determined to regain control of France without spilling a drop of French blood – all the more reason to allow people to think me French. If the worst came to it, I thought, I would just shout *Vive l'Empereur!* with the rest of them and look to slide out at the first opportunity.

Having resolved to go on the offensive, Ney was in a fever to start planning his campaign. We spent that evening poring over maps and troop lists, issuing orders and doing everything we could to get all available troops and supplies to Lons-le-Saunier as soon as possible. We were joined that night by another general, a man called Lecourbe. He was a revolutionary veteran who had been dismissed from the army by Bonaparte, suspected of being involved in some plot. He harboured a deep resentment of the emperor and after all the orders had finally been written he sat with Ney drinking brandy and talking of old times.

"Are you sure the men will follow you?" asked Lecourbe at one point. I pricked my ears up at that for it was a question heavily on my mind too.

"Of course they will fucking follow me," growled Ney, the coarse trooper in him more apparent when he was drunk. "I will fire the first shot myself and then they will join me. If just one tries to declare for the emperor, he will have my sword through his body up to the hilt."

I went to my room that night more convinced than ever that disaster was in the offing. I would have slipped away that night but Bourmont had told us that as a precaution he had placed sentries he could trust at the gates with orders to stop anyone trying to leave. He was worried about some of his own men trying to join the emperor, while I was thwarted from travelling in exactly the opposite direction. In the morning Ney decided to write to the king to update him on his plans. He did not want to tell d'Artois in case the duke dragged us into some strategy of his own.

"The men won't stand for d'Artois, but they will stand for me," he insisted as he put his seal on the despatch. Naturally I offered my services as courier again, only to be rebuffed once more. "You are my only staff officer," snapped Ney irritably. "I need you by my side. Find some junior officer to take it." I did, but I took a moment to add my own letter and got the young officer's word of honour that he would deliver it personally. My note was to Louisa, telling her to get out of France with my son as soon as possible as resistance in the south was crumbling and civil war looked certain. I had written the note in French and with my French name in case the courier or someone else decided to read it. I did not doubt that if Louisa got the message, she would pass the warning on to the embassy. I just hoped that my postscript that, 'I would join her as soon as I could,' would not prove unfounded optimism.

We left for Lons-le-Saunier that morning, changing horses at Poligny. There Ney was greeted by a local official who sought reassurance that all would be well. Ney repeated to him his promise to the king to bring Bonaparte back to Paris in an iron cage.

"It would be better if you brought him back dead in a cart," the man suggested.

"No, no," replied Ney laughing. "You don't know Paris. The Parisians must see him beaten and humiliated. It will be the last act of his tragedy, the denouement of the Napoleon epic."

He was in a strange mood on that journey. His eyes gleamed with excitement and despite the odds of any future battle being against him, he seemed in remarkably good humour. It was as though he was relishing the part he thought he would now play in history. He was free of d'Artois and determined to show that he was the better of his former master. He spent most of that journey riding alongside one of the two generals, but at one point he dropped back to ride with me. It was evening then and bitterly cold with a freezing wind whipping our faces, but when I commented on it he just laughed. "I can tell you were not with us in Russia, Colonel, then you would know what cold really is. He talked for a while about the Russian campaign and if anything his stories served to chill my bones even further. But as he harked back to those times with a fond regard, I decided to ask the obvious question.

"You served alongside the emperor for so long. Do you have no misgivings at all about facing him in battle?"

"No," he said without hesitation. He gave me a stern glare before adding, "I looked the emperor in the eye and told him when I could no longer serve him. I might not have royal blood like some, but I am a man of honour and I have given the king my word to deliver the emperor as a captive. I have always done what I think is best for France." His tone softened. "I don't think too much about these things, Colonel, if you think too much you will not get anything done. Trust to your instincts and do what you think is right. That is the only way you can look in the mirror and be proud of what you see." He must have thought that I was having doubts myself and his little speech was intended to allay them. He reached across and slapped me on the back before adding with a grin, "Keep warm, Colonel." Spurring his horse forward, I thought he would return to riding alongside the two generals in front, but instead he rode past them and cantered away at the front of our party alone. He evidently wanted to do some thinking of his own after all.

It was gone midnight by the time we arrived at Lons-le-Saunier. There was no army barracks there and so we put up at the inn in the centre of the town, a place called The Golden Apple. Soon we were shown into what in an English pub would be called the snug, a small comfortable parlour with a roaring fire. Having thrown off our greatcoats to better feel the heat, we moved towards the small hearth. The two generals initially took the prime positions, leaving a gap between them for the marshal. But Ney insisted that I take the centre space with him to share the warmth. We must have stood in virtual silence in front of that blaze for five minutes, it was bliss. Teeth slowly stopped chattering, muscles ceased shivering and feeling came back to hands and feet. Then the landlord came in with four cups of a hot broth. He stopped short when he saw all the decorations and marks of rank on Ney's uniform. His eyes darted cautiously between us; he was clearly wondering if we were for the king or for Bonaparte.

"Beg pardon, sirs, I had no idea that I had so many generals in my humble establishment. Are you heading north or south, gentlemen?"

"South," replied Ney firmly. "In the service of the king."

"Ah, in that case, gentlemen, would you be interested in meeting a Monsieur Boulouze? He is a merchant who arrived earlier this evening from Lyon. He will have turned in for the evening, but I am sure for you he would arise again."

A bleary-eyed Boulouze showed himself a few minutes later. His initial scowl of irritation at having been dragged out of bed by his landlord in the middle of the night to speak to some army officers, transformed instantly when he saw Ney.

"Marshal Ney, 'pon my soul, it is an honour to meet you, sir. I have seen you several times in Paris and have always been grateful to you for bringing the country peace and prosperity." He shook Ney warmly by the hand as he added, "I remember well how you persuaded the emp… I mean General Bonaparte to abdicate before. I know we can rely on you to stop this current madness."

Despite his fatigue from the ride, Ney grew an inch at the compliment and gestured for the merchant to take a seat. "The landlord tells me you were at Lyon," he prompted.

Boulouze settled into the chair, clearly pleased with himself that the great Marshal Ney was interested in his account. "I was there when General Bonaparte arrived, sir, and a few days before. As soon as we heard he had landed the rumours started. There were stories that the king was going to restore estates to their old aristocratic owners and that they would be able to charge new rents on all those living on their lands. People went to the Comte d'Artois to get him to deny it but he refused. I told those that would listen that if Bonaparte was back it would be war again for certain, that the allies would never let him regain the throne, but many people told me I was wrong. The British navy had allowed him to escape from Elba, they said, he could not have got away otherwise. Then the proclamations started to appear all over the city saying that all the allies supported his return."

"Was there any resistance at all?" asked Ney quietly.

"No sir, the royalists had all fled long before General Bonaparte arrived." Boulouze looked embarrassed as he added, "The army led the cheering, sir, but the people gave the general a good welcome too. The general reviewed his troops in the central square like the old days and gave speeches. I heard him say that he had the support of Austria and that the empress and his son will come from Vienna."

"That is just some of his usual boasting." Ney tried to sound dismissive but he did not sound convincing.

"One of my friends heard the general say that they would march on Paris with their hands in their pockets as it was all arranged for them to get there."

"Well it is not all arranged," said Ney more confidently. "I can tell you that for certain. For the king himself has tasked me to stop Bonaparte and that is what I shall do."

"So the king is still in Paris?" asked Boulouze, who had clearly heard otherwise.

"I am sure he is," replied Ney sounding less confident. "Now, Monsieur Boulouze, I thank you for your information but I should let you return to your bed." He turned to the rest of us. "You should retire to your rooms too, gentlemen, it has been a long day. We will discuss developments in the morning." Ney showed no sign of getting up himself, instead stretching his feet out from his chair before the fire. We took our leave and I was the last to go through the door. As I did so I looked back and saw him pulling a paper from his pocket, it was Napoleon's proclamation I had given him the previous day.

Chapter 13

The next morning I was awoken by the rattle of wheels on the cobbles outside my window at the inn. Looking out I saw another liveried coach had pulled up, but at least this time the occupant was getting out. The man was dressed in an army uniform that dripped of gold braid. With a powdered wig and an ivory-topped cane instead of a sword, it did not take great powers of deduction to guess that despite his senior rank, he was likely to be one of those royalist officers who had never stepped on a battlefield. I hurriedly dressed and went down the stairs to the parlour, where raised voices indicated that Ney's meeting with the stranger was not going well.

"How dare you take that tone with me," Ney was roaring at the aristocrat as I slipped into the room to stand beside Bourmont and Lecourbe, who had got there before me. "I am a peer and marshal of France, the Prince of Moscow and Duke of Elchingen, not your blasted footman."

"I have no wish to cause you any offence, sir," replied the stranger in a way that implied he really could not give a damn if he did. "But you will understand that your commanding officer, the Comte d'Artois, is puzzled why you should be gathering all available troops here, on the path expected to be taken by your former commanding officer, when he had anticipated that you would fall back to join him to defend Paris."

"What exactly are you suggesting, sir?" Ney's voice was low with fury. The fingers of his right hand clenched into a fist and I saw the newcomer notice and step back a pace.

"I am merely pointing out that some..." and here he waved his hand airily to indicate others rather than himself, "...may consider your actions...err...unusual."

"They may be unusual in your army, sir, where commanders lose control of their men and then run before the enemy arrives. But in my army, if you want to attack someone you gather soldiers together and put yourself in the path of your enemy."

"But surely you should inform your commander," interjected the stranger.

"I did," Ney shouted. "The comte has no army left; the king is my commander now and I have written to him with details of what I intend. Now, sir, get your aristocratic arse out of my presence."

The noble spluttered with indignation, but before he could say anything a grinning Lecourbe stepped forward. "Let me guide your aristocratic arse back to your carriage," he said with a grin before grabbing the man firmly by the arm and steering him out of the room. Lecourbe had been talking on the ride the day before about his days as a revolutionary soldier. It was clear now that he was on the royalist side more due to his hatred of Napoleon than any affection for his king.

"Who was that man?" I asked Bourmont as they left the room.

"The Marquis de Saurans, he is another aide de camp of the Comte d'Artois."

"He is a bloody fool," interjected Ney. "Just like the rest of them. They have no idea how to command an army." He picked up a piece of paper from the table. "This is how you speak to an army: '...the eagle with the nation's colours will fly from village spire to village spire, even to the towers of Notre Dame.' That is how the king should write to his men. Instead, he sends his brother and fops like that. Men too proud to let me even sit in their carriage. Look at the mess of things they made in Lyon, a city that had been fervently for the king. They have disbanded most of the Imperial Guard and insulted the rest of the army with new regimental names and incompetent officers. Bonaparte shows them how to lead, how to inspire, how to…"

"Sir," interrupted Bourmont, a stricken look on his face. "You are surely not considering abandoning the king; you have given your oath."

Ney gave him almost a look of pity. "I have given more oaths to Bonaparte in my time, but you need not worry. He will never forgive me for forcing him to abdicate. He would probably rather take my head than my hand. Now leave me, gentlemen, I would like some time alone."

It was a Sunday morning as I remember, but there was no rest for us that day. Bourmont, Lecourbe and I were busy sending orders to hurry troops and supplies, organising ammunition and gathering artillery. If we could have trusted our own men it would have been an ideal time for me to slip away as I rode between various depots and encampments. Unfortunately we could not and Bourmont had already organised the few men he did have faith in to patrol the outskirts and the roads to stop deserters. He also decided it was necessary to give us an escort of loyal royalists for our own protection, given the increasingly truculent mood of the men.

While I wanted to escape to Paris and then to England, I reluctantly had to accept it was necessary to bide my time for a while. One of our couriers had been roughed up by some Bonaparte-supporting soldiers on the road to Paris. He had been forced to use the flat of his sword to escape. The roads would not be safe for anyone heading north when many soldiers were heading south to join their emperor. Bonaparte was still several days away, but it was already obvious to me that despite what Ney thought, the men would not fight against their emperor.

It was not just the men; on the Monday Ney ordered the arrest of an officer who had called out *Vive l'Empereur!* at one of the cafés. Other officers were reporting increased agitation amongst their commands with soldiers refusing to obey orders, the tricolour being displayed and Bonaparte's proclamations being widely circulated. One of the patrols brought in a dozen soldiers they had intercepted trying to desert to the emperor and their commander showed me a handful of the tricolour cockades that the men had kept in their packs from the old days. I tutted in sympathy with him, but kept one of the cockades all the same. I told the officer I would show it to Ney, but I put it in my pocket to use when it came necessary to change loyalties myself.

By Monday evening it was obvious to all but the most fervent royalist that the situation at least in Lons-le-Saunier was lost. Reports were coming in that Bonaparte now had fourteen thousand men whereas we had six thousand at most and nearly all of those would be reluctant to fight, particularly against such overwhelming odds. Then we received a message from the nearby town of Bourg to say that the 76th Infantry stationed there, who had been ordered to join Ney, had instead displayed their old colours and marched off to join Napoleon. The mood was now getting ugly in the town and that evening a young officer was brought to the inn. He was one of the trusted royalists and had been badly beaten by soldiers. He was covered in blood and likely to lose the sight of one eye.

The marshal grew more morose and unsure what to do. Bourmont and Lecourbe suggested that they should take the few remaining loyal troops and march to Chambery where it was rumoured a Swiss army was coming to help the king. Ney flew up at that, swearing that he would never join a foreign army against France. He stomped up to his room and I almost felt sorry for him, for he had painted himself into a corner. He was sure the emperor would not welcome him back and while he felt a sense of loyalty to the king, he hated most of the courtiers. Now his own command was almost certain to refuse his orders to fight. Tomorrow, I thought, would be the day that things would collapse. Bonaparte would be a day nearer, the men verging on open revolt and the few loyal troops would be more than stretched to keep a lid on things. It would be easy then to divert my escort elsewhere and get away. I would ride north as soon as it was safe – my rank would see me past the checkpoints. I patted the tricolour cockade in my pocket; I would need it once outside of the town and possibly sooner if things turned nasty.

The Golden Apple hotel was busy that night, full of officers and civilians speculating on what might happen next. Thinking it might be my last night of comfort before several days of travel, I ordered wine and food and settled down to talk to Bourmont and two other officers. None of us noticed two men in civilian clothes arrive, who then had a message passed up to Ney's room. Shortly afterwards they were shown upstairs.

The strangers were not there when Ney summoned me to his chamber just after midnight. But the presence of extra dirty plates and glasses indicated that he had dined with someone. Ney looked agitated and tense, his hair dishevelled. The bed was disturbed as though he had retired, could not sleep and got up again.

"Moreau," he said as I entered. "Sit down and join me for a drink." As I sat he watched me carefully as he filled two glasses. He appeared to be trying to weigh up something in his mind. "The other night, on the ride here," he said at last, "you asked me if I had any doubts about fighting the emperor. Do you have any doubts?"

Well I might have drunk the best part of a bottle of brandy downstairs that evening, but I was not drunk enough to miss the danger here. Did he suspect my allegiance? I still remembered his threat to run through with his sword any officer who shouted his loyalty to the emperor. Unconsciously my eyes flicked across to where the weapon lay on a chest at the bottom of the bed. "Well, sir," I said at last, "like you I have served the emperor for many years and in several campaigns, but I have also given an oath of loyalty to the king."

Ney smiled at my obvious evasion and without a word pushed a paper across the table towards me. I looked at it expecting to find some new order from the king or d'Artois, but instead felt a jolt of shock as I noticed the signature at the bottom of the page. Then, taking a deep breath, I read the note in full.

Mon cousin. My major-general sends you your marching orders. I have no doubt that on receiving news of my arrival at Lyons you have already made your troops resume the tricolour flag. Execute Bertrand's orders, come and join me at Chalons. I shall receive you as I did on the morrow of the battle of Moscow.

Napoleon

I sat stunned for a moment at the audacity of it. Bonaparte must know that Ney was planning to stop his advance – he probably had far more spies amongst our men than we did amongst his. Perhaps he even knew about the rift between Ney and d'Artois and he surely was aware that most of Ney's command were reluctant to fight against the man who had led them to so many victories. But you don't get to be the emperor ruling Europe without knowing how to manage your men. Threats and promises of retribution would not have intimidated Ney.

They would only have made him more stubbornly determined to resist. So instead Napoleon appealed to his pride and his love for *la gloire*, giving him the opportunity to make a fresh start.

God knows what Napoleon had said to Ney after the battle of Moscow, but the reminder of their former campaigns together and the title the emperor subsequently gave Ney had evidently struck home. I looked up at the marshal; he was as excited and confused as a dog with two sticks. Or in this case, a marshal with two batons; one given to him by his king and another from his emperor. On the one hand, he had given his oath and he prided himself on his integrity. But the royalist leaders treated him and his wife with contempt. On the other hand, he had felt trapped before, and this offer gave him an escape. He would be a valued marshal of the empire again, albeit one who some men would never truly trust. "So," asked Ney impatiently. "What do you think?"

I have often wondered what would have happened if I had called Ney back to his duty to the king. I flatter myself that I could have done it, for while he was brave, he was not a shrewd man. I would just have had to throw some of his earlier phrases back at him and suggest that his name would become a byword for treachery, which it did in due course, for some. That was undoubtedly my duty as a British diplomat, but there were other factors to consider, chief among them preserving the precious skin of yours truly.

For if Ney stayed loyal to the king and word of this offer got out – and who knew what other imperial messengers were passing among the ranks – then life would get deuced dicey for his one staff officer. I remembered all too well the blood-soaked royalist I had seen earlier that day. The army was still certain to go over to the emperor whether Ney was with them or not. A refusal would just mean one less marshal for the emperor to command. Bonaparte may even have sent cavalry patrols to cut roads to stop Ney and other royalist officers escaping if he chose to stay loyal to fat Louis. But if he threw in his lot with the emperor there would be harmony among the ranks of the army and more importantly, safety for your humble obedient.

So it seemed to me that my duty, at least as far as I was concerned, was clear. Looking at his expectant face and taking into account his opening question, it was obvious what he wanted me to say. Bonaparte knew his man well, for if Ney had wanted to be talked into staying loyal to the king he would have sent for Bourmont rather than me. So for an answer I reached into my pocket and without a word, put the tricolour cockade on the table before us.

"I knew it," said Ney grinning. "We have served too long under the tricolour to turn against it. Some of the others, though, will be harder to convince."

I gestured to the plates still on the table. "Did his messengers say anything else? What are your orders he mentions?"

"I have a proclamation to read to the troops tomorrow and then we march to Chalon." A look of concern crossed his face as he added, "They still say that his escape was arranged with the allies. Did you hear any rumours when you were in Paris? I can't see how he could have escaped Elba without British help."

I had been puzzling over that one for I knew that the British had an ambassador on the island specifically to keep an eye on Napoleon. He could have been silenced but there was also a British naval squadron cruising around the island as well as royalist French naval patrols. Surely they should have been able to stop the emperor's escape. That was what they were there for. Had I but known it, the emperor's ship had passed within hailing distance of a French naval brig, but had convinced them that they were on a trading voyage. Meanwhile, the British ambassador was visiting his lover in Naples.

"I did not hear anything in Paris, only talk of the Duc d'Orleans. But I cannot believe that the British government would deliberately let the emperor escape."

He gave a deep sigh. "It will be war for certain. But at least this way it will not be Frenchmen fighting Frenchmen in a bloody civil war with foreigners joining the royalists to pillage our country." He smiled again. "With the emperor, we have the best army there is and we have beaten their alliances before. Who is to say we cannot do so again."

"Most of the army has been disbanded," I pointed out.

"True," agreed Ney, "but the allies have disbanded their armies too. We will be defending the sacred soil of France. Men will come back to their regimental eagles with more passion to defend their homes."

"I am sure you are right, sir," I said while privately thanking my stars that I would not be there to see it. For Ney's unexpected conversion could only be good news, at least for Flashy. There would be no imminent battle and with Ney by Napoleon's side, I doubted many soldiers would stay with the king. The royalists would be forced to flee again. But Ney was right: no country was in a state of readiness for war. There would be months of negotiation and posturing, leaving plenty of time for me to slip away. If the channel ports were closed I could travel through the Low Countries and reach England that way. Indeed, if I were to witness Ney's meeting with the emperor, it could still be something to boast about in diplomatic circles when I got home. Then when the shooting finally started I could watch the soldiers march through London to battle, while sitting safely behind a window in the Foreign Office.

I confess I did not give a thought to the poor bastards in red coats who would have to fight again. Many would probably be pleased at the prospect for it meant regiments would be raised again and promotions for those that lived through this new conflict. I had done my share of facing French columns. It was time for someone else to have a go, while I stayed safely out of the way. I must have been grinning at the thought for Ney looked at me and said, "I don't think I have seen you happier, Colonel. But while us war horses relish the prospect of battle, there will be others who do not. Send Lecourbe and Bourmont to see me in the morning, but it would probably be best if you do not warn them what I am to say."

Chapter 14

I don't know what Ney told Bourmont and Lecourbe the next morning,
but to my surprise they did not ride straight away to Paris to report
Ney's treachery. Bourmont even arranged to have all available troops
paraded that morning on the outskirts of town. At eleven Ney appeared
in the yard of the Golden Apple in his best uniform and, flanked by his
two generals they rode to the assembly. I followed on a few yards
behind with the officer of the escort and several other officers who
were on Bourmont's staff. It only took five minutes to get to where the
men were formed up but I don't recall anyone speaking on the way.
Bourmont must have told some of his officers, but those who knew
what was about to happen were unsure of the real loyalty of those
about them.

The troops were arrayed on the Place d'Armes in a hollow square.
There were two regiments of infantry and six squadrons of cavalry,
some three thousand men in all. But word had spread of some
important happening and the people of the town had come as well in a
large crowd that went around two sides of the square. The noise from
the gathering increased markedly as we came into view. The clamour
was not just from the townspeople; officers and sergeants could be
seen going up and down the ranks to still disquiet and in a couple of
places I could see men being shoved back into line after they had tried
to call out to their comrades. They were in a black mood and if we had
been about to order them to march against their emperor, as most
seemed to be expecting, then I had little doubt that we would be facing
a mutiny. But Ney was unconcerned as he dismounted just outside the
square and then, gesturing for us to follow suit, he led us on foot to its
middle.

Ney stood still in the centre and slowly looked around at all of the
men watching him. There was silence now, everyone waiting to see
what would happen next. Ney took a paper from his pocket and then
nodded to two drummers in the front rank who both did a drum roll.
Then after another interminable pause, Ney slowly drew his sword,
resting the blade against his shoulder and began to read. "Officers,

non-commissioned officers and soldiers, the cause of the Bourbons is lost for ever…"

That was as far as he got before the cheering started. We were surrounded by shouts of *Vive l'Empereur!* and men waving swords and muskets and throwing their hats in the air. As far as I could tell, the cheering of the soldiers was echoed by the crowd beyond. Ney waited a full minute for the initial tumult to die down before he started to read again.

"The lawful dynasty adopted by the French nation is again to be seated on the throne. It is to the Emperor Napoleon that it belongs to rule over our beautiful country. Soldiers, I have often led you to victory. Now I am about to lead you to the immortal phalanx that the emperor is leading to Paris."

He waved his sword above his head to signal his speech was over and the cheering was renewed and this time, the lines of men broke and rushed towards us. In a moment we were surrounded by men of all ranks, shaking our hand and slapping us on the back. Ney, wild-eyed and laughing was pushing his way through the throng, and hugging men as he went.

One man stood out, however, as he was not laughing or cheering. It was an officer called Dubalen, the colonel of one of the infantry regiments, and he was forcing his horse through the men towards Ney. He looked livid with fury and when he got close to Ney he shouted down at him

"Marshal, my oath of loyalty to the king will not allow me to change sides so easily. I give you my resignation."

"I won't accept it," cried Ney. "But you are free to go, get away quickly… No, leave him alone." This last remark was to a sergeant who had heard the exchange and who was reaching up to pull the colonel from his horse. "Go man," urged Ney to the colonel. "Let him pass," he added to the men around him.

The colonel spurred his horse through the throng and reached the main street of the town. But once there, several dragoons rode wildly after him. They must have guessed that the colonel was staying true to the royalist cause and had not heard Ney's instructions in all the noise.

One of the dragoons overtook the colonel, but Dubalen's sword flashed out and the trooper fell with a nasty wound to the head. The colonel escaped without any further pursuit. That was the only royalist I saw that day. There probably were a few among the townspeople, but with three thousand armed men cheering the emperor, they wisely decided to keep their feelings to themselves.

The soldiery drank the town dry that night and I attended a dinner hosted by Ney at the Golden Apple. By then he was strangely subdued, but he was the only one. We had avoided a mutiny, a battle with Bonaparte and the chances of a civil war within France were receding fast. This meant that the precious skin of your correspondent looked set to be preserved for a bit longer. Some speculated on why the British had let the emperor escape and all seemed convinced that 'perfidious Albion' had done so through some unknown self-interest. I still could not see what and when I raised the prospect of another war against the combined might of the allies, my brother officers did not seem the slightest bit concerned. With their emperor at their head again, they felt confident that they could beat whatever the allies threw at them. They talked of battles at the end of the last war when the emperor had marched and counter marched and repeatedly beaten much larger enemy forces. There was still resentment that Paris had been surrendered to bring an end to his first reign, when many in the army apparently felt that they could still have won.

The next morning, my hat adorned with the tricolour cockade, I joined the men as they prepared to march to join their emperor. As I surveyed the ranks I was surprised by how many tricolour-adorned helmets there were. At least half the men present had evidently tucked the old emblem away in their packs in the hope that they would need it again. The soldiers were in high spirits, but Ney, now in a more mercurial mood, dampened them down by sending them back to their barracks to smarten themselves up.

"You will not embarrass me in front of the emperor," he roared at them before promising to break down to private any sergeant whose company was not in good order within the hour. With much grumbling, we set off at lunchtime for a three day march, not to

Chalon but to Dijon, as Ney received new orders from the emperor while his entourage continued to speed north.

It was a strange progress for the morale of the men was higher than that of the officers. While I was happy just to be heading north in safety, Ney grew gradually more tense and irritable as he got closer to his emperor. His temper was not improved by a steady attrition of his staff. Bourmont disappeared quietly on the first night. Lecourbe, who had no plans to leave, told me that his fellow general could not stomach breaking his oath again and was going home. The next night a number of Bourmont's officers followed his example. I was tempted to join them but thought that I might at least stay for the meeting of marshal and emperor so that I could salvage something from the experience to earn diplomatic credit.

Ney glared at the dwindling numbers around his table at breakfast the following morning and then walked off to his room for an hour to start writing something he called his 'justification'. When we reached Dijon that evening we found orders for the men to rest there but for Ney to join the emperor at Auxerre, which was less than a hundred miles from Paris. The marshal shut himself away again to continue his writing and the next morning he and I set off together for Auxerre. The rest of his army was left to enjoy a day of rest to repair boots and uniforms before a further march north.

I think we both felt a sense of apprehension as we rode into the town to meet the emperor. Ney had been lost in his own thoughts most of the way and had barely spoken to me at all on the journey. When we stopped he would borrow a desk and ink and scratch away again on his 'justification', which now stretched to nearly a score of pages. Once when he had gone off to the privy I took the chance to read a bit of it. It started with, 'If you continue to govern tyrannically I shall be your prisoner rather than your partisan', and continued with pages explaining why he had found it necessary to insist the emperor abdicate before and the reasons he was obliged to abandon the king to serve him again. It was a long rambling piece with lots of crossing out and scruffy blots of ink. It seemed to me that it was more to convince the marshal that he was doing the right thing than the emperor.

By then I had been masquerading as a French officer for nearly five months. I was well established in the role and accepted as such by all those around me. But I could not help but feel a sense of unease as the moment of meeting the emperor approached. I had been introduced to him once before, as an English spy, no less, but that had been twelve years ago at a crowded embassy reception. He must have been introduced to hundreds of people that night alone. Surely he would not remember me from that long ago. I had been a callow youth of twenty-one back then; now I was a veteran of numerous battles.

As we entered the town of Auxerre many recognised Ney and cheered him as he made his way to the town hall. He was in his full uniform and word must have spread that the marshal was bringing his army to join that of Napoleon. If they had known that earlier he had been planning to oppose the emperor, they tactfully chose to ignore the fact. The town hall or *Hotel de Ville* was protected by huge grenadiers of the Old Guard, who, with their bearskins, looked at least seven feet tall. Their boots slammed down on the flagstones as they presented arms to Ney, but the hard look on their faces hinted that these men at least knew Ney's loyalty was in doubt.

Bonaparte did not keep us waiting long. Within minutes an aide was showing us up a grand staircase and into a large reception room. There we found a group of officers at the far end gathered around a large table covered in maps. As a colonel, I was the most junior officer present and no one paid any attention to us as we paced across the room. Our boots made a clacking sound on the wooden floor and spurs jingled, but not one head looked up. It was obvious they knew we were approaching, but all were waiting for the emperor to notice us first. Ney came to a halt a few yards from the group and I stood a respectful half a yard behind him. He looked awkward standing there with his justification clutched tightly in one hand.

"Ney," said the emperor looking up at last. "I am glad that you decided to join us." There was a wry grin at the edge of his mouth as though he realised that his erstwhile trusty marshal had been given little choice. Then he stepped around the table towards us, holding out his hand in greeting. That was when I realised quite how fat he had become. I had seen drawings, of course, and already knew that the slim, long-haired and energetic first consul I had met in Paris had become a short-haired and plump emperor. He wasn't as fat as the king, of course – only a whale matched that level of obesity – but instead of a bit of a paunch, there was now a round pot belly straining against his waistcoat buttons.

"It is good to see you, my friend," said Napoleon gripping Ney's hand. "Have you brought me many troops?" he asked although I suspect he knew exactly how many men we had.

"Yes sire," replied Ney shifting uncomfortably.

The emperor turned back to the men at the table. "We should write to the king to tell him not to send us any more reinforcements, we have quite enough." They all laughed at that with a few curious looks at Ney, for it was obvious that the emperor was also reminding him of his former loyalty.

"Sire, I must present you with this," muttered Ney thrusting forward his much laboured on justification.

"What is it?" asked the emperor flicking through the first few pages. He frowned as he must have scanned the phrases about his tyrannical government as well as the explanations of Ney's behaviour. He shook his head slightly in resignation before half turning and throwing the document on the table. "What need do I have of a justification from you?" He put his arm now around Ney's shoulders. "We have fought together for far too long for that. It will soon be like old times with us chasing our enemies before us."

"But sire," Ney started and I guessed that he felt the situation slipping away from him. He had probably planned some sort of speech along the lines of his justification, but that had all been swept away.

Bonaparte, no doubt suspecting the same, decided to deftly remind the marshal where the power lay in the room. "Unless, my friend," he prompted gently, "you still want to take me back to Paris in an iron cage?"

Ney jerked back as though stung by a bee – and he had, for the bee was one of Napoleon's imperial symbols. "No sire, I never said that." There were some smirks around the table now, for Ney was admitting he was aware of the story. While I had been there to hear him say it, I was sure that reliable reports of Ney's boast had reached the emperor too. A film of sweat had broken out on Ney's brow. He might be the bravest of the brave, but it seemed he was frightened of his emperor. Bonaparte watched him with a look of mild amusement, probably relishing his control over his headstrong general, while Ney shifted uncomfortably, at a loss for anything more to say. Then of all the cursed luck he suddenly remembered me. "Sire, I would introduce Colonel Moreau, on my staff."

"You are most welcome, Colonel," said the emperor turning to me.

I had a sudden moment of panic. What was the etiquette for meeting a commanding general who was also an emperor? Do you salute or bow? Unsure, I did both, snapping to attention and then giving a stiff bow, while muttering, "Your majesty." But when I straightened up I found Bonaparte's eye's boring into mine.

It was only at that moment that I remembered. The face and the body had aged a lot since I had last seen him, at the Austrian embassy, but the eyes were still the same. They had carefully examined me back then too. Only now did I recall that at the time it had seemed as though Bonaparte had been trying to memorise my face. I had been introduced to him then by Wickham, Britain's spy master and now here I was masquerading as one of his officers, without even the hint of a disguise. For the first time in my life, I wished for a disfiguring scar or something that would have changed my appearance. I had scars on my chest and leg, even a wound on my arse, but apart from a feint scar on my forehead, my face had survived untouched. I too felt sweat break out on my own brow. Surely he recognised me and I half expected his next words to be, 'How is Mr Wickham?' before ordering my arrest and execution. It was a matter of course on all sides for spies in enemy uniform to be shot. But instead, he just gave a slow nod of greeting as he watched me, more with curiosity than hostility, and then turned back to Ney.

"Come, walk with me and tell me of your journey." The two of them turned and began to pace up and down the far side of the room, stopping occasionally to look out of the windows as they talked in low tones. I was left there still sweating and literally shaking with fear.

"You have not met him before, then?" said a voice beside me. I turned to see a tough, wiry man in a general's uniform holding out a glass of brandy for me.

"No sir," I said gratefully taking the goblet and gulping some of the spirit down.

"It is often like that when people meet him for the first time. I have been as close to him as anyone this past year and it still gives me a start sometimes when he remembers something I said or did months before." He held out his hand. "Cambronne," he said by way of introduction. I realised that this was the general that Napoleon had taken with him to Elba to command his Old Guard. "Oh, and we salute the emperor," said Cambronne grinning. "Civilians bow." He turned back to join the others at the table while I strolled around it to warm myself by the fire. I wanted as many people between me and the emperor as possible in case he glanced back in my direction. The fire was burning well and as I warmed my hands in the heat I looked down. In addition to the logs, a fresh wad of kindling had recently been added, which looked suspiciously like Ney's justification.

Chapter 15

I felt a weight lift from my shoulders when Ney and I finally left that room. At every moment we had been in it I had half expected the emperor to wheel around and point at me, shouting 'Arrest that man!' But it appeared he had forgotten me for he did not give me a glance as I followed the marshal out of the door. The experience had shaken me more than I liked to admit. It was a long time since I had been in that kind of danger and now I just wanted to get away. I suggested again that I should ride to Paris, this time with messages for Ney's wife as he was to return to his army and slowly march it north.

"She will want to hear from you why you have changed sides," I prompted, "rather than read about it in the *Moniteur*." To my surprise, he agreed. But before I could celebrate my good fortune he mentioned that there had been some trouble in the capital with royalists turning on suspected Bonapartists.

"My wife will have gone into hiding with reliable friends," he told me. "It would be wise for you not to arrive ahead of the advance guard or you will not find her anyway. Some of the Old Guard will march off ahead of the emperor for Paris the day after tomorrow; you had best join them."

This meant staying with the emperor's party for a day. But he now had ten thousand men, surely, I reasoned, I could keep out of his sight among them. Then once I was in Paris I could get someone to deliver the messages to the Princess of Moscow, or Madame Ney as she was known to the royalists, while I checked that my own dear wife had left the city.

We had heard that royalists and foreigners were leaving Paris in droves, without difficulty as the Bonapartists were happy to see them go. Napoleon had publicly repeated he wanted to regain the country without spilling a drop of blood. I was sure Louisa would have headed north with the embassy staff, but I would visit the hotel first to be certain, and then head to the channel ports myself. I reached into my pocket to check that the white royalist cockade was still there for when I would need to change sides again.

Bonaparte left Auxerre at nine the next morning. It was one of the most inspiring things I ever saw. There was a big black carriage and around fifty mounted officers in the yard by the town hall waiting for him to leave, one of whom was skulking at the back to keep out of the way. We could hear a crowd of some two or three hundred people waiting in the market place at the front of the building for a glimpse of their emperor. They gave a roar of delight as he appeared mounted on a white horse and the rest of us dutifully followed him out into the square. He was riding through the crowd, occasionally raising his hat to those cheering him, while he looked closely at all those around him. The rest of us rode two or three abreast in a column starting ten yards behind him. Despite my best endeavours, I had ended up further forward than I had intended, in the fourth or fifth row of men, with a colonel on one side and a major on the other. I did not know either of them; Ney had left for his army earlier in the morning.

We were all progressing through the square when the emperor pointed at a man in the crowd and reined in his horse. The emperor shouted something I could not catch but the noise of the crowd started to drop as they wanted to listen. Then I distinctly heard him shout, "Yes you are Duroc, we were together in Italy."

"Yes sire," came a voice from an unseen man in the crowd. Then the emperor called for someone to hold his horse while he dismounted.

"Italy," I muttered, half to myself. "That campaign was nearly twenty years ago. Surely he cannot remember a soldier from that far back."

The man in front of me turned around and grinned. "Yes he can," said General Cambronne. "I have seen him do this many times, he has an incredible memory. Watch him with this crowd and you will understand why he is an emperor."

The crowd was clearing around the fellow I took to be Duroc. He was a grey-haired old man in his fifties, but he brought himself up smartly to attention and saluted as his emperor approached. Napoleon ignored the salute and swept forward to embrace the man in a hug as though they were long-lost friends. "This man," called Bonaparte to the quietening crowd, "stood beside me in Italy." He looked down at the man and added, "I saw you at Arcoli, didn't I? You broke your arm there."

The man could only nod. He looked as though he was experiencing a moment of religious rapture, but managed to hold up his right arm by way of confirmation.

"My friend Duroc," shouted Napoleon to the crowd, "was beside me when we charged our enemies at Arcoli, sweeping them from their fortifications. When I took command in Italy the army was dressed in rags and few even had boots. They had not known victory. Once I arrived they did not know defeat." There was a rousing cheer at that but Napoleon waved them to silence so he could continue. "Did we plunder and loot that country?" he asked. If he was looking at Duroc for support he was on a sticky wicket, for the man still had the countenance of a stunned ox. Quite a few of the crowd looked uncertain too. So the emperor answered his own question. "No. We took gold certainly but for uniforms and boots." He was interrupted by a comment from Duroc, who was now gazing adoringly up at his emperor. I could not catch what he said but it made the emperor laugh with delight and give the man another hug. "My friend reminds me that I issued a proclamation calling for boots before bread. Well, we got boots and we marched further and faster than our enemies. We vanquished them everywhere we found them until Italy was free. Then we gave the people of Italy their own republic and their freedom." He paused again as another cheer ran around the square and used the time to shake hands with Duroc and swing himself back up on his horse so more could see him.

"The allies are wary of me," he continued, "because I have brought France glory, justice, science and a society where a man rises on his merits and not through his birth. Comrade Duroc can tell his grandchildren how with courage he helped me in my hour of need. What will you tell your grandchildren? Will you explain that your freedom was stolen by a puppet king imposed on France by its enemies? Will you tell your children that you sat back while liberty was snuffed out like a candle and meekly allowed the old ways to return?" Each question had been answered by a chorus of "No," but

111

now the emperor paused again until you could have heard a pin drop in that square. "Or will you join me in defending our liberty and the glory of France?"

There was a deafening cheer then that echoed off the stone walls. If you had been there I swear that, like me, you would have felt the hair stand up on the back of your neck. God, I was not even French and I was stirred. If he had asked them at that moment then every last one of them in that square would have followed him into the gates of hell itself, and even Flashy would have doffed his hat to wish them well.

"Do you see?" asked Cambronne craning round again and shouting over the noise. "*That* is why he is the emperor."

There is no doubt that Bonaparte was a great general, and despite what our people say, he was a very capable politician, but he was a performer too. Maybe that was the secret to his success on the battlefield. It was not just that he could see an enemy's weakness; he could inspire his own men to exploit it. Certainly Wellington thought his presence was worth forty thousand men on a battlefield and given everything I have seen, I would not disagree.

We rode out of Auxerre and as soon as we were out of sight of the town the emperor stopped and climbed inside his carriage. Secretaries came and went from the vehicle as we travelled and once when I rode past it I saw him inside dictating a report. We stopped at three more towns that day and each time the same thing happened. Bonaparte would mount his horse just out of town and as riders had been sent on ahead, there would be a crowd waiting in the square. Each time he found a familiar face and gave a similar rousing speech. I was getting increasingly alarmed at his uncanny memory, at least, that is, until we got to the last town.

There the emperor found a familiar face that he claimed had been with him at Austerlitz. The fellow looked increasingly uncomfortable as Napoleon reminisced about how they had beaten the combined might of Russia and Austria there together. I doubted the man had been there at all, and certainly not leading the charge. But even if the emperor had chosen some unwitting stooge this time, his speech had the same effect on the populace as in the other places. I also suspect that even today there are children being brought up in a town south of Paris, convinced that Grandpapa was the real victor of Austerlitz with perhaps just a little help from General Bonaparte.

The next day Cambronne happily agreed for me to join his advanced guard. There were already a number of other officers in the party, keen to go on ahead and prepare for the emperor's arrival. The bulk of the force, though, was the five hundred men of the Old Guard that had gone with their emperor to Elba. Already their number had been augmented by at least a hundred former soldiers of the Guard, who had flocked to their old eagle as soon as they had heard that their emperor had returned. They formed extra ranks at the rear of the column. Some had kept their old uniforms, which they were now wearing proudly, but others only had bits of uniform or civilian clothes. You could tell they were guardsmen, though, whatever they were wearing. Most of the soldiers were adorned with gold earrings and nearly all had long drooping moustaches, which was the fashion in their ranks. But it was the precision and speed with which they marched that gave them away. I have not seen any other soldiers march at such a fast pace and keep in perfect time. They did it without any conscious thought, as though it were second nature to them, which it must have been after so many campaigns.

Without thinking, I complimented Cambronne on his command and if it was possible given his already erect stature, he stiffened further with pride, before a curious frown crossed his face. "Surely you have marched with the Old Guard before, Colonel?"

"Not in Spain, sir," I said hastily to cover my error. "If there were Old Guard regiments there I never had the honour to march with them."

"Ah, you should have seen them before we went to Russia," Cambronne said wistfully. "Thousands of the finest soldiers that ever marched." He gave a heavy sigh before adding, "But courage could not vanquish the cold."

That was the closest I ever saw any member of the Old Guard be critical of Napoleon. From what I heard, some fifty thousand members of the Imperial Guard marched into Russia and less than one in ten came back. The Imperial Guard consisted of the veteran elite in the Old Guard together with less experienced Middle Guard and Young Guard regiments. But even these junior regiments took only the best recruits from the wider army.

Quite what they would have done if they knew that a British spy was marching in their midst did not bear thinking about. For despite their suffering over recent years, there was no doubt as to their commitment to the cause. I saw that for myself when we reached a crossroads where the toll gate keeper was defiantly flying a royalist flag from his window. He may have thought differently about that had he known who was marching up the road towards him. With a growl of indignation, a squad of soldiers was sent off to deal with the matter as the rest of us continued past. The door of the cottage was kicked in, the flag torn down and there was the sound of smashing furniture and the scream of a woman. The soldiers emerged a few moments later. There had been no gunfire and their bayonets looked clean. They had obeyed their emperor's edict that not a drop of blood should be spilt for his return, although several were pushing loot, including a dead chicken into their packs.

Certainly there was some killing over those days, for we passed the corpses of two white-coated royalist officers hanging from a tree beside the road. Cambronne ordered them cut down and buried so that the emperor did not see them when he followed later. The roads were generally quiet but in towns and villages there would be small crowds of people, who even if they weren't Bonapartists, found it politic to cheer on our formidable band of men. Most were genuinely pleased to see them and everyone asked when the emperor was coming. The size of our band was steadily growing too, for in most of those villages another handful of veterans waited. Several had tears in their eyes as they watched us march towards them and then, calling out greetings to comrades in the ranks, they would step in and join the last lines of men marching along.

I vividly remember going through one town, the day before we entered Paris, and seeing a grizzled old veteran standing by the side of the road with a sack in his hand. He had the tall erect bearing of a

114

guard, not to mention the moustache and the earrings. I thought he would join us too until I looked down and saw that he also had a wooden leg. I stood to one side to see if he would indeed try to march with us but as the final half-uniformed ranks went by he hobbled up to a guardsman who was still in civilian clothes and handed him this sack.

"Show it glory again," the old man had shouted as he limped along after the column. The soldier who had taken the sack had not even broken stride until he looked inside it. Then he stepped out from the ranks and came back to the old man.

"I will, brother," he replied fiercely as he embraced the old man. "It will see glory or my death," he declared. You could tell he meant it too. Then he reached inside and brought out the carefully brushed bearskin hat worn by the Old Guard. As I watched the soldier run after his comrades, I thanked my stars that I was no longer in the army. There was no Russian winter to stop them this time, some poor devil would have to do it with a bayonet, and I did not fancy their chances. At least, I thought, it would not be me.

Chapter 16

We were just ahead of the emperor when we reached the outskirts of Paris. While he was travelling in his carriage, he did not set off until nine each day and stopped at every major town to give one of his speeches. By starting shortly after dawn and with their fast marching pace, the steadily growing column of the Old Guard had kept in front.

It seemed that every soldier in Paris was on the streets of the city to welcome us and many streamed past us down the road to get their first glimpse of Napoleon. There were plenty of civilians cheering on the streets too, but as I looked closely I saw a few worried faces amongst them, particularly when I looked up at the windows above the shops and businesses. From there, faces had mixed expressions. They perhaps had seen beyond Bonaparte's bluster and as business owners, they had more to lose. They rightly suspected that his return would inevitably mean a resumption of war. I did not know it then, but the allies at the Congress of Vienna had already issued an edict declaring Bonaparte an outlaw who must be overthrown; which rather ruled out their involvement in his escape as he had claimed. If he was to keep his throne he would have to beat the combined might of the allies – but as his supporters would not hesitate to point out, he had done that before more than once.

While the Old Guard turned towards their barracks, I thanked Cambronne for his company and headed towards the hotel I had not seen for nearly a month. I was certain that Louisa would not be there, but I needed to check. Then I would head north. If the channel ports were still open, God willing, within a few days I should be back on the shores of England. Then France could do what it pleased. I would be tucked up safely in Berkeley Hall, facing nothing more dangerous than the bad breath of my tenant farmers.

Of course plans rarely go that smoothly and I found my first obstacle at the hotel door. It was locked shut and a notice pinned to it announcing that the hotel was closed while the staff went to welcome the emperor to the city. I stood on the step considering what to do. Surely Louisa would not have waited for me? Perhaps I should just head north now? But she may have left things for me at the hotel and some civilian clothes might prove useful later on in the journey. There was also a favourite silver-handled razor I had not packed when I went with Ney, which was probably still in my room.

A silver-handled razor! It was worth a guinea at most; even now I could weep at what that cost me. For with hindsight I should have abandoned the crown jewels in that room if necessary and headed north to the coast. But of course I did not know that then and an extra hour or two before I started my journey did not seem to make a lot of difference. I felt in my pocket; I still had the letter from Ney for his wife. I could at least deliver that while I waited. We had heard on the way into the city that the Napoleonic elite were gathering at the Tuileries Palace and so I headed there. A letter bearing the seal of Marshal Ney was all I needed to be shown into the royal apartments. Soon I was passing through the anteroom that Ney and I had waited in to see the king. It seemed an age ago but it was less than a month before. From the audience chamber itself, I could hear squeals of laughter and occasional cheering. It sounded as though the party had started in there already, but I could never have guessed the scene which would be revealed when I pulled open the door.

I almost fell over the first woman. Judging from the silk dress and bejewelled tiara she wore, she was one of the imperial courtiers. But instead of standing in their finery, all of the women and quite a few of the men in the room were all down on their hands and knees working industriously on the carpet.

"Don't just stand there," the woman at my feet barked at me. "Find a knife from somewhere and help. We need the carpet all finished before the emperor gets here." It was only as she sat back to talk to me that I was able to see what she was doing. She had been using a small knife to pick at the stitching around one of the royal Bourbon *fleur de lys* sewn all over the carpet. But from under the edge that she had pulled off, I could see that there was something underneath. It was a bee, Napoleon's imperial symbol that had been woven into the carpet when it was made. Clearly Louis had not wanted to pay for a new carpet and so he had got his people to sew his emblem over the top of the Napoleonic one.

"Yes ma'am," I replied for I noticed nearer the middle of the room a familiar face. There, crouched on the floor and scratching away at some stubborn stitching, was the Princess of Moscow. She looked up and grinned as I came over.

"I see you have made the acquaintance of the Duchess of Auerstaedt," she said gesturing at the woman who had hectored me as I entered the room. "She is almost as fearsome as her husband." I had no idea who the Duke of Auerstaedt was and it must have shown on my face for she added helpfully, "Marshal Davout. Now get down and help or she will tell us both off. Here, have this," she said, passing me half of a pair of scissors and gesturing to a *fleur de lys* still undisturbed on the carpet.

"Your husband sent me to give you this note to explain why he changed sides," I whispered as I got down beside her. I passed her Ney's letter and with nothing better to do I picked up the scissor and started to attack the silk patch on the carpet.

"Oh, I thought he would," the princess admitted airily as she tucked the letter unread into some fold of her dress. "While my poor mother would have been heartbroken that the king was forced out again, we were not happy in his court. The emperor will be much better for France." Her bright blue eyes looked appraisingly at me. Then she stopped attacking the carpet for a moment to ask, "So, Colonel Moreau, where do your loyalties truly lie? Michel tells me that no one knows of your past but you have links with the British. You served my husband as a royalist officer and were appointed by Clarke, who has gone to Ghent with the king. Will you stay or will you quietly slip away for the border too?"

Well that caught me off guard. I had thought that the princess was concentrating on nothing more than the needlework before her. But she had not lived through the Revolution, the Terror, the formation of a republic, an empire, a kingdom and now an empire again without developing an acute political awareness. As I comprehended this I saw that she was watching my reaction closely. I was surprised that Ney had evidently shared what he knew of my background with her. He obviously valued her judgement. I would need to be convincing.

"I swear that I have no loyalty to Louis and I detest Clarke. I would not follow him anywhere," I answered honestly.

"I believe you," the princess replied, but before I could relax she added perceptively, "but I suspect that you have no great love for the emperor either. You are simply trying to stay afloat in the political storm that is blowing across France."

"I can assure you, Princess," I started to protest, but she held up a hand to forestall me.

"I intend no criticism; many in this room are the same. You probably have heard that the Congress of Vienna has declared our emperor an outlaw. That means sooner or later it will be war, France against all of them."

"I am sure we can still win, Princess," I replied dutifully while thinking that the allies were working fast. They must have all still been together in Vienna when they had heard that Bonaparte had landed, which would have saved weeks of negotiation with couriers riding all over Europe.

"I pray you are right, Colonel," murmured the princess so only I could hear and then she gestured to the surrounding throng. "These are all people who have risen in the emperor's service. The Duke of Auerstaedt, Marshal Davout, was a junior lieutenant at the time of the Revolution, you know my Michel was a cavalry trooper, Soult was a private and the Comte d'Erlon over there was a locksmith. I don't need to tell you that men follow Napoleon because there are no limits to the heights that they can rise to if they are lucky and serve him well. They could become princes or, like Murat, rise from a haberdasher's clerk to king of Naples."

"The emperor is a generous ruler," I agreed.

"You don't understand what I am telling you," interrupted the princess irritably. "The higher a man rises the more he worries about keeping what he has got. Already three of the emperor's old marshals have decided that he cannot win and have declared for the king. Another three have ruled themselves out of campaigning on either side as they are too old or ill. A further two are out of the country and who knows if they will come back. My Michel could never go back to the king now, even if he wanted to. But some of these," and here she nodded with her head at the crowd while stabbing viciously down on another *fleur de lys*, "will be trying to play both sides to protect their position whatever happens. Now the emperor is in the ascendancy they are here, but if things start to go wrong they will desert him like flies on a waking dog."

I had initially taken the princess as a simple wife and mother who was content to let her husband manage affairs. But I realised now that she was an astute judge and probably a guiding hand in Ney's career. Maybe that was the reason he appeared so lost when he had to make big decisions without her. I thought it would be foolish not to take advantage of her judgement; it would be useful information to take home. So I asked, "Do you think things will go wrong?"

She stopped picking at the last *fleur de lys* near us while she considered the matter seriously. "No," she said at last. "I think that the allies will underestimate the emperor. Men always fight harder when they are defending their homeland." She looked sad for a moment as she added, "Men like my Michel would rather die than let the empire fall again. They know only ruin and disgrace await them if the king comes back."

We were interrupted by a shout from the end of the room and there was the sound of distant cheering. The emperor had arrived. I tore the *fleur de lys* I had been working on off the carpet and looked around. They were now nearly all gone with just a handful of people still picking away. Others were moving towards the door and the sound of cheering was getting louder. I helped the princess to her feet and we both joined the throng near the big double doors. Grinning guardsmen were gently pushing the crowd back to make way for the procession behind them. Then the noise redoubled as Bonaparte appeared.

He was being carried on the shoulders of at least half a dozen men with others reaching up to support him. Lying half on his back he had his arms up in the air as though feeling his way through a dark room. There was a sublime smile on his face and, to my surprise, I saw that

120

his eyes were shut. It was as though he was concentrating on just the sensation of returning to his palace. I was jostled by the crowd as he went past. Dozens more people were coming into the room behind him until you could barely see the carpet that had been so painstakingly 'de-Bourboned'. Eventually, amidst continued cheering, he was delivered back to his feet on the dais at the end of the room. I saw him look at Louis' huge throne and grin with amusement. It must have been vastly bigger than the one he had seen there before. The emperor would have looked like a lost child if he had sat in it. A group of army officers started chanting *Vive l'Empereur!* as they stared at their commander in chief with an almost feverish excitement. Many of the civilians were joining in, but I saw a few at the back with more anxious expressions. Napoleon let the chant continue a few moments and then, smiling again, he held up his hands for silence.

"Thank you, my friends, thank you," he called to quieten them. "The people of France have called us back and we have much to do."

"Lead us to beat the allies now, before they are ready," called out a voice from the crowd.

"No, no," replied the emperor grinning. "The people want peace; the world wants peace and not war. We will do our best to give it to them." There were confused glances between many of the army officers present at that, but the emperor continued. "I will write to the allies promising I will respect our 1799 borders and asking them to do the same. Then we will develop a new constitution to give France a stable government and remove the Bourbon injustices. We will bring a new age of science, industry and enlightenment to France. We will make her great again."

There was more cheering at that, perhaps slightly muted from the army officers, but when I looked over my shoulder at the sombre group at the back of the room I saw at least half of them clapping enthusiastically. The rest looked either puzzled or downright suspicious as though they could not believe that a leopard could so completely change its spots. I did not blame them, for it seemed to me that the little speech had been entirely for the benefit of the allied rulers, who all doubtless had their spies in the room. If the Princess of

Moscow had heard that the allies had declared Bonaparte an outlaw, then he must have heard it too. He must have known that peace with him at the helm of France was unlikely. Perhaps, I wondered, that was why he was also announcing a new constitution; so that he could persuade the allies that he now ruled as part of an elected government.

Before I could consider this anymore, a glass of champagne was pressed into my hand by a court flunkey who was precariously balancing a tray of them as he pushed through the excited crowd. I caught a glimpse of the emperor stepping down from the dais to greet his new court and the next thing I knew a young woman had literally thrown herself into my arms.

"Isn't it wonderful," she gushed. "I don't know when I have been this excited." Most of my champagne had gone down the back of her dress, but she did not seem to notice. I had to put my arm around her to stop her falling, but I did not mind that for she was an absolute beauty.

"It is a historic day, Miss," I replied grinning. For you could not help but smile at her. She was nineteen or twenty, I guessed, and bursting with excitement.

"Do you think the emperor will come this way?" she asked before continuing without giving me a chance to answer. "I have met him once before at my aunt's wedding but that was years ago. He was very kind but my aunt says that he can be very angry sometimes too."

I looked into the crowd about us but there was so much movement it was hard to tell where the emperor was or in which direction he was going. I had no wish to run into him again, but any thought of leaving was dispelled by the shapely stunner at my side. I thought perhaps I could stay a few minutes longer. "He was kind to me when I met him too," I told her. "But he will have a lot of people to meet today."

"I think you are so lucky being a soldier. You must have fought many battles with him and you are a colonel so you must have been brave." Her bright eyes sparkled with interest as she licked her lips and asked, "What is it like going to war with the emperor?"

Of course, I had no idea, but I could make something up. I thought she was the romantic type who wanted to hear tales of heroic valour rather than the gritty reality of blood and men screaming in agony, but

122

as I tried to think of a tale to tell she asked, "Have you been wounded?"

"Yes, I was wounded fighting in Spain. I was shot through the chest, I nearly died." That at least was true although it had been a French musket ball that had nearly carried me off.

"You poor man." She bit her lip, hesitating, and whispered, "Can I see the scar?"

At another time and place, I would not have hesitated to use that as an excuse to take her to some quiet spot in the palace to show her a lot more than my scar. But then I wavered. I had Louisa back, although I suspected that she might have been unfaithful already. Was I going back to my old ways? By Christ, though, this girl was pretty enough to tempt a cardinal away from his vows… "I can't show you here," I gasped hoarsely.

"Let me feel it through your shirt, then," she whispered, and she reached up to press her small warm hand to my chest. I felt her fingers delicately trace the scar lines of the star-shaped wound and gazed at the look of rapt concentration on her face as she tried to imagine what she could not see. "You were so brave," she murmured as I felt desire course through me. I forgot everything else at that moment, felt only her body close to mine, her fingertips exploring the wound that had nearly killed me and her expression of wonder that I could have lived. If I had not been quite so rapt and aroused I might have noticed the disturbance in the crowd about us. But I didn't, which made what happened then all the more startling.

"Ah, Colonel Moreau, it is good to see you again." It took a full second for my mind to adjust. In one moment I was lost in a delicious fantasy, imagining the girl touching me naked and the pair of us indulging in the most licentious debauchery. But in the next moment I realised that the man who had once ruled all of Europe was staring at me with a curious look on his face, while several about him were glaring indignantly at my inattention. Then as I finally remembered that *I* was Moreau, I snapped myself to attention.

"I am sorry, sir…" I stammered but the emperor reached up and patted my shoulder.

"Do not worry, Colonel, even an emperor knows he will be outshined by such beauty." He turned to the girl. "Mademoiselle, it is only when you are old and grey that I will be able to get men to pay attention to me again."

The girl blushed a deep pink and dropped into a curtsey. "Pauline Leclerc, Your Majesty, I am so sorry."

"Don't be," replied the emperor genially. "You brighten up my court." Then he turned back to me. "Now, Moreau, your face seemed familiar when we met at Auxerre. Where have I seen you before?"

If a man's bowels can summersault in terror then mine did then, for this was exactly the situation that I had been trying to avoid.

"I…I do not think that we have met before Auxerre, sire," I said hesitantly feeling my mouth go dry as mounting panic set in. In a moment he would remember and then it would all be over. The emperor frowned now in irritation and started to search that prodigious memory of his. But then rescue came from an unlikely source.

"The colonel has a terrible chest wound, sire." Pauline spoke up while keeping her eyes cast down at the emperor's feet. "He nearly died from it. Perhaps you saw him while he was unconscious as you visited the wounded after a battle?"

"Yes that is possible, I suppose," said the emperor smiling at Pauline and raising her chin so that she looked at him." Relief washed over me for a heartbeat until he frowned again. "No, that was not it. I am sure we have spoken before."

He reached up and I thought he was going to pat my shoulder again before I felt a sharp pain in my earlobe as he pinched it hard. I may have winced in pain, although I have been told since that having your ear pinched by the emperor was a valued sign of comradeship. "Observe, gentleman," he said to those about him, "the man who forgets a meeting with his emperor. I suspect he remembers all too well and I have reprimanded him for something." He grinned at me and started to move away but called back over his shoulder, "I will recollect our meeting, Colonel, sooner or later."

Already others were talking to him and I felt my muscles relax. Unless his memory came back damn fast it would be too late: it was time for me to go. I was turning to leave when the girl I now knew as Pauline grabbed my arm.

"You did know the emperor and he knew you." She reached up and kissed me then. I tasted wine on her lips as she pressed her body against me. Now that the danger was past I felt that familiar feeling of recklessness and there were other memorable feelings too. I reached down and squeezed one of her breasts and she gave a small groan of desire.

"I never did show you that scar, did I?" I whispered.

"No," she giggled. "And you are much rougher with my chest than I was with yours."

"Let's find a quiet corner where I can check you over for scars too."

Chapter 17

We moved discreetly to the nearest door and found ourselves back in the anteroom, which must have had at least a dozen people in it. There was an unguarded door leading deeper into the palace and we headed in that direction. We were giggling like schoolchildren when we pushed it open, only to find two generals and a civilian deep in conversation. From the way they glared at us and then quickly stepped apart they were clearly up to no good, but we did not care. Laughing, we ran on to the next room and found it completely bare. I don't just mean of people but of a single stick of furniture too. That is the trouble with these big palaces; few monarchs can afford to furnish all of the rooms. If I was going to couple with this prime piece I wanted something a bit more comfortable than a marble floor and so we went on to the next door. As she held up her skirts to run, the minx was calling back to me, telling me just how she would like to be taken. By God she was brazen, just the way I like 'em. By the time we had got to the next room I had so come to the boil that I would have had her on a marble staircase if that was all that was available. But no, it was a room full of huge crates; those still open showing the belongings of the previous occupants of the palace. There were half-packed life-size statues of kings and princes, stacks of portraits, mounds of clothes, shoes, even a rack of wigs. Of particular interest at that moment was a stack of what may have been priceless tapestries, which were piled conveniently to make a mattress.

We were all over each other in a moment. She undid my belt with practiced ease and was soon working to undo my breeches, while I had one tit out and was munching down on it and hauling up her skirts. She had half torn open my shirt – it appeared that she did actually want to see the scar – when we heard the voice.

"Pauline, Pauline, I saw you. Come back here this instant. You will not bring disgrace on this family again. Where are you?"

"It is my Aunt Louise," gasped the girl pushing me away and tucking her breast back in her dress. "Quick, go, she must not find you here."

There may be other men who would stay to help defend a girl's honour in this situation but I am not one of them. Grabbing my belt with one hand and holding up my breeches with the other, I was off, darting into the maze of packing cases.

"There you are," I heard the woman call as she entered the room and found Pauline. It was a strident voice which sounded vaguely familiar. "What is it with you and men in uniform? Where is he, then?"

"I don't know what you mean, Aunt, I just came to take some air. It was very hot in the room with the emperor." This was followed by a slapping sound and a shriek of pained surprise from Pauline.

"Do you take me for a fool?" the older woman scolded. "Did I not just glimpse you with my own eyes running in this direction with some army officer? Now, where is the rogue?" There was the noise of banging wood now. I imagined her throwing open one of the crates of statues to see if I was hiding inside. I looked around for a hiding place and saw another mound of clothes. I quickly and silently burrowed into them.

"Where is he?" The older woman was almost screeching in fury now and I heard Pauline say, "He's gone," between sobs. Another crate slammed open nearby and I twisted feverishly in the confined space to do up my breech buttons and tuck my shirt in so that things would look less incriminating if the aunt did find me.

There was the sound of more crate lids being thrown to the floor and then a clatter of what must have been a stack of portraits being pushed over. She was getting closer and I held my breath to keep my pile of clothes absolutely still.

"Where are you, you wretch!" her voice shrieked at me from nearby and I felt something fall on my pile.

Panic started to rise in me, but then I calmed myself. What could an old woman do? I would push her away and then I would be out of the palace. Then free of Paris and soon all of France. She could threaten what she liked; she would never see me again. There was the smash of some vase she must have dashed to the ground in her fury and then her voice rang out. It seemed to come from directly over my head.

127

"I know you are in here, you villain," she snarled. "So listen carefully. If you come near my niece again you will find yourself transferred to latrine guard duties for the rest of your miserable career. And if you think I am bluffing think on this: my husband is about to be announced as war minister in the emperor's new government."

I breathed a slow sigh of relief as their footsteps receded, which was swiftly followed by an idle curiosity as to who this new minister was. When the room fell silent I counted slowly to a hundred and then started to pull the clothes away. Instead of the ceiling, I found a disapproving face glaring down at me. It was a fallen portrait of an angry French king, now lying across my pile of clothes. I pushed it up against another stack of pictures; judging from his attire, it was probably Louis XIV. I could not help feeling that given his own reputation as a womaniser, his stern glare was a tad hypocritical.

I had to return the way I had come and peered cautiously around each door before entering the room. When I reached the chamber with the two army officers and the civilian, who were still deep in their intrigues, one of the soldiers cackled in delight.

"Ah, here he is, his weapon unfired and his target stolen away." I gave them a rueful grin as I entered, to be met by a steely glare from the civilian and a guffaw from the other officer.

"Have they gone?" I asked

"Yes," said the first officer. "Young Venus has been dragged home in disgrace by the gorgon. But don't worry, there will be plenty of others. With the emperor back and Paris full of soldiers, few pretty girls will sleep alone tonight."

"That one will," muttered the civilian. "She will be locked alone in her room tonight and you would be a brave fool to try and disturb her."

"Oh I have no intention of risking any more trouble tonight," I told them as I went past, and I meant it too.

I was soon on the street outside the Tuileries and breathed a sigh of relief. I had dallied long enough; it was time to go home. It was already getting dark and too late to set out that night. I thought I would spend one final night at the hotel and then leave first thing in the morning.

When I reached the building I was relieved to see that the hotel door was now open. The emperor duly welcomed, it was clearly back to business as usual. I still had my key in my pocket and hoped to get up to my room again and slip away in the morning without being seen by anyone. I peered cautiously around the entrance hall. It was deserted apart from another guest reading a paper by the fire. I was halfway across when a voice called out in an urgent hushed tone.

"Monsieur, Monsieur, quickly, this way." I looked around; the guest was still reading his news sheet and for a moment I could not see who had spoken. Then I spotted the hotel manager's face peering around his office door. I had met him before, when we had arrived at the hotel and he had shown his new wealthy English guests to their suite. Since then he had given me the odd curious glance when he had seen me in my French army uniform, but I had brushed away any questions with the explanation that I was now a liaison officer. He had always borne a sad expression, but now he looked like a grief-stricken bloodhound as he gestured urgently for me to join him.

"Look, if it is about the bill..." I started but he flapped his hand dismissively at the thought.

"No, no, Monsieur, your wife has paid until the end of the month. I thought I had missed you. Thank goodness I looked out when I did. Here, sir, take a seat, it is a matter of the utmost urgency."

I sat down in a creaking wooden chair feeling a growing sense of unease. "Well, what is it about, then?" I asked impatiently. "I am leaving first thing in the morning."

"No, no sir, that is impossible," he replied as he pulled a key on a chain from his pocket and unlocked a sturdy strong box. "Now, where is it?" he muttered as he started to rummage about in its contents. "Ah, here." He turned to me, his flabby features stretched into a smile of sorts, and proudly presented me with a letter. For a brief moment I entertained the hope that it might be from Louisa, but then I saw the official embassy seal. Sensing danger, I snatched my hand away without taking it.

"Now look here, I am an officer in the French army, I want nothing to do with any intrigues of the British embassy." I was going to ride for the coast come hell or high water. The only reason the embassy would contact me now would be to keep me in France, probably on some half-baked new assignment that the novice ambassador had dreamt up in his bath. Well they weren't getting me caught up in their intrigues again. I gave the hotel manager a stern look and continued, "I suggest that you throw that in the fire and we will just pretend that we never met. Tell them you did not see me and I will leave in the morning."

The smile on his face melted away into a look of intense disappointment. "You are a British spy," he said speaking for the first time in English. "Do you think I am a fool? A British liaison officer would wear a British uniform not a French one. I saw you arrive as an Englishman, I saw you go to the embassy and then suddenly pffft," he gave a flourish of his hand like a conjurer revealing his trick, "you are a French officer with a different name."

"What is it to you what I am? Even if I were a spy, as a French citizen you should not be helping me." I thought perhaps I could intimidate him into letting me go and so I stood up, straightened my uniform and added, "As a French officer, perhaps I should report you for your behaviour."

He did not look the least bit alarmed as he shook his head slowly. "We both know that you will do no such thing. I know what is in the letter and you will read it. Then I will tell my contact with the British that the letter was received. If you refuse to open it then I will tell them that too and you can suffer the consequences of your refusal to help your country when you reach London."

"Dammit, why should you care what I do?" I had been so close to escaping and now the net was closing around me again. I looked at the letter with suspicion; for all I knew it could have contained orders to assassinate the emperor or kidnap him and take him to London.

"Because the emperor cannot possibly win against all the allies working together. Soon the British will be back in their embassy and they will know that I am a reliable friend amongst the people of Paris." He held out the letter again, and this time I reluctantly took it. The edges of the seal were slightly proud of the paper. Someone, presumably the manager, had slid a hot knife blade underneath to open the letter without breaking the seal and then tried to stick it down again. Having done the same trick myself, I knew that the edges of the seal never looked quite right unless you used some hot wire to melt the wax at the edges.

The manager, knowing what was in the letter, was determined I should read it. That meant almost certainly that it could not be good news. It was addressed to me just by the initials TF and I snapped the seal and unfolded the letter with a sense of deep trepidation.

TF

Uncle Arthur sends his compliments and requires you to continue in your current duties rather than return home. A mutual friend will send details of how to contact him through the bearer of this note.

S

I guessed the 'S' was Stuart, the new ambassador. It was all cloak and dagger with no names and only the seal to prove it came from the embassy, but I did not doubt it was genuine. I had reluctantly acted as a spy for 'Uncle' Arthur Wellesley, now the Duke of Wellington, before. With every royalist fleeing the capital he would be delighted to have a man he thought was a valuable agent, disguised amongst the emperor's men. But it left me trapped on the wrong side of the English Channel. The manager was right about another thing: for all the emperor's claims of wanting peace there would be war sooner or later. Probably sooner. And what of the emperor and his legendary memory for names and faces? Would he ever remember where he had seen me before? It was like holding a mortar shell with a sputtering fuse: you did not know when it would go off or if it would go off at all, but it would be catastrophic for me if it did.

For a moment I felt sick with despair. Why oh why had I come back to this wretched hotel at all? Now some diligent frog toady to the embassy had got me by the balls and was dragging me from the frying pan into the fire. But then I started to think. I had only been ordered to continue my current duties and no one at the embassy knew precisely what they were, just that I was on Ney's staff. Surely I could persuade him to send me on some tedious assignment somewhere which would

131

keep me well out of danger and of course away from the emperor's beady eye.

I realised with a sudden chill that I certainly had to move for I could not stay at the hotel. As the manager had proven, too many of the staff would remember me either as an English guest or a French royalist. As if reading my mind the manager spoke again.

"You cannot continue to reside here. I have arranged new accommodation for you at a lodging house on the other side of the city."

"But this *mutual friend* mentioned in the letter, whoever the hell they are, how are they going to reach me?"

"Don't worry, Colonel," said the manager. He was speaking French again and wore a prim smile of satisfaction now that he thought his obligations were being met. "I will personally forward on any correspondence or messages to your new address. Everyone else at this hotel will think you have left."

Chapter 18

For the first month my plan worked perfectly. Things only started to go wrong when I let an organ other than my brain influence decisions. Ney arrived in Paris three days after Napoleon. In the intervening time, I had discovered who the mysterious new war minister was. It turned out to be Marshal Davout. I was at last able to place that familiar voice I had heard from under the clothes as the doughty noblewoman who had accosted me when I had first entered the throne room. Davout was fiercely loyal to his emperor. Ordered to hold the Hamburg area during the first allied invasion of 1814, he had held off all allied forces and surrendered only after Napoleon had abdicated. He was also the only French marshal who had not sought a position under the Bourbons, preferring instead to retire to his country house.

While Davout's loyalty to the emperor was beyond question, the same could not be said for Ney. I spent some time in the officers' mess at a local barracks where I heard much debate at his damascene conversion from king to emperor and his commitment to fighting the allies. Davout evidently felt that it would be best for his old friend to be out of the way for a while. So on the day Ney arrived in the city he was given orders to leave at once and carry out a tour of inspection of defences in the north and east of the country.

While the marshal was morose at this further evidence that he was not trusted, I barely hid my delight, for this was excellent news. Accompanying my chief I would be away from Paris and the curious gaze of the emperor for at least a month. Not only that, but I was then ideally placed to send my own report on France's defences to the allies as though I was diligently doing my duty as a spy.

So we set off on our expedition and I'll vouch that an enemy agent has never been given an easier time to do his work. Ney and his trusty aide were welcomed at every town, given excellent food and board along with guided tours of every dilapidated fortress, gun emplacement and bastion across north-eastern France. I would make notes of my own and add to them the observations of Ney as we went around various battlements. Sometimes the governors of fortresses would provide me with their own lists of guns, calibres and ammunition stores to save me even that effort and ensure that the right details reached Paris. It was absurdly easy and it would have been almost pleasurable if Ney had not been in such a tearing hurry to get the job done.

As March turned into April, the news sheets and bulletins from the capital showed that the pace of government had changed dramatically from that under the fat, indolent king. Even from a hundred miles away it was clear from what we read that the emperor was frenetically working to transform France before the allies had the chance to react to his return. Unpopular taxes were revoked, royalist land and assets seized, appeals made to the allies for peace, public works started and new ministers appointed.

There was still some opposition, a revolt against the emperor's return in the more royalist south had been put down by a former aristocrat cavalry general called Grouchy, while another uprising simmered in the west of the country. But even where people were not openly in rebellion, the emperor's return had ignited a wide array of conflicting hopes. The Bonapartists wanted a return to the glory days of the empire; Jacobins wanted to go back to the fiery principles of the Revolution, while most of the landed middle class just wanted a period of peace and prosperity.

To keep everyone happy, Napoleon launched the work to create a new constitution. To show that it would not simply be a puppet to his rule, he put one of his most outspoken critics in charge of drawing it up. I confess I was surprised, I did not expect him to give up that much control of France, but when I mentioned that to Ney, he just laughed.

"He has not given up any control," the marshal told me. "If he wins the coming war then he will be unassailable and he will be able to do what he likes regardless of the constitution. And if he loses the war then it will not matter." It was a cynical response from an increasingly cynical man. For several evenings now I had endured Ney bemoaning how Napoleon, for whom he had risked his life so many times, would no longer even receive him. He had been sounding as bitter as he had done when he had been waiting to attack his old emperor.

134

"You are sure it will be war, then?" I asked. There had been speculation in the papers that if France formed some kind of constitutional monarchy, such as we had in Britain, it might be enough to appease the allies.

"Of course there will be war," growled Ney as we stood alone together on the battlements of some forgotten fortress. I cannot remember which town we were in now, but it was a grey miserable day with a steady drizzle of rain and the wet stonework and guns looked similarly depressing. I reached out and tugged on a loose stone on the edge of the battlements. The rock moved and then tumbled down into the moat below with a splash.

"Then why is it just us inspecting the fortifications?" I asked. "Surely there should be teams of engineers strengthening them?"

"You have not fought with him, have you?" asked Ney with a softer tone to his voice now. "He will not stay still in a fortress. He wins because he can move faster than his enemies, strike them when they least expect it and confuse them as to his intentions. He cannot do any of that hiding behind stone walls." He grinned ruefully at me. "Don't lose hope, Colonel. You don't know him as I do. He is at his most dangerous when his enemies think he is beaten."

"But if the allies unite against us, will we really still stand a chance?" I asked.

"Not if he waits much longer. We should have launched an attack as soon as he got back to Paris to catch them off guard. Instead, we are wasting our time out here." Ney picked up a lump of loose mortar from between the stones and hurled it out over the moat in frustration. "Every day he waits the allies get stronger. The British and the Prussians are gathering men near Brussels. They will soon have more than we can hope to muster."

"What about the Russians and the Austrians? There has been little about their armies in the papers."

"The Russians will take months to get here and the Austrians will make a lot of noise, but will hold back to see who is winning."

"Why would the Austrians hold back?"

"Because they are cunning bastards and the emperor's heir is also the Austrian emperor's grandson. They know that Napoleon will do anything to get his son back, so they will look to gain whether we win or lose." Another flurry of rain soaked us and Ney snarled his annoyance and picked up another rock to fling over the moat. He issued a string of oaths he must have learned in his trooper days before exploding, "What a God-awful waste of time this is. We should have chased the Prussians half way to fucking Berlin by now."

I had long since discovered that patience was not one of Marshal Ney's strong suits. While I would have been content to sit out the whole war on this pointless but completely safe exercise, he found it immensely frustrating. He had irrevocably tied his fortune to the emperor, but now had to stand and watch as, in his view, the chance of victory steadily diminished.

I will spare you the details of that tedious tour. Each night I would draft a report of the day's observations and keep some notes back for my own submission to Wellington. Ney would sign the report, often without bothering to read it, and then it would be submitted to Paris. Ney was always insistent that we listed where we were heading next – he did not want any delay in receiving the hoped for recall from the emperor. But while couriers did arrive, mostly from Davout, who made a point of keeping his old comrade informed, nothing came with the longed for imperial seal. In the end, I think it was Davout who summoned Ney back to Paris.

We arrived back in the city in mid-April and by then any pretence at hoping for peace had passed. In every barracks and officers' mess, there was a hive of activity as old soldiers and former prisoners of war re-enlisted, new recruits were trained and all were equipped with weapons and uniforms. Old commanders were being brought out of retirement. Grouchy the young general who had beaten the royalists in the south was made a marshal and even General Bourmont, who I had expected to have fled with the royalists, turned out to have stayed in France and retained his division. My old friends Lagarde and de Briqueville had both been given new units, but when the Prince of Moscow, Marshal of France and hero of countless battles finally had a

136

private audience with his emperor, he walked away without command of even a squadron of cavalry.

Ney had endured enough and decided to retire back to his country seat at Coudreaux. I had supposed that this would leave me free to tool around Paris without any duties, and so it would have if I had not been led astray by my loins. We were sitting in Ney's Paris house when a note arrived from Davout. Ney was set to leave the city the following day and the war minister was inviting him for a farewell dinner.

"You are welcome to come too," said Ney passing me the note. "But there will be just Davout and some friends and family present. No one will mind if you cannot accept." I was about to decline when I remembered the delectable Pauline. As Davout's niece, there was a good chance that she would be present. I had unfinished business there and she had been game before her aunt had arrived. I hesitated briefly, wondering if the aunt would recognise me from the glimpse she'd had of us together that night. But the fearsome duchess had also seen me with Ney's wife and I suspected that if she had recognised me, I would have heard about it by now. No, Pauline was too pretty and willing to ignore. The dinner would be the perfect opportunity to arrange an assignation to pick things up where we had been forced to leave them.

"I would be honoured to accept," I told Ney before leaving to get myself spruced up for the evening. A few hours later, wearing my best uniform with buttons and sword hilt polished to a gleam, I found myself stepping into the war minister's drawing room. The man himself welcomed me, giving my efforts at presentation a cursory glance like a schoolmaster checking the cleanliness of boys before they entered the refectory.

"Glad you could come," he said gruffly. "You have been a valuable aide to the marshal." He started to steer me towards a group of army officers, including Ney, on the far side of the room. "Now, apart from the marshal, who here do you know?"

He probably thought that I was some ambitious little sycophant trying to ingratiate myself with him, but instead of studying the officers my gaze had strayed to the group of ladies by the fire. To my delight Pauline was there, sitting between two elderly ladies and struggling to hide that she was bored to death. Sensing my gaze she looked up and beamed with delight.

"Why, Colonel Moreau, what a pleasure to see you here."

"The pleasure is all mine, ma'am," I responded gallantly as she got up and came towards me.

Davout had stopped and was watching the pair of us with a puzzled frown. "I had no idea you knew my niece," he said as he gave me a new appraising look. He was clearly changing his mind about my motives for being there and asked, "Where did you meet Pauline?"

"Yes I would be interested in knowing that too," came a new voice. When I turned around there was the minister's wife, the Duchess of Auerstaedt, glaring at me with unbridled suspicion.

"We met at an art gallery," I said, mentioning the first place I could think of where a respectable young lady might mingle with an unintroduced stranger.

The glare from the duchess only darkened and her lips compressed into a tight line of disbelief.

"Well it was not so much a gallery as an exhibit," said Pauline brightly as she put her arm through mine. "We met at the Elephant of the Bastille." The lips relaxed slightly as though this was more plausible, but I still felt as welcome as a turd on a crumpet. At least I had seen the Elephant of the Bastille, which meant I could answer questions if pressed. The old Bastille prison, which had been stormed at the start of the Revolution, had been torn down and there had been much debate as to what would replace it. The emperor had finally approved a huge statue of an elephant as a fountain, with water spurting from its trunk. It was to be a colossal structure – you could have ridden a real elephant underneath it – and consequently it would cost a fortune to make in bronze. While the base had been built, plans for the casting had been put on hold. Instead, a full-scale model had been built of plaster, which was now on display. I had seen it when touring Paris with Louisa; we had been shown around by a guard who lived in one of the animal's legs.

"Yes, it is magnificent," I agreed supportively, "I am greatly looking forward to seeing the finished version."

138

"And when did you see this creature?" enquired the duchess.

"Oh, it was last week," replied Pauline to her aunt, without a moment's hesitation. "When you were away with your friend Caroline. Now I must show the colonel your drawings by Blondel, he is one of the colonel's favourite painters." Pauline turned and winked at me, evidently very pleased at her deception. In doing so she did not see Ney cock an eyebrow to me over her shoulder. A week ago we had been inspecting the fortress at Verdun, a place not known for its art collection.

We went and pretended to be interested in some faded drawings of some characters wearing medieval armour, while Pauline apologised for being dragged away at the Tuileries.

"My aunt watches me like an old hen guards her chicks," she complained. The old bird in question was still glaring suspiciously at us from across the room.

"Well she surely cannot complain about your new interest in the arts," I grinned conspiratorially. When do you next think you might be allowed to visit another gallery? I thought we might spend some time studying the human form." She giggled at that and we made arrangements to meet the following week.

Davout must have known that Pauline was lying as he had received the reports I had written at Verdun, but he did not say anything to his wife. Instead, he joined Ney and the two marshals talked together. If they glanced across at me as they did so, I did not notice for I was too distracted by matters closer at hand. That was even more the case when we went in for dinner; Pauline moved the place cards so that we were sitting together and then her fingers began to tease me delightfully under the table. It was a struggle to concentrate on the conversation at all. At one point someone asked me what I had thought of the latest exhibit from the artist Blondel. Thinking back to the earlier drawings, I replied that the armour was very realistic.

"Armour?" repeated the duchess in an acerbic tone. "I am not sure what picture you were examining, Colonel, his latest painting is of a Circassian girl entering her bath."

Apologising for being out of date with my art appreciation, I promised that I would make time to see this new work at my earliest convenience.

Pauline, rubbing the inside of my thigh under the table, added that she would be delighted to come with me, but at this Davout intervened with a wry smile.

"I regret, Colonel that you will have no time to wander around art galleries in the coming months. My friend here," he gestured at a grinning Ney, "has kindly agreed to attach you to my command. As you know we have an army to rebuild and the marshal assures me that you are a very capable staff officer. While it will disappoint my niece, I will need your total commitment to the cause."

"Surely you will give the colonel some time off on leave?" protested Pauline as I sat stunned at this unexpected development.

"I am sure that the colonel will appreciate," interjected the duchess, "that he is *very fortunate* to be appointed to the ministry staff." She gave me a glance that clearly implied that she did not think I deserved such good fortune. "It will be good for his career and if the colonel is given leave, I very much doubt you will be available to join him." The duchess exchanged a meaningful look with her husband and I was certain that this would be the case. Both Davout and Ney were staring at me expectantly. Whether Ney genuinely thought he was doing me a favour or was just trying to keep my lecherous hands off his friend's niece it was hard to say. It was clear that I had been out-manoeuvred by the pair of them. But try as I might, I could see no alternative to accepting. To do anything else would immediately have aroused suspicion.

"I would be honoured to join your staff, sir," I offered as a hand under the table was snatched away by its owner. So it was that a reluctant spy was given one of the most coveted jobs, right at the heart of the preparations for war.

Chapter 19

A lot of people have criticised Bonaparte for using Davout as war minister, when his skills on the battlefield would have been so welcome later in the campaign. Ney had previously told me that at Auerstaedt, where he had won his dukedom, Davout had beaten the main Prussian army with his single corps despite being outnumbered by more than three to one. But as I was to discover, he was methodical, driven and disciplined in matters of administration too. Without Davout at the War Ministry, I suspect that there would have been no Waterloo campaign, for half of the French army would still have been waiting for uniforms, weapons or ammunition.

I spent two months toiling under his command and I don't think I have worked so hard for the service of any country. The army had more than halved in size under the Bourbons, but now Napoleon was demanding a huge increase in numbers. As well as garrisons for all the defensive positions, he wanted an army to campaign with, all equipped and ready to fight by the beginning of June. I could not see how it could possibly be done but Davout was determined to succeed. He slept most nights in his office and by day was everywhere with lists and plans. He even had charts on a wall that he would mark off each day. And of course he drove his staff just as hard as he drove himself. We could not delegate to others, we had to check things were done ourselves and only then would a task be marked as complete. It seemed a hopeless endeavour as no sooner had we confirmed that a regiment had been supplied with uniforms than we would be told that two more regiments had been raised and also needed equipment.

I remember that we had workshops across Paris, Lyon, Toulouse and Bordeaux that were making one thousand two hundred and fifty uniforms a day. They had to be supplied with the right patterns, cloth and dyes, not to mention buttons and badges. Then there were cross belts and musket slings from the tanners and twenty thousand muskets a month from various armouries and foundries.

Horses were being requisitioned from all over the country, musket cartridges made by the million and new guns cast, while more were

141

gathered from a virtually decommissioned navy. There was always particular attention paid to artillery, not least because the emperor was trained as a gunner and always used his cannon to full effect in battles. I well remember when he decided that a particular regiment should have two more batteries of guns. I spent much of the following week moving naval guns, ball and powder, onto carts and getting them transported to their new barracks. At the same time scores of carpenters and wheelwrights were busy building the gun carriages and caissons while dozens of horses and ammunition wagons were gathered, not to mention men with all their uniforms, supplies and equipment.

In two weeks all was ready for the emperor's inspection, even if some of the paint and varnish was still wet when he arrived. I confess to a feeling of pride as I looked on those neat files of men and equipment that I had toiled so hard to put together. I made sure that I was out of sight, though, as his carriage pulled into the courtyard. It was no cursory review; he went through everything as though he were the commanding colonel. He appeared pleased with the result. But when I eventually returned to the War Ministry, Davout handed to me a note he had received from Napoleon. It pointed out that the gun carriages did not have the little pots of grease they should have to keep the wheels lubricated. I remember thinking that he was an ungrateful bastard at the time, although without grease the wheels would have seized within a few miles and the unit would have been stuck impotently miles away from the enemy.

Looking back, it was that standard of detail and professionalism that made all the difference to the French army in the weeks to follow. Without it, the allies would easily have pushed aside a disorganised rabble of troops. But the emperor had ambitious plans, and to achieve them he needed one of the best armies he was ever to command. With my help, he got it too.

I was so absorbed in my work that I sometimes forgot that I was a British spy. I suppose I could have looked to sabotage things, but I would not have lasted long if I did. Davout had everything checked before tasks were marked off as done on his lists. He was known as a ruthless commander, having had a number of soldiers shot for disobedience during his defence of Hamburg. There was a constant fear of royalist sympathisers; General D'Erlon had one arsenal temporarily closed and thousands of cartridges checked after suspicions that they were deliberately producing dud ammunition. I had still not received any further contact from the British so had no means to feed back information even if I had wanted to. In any event I did not have time to think, constantly on the run from one task to the next. So it was that one evening in late April I was walking wearily through a square back to my lodgings when I heard someone calling my name. I had half turned before my tired brain registered the fact that I was being summoned in English and with my English name.

"Flashman...ah, Thomas, it is you. Bless my soul, I never expected to see you here." The caller grinned at me happily and was getting up out of his chair in front of a nearby café and gesturing for me to join him.

If he never expected to see *me* in Paris I could return the feeling a hundredfold. For there, bold as brass in front of me, was Lord Byron's friend Cam Hobhouse. For a moment I was speechless, for I had last seen him in Seville during the Peninsular War. I hesitated for a second as six years previously I had pointed the British authorities in Hobhouse's direction to divert them from discovering my own involvement in the Mary Clarke scandal. As a result, he had been obliged to flee the country, which is why I had seen him in Spain. But his welcoming grin indicated that he had never discovered my involvement in his involuntary exile.

"What... What on earth are you doing here?" I stammered and then blurted out, "You surely are not still hiding from the Clarke investigation? That was years ago."

"No, no, they have forgotten about that now. I am here to support the tree of liberty."

"The tree of what?" I asked puzzled.

"The cause of liberty, Flashman!" he cried enthusiastically while gesturing around him. We were speaking in English and several nearby were watching us curiously. "Enlightenment has been re-born

143

in France and it must not be extinguished. This is now a land where men can rise on their talents and not through an accident of birth, where science is encouraged and respected and where men of the arts," and here his chest puffed up a little to signify that he thought he was one, "are valued."

"Indeed," I agreed, still not sure what the buffoon was doing in what would soon be an enemy capital.

"France is the new Promised Land, Flashman," he enthused, "and the emperor is just the man of destiny that we need to lead the way."

"There are some in London who would disagree," I pointed out.

"Of course, our corrupt and self-serving politicians and rulers will try to resist," Hobhouse scoffed. "But they cannot resist the people and the masses are tired of war and they want peace. They also want a government of merit and many are now watching enviously across the channel."

"Really?" I queried for this was news to me, but then England had largely been at peace when I was last there.

"Of course, many are greatly impressed with the emperor's new approach to government. How many sovereigns have had a chance to reflect on their governance while out of office and then regain the crown? It is unique and the emperor's choice of one of his critics to draw up his constitution shows clearly that he now intends a more enlightened rule than before. It is the obligation, no the duty of all humanity to support him, not just in France but across Europe, the world, even."

"Indeed," I agreed again, while reflecting back to Ney's more informed assessment of Napoleon's motives. I knew Hobhouse as a failed poet and a pompous idealist and clearly his judgement was at fault here too. "Support from across the world?" I queried. "Do you think he will try to conquer Europe again?"

"No, he won't need to for the people want to follow the example he has set. In England the government is teetering on a knife edge. The Tory support for more fighting with France is ebbing away. The public is tired of war and the taxes needed to pay for it. As we are already being taxed on the light that comes into our homes, people wonder

144

what else they will be asked to pay for. Samuel Whitbread has not only promised them peace but many of the same enlightened policies that the emperor has introduced."

"Forgive me, I have been out of the country a while, but who the hell is Samuel Whitbread?"

"He is the leader of the Whigs and if the British army is to suffer just one major defeat he will be the next prime minister and saviour of liberty. We will have a lasting peace and join this modern age."

I sat back feeling a little stunned. When I had last been in Britain we had been at peace and the Tories were in the ascendancy. No one was even mentioning this Whitbread fellow. But now his time had come and I could easily imagine he would get a lot of support. I had been resentful about the window tax myself. "But wait a minute," I said remembering something. "Don't you have a brother in this British army that you want to see beaten?"

Hobhouse had the grace to look embarrassed before he admitted, "Yes, he is with the forces gathering over the border, but obviously I hope he is spared." It was a hope that was to turn out to be forlorn. Years later I read the diary that Hobhouse published of his time in Paris. He does not mention me, presumably to spare embarrassment given what followed, but he admitted that he was celebrating what he thought was the emperor's victory at the very time this brother was dying from his hero's attacks. But now he looked at me with a curious frown. "I say, Flashman, I have to admit that I am surprised to see you here and in the emperor's uniform. When I last saw you it was in British red. You never struck me as a man of strong political principles, if you will pardon me for saying. And by your own admission, you had not heard of Samuel Whitbread, yet now here you are in French service."

It was an inevitable question and despite desperately wracking my brains for a good answer as we had talked, I had still not come up with an explanation that would serve. "Oh I may not be a man of politics," I admitted airily. "But when you have seen what I have seen on the field of battle and afterwards, well it changes a man, you know."

"I see," replied Hobhouse, his frown deepening to indicate that he patently didn't. So I pressed on before he could ask any more awkward questions.

"Do you remember that dog you gave me in Seville?"

"Oh yes," he cried brightening at the memory "Viriates, ghastly creature, wasn't he. I am sorry about that, I hope you managed to get rid of him quickly."

My feelings towards Hobhouse suddenly soured as I thought back on the great Irish wolfhound I had renamed Boney. He had been one of the best comrades a man could have. "I had him for two years and he saved my life more than once, in fact he died saving it."

"Good grief!" exclaimed Hobhouse. "To have your life saved by a dog, how extraordinary." Then he noticed the people at nearby tables who were still watching us curiously and added in a lower tone, "I say, Flash, do you find the people here welcoming? Some have been decidedly off with me." This from a man wearing a British-made tweed suit, who could not have looked more English if he had worn a sash with the words 'John Bull' on it.

"Well you must have seen the papers. The British are being blamed for continuing the war and depriving the emperor of his peaceful reign. They probably struggle to believe that any Briton is quite as enlightened as you." I did not like the hostile stares either. The last thing I needed was anyone asking questions as to the background of the French colonel seen speaking to this unlikely British visitor. "Well, duty calls," I said getting up. I have to report back to the barracks, but perhaps I will see you here again?"

"Yes to see a friendly face would be most welcome. I take tea here most afternoons."

"Then I may well see you again," I said shaking his hand before I walked away. Inwardly I resolved never to go near that café again. Hobhouse was clearly a naïve fool but he could easily give me away by accident, or design if he suspected I was betraying his precious cause of liberty. But there was no French Colonel Flashman and so people would struggle to tie me to the colonel seen speaking to the strange Englishman. You could not be too careful, though, and so I

146

took several detours on my way to my new lodgings, just to make certain I was not being followed.

As I strolled the streets I reflected that if Hobhouse was right, the news from England gave Napoleon more than a little cause for hope. I had never paid much attention to the Whigs; they had been in opposition for years and being a bunch of largely eccentric liberals, had looked unlikely to ever form a government. We had been fighting France on and off for over twenty years at a huge cost in terms of blood and gold. I had been in Canada when peace was declared but had heard of the celebrations when I got home. The thought of another prolonged war with France might well have driven many into the welcome arms of the government's opposition; especially if men like Hobhouse were spouting idealist nonsense about France being a new Utopia.

Chapter 20

April turned into May and if anything I was working even harder. Yet more muskets were demanded by the emperor and armouries could not keep pace with demand. New workshops were set up and broken weapons were collected from around the country for repair. I remember one shipment of forty thousand weapons appearing. Rumour had it that they had been delivered secretly from Britain after a manufacturer had been paid handsomely for the urgent order. I cannot say if that is true, but I do know that the French workshops could not have produced them on top of what they were already making.

While the British might have been well paid, other suppliers were not and many were pressing for payment. Money was constantly in short supply with many merchants reluctant to accept promissory notes given the precarious state of the government. Meanwhile the emperor was unceasing in his fresh demands for new units and for things to be done even faster. Davout was working around the clock and increasingly short-tempered. He and the emperor had furious rows about what was possible and most of the time I was simply glad to be out of the way, chivvying along some harassed factory owner. It must have been mid-May when I got back to my lodgings one evening to find the letter I had long feared.

It had been pushed under the door. There was a different, unfamiliar seal on this one but, like the embassy letter, it had previously been removed so that the letter could be read and then clumsily stuck back down. With a slightly trembling hand, I broke it open. It was addressed on the outside to Colonel Moreau but inside the first words I read were '*Captain Thomas Flashman*'. Well I held the rank of major with the British but it was not that which sent a chill of alarm through my veins. Here was written proof that Moreau was a British spy and it would be my death warrant if it fell into the wrong hands. I already knew that someone other than the sender had read it. I just had to hope that it was the manager of the hotel by the embassy and no one else, for he already knew my secret. I was about to look through the window to check that my current lodging was not being watched when my eyes scanned the rest of the letter and my blood began to boil with rage.

Captain Thomas Flashman,

I have been appointed by His Grace to be the head of intelligence for the coming conflict. He has informed me that you are up to your old tricks of masquerading in enemy uniform. I gather that you are even using the same name as when we were together in Paris. No doubt you are spending your time shirking and fornicating as you did before, but should you find out anything useful you can send it to me via the address written on the enclosed card.

Colonel Colquhoun Grant

PS Don't think I have forgotten how you abandoned me in Brest. If you are captured and shot as a spy it will be nothing less than that what you richly deserve.

Grant the vain, arrogant dunderhead in charge of intelligence. Doubtless he had used my full name and what he thought was my army rank in the hope that his letter would fall into the wrong hands. But if it had, I reasoned, they would not have delivered it. Instead, they would have simply arrested me. Oh, I don't deny that I had given Grant cause to hate me. If you have read my previous memoirs you will know that I was sent to rescue him, but due to his stubborn stupidity we had ended up in Paris. I saved him there too only to have him threaten me with a court martial. So I had left him in Brest, waiting for a rescue that would never come, while I escaped on an American ship. Ironically, that took me directly to a new conflict while he later managed to escape to safety. Well I decided he could go to the devil, for pigs would fly before I gave him any help. He was bound to claim any credit for himself while he would take every opportunity to serve me ill. So I burned his letter and the notes I had taken of the northern fortresses and French war preparations. I had thrown the little card with the address on into the flames too, but on impulse, I snatched it back. The corner was burnt but it was still readable. Even though it came from Grant, it seemed foolish to throw away the details of the only friendly agent I had. I hid it under a loose floorboard. With the

149

benefit of hindsight, many lives might have been saved if I had burnt that too.

Were it not for the fact that I knew the border was now guarded I would have left Paris then and there. But I already knew far too much about French military preparations and my absence would be quickly noticed. Men would be sent to find me. Davout despised traitors and treachery and I could expect no mercy if I was caught. The safest thing was to carry on as I was and hope for an opportunity to escape in the confusion following an allied invasion of France – for that seemed the most likely outcome. Already the allied armies around Brussels exceeded those of the French and that was before the Russians and Austrians arrived on the scene.

Things were still moving quickly in France. At around the same time I received Grant's letter, an election was held to approve the new constitution. It established new elected chambers of government, guaranteed civil liberty and press freedom and the emperor claimed it would form the liberal foundation of his new regime. The constitution was overwhelmingly approved, officially by one and a half million votes to less than five thousand against. The ballot was suspiciously one-sided, although most were certainly in favour. But having been passed by the people, the inauguration of the new constitution had to be marked by a grand ceremony.

The event was called the Champ du Mai, to be held on the 1st of June. It was a huge affair with the elected representatives being sworn in, a church service and a distribution of eagle standards to regiments. Over forty-five thousand troops would be in attendance and the emperor was insistent that they were immaculately equipped to avoid any blemish to this national spectacle. So instead of worrying about my role as a spy and the downfall of France, I found myself fully absorbed into the preparations. When I could have been risking my neck eavesdropping on meetings, I was instead resolving the great brass button shortage that threatened to bring a *déboutonnée* scandal to the inauguration of the state. Ironically it was my diligence in this work, which was intended to keep me safe, that led to the greatest danger.

150

The first I knew of anything unusual was when I was summoned to Davout with the latest numbers of the little brass circles, the numbers that had been embossed and those buttons that had been completed and distributed. I will have you know, dear reader, that making a brass button is no simple task. I was feeling quite pleased with myself for at last all the new regiments getting their eagles would be properly dressed, when a week before they had seemed destined to resemble a bunch of well-armed vagrants. The marshal gave a brief nod of approval when I reported, which for him was glowing praise.

Then he ordered me and two other staff officers in the room to join him in his carriage for a meeting to discuss the preparations. Little was said on the journey and if the other staff officers knew where we were going they said nothing. Davout buried himself in his papers, checking that he could find any of the figures he needed easily. It was only when we went through the palace gates that I realised where the meeting was. It was at the Tuileries, which meant almost certainly Napoleon: a man I had tried to avoid for the last two months, would be present.

"Are we to see the emperor?" I asked nervously, while wondering if there was still time to feign illness to avoid the encounter.

"It is a state council meeting," barked Davout glaring at me and then at the others. "You will stay in the background, is that clear?" If he thought I was ambitiously going to try to attract the imperial eye, he could not have been more wrong.

"Yes sir," we chorused. Never have I been more enthusiastic to obey an order for I would do everything I could to ensure that the emperor did *not* notice me and start to delve into his memory again.

"You are here simply in case the emperor requires further clarification on details," continued Davout as the carriage came to a stop. "You are only to answer questions if directly asked by the emperor or myself."

"Yes sir," we repeated dutifully as we began to climb down from the carriage. We entered a marbled hall with a colonnade of pillars. I joined a group of staff officers and attendants that congregated at the edge of the room while Davout strode on to join the ministers that were standing around a large table. The emperor was not yet there, but I recognised Soult. Half of the ministers were in uniform and the rest were civilians, most in expensive clothes, some with decorations pinned to their chests or sashes. The ministers talked quietly to each other while waiting for the meeting to start, although I noticed one small fellow dressed entirely in black standing aloof from the rest. He looked like a crow amidst a flock of brightly coloured parrots and was watching the others with a look of wry amusement. I realised that he was the civilian that I had seen talking to the two generals when I had been with Pauline in the Tuileries. He evidently remembered me too, for as his eyes scanned the group of assistants and staff officers at the edge of the room, he saw me and gave the briefest nod of recognition. It was the only interaction he had with anyone in the room, for the rest of the ministers ignored him. Not one spoke a word to him or even stood within a few feet of him. It was as though he had some contagion that they did not want to catch.

There was a sudden crash of boots on the marble floor and peering around a pillar I saw two tall grenadier guard sentries standing on either side of a door on the far wall. They were presenting arms as the door swung open and I had the briefest glimpse of the emperor striding into the room before I shrank back behind the nearest marble column.

There was very little debate or discussion. Napoleon got straight down to business with a series of questions about the Champ du Mai event, checking who would make speeches, when he would see them in advance, which regiments would receive eagles and a host of other details. If any of the ministers were vague in their replies he would impatiently demand facts; nothing would be left to chance. Davout had come well prepared with the information he needed and had easily answered all of the emperor's questions until he was asked about the risk of an uprising in the more royalist Vendée region in the west of France.

"I am reinforcing garrisons there, sire with another ten thousand men," declared Davout briskly. "They will be able to quell any unrest before it can take hold."

"There will be no revolt," said a new voice calmly and peering round I saw it was the man in black speaking.

"How can you be so sure?" demanded Davout with more than a hint of aggression. He clearly did not like the man in black. "They would like nothing more than to rise up while we are engaged elsewhere."

The stranger ignored the hostile tone and picked at something under a fingernail before replying. "Because my emissary has convinced them that you will be beaten by the allies and that an uprising now would be an unnecessary waste of royalist blood." There was a moment of stunned silence around the table at the suggestion of defeat, but the stranger did not seem the slightest bit concerned. He gave a weary sigh before continuing. "I would be grateful for confirmation from the marshal's garrisons in the region, but I think he will find that the rebel bands are already dispersing. The few who stay loyal to its leader could be contained with a single regiment of dragoons.

"The Duke of Otranto has his own methods, gentlemen." It was Napoleon's voice again. "Davout, confirm the rebel groups are disbanding and if they are, bring those regiments back. We need all the men we can get." There was a rustle as the emperor checked his papers and then he asked "What of Berthier?

"He is still in Bavaria, sire," replied Davout. "We are not sure if our messages are getting through to him."

"Well send someone reliable to speak to him in person and bring him back," snapped the emperor. "I must have Berthier; he is my right hand on campaign. He always knows what I want done."

"Yes sire," replied Davout. I knew of Berthier. He was another of the old marshals who had not returned to France to re-join the emperor. He had been Napoleon's chief of staff for over twenty years, making sure that every regiment was where it should be in any battle.

"Now," continued the emperor, "move those papers off the map and tell me about our enemies."

Davout shuffled through some of his papers before replying. "We believe that the British and Prussian armies each number around one hundred thousand men. They are spread over a ninety mile front with the British centred on Brussels," he pointed at the map, "and the

Prussians at Namur to the south-east. Half of the British force is actually made up of German and Dutch regiments and many of the Dutch forces previously fought for Your Majesty. Even some of their British regiments are new and untried in battle. The Prussians similarly have a large proportion of untested militia. The Russian army of a hundred and fifty thousand is starting to cross Prussia but it is unclear when it will arrive, while the Austrians are indicating that their army of another hundred and fifty thousand might be ready to campaign at the end of July."

It was a huge force of half a million men marching on France and I could not help but peer briefly around at the emperor to see how he was reacting to what seemed a death sentence to his new empire. He was staring down at the map as though he could see on it the forces slowly converging towards him. "How many men do I have now?"

"In addition to the men guarding our borders, sire," Davout spoke the number in almost a whisper, "one hundred thousand men."

I could understand now how the Duke of Otranto had persuaded the royalists to stop their revolt, for it appeared a truly hopeless position.

"Many of our enemies are raw recruits," said Marshal Soult, speaking for the first time, his chin jutting belligerently out as he added proudly, "while nearly all our men are veterans of at least one campaign." He looked around challenging anyone to disagree with him, but most just stared down at the map with the emperor.

"I need two hundred thousand men," Napoleon said quietly as though half to himself. Then he looked up at Davout and spoke with more conviction. "You must get me two hundred thousand men. Raid every depot, replace the border forces with raw recruits if you have to, but I must have two hundred thousand men ready to attack by the end of June."

"Attack?" gasped one of the civilians. "But sire, even if you get that number of men, you will still be outnumbered more than two to one by the forces of our enemies."

"It will be Leipzig all over again," muttered one of the staff officers standing near me. I did not know it then as it had been fought while I had been in Canada, but the battle at Leipzig was the largest ever fought, then or since. Over six hundred thousand men had come together, with the French outnumbered two to one. While they had suffered lower casualties, the French had still been forced to withdraw.

"No," whispered another of the men. "At Leipzig we faced all of our enemies massed together. This time we will pick them off one at a time." There was other whispering and muttering among the small group of staff officers around me. They had stiffened at the mention of action and several were grinning in delight at the prospect. One or two, though, looked worried and their concerns were perhaps expressed by the civilian at the council table.

"Surely we should be considering a more defensive strategy, sire..." he continued, to a snort of disgust from Soult

"When has that served us well?" the marshal demanded. "We must have the advantage of surprise and attack."

"What does the enemy expect us to do?" the emperor asked Davout.

Davout glanced down at his papers, but he already knew that no answer would help him there. "I do not know, sire, but they must have confidence in their strength of numbers."

"They do not think we will attack." It was the man in black, this Duke of Otranto speaking again. "In fact they are busy planning their own assault on France. The Prussians want the British to joint them in an attack during June as the cost of maintaining their huge army in the field is bringing their nation close to bankruptcy. But the British are content to wait until July. They do not trust the Prussians to observe the Vienna treaty boundaries and so welcome the fact that the Prussians will not be able to afford to raise another army for a while." He gave a little smile before adding, "The delay also gives the Duke of Wellington more time to seduce every woman in Brussels society with loose morals."

The civilian burst out again, "How do you know all of this?"

It is my job to know it." Otranto looked the civilian in the eye and held his gaze as he added with a hint of menace, "You would be surprised at just what I know."

The civilian shifted uncomfortably but did not give up. "If you know that about our enemies, they will have their spies among us too.

Many with royalist sympathies remain in France. We cannot hope to attack without our enemies being forewarned."

Davout looked down at his papers and appeared pleased to have some information to contribute to the conversation. "I have heard that a man called Colquhoun Grant is heading up their intelligence gathering."

"I knew that devil in Spain," Soult conceded grudgingly. "Until we captured him, Wellington always knew where our forces were and where they were going. He escaped from captivity too. We will need to be wary of him." I was annoyed beyond measure at this high regard Soult had for Grant. It was Grant's Spanish guide León who had done the valuable intelligence gathering and he had been shot when Grant was captured. The bastard had only escaped captivity with my help – not that I could boast of that accomplishment here.

"This Colquhoun Grant is a fool," said Otranto dismissively and to my surprise I felt myself warming to this strange man. "Nearly all of the agents he has recruited are French-speaking from the border area. Most want France to be victorious and they are only passing on the information I give them."

"Ah, but you said *most*," said the civilian triumphantly. "It will only take one royalist to reveal our plans. How can you stop them sending messages to the British?"

"I have no intention of stopping their messages," replied Otranto calmly. "In fact, I correspond with Wellington myself; he believes I am helping the royalists." There was another gasp of astonishment from nearly everyone in the room at this extraordinary revelation. One of the men near me swore vehemently at this apparent treachery and even I risked leaning forward around the pillar to catch a glimpse of Napoleon's reaction. He was staring intently at Otranto like a man playing cards and holding kings and wondering if his opponent had aces.

"I trust," the emperor said at last, "that I have more reason for confidence in your loyalty than my enemies."

Otranto did not bat an eyelid before calmly replying. "Your Majesty will remember that I was among those who signed the execution order for the old king. The royalists will never forgive me for that. I believe I have always given you sound advice, I counselled against your invasions of Spain and Russia, which have greatly diminished our forces and just now I have returned ten thousand men to your army by preventing a revolt in the Vendée."

"So why do you write to our enemies?" demanded the civilian.

"To spread doubt and confusion. My agents are constantly sending them reports of our preparations, some true and some false, so that any report from a royalist is just one of many. They will receive so much information that it will be hard to judge what they can rely on." He paused before adding casually, "But as an added precaution one of my men is working in the office of this Colquhoun Grant. He can remove messages or add more as necessary." He looked pointedly at the civilian before concluding, "I have been watching and spreading confusion among our enemies for many years. Giving them too much information is always more effective than trying to leave them with too little."

I peered around the column again to see how this was being received. Napoleon was nodding slowly in agreement and the others around the table could see the sense in Otranto's claim. "We must leave you to do what you do best," said the emperor enigmatically. "Now we must consider what I do best and that is beating our enemies in the field." He turned to Davout. "Can you get me two hundred thousand men ready to campaign by the end of June?"

"One way or another it will be done, sire."

"Then, gentlemen, we will prepare to attack our enemies at the start of July. By then the British and Prussians will be distracted preparing for their own assault and the Austrians and Russians will have yet to come to their aid."

I stood there stunned at what I was hearing. I had come expecting to listen to the preparations for the Champ du Mai celebrations, but instead here I was eavesdropping on the most powerful men in France as they planned a surprise attack on the forces of my own country.

The group of staff officers I stood amongst were all slapping each other on the back at the news. My hand was shaken by at least two of them as they congratulated themselves on being there at this historic moment. They had no doubt that victory would be imminent.

"Our attack will be the last thing they expect," one of my new colleagues whispered as we watched the cabinet meeting come to a close. "Our veterans will tear through their inexperienced troops," he assured those standing around me. If they caught the allies unprepared I had a horrible feeling he would be proved right. I remembered Hobhouse telling me that the British government could fall with one major set-back. If the supply of gold from Britain to the other allies dried up then it was likely that the alliance would fall apart. Prussia was broke, the Austrians would negotiate a deal using Napoleon's son as leverage and the Russians could not maintain an army so far from home for long.

I went with Davout and the rest of his staff back to the carriage with my head in a spin. I had spent so long in France that my loyalties were divided. I did not doubt that France would be better off under Napoleon than the fat King Louis, not to mention the aristocrats who wanted to wind the country back to the past. But equally, I was not fooled by the emperor's protestations of wanting peace. If he beat the allies he would be secure on his throne. Then he would make plans to rebuild France and in due course, he would expand his empire again.

I did not give a stuff about the 'Age of Enlightenment,' principles, constitutions or politics. But what I did care most passionately about was preserving the precious skin of one T. Flashman Esquire. That delicate hide had already been pierced more than once fighting the French. With my ill fortune, it seemed to me that if war were to continue there was every chance it would be endangered again. With a nauseating sense of fear I realised that there was only one way to guarantee long-term peace and that was to ensure that the French attack did not have the element of surprise. And the only person who could do that was me.

Chapter 21

It was a small terraced house in the Montmartre district of Paris, certainly not the typical location to hold the future of Europe in the balance. I had walked past both ends of the street from different directions. I had even loitered for a while at one end of it, at least until some local tart thought I was there looking for company. I could not see anyone else watching the house, but it was overlooked by at least half a dozen other properties. It was the address on the card given to me by Grant. From what I had heard from Otranto, it was likely that his men were either watching the house or perhaps the person who lived there was one of his agents. But this was the only means I had of getting a message to the British. I had already decided that I would not send anything addressed to Grant, for that was certain to be intercepted. Instead, I planned to write directly to Wellington, but that still relied on the courier being loyal. If they were an agent then I would be seized with no doubt torture to follow and execution if I survived the agonies of my interrogation.

I had already considered and dismissed the idea of making a bolt for the border on horseback myself. It had turned out that I was not the only one at the cabinet meeting with a link with the allies: a ministerial official called Calvet had already tried a midnight ride towards Brussels to warn them. I saw the orders for increased cavalry patrols to find him. They were scouring the countryside and a day later came the report that he had been found. Bizarrely he had been discovered dead in a barn. I could not run; Davout had his staff report to him daily. My absence would be noted in a few hours and a message on their semaphore signalling stations would swiftly outrun a man on horseback. It was not worth the risk. So it was that for the five days following the cabinet meeting I had dithered over what to do. Not that I had been given much time to think with the continued frantic preparations for the Champ du Mai on top of other work to get a fighting army of two hundred thousand men ready by the beginning of July.

So it was that early on the morning of the 1st of June, the day of the Champ du Mai itself, I was once more walking hesitantly past the Montmartre street. I was still in a flurry of indecision and thinking of the carefully worded letter I had written and hidden under the floorboards in my rooms. Napoleon's plans were precisely the information that I had been left in Paris to discover. If it was ever revealed that I had been in that meeting and did not try to pass them on I would be ruined. But as far as I could see, if I did attempt to get a message out I was most likely to be caught. There would be no public trial – Napoleon and Davout would not want to reveal that the British had a highly placed agent. My fate was likely to be a shot or a blade in some grubby basement and then an unmarked grave.

For the umpteenth time, I felt my resolve melt away and hurried back into the heart of the city. The ceremonies were to be centred around the *Ecole Militaire*, the military school in the centre of Paris. Huge staging had been built around the facade with seating for dignitaries and the five hundred members of the newly elected houses of government. No less than forty-five thousand troops, perfectly buttoned, I might add, would also be arrayed there to receive eagles, while thousands more members of the Imperial Guard would line the route from the Tuileries and serve as the emperor's escort.

I will admit that I felt some pride when I saw those immaculately arrayed ranks of men and I had to remind myself that they were the enemy. I had worked hard to ensure that they were fully equipped, but now I had nothing to do but enjoy the spectacle myself. The public and officials were already arriving; it was to be the biggest state occasion for many years and most were getting there early. Slowly the crowds built until there was barely room to move and then the thunder of a hundred cannon from the Tuileries announced that the emperor had started the procession. It took over an hour for him to cover the short distance. The cheering of the crowd was virtually drowned out by gun salutes from various batteries put in place to defend the city and half a dozen regimental bands. No less than nineteen state coaches pulled into the square to deliver members of the emperor's family and ministers before a huge gold vehicle conveying the emperor finally hove into view. Four marshals of France rode alongside it as personal escorts, including Ney, who had been drafted in especially for the occasion. The cries of *Vive l'Empereur!* redoubled as the coach came to a stop at the end of the carpet and Napoleon finally stepped into view.

I suppose after an entrance like that it was almost inevitable that the emperor's appearance would be something of an anti-climax. He looked tired as he stepped down and was trying to adopt a stern, magisterial demeanour. But what really took your breath away was that amongst all this martial splendour, he had decided to arrive dressed like some prize frosted plum. It was a purple velvet confection, with white ermine around his shoulders and a black hat adorned with lace and so many white feathers it looked like an explosion in a dovecote.

"What on earth is he wearing?" I asked the man beside me. I had to shout the question over the roar of the crowd.

"They are his imperial coronation robes," he bellowed back. Then he gestured at the cheering people in the stands and yelled, "Everyone in Paris must be here." I nodded in agreement and then I was struck by inspiration. He was right, there were hundreds of thousands watching the ceremony and lining the route. The streets would be empty; there would never be a better time to deliver my message. The courier might be watching the ceremony too, but that did not matter, I would slide the message under the door. Indeed if they had been turned by Otranto, it would be better if the agent did not see me. I would have done my duty and if things miscarried, well it would not be my fault. That would be Grant's responsibility as it was his courier.

"I just need to check on something," I shouted to my companion and turned to start working my way back through the crowd. That was easier said than done as every conceivable vantage point had been taken, but eventually after a lot of pushing and shoving I was clear. The surrounding streets were thronged with people too and it took over half an hour to get back to my lodging. I quickly changed out of my uniform into clothes that I thought would be less conspicuous and put the message in my pocket. Then as I left I found a grubby coat and wide-brimmed hat on a peg in the hallway and put those on too. They would hide my clothes and leave my face in shadow if anyone was still watching the house. Then I was climbing the hill back up to the Montmartre district of the city and increasingly feeling like my heart was up near my throat.

I doubt I passed more than a dozen people between my lodgings and the courier's address, but that only calmed my nerves a little. I was out of breath when I got there. I was not sure if that was due to the steep streets or anxiety, for the closer I got the more I appreciated the risk I was taking. When I reached the end of the now familiar street I hesitated once more. I was in a blue funk by then and very nearly turned around again. Only by reminding myself that I had to do something to get a message out and I would never get a better chance, did I find the courage to go forward.

Every window I passed was empty. The only sound, a dog barking in a yard behind the terrace. The houses opened directly onto the street and I looked carefully at the fronts until I found the one I wanted. I strode over to it as casually as I could and nonchalantly bent down to push my note firmly under the door. I heard the wax seal skitter over the tiles inside as I stood up, feeling a weight of responsibility fall from my shoulders. That was it, I had done my duty. I pulled my hat a little lower and tried to slouch a little more as I began to saunter away. Two paces, then three and still not a shout to stop or the sound of boots running in pursuit. Then came a sound that seemed as ominous as the cocking of a gun, for I heard the noise of the door being unlatched behind me.

"Hello, Monsieur." If it had been a man's voice I would probably have made a run for it, but it was a woman's and I instinctively turned to look. And what a woman! She was in her early twenties, blonde curls escaping down her cheek from under her mop cap. Her cornflower -blue eyes were wide open with a look of innocent enquiry and as I ran my gaze down her shapely body I saw that she was holding my letter in her hand.

"Are you the courier?" I blurted out and watched as a shadow of fear crossed her face as she glanced quickly up and down the street.

"Quickly, Monsieur, come inside," she replied gesturing for me to follow her into the cottage. "Were you followed?" she asked as she shut the door behind me.

"No, I checked several times on the way here but everybody seems to be in the city watching the ceremonies."

"Yes, I wanted to go but my father said I must stay here while he is away. Please take a seat. Would you like some wine?"

"Thank you, but are you sure this house is not being watched?" I sat down, torn between a desire to know that she could get the message out and an urge to be as far away from this little cottage as possible now that the note was out of my hands.

"Don't worry, we know all of our neighbours and we look after each other. You will be quite safe here." I relaxed slightly and took a deep draught of the offered wine. The girl was an uncommon beauty and while many such stunners have learned to use their looks for their own ends, there were no such flirtatious glances from her. With danger apparently past I felt a familiar stirring in my loins.

"Do you live here with your husband?" I probed.

She paused in her tidying up of the small room and crossed herself as she almost whispered. "No, my François was killed in Russia three years ago. He did not want to be a soldier, but they made him go and now he is dead. I have lived here with my father ever since."

"And is your father the courier?"

"Oh…I…I am not allowed to say."

I could not help but laugh at that. "What do you mean you cannot tell me? You invited me into your house when I asked if it was you, so you obviously know."

"You could be an agent from the Ministry of Police," she retorted.

"If I was you would already be under arrest and anyway would an agent deliver a letter addressed to the Duke of Wellington?" As I said the words I thought that in fact, that would be an excellent way to confirm someone was a courier. But I was already getting the impression that the girl was not the sharpest knife in the block and I doubted she would notice. She bit her lip in consternation and looked down at the letter, now on her table, apparently noticing the address for the first time.

"I don't know," she murmured half to herself. She reached up and tucked the escaped curl back under her cap, her clothes tightening over her ample breast as she moved. My mouth went dry as I watched her body move under the simple cotton blouse. It had been months since I had been with a woman, with only the frustrating experiences with Pauline in between. I could not remember when I had wanted one more.

"Come and sit down beside me," I said hoarsely patting the bench before taking another sip of wine.

"My father says I must not tell anyone what we do," she declared as she sat down.

"I know," I soothed. "Tell me, do you want to see Napoleon beaten?"

"Oh yes, more than anything!" The gleam was back in her eye now. "If it had not been for him then my François would still be alive. We had only been married for six months when they took him away and we had been so happy. I hate the emperor and all of his generals. We rejoiced when he was beaten and the king came back, but now everything is ruined again."

I shifted round to face her and reached out to grip her shoulder, feeling her warm flesh under my fingertips as I looked her in the eye. "The letter on that table will get rid of Napoleon once and for all."

"Will it bring back the king?" she whispered, glancing at the letter with awe as though it had transformed into the Holy Grail.

Yes, the king's whole future rests on your beautiful shoulders," I caressed her collarbone with my thumb… and your father, if he is the courier."

She flushed at that and got up, taking that comely body away from me. "Yes, my father is the courier. He is a leather merchant and takes messages hidden among the hides in his cart. He has a skin with a secret pocket in it. He has been stopped many times but they have never found it."

164

"Excellent. But this is really important. I know he normally gives his messages to a Colonel Grant, but it is vital that he gives this letter to no one else but General Wellington. The general will reward your father well, for the message inside ensures his victory. With Napoleon beaten the king will return to the throne – you can see how his fate rests with you."

"I will tell him," she assured me solemnly. "He will be back tomorrow and he can be in Brussels in a week." That, I thought would be fast enough to give Wellington plenty of warning of what to expect. But given everything Otranto had said, I still had a nagging doubt that things were not as secure as the girl promised.

"Are you sure that no one is watching you or your father or suspects what you are doing?"

"I am certain. Only my friend Amélie, who lives next door, knows what my father does. She has an uncle that does the same, but I will make sure that it is my father who takes your message."

"But agents of the police…" I started only for her to mutter some incoherent curse, cross herself and spit into the fireplace.

"That devil Fouché will have to kill me to stop the return of the king," she vowed her eyes ablaze now with a sudden passion.

"Fouché?" I asked puzzled. "But surely he is now long gone." Fouché had been in charge of the secret police when I had first visited Paris back in '02 during the peace. I had been with Wickham, Britain's spymaster then, who had viewed Fouché as a formidable opponent. But when I was back in Paris in 1812 there had been a new man in charge.

"No, he has come back again to serve the usurping tyrant that sits on his stolen throne. He is the very devil. They say he has files on everyone, even the emperor, and that he blackmails and schemes to get his way."

There must be fine old times if Fouché and Otranto get together, thinks I. But aloud I said, "Come now, he can't be that bad. I know of at least one person in the government who I suspect could keep this Fouché in check."

She laughed in scorn at that. "You must be a foreigner to say such a thing. Have you heard of Robespierre and his Committee of Public Safety and their Reign of Terror during the Revolution? They thought they could keep Fouché in check and yet he sent them to their own guillotine."

"Really?" I asked astonished.

"I tell you he is the very devil. He trained to be a priest but when the Revolution came he joined the Jacobins and persecuted and killed many priests. He was the revolutionary leader in Lyon and once chained two hundred people together and executed them with grape shot from cannon. When the Committee of Public Safety reprimanded him, he knew his days were numbered and so he plotted and schemed with all of their enemies to bring them down. Then he served Bonaparte for years until he started to plot against him too."

If I had not been quite so distracted by those splendid bouncers heaving away under her blouse as she got into her passion, I might have paid more attention. But I didn't. Now the danger was past my mind and body were working to their own end. I conjured what I hoped would be a winning smile. "Well let's not worry about him. Why don't you pour us both some more wine and sit back down here." I patted the seat beside me.

"No, you must go. If the king depends on your letter, you must not be seen here."

"But there is no one outside…"

"No, you must go." She was virtually pulling me up from my seat and pushing the wide-brimmed hat I had discarded back in my hands as she guided me to the door. In a second or two I was back out on the step. Well, this was really too much. Twice now I had been brought to the boil by some scheming female only to be let down. Well, perhaps not scheming in this case for she did not seem that bright, but that just made it all the more infuriating. Dammit, if I could not win her by charm, I resolved to win her by guile.

"Stop," I whispered urgently. "Don't look, someone just peered around the end of the street and then ducked back. It might be one of Fouché's men." Of course there was no one there at all, but she did not

166

know that and it seemed a capital idea to play on her fears. "They must have heard the door open and looked round to see me standing on the step. Quick, put your arms around my neck and kiss me as though I am your lover."

"What!" she gasped indignantly.

"Look, girl," I warned sternly. "The king's life and his crown could depend on whether you kiss me right now. Do you want the death of the king on your conscience?"

"No, no..." The poor girl looked confused – she could not understand what was happening.

"Quickly now," I urged, not wanting to give her time to think.

"For…for the king, then," she muttered as she leaned forward and placed her arms around my neck and gave me a delicate kiss on the cheek.

"On the lips, girl," I muttered before twisting to plant my mouth on hers while pulling her towards me. She had a scent with a hint of lavender and as I breathed it in I reached up to grab one of those firm ripe breasts. She stiffened at that – as did I – but for a brief moment I felt her press herself against me and her mouth opened as though remembering some long-forgotten pleasurable experiences with her husband. Then she pushed me away.

"No, we mustn't." As she glared at me indignantly I took another swift glance at the empty other end of the street and started as though I had seen something.

"Surely you saw that one?" I turned back to face her angry glare and struggled to ignore that delightfully heaving bosom. "We must give them no cause for suspicion. If I am caught then you and your father would be at risk and the king would be doomed. Quickly, inside, pretend you are welcoming your lover home." I pushed her bodily into the house giving her very little opportunity for any acting. "Have you a place to hide the letter?"

"Yes, of course," she said and rushed over to the hearth where she lifted a loose stone and started to slide my letter underneath. I did not stay to watch but bounded up the little staircase to the floor above. There were just two rooms, a small one at the back, which I guessed

167

was hers and a larger one with a double bed at the front that must belong to her father. By the time I heard her shoes clacking up the stair boards I was staring out of the front bedroom window.

"Is there a passage behind the houses in front?" I asked. I had already seen that there was one behind the row of houses I was in and so it was a reasonable assumption.

"Yes, why? And what are you doing in here?"

"I thought so." I pointed at the house opposite. "One of the devils is watching us at this very minute through a telescope, I saw light glint off the glass."

"What? Now this is madness. That is Madame Celeste's house, of course she is not an agent of Fouché." I thought for a moment that I had overcooked it then, but she squinted across the street and added hesitantly, "I cannot see her in there."

"Of course not," I pounced on the opportunity. "She is either at the ceremonies or the agents have taken over her house. For her sake, we must do nothing to alarm them."

"I don't understand what is happening." She was sounding more hesitant now and I stepped closer.

"Unless Madame Celeste has a tall son with a telescope who watches your father's bedroom, there is an agent of Fouché watching us right now." I pulled off her mop cap and her long blond tresses fell down onto her shoulders while those cornflower-blue eyes stared at me with a surprised innocence. If this girl had been without a man for three years since her husband died, I thought it had been a shocking waste of beauty. Something I was all too keen to rectify. "We must convince them that we are lovers," I assured her. "A couple who have slipped away from the ceremonies for a private assignation. Otherwise, they will get suspicious and everything will be lost." I took hold of her then and kissed her again. She hesitated at first and then slowly she put her arms around my neck. This time, she did not push me away as I reached up to cup one of those wonderful breasts. I felt a tremble pass through her body and it was not from fear as she suddenly pressed both her lips and her body hard against me.

By George, this was capital, I thought as she broke the kiss to whisper in my ear, "Are you certain they are watching?"

"I would never ask this of you if there was the slightest doubt," I assured her as I pushed her back towards the bed.

"We must do this for the king," she murmured as I lowered her down to the covers. She was breathing heavily by then and while she was playing the coy and reluctant bird, I know women. She was just searching for an excuse to justify what she had probably wanted all along. "Heavens, girl," I gasped as I started hauling up her skirts with one hand while unbuttoning myself with the other. "He will probably give you a medal for this afternoon's work."

"It is my duty, then," she sighed, before squealing, "ooh what is that!" as something poked at her.

"Consider it the royal sceptre," I growled as she reached down between my legs to grab the offending item and two royal orbs.

As it turned out she was quite an ardent royalist and once she had got over her initial shyness, she willingly took up all of my suggestions and even suggested a few salutes of her own to her monarch. As the waves of pleasure reached their peak she arched her back and shouted out, *Vive le Roi!* It was a good job Fouché's men were not across the street, for they would have certainly heard her.

I have always said that patriotism has its place and for me, it was never more finely expressed than in that little room in Montmartre. The revolutionary principles of *Liberté*, *Fraternité* and *Egalité* are all very well, but they are a bit too virtuous for me. If kings, even fat ones like Louis, can inspire pretty blonde girls to go to extraordinary lengths to express their devotion, then I agree with her: *Vive le Roi!* That girl literally bent over backwards to please her monarch, as well as forwards and on one side and then the other. Every oath of allegiance I have seen since has seemed rather tame.

Afterwards, she fetched up the wine and I found a cigar and we lay together, with me reflecting that this espionage business does have its upsides.

"Do all royal duties give this much pleasure?" she giggled.

"It certainly beats standing guard at the palace," I agreed.

She gave a little purr of desire and added, "Fouché may have helped kill one king but if we have to do this, I don't mind stopping him kill another."

"What do you mean, he helped kill a king?" I asked feeling a sudden unease.

"He was one of those who signed the execution warrant."

A chill feeling spread down my spine as I queried, "This Fouché, does he have another name?"

"Yes. When the emperor dismissed him before, even he did not dare send him away in disgrace. So Fouché was made a duke of somewhere in Italy."

"Otranto," I whispered in growing horror.

"Yes, that was it," she agreed happily, snuggling into me. It fitted. Of course it bloody fitted and I cursed myself for not having seen it before. Those same eyes that had stared into mine at the cabinet meeting had watched those poor wretches blown apart by canister on his order and countless other conspiracies over the intervening years. A moment before I had been considering a second patriotic tribute. But now I just wanted to be away from that house and any hint of intrigue. I got up slowly and peered around the curtain at the road outside. There were a couple of women walking up the street with half a dozen weary children. They must have come back from the ceremonies in the city. It was high time I was back in the ministry; I would find some quiet corner and claim I had been there all afternoon.

"I think they have gone," I told the girl. "But to be sure I will go out the back door. That way when I emerge from the alley at the end of the street, if anyone is there, they will not know what house I came from." It was absurd, but while I had made up the existence of Fouché's agents before, I was now more than half convinced that they might exist.

"Wait a minute," the girl called as I started to pull on my clothes. "I don't even know your name." She giggled again, "When the king summons me for my medal, I need to know who he should give the second one to." Tempting though it was to fantasise about the Cross of the Order of Joan of Arc pinned on my left tit, awarded for fornication

170

above and beyond the call of duty, I had no intention of giving her my real name or even my French one.

I hesitated a full second before I replied, considering my options. Now I knew that Fouché and Otranto were one and the same, I did not doubt that sooner or later his agents would genuinely come knocking on the door. If they got their hands on the message I did not want them coming after me. I could have given her a made up name but they would have swiftly discovered it was false and then tried to track down the real culprit. Far better to give them a genuine person.

"Hobhouse," I told her. "My name is Cam Hobhouse, but you must keep that to yourself."

"What a strange name, Cam 'obhouse," she repeated and then she added, "must you go now? Maybe one day I will be Madame 'obhouse?"

"It is quite possible," I assured her. She said the name very prettily and as she lay there naked on the bed pouting up at me with her blonde hair tousled across the pillow, I nearly tore my clothes off again. Lust and fear battled among my wits for a moment, before fear won by a head and I reluctantly picked up my coat. "I have to go," I assured her, "but I will be back as soon as it is safe."

A minute later I was disappearing down the alley at the back of the house, having checked that both ends were clear of agents. I reflected that this was the second time that I had framed Hobhouse for something that I had done. The first time he had been forced to flee the country and I had a twinge of conscience about his fate this time. If Fouché had anything to do with it, I suspected our friend Hobhouse would discover that the new French republic was not quite the bastion of enlightenment he supposed. It would serve the naive idealist right to have a dose of reality. Perhaps he would then run off and join his brother with the British forces. They were bound to question him, I thought, but as he knew nothing he could do no harm. Even if he mentioned his friend Flashman in a French army uniform, there was no way to connect that to me.

Chapter 22

I realised as I hurried away that I had not even bothered to ask the girl her name. Not that I cared too much about that, for I never really intended to go back. It might have been callous indifference, but I think it saved my life a few days later, as you will see. No, all I cared about was getting away without being seen and that message reaching Wellington. The girl had assured me that her father would take it personally the very next day and she was in no doubt as to its importance. I went back to the ministry that afternoon and as my fellow officers appeared, mostly drunk, a while later, I was easily able to convince them that I had been a good little toady swot and diligently working through the day.

The next morning I went to extraordinary lengths to check that I was not being followed, but there was no one. Everything was as before. That evening I hired a coach and had it drive through the square where I had met Hobhouse. I half drew the blinds and hunched down in the shadows; sure enough he was there, sitting at the same table as before and poring over a pamphlet with another bookish fellow. I sat back against the leather seats of the carriage and grinned for it seemed we had got away with it. By now the message should be hidden in the leather cart on its way to Brussels. I could easily imagine Wellington's reaction when he saw it: the contents were just the information he wanted. It would save him from a humiliating defeat and possibly the collapse of the alliance. I had saved his armies with messages from behind enemy lines before, but this was possibly the most important campaign of the age. It would set the seal on my diplomatic career. There would be honours and recognition and, just as importantly, it would reveal Grant to be an incompetent halfwit. The icing on the cake was that Davout had announced he would remain in Paris as war minister when the campaign started, so as one of his staff officers I would stay safely in the capital while the rest went off to fight.

I was much more relaxed the next day, which turned out to be a mistake. The pace of work at the ministry had, if anything, increased as the marshal pushed everyone to get troops ready to meet the emperor's target. By evening I was exhausted when I reached my lodgings. If I had been more alert I might have noticed the polished black carriage parked across the street, but probably would not have, for coach drivers often waited there for patrons who were visiting the nearby theatre. The first indication I had that anything was wrong was when I reached my landing and saw that the door to my rooms was open. There were candles flickering inside and the low rumble of male voices. I cursed myself for not carrying a pistol that day. The only weapon I had was my sword. It was not my trusty gold-hilted blade that I had carried for years – that still hung over the study fireplace in Berkeley Hall. I had left it in England when I came to France, thinking that my soldiering was behind me. Now I carried a cheap utilitarian sabre. I slowly reached down and started to pull on the hilt. The steel made a scraping noise against the throat of the scabbard and the voices inside my room stopped at the sound. There was silence for a moment, but then I heard a boot scrape in the hallway below. I chanced a glance over the bannister to see a heavy-set man staring back up at me. He made no attempt to climb the stairs; it was obvious that he was there to catch me if I tried to make a run for it. I felt a trickle of sweat run down my spine, I was trapped.

With the blade now free and held out in front of me, I took another step forward so that I could look through the door into my room. God knows what I had been expecting, but it was not a half-eaten roast chicken and basket of bread on my table with glasses of wine. A man I had not seen before sat facing me. He smiled as I came into view and beckoned me to enter my own room.

"Please, don't keep us waiting, Colonel." The voice came from the end of the table that I could not see. I reached out with my sword point to push the door further open to see the speaker and almost instantly wished I hadn't. For there, sitting in my best chair at the end of the table, was none other than Joseph Fouché, Duke of Otranto.

My guts did a proper polka of terror then for the thought of this encounter had given me a nightmare just two evenings before. "What... what are you doing here... sir?" I croaked.

"Ah do come in, Colonel. Marcel, don't just sit there, give the colonel some of the chicken and pour him some wine. He must be hungry after a long day at the ministry." Fouché smiled as he gestured to the plate of chicken bones in front of him. "I must apologise, Colonel, you were such a long time that I ate my share without you." He was a small thin man, a bony face with grey hair and sideburns; he looked almost rodent-like. In other circumstances you would not have given him a second glance, but I noticed that his smile did not extend to his eyes. There was no warmth in them at all and I could not help but wonder at all the secrets he knew and how many men he must have looked at before arranging their deaths.

I stepped over the threshold and looked about me. There was just Fouché and the man Marcel in the room and a quick glance showed that my possessions had been expertly searched.

"What do you want with me?" I asked, although I was not sure I really wanted to hear the answer. But Fouché just ignored my question.

"Marcel, take the colonel's sword and show him to a chair." I felt the sword prised from my fingers. There was little point in resisting for they were bound to be better armed than I. The servant simply put the weapon on the sideboard as though they were unconcerned if I snatched it up again. Then he was guiding me to one of my own chairs and I was firmly seated in it. The man remained standing behind me, and I turned from him to Fouché, wondering what would happen next. Fouché looked calmly back at me. "The chicken is very good." He seemed determined to continue the act of the welcoming host, notwithstanding that he had come uninvited into my room. "You could drink from my glass if you are worried about poison." That was the first reference to this meeting being anything unusual. "Some people feel a little uncomfortable about my...er...hospitality," he added.

My mouth had gone dry and I had enough sense to realise that if they wanted to interrogate me they would hardly poison me first. So I reached forward and took a sip from my own glass. I felt some virtuous outrage would be in order if I was to maintain my pretence of

174

innocence. "Perhaps if you did not break into their rooms, they would feel more comfortable about meeting you."

"You may be right, but I don't think that either of us want people knowing about this meeting." He looked up at the servant. "Are you sure that this was the man you saw?"

"Certain, sir," came the voice from behind me.

"In that case, you can leave us." His gaze returned to me. "I am sure the colonel will not be a problem. Wait on the landing."

That exchange sent my mind reeling. Where had that servant seen me before? Had they really been watching the girl's house when I had been pretending to see them? Dear God, I thought, at any moment now he was going to bring out my letter to Wellington and then he would triumphantly reveal me to the emperor as an unmasked spy. I could expect no mercy after that. My mind was racing away to horrifying consequences so when the axe did fall it took me completely by surprise.

"I thought we might talk about Madame Chambord." Fouché said the words in a conversational tone but he was watching closely for a reaction.

"Eh?" was absolutely all I could say in response. I had been expecting accusations and revelations but instead he wanted to talk about someone I had never heard of. Confusion must have replaced fear on my features and it would not have taken a skilled interrogator to realise that it was genuine. "I… I have never heard of the woman," I managed to stammer. As the words left my lips I had a gut-churning realisation of who she might be, but I managed to hide that by furrowing my brow into an even deeper frown of indignation. "Look I don't know what this is about, but I have had a long day and I would like to go to bed. I really do not have time to keep up with society gossip. So unless there is something else, I would be much obliged if you would take your leave." It was a rude and impertinent way to speak to any duke, especially one as powerful as Fouché, but I realised that my only hope of surviving this encounter would be by dissembling and bluster.

175

"There is indeed something else, Colonel. Fouché spoke in a measured, calm tone, like a country surgeon keeping his patient calm before an amputation. "But I confess you surprise me. Perhaps I have been misinformed and your friend Mr Hobhouse was not being watched effectively the other day after all. That will be most unfortunate for someone." My guts did a backflip at the mention of Hobhouse being my friend and even though I swear my face did not change, Fouché noticed somehow, for he gave a little smile of triumph. "You are not going to deny knowing Mr Hobhouse, I trust, Colonel?" His eyes flicked to the door behind which his servant stood. Was he bluffing? Was this a trick to get me to admit the association or had his man really seen me talking to Hobhouse? If I had been spotted then my goose was probably cooked, but could I afford to call his bluff? I decided to hedge my bets.

"I think I may have met a man called Hobhouse, it is a strange name. But I certainly would not call him a friend."

"Oh come now, Colonel." Fouché moved his plate and underneath it I saw he had some papers. He looked at the top one and continued. "You met him at the *Café Angelo* a month ago and spent a quarter of an hour talking to him. I am told you spoke in English so my agents did not know what you were saying, but they tell me you acted like old friends. I suspect that you must have met him secretly at least once since then."

"Ah yes, I remember now." It was poor acting and we both knew it, but all I could do was fall back on the explanation I had used in the past. "My wife has English relations; I think he is someone I met through them. We stayed in England briefly after the Revolution. That is where I learned English."

"I see, then perhaps you can explain this." Fouché picked up another paper from the small pile in front of him and passed it across the table to me. At least it was not my letter, I thought, as the paper was unfolded and then I saw the words and my blood froze. For it was a copy of my message, every single word.

Uncle Arthur,

Overheard <u>very</u> senior officers talking about French attack on British and Prussian forces. They aim to invade at the beginning of July and by then will have two hundred thousand men.

Emperor keen to have Berthier re-join him.

Your nephew TF

PS Regards to Madame Freese

I felt the colour drain from my face and I probably went all the paler knowing that Fouché, the master interrogator and schemer, was watching every muscle twitch. How much did he know and what did he only suspect? "This gives away the emperor's plans," I gasped. It was not difficult to sound shocked.

"Plans the emperor revealed at a meeting you were in. Then either you or Mr Hobhouse delivered the plans to Madame Chambord to be taken to the British."

"That is an outrageous lie! It must have been Hobhouse and he certainly did not get the information from me!"

"Let's not waste each other's time, Colonel. We have been watching this man called Hobhouse for weeks. If he is a spy he is either very brave or very stupid as he makes no attempt to hide his nationality. He has not been near anyone from the cabinet meeting with the possible exception of you. Madame Chambord's neighbour works for me. She tells me that Madame Chambord slept with a man who gave her this message and told her that his name was Hobhouse. The description of that man matches you more than Mr Hobhouse, who, my watchers tell me, has not been near Montmartre since he arrived in Paris."

"This is absurd. I have already told you that I do not know Madame Chambord. There were lots of people at that cabinet meeting; perhaps one sent a message through a servant to this Hobhouse, knowing he was British." I was desperate and clutching at straws now, for the evidence against me was overwhelming. "Have you questioned this Hobhouse? Does he say I gave him the message? Perhaps the British have sent a new agent to Paris who is using his name?"

"There were indeed lots of people at the cabinet meeting and I have files on them all. I knew that Calvet was going to try and betray the emperor before he did, which was the reason I had him poisoned. I could not have him delivering the information to General Wellington before me. But don't worry, your message will also be delivered to add further confirmation."

For a moment the significance of what he was saying did not sink in. I was still trying to think of a more plausible excuse for my actions when I realised that Fouché was also admitting to giving information to the British. "What? You have betrayed the emperor's plans to the British?"

"Of course. Tell me, who is Madame Freese?"

I was so shocked I nearly told him and that would probably have sealed my fate. She had been the mistress that Wellington and I had shared in India and only we knew that. It was my way of telling the British commander that the message was genuine. Instead, I just blurted out the question uppermost in my mind: "Why?"

"Isn't it obvious? If the emperor loses I want the British to know that I am helping the allied cause."

"But you said to the emperor that the royalists would never forgive you for signing the old king's death warrant."

"They won't but I might be too useful or too dangerous for them to dismiss easily."

"And if the emperor wins?"

"I have given him ten thousand men for his campaign, which might have made the difference. And I will continue to serve him loyally." With just a hint of irony he added, "As I do now."

I sat there stunned for a moment. Whoever won the coming conflict, Fouché was determined not to be on the losing side. Then another thought struck me: Why was he telling me this? I have always been suspicious of devious bastards who tell you their plans. It normally means that they are not expecting you to live long enough to interfere with them. But almost inevitably he was one step ahead of me.

"You are wondering perhaps why I am not worried about you betraying me?"

"The thought had crossed my mind."

"Whoever you really are, Colonel, you're not the career soldier you pretend to be. You have no evidence that I betrayed the emperor whereas I have a lot of information and witnesses that would prove it was you." He gave a long weary sigh. "When I was younger and an idealist I killed traitors. But as I have grown older and wiser, I have found that it is far more useful to keep them alive." He gave me a long calculating look before continuing. "I don't think you would dare betray me because you know it would end badly for you. So if the allies win I will be able to show that I protected their agent in Paris. You may also be interested to know that Marshal Berthier will not be joining the emperor. Two days ago he fell out of a high window in Bamberg and was killed."

"Bamberg, but that is in the middle of the German states. How could you know so soon?"

"Fouché gave a cold smile. "Fortunately one of my agents was on hand with a messenger pigeon."

"How very fortunate for your agent, if not the marshal." I hesitated before asking my next question, but I had to know. "You told me what will happen if the allies win, but what happens to me if the emperor is victorious?"

"If the emperor wins you will belong to me. You will be one of several people telling me what I need to know at the War Ministry." He got to his feet, picking up the papers from the table and putting them in his pocket. "Now, I had better go as you are anxious to get to your bed." He grinned. "Sleep well, my friend."

My mind was still swimming with what he had told me, but as he got to the door he turned back. "Tell me," he said with a curious frown. "You must know him. Is this Colonel Grant really as stupid as my agents claim?"

How I wished I could tell him that compared to his own intrigues, Grant had the addled wits of a syphilitic baboon. But instead, I tried to maintain a blank expression and replied, "Grant? I have no idea, I have never met the man."

Chapter 23

I remember Grant telling me once when we were in Paris together, that he thought he could withstand torture and would never talk. Just the other week a similar ass at the Reform Club – God knows what I was doing there – told me that he thought torture of the mind was far worse than torture of the body. Well unlike those imbeciles, I have sat in a dungeon waiting for some bastard to stick red-hot metal implements where they were least wanted to make me spill my secrets. I know that I would have said whatever it took to stop the pain, whether it was true or not. It was a lesson I suspect citizen Fouché had long ago learned: intimidation and blackmail were far more reliable inducements than a henchman with red-hot pincers.

I did not get a lot of sleep after he left. I spent most the night pacing my room trying to work out what he knew, what he was only guessing and what he might do about it. My first thought was to make a run for it, but if they were not watching me before, Fouché's men would certainly be watching me now. I would soon have them on my tail and then Davout would have the army after me as well – my actions having proved to all that I was a traitor. Perhaps that was what Fouché wanted, a convenient gull he could blame his own treachery on if Bonaparte won.

But I realised that if I stayed Fouché could expose me any time he wanted. While he did not have conclusive proof now, he only had to wheel out Hobhouse in front of the emperor and that deluded fool would happily tell his hero that I was once a British officer. I suspected that it would not be hard to trick Madame Chambord into confirming I was the man who deceived his way into her bed and then I would be properly sunk.

I even began to wonder if Fouché really had sent the messages to Wellington or whether that was just a trick to get me to confess. But eventually I came to the conclusion that if he was loyal to the emperor he would just have had me arrested. It was far more likely that he was using me to play both sides. That did at least mean that I could be sure that my note would reach the British. Relaxing a bit, I realised that

Fouché was unlikely to make a move until he knew who had won the coming conflict. Now that the allies had details of the emperor's plans the odds had to be in their favour. If the British were victorious I would be safe from Fouché and the hero of the hour. I sat back and began to calm myself by imagining the honours that would come my way. I could not help but smile in that dark room as I thought how furious Grant would be at my success. If only I knew that my assumptions were built on foundations of sand.

A week passed and I will say this about Fouché's men, they were deuced discreet. Even searching for them, I only spotted my tail a handful of times. Mind you I was busy; preparations were continuing at a rapid pace and a growing force was amassing at the border. They had orders to break up roads into the country and give the impression that they were preparing for a defensive campaign. I almost felt sorry for some of my companions, who worked so hard on their 'secret' attack plans, little realising that it was all in vain… and then my world came crashing down.

Possibly I was so taken aback by events as the moment that immediately preceded the catastrophe was equally unexpected but pleasant. It was a Sunday that it happened, the 11th of June 1815: the day everything changed. After checking on progress at an arms factory I had not arrived at the ministry until eleven. There I found a message saying that Davout wanted to see me, but it was not urgent and his aide said he would be free at two. At the appointed hour I knocked on the mahogany door of the marshal's office. It opened a moment later but before I could enter half a dozen generals came streaming out of the room, all whispering excitedly to one another as they hurried away.

"You wanted to see me, sir?" I asked.

Davout was by his large table on the far side of the room, halfway through rolling up a large map. "Ah, Colonel Moreau, come in, come." Compared to his normal strict schoolmaster demeanour, he was in a surprisingly genial mood and he stopped rolling his map and dropped it back on the table where it immediately unfurled itself to lay half rolled across other papers. "I will show you this in a minute; you deserve to know what is happening. But first I have something for you.

He stepped across to the huge ornate desk and picked up a small blue leather box. "It is at the emperor's personal request that you have this. He wanted all of my staff officers to receive one. Some have them already, but you most certainly have earned yours." He held out the box to me with his left hand and proffered his right to shake mine. For the stiffly formal Davout, this was an unprecedented level of intimacy and I half feared that he would get carried away and start kissing me on both cheeks in that awkward Gallic manner. But instead, he recovered himself and snapped, "Well open it, man!" in his more usual brusque style.

I undid the clip, lifted the lid and could not help but gasp in surprise. For there on a red velvet lining was the pointed white cross of the *chevalier* rank of the *Légion d'Honneur*. It hung on a red ribbon with green enamel oak leaves around the cross. It was the decoration that every French soldier, of any rank, wanted and at that moment I felt truly honoured. I have the thing still and wear it on special occasions. Other British soldiers have earned them since, of course, especially for this Crimean nonsense. But theirs were issued much later and look different. I suspect that I am the only British soldier to have the cross with the profile of Napoleon in the centre. I was still staring at the bauble when Davout called me across to the map table, where he was pinning the chart down with weights.

"This is our plan of attack," he announced.

"But isn't it too early to make a plan?" I asked. "The allies could move a lot of their forces in the next three weeks."

Davout was smiling like a man with a secret he was desperate to share and abruptly I got a nasty sense of foreboding. "It would be if we were attacking in three weeks but we are not. The emperor left this morning to take command; we are starting the attack now."

It took me a full second to comprehend what he had said and then I was aghast. "But he can't," I blurted out. As the implications of what this meant sank in I was appalled. I had spent ages fretting about getting a message to Wellington to warn him about the French plans. Now when I had finally succeeded the plans had changed. Instead of helping the allies I was deceiving them and leaving them more vulnerable.

"What do you mean he can't?" Davout was staring at me with a puzzled expression; no wonder, for the emotions struggling across my face must have been a picture.

"Well..." I struggled to recover my composure. "What about the cabinet meeting? We only have a hundred thousand men, half what the emperor wanted."

"We have over a hundred and twenty thousand men and the emperor thinks that will be enough. It will have to be. He did not trust those at the council to keep his plans secret. You know that Calvet tried to warn the allies and he is uncertain of Fouché's loyalty. So he is launching the attack now to keep the element of surprise."

"Oh, I am sure he will have that," I muttered before adding, "but surely we cannot win with a force that size. The Prussians and British outnumber us by more than two to one and then there are the Austrians and Russians."

"That is if we fight their combined army," explained Davout. "Look here at the map." It was a large-scale chart showing north-eastern France and the Low Countries. If I had been expecting a complicated strategy of various corps marching in different directions I was destined to be disappointed. There was just one thick arrow drawn on it starting at Charleroi near the border, marking a straight line up the road towards Brussels. "This road marks the dividing line between the British and the Prussians," Davout explained. "If we can get between them the British will retreat west towards the coast as they will not want to be cut off from their supplies by sea. The Prussians, on the other hand, will retreat east, back towards Prussia."

"And does the emperor think that they will simply let us march straight up the road between them?"

"Their forces are dispersed over an area of ninety miles so that their men can live off the land without running out of supplies. They do not expect us to assault their positions; they do not even regularly patrol the border. They are convinced that it is they that will be making an attack." I felt more than a twinge of guilt at his words for I had helped lull them into their complacency.

"They will need at least a day to concentrate their forces," Davout continued. "If things go to plan they will not have that time. The emperor intends to push the Prussians to one side and march on Brussels. Half the British army is there and we can beat it. The capture of Brussels will show our enemies that the emperor is as strong as ever. Many of their soldiers who once fought in our ranks will think twice about taking up arms against us. After a taste of their new rulers, some might even re-join our units."

"What about the other allies?" I asked.

"Once we have beaten the British we can turn on the Prussians but they will probably retreat ahead of our army. The Austrians will not attack on their own and the Russians are still at least a month away. The emperor hopes having shown his teeth, he can sue for peace to buy us time to rebuild France and the army."

I could not help but be impressed at the audacious approach. It was a good bold plan and in hindsight, it was something I should have expected from a general like Napoleon. But it depended on being able to march a huge army of over a hundred thousand men right up to Wellington's front door without him noticing. Surely even someone as dim as Grant would have picked up news of an approaching force of that size. He must have *some* reliable agents and there must be Prussian and British troops on the border who would see huge numbers of men gathering on the other side. Even if that did not work there were dozens of men in the French army who were suspected of having royalist sympathies. It would only take one of them to slip across the border and the element of surprise would be lost.

Even if Grant did not detect the enemy force, surely Fouché would. No one had a better spy network and he had already boasted of other informers in Davout's ministry. Unless he was lying, Fouché probably knew of the change in plans already, but I had to get a message to him to make sure. I could hardly walk out of the War Ministry and straight to Fouché's office without raising suspicion. I would need to find another way. The prospect of another stroll to Montmartre seemed quite appealing. This time I would call in first at Madame Chambord's neighbour, who I now knew was Fouché's agent, to give her the message. They would need to be quick if the emperor was already on the road, but a man on a fast horse would out-run a carriage. They were bound to have closed the border now, but Fouché would know of ways to get through. Yes, I thought, that is what I would do first and then it would be time for Hobhouse to visit Madame Chambord again. After all, with the army now on the march there would be little for us to do at the ministry apart from round up reinforcements as they became available. I was just remembering that naked body and blonde hair spread out across the bed when I realised that Davout was still speaking to me.

"...He has no command but the emperor has invited him to join the army. Perhaps a position can be found for him there, but you should make no promises, Colonel, that is important."

"Er, yes sir," I agreed while desperately trying to recall the earlier part of this conversation that I had not been paying attention to. Who the hell was he talking about? Perhaps a location would give me a clue. "Where will I find him, sir?"

"Well you were on his staff, you should know where he spends his time," replied Davout irritably. "He was in Paris yesterday but if he is not still here he will be at his Coudreaux estate. Find him and take him to the emperor's headquarters as quickly as you can."

To my horror, I realised that I was going to war after all.

"Wake up," hissed a voice. "You are leaning on the marshal."

A boot kicked my leg to reinforce the words as I came reluctantly to consciousness. I sat up and opened my eyes to see an indignant officer glaring at me. He was wearing an unfamiliar red uniform, which disconcerted me for a moment until I remembered who he was. His name was Colonel Heymès and he was an insufferable toady.

I had located Ney at his Paris home and had given him Davout's message. The Princess of Moscow had been almost reluctant to bring me into her husband's presence, perhaps fearing some new slight from the emperor to further depress him. I found Ney in his study staring morosely at an unlit fireplace, an unread newspaper on his lap. He was the very picture of dejection. A moment later the news had transformed him back into an energetic marshal of France.

"At last!" he had roared and he actually hugged me, his stubbly unshaven cheeks rasping my face. "Now I will remind them all how I can fight. What command has he given me?"

I reminded him that the message was simply to report to the emperor's headquarters at Avesnes, but he was barely listening. He rushed off calling for his uniforms and campaign chest. The princess stared indulgently after him and then she too hugged my arm.

"Do what you can to bring him back to me safely, Colonel," she urged. "Now, I must get the cook to pack some food for your journey."

He had no horses at the Paris house, but it was a hundred and fifty miles to Avesnes and so he decided to hire a carriage. He had also insisted on bringing with us his friend Heymès, who he had campaigned with in the past.

We had been bouncing along in that carriage to make our rendezvous with the emperor for a day now and it had not been a comfortable journey. It had rained for much of the previous day and the roads had been busy with carts and wagons heading in the same direction as us, so progress had been slow. I straightened up and tried to stretch my stiff limbs. The blinds were down but the drumming sound on the carriage roof confirmed it was still raining. If Heymès had intended to prolong the marshal's sleep he had failed.

"Well, Pierre," growled the man beside me on the seat. "Now you have woken us both up perhaps you could tell us where we are." The marshal reached forward and pulled on a cord that raised the leather curtain covering the window on his side of the compartment. A grey light shone through the glass, which had misted up with the breath of three men through the night.

"I think we are near Saint Quentin, Marshal," said Heymès.

Ney tried to clear the glass with his hand, but with water on both sides of pane, it was still hard to see outside. With a grunt of irritation, he unhooked the leather strap that lowered the window. A blast of chill air invaded the carriage. I raised the blind and lowered the window on my side too. It was raining hard and rivulets of water ran down the gutters of the road. We were passing a cart that according to the number painted on its canvas side, belonged to the 23rd regiment, but it would be a while before it caught up with the column. It had its axle propped up on a log and a wheel missing.

"Would you like some food, Marshal?" asked Heymès opening a hamper at his side. "There is some chicken left and some slices of ham. The bread is stale but could still be eaten."

"No," said Ney cutting him off. "I want a piss. Tell the coachman to stop under those trees up ahead." He turned to me, "Have you ever gone on a campaign in a carriage before, Moreau?"

"No, I haven't," I admitted.

"Neither have I and I don't like it. We need to find some horses at Avesnes; I want a saddle between my legs, not a hamper of ham."

Having watered the trees we climbed back into the carriage, our clothes damp, to continue the journey. Ney sat forward eagerly, often putting his head out to look for any signs of the gathering army up ahead. He and Heymès talked of old campaigns with the excitement of children going on some adventure. I struggled to share their enthusiasm.

Heymès' uniform did not help, for it looked more British than French. The red cloth reminded me that the 'enemy' we were on our way to fight were my own people. It had all been a little unreal when I was in my nice safe billet in Paris. I had concentrated on gathering equipment and supplies with little thought as to who they would be used against. After all, the British commander himself had asked me to stay behind enemy lines. But now I knew that the information I had managed to pass on had only served to deceive the allies. On top of that, instead of being safely in the enemy capital I was reluctantly anchored to possibly the bravest lunatic in the army. The prospect of a quiet war was receding fast.

I had a strong sense of divided loyalties. I did not want the British to be beaten, but equally for the first time in my life I did not want to see the French defeated either. A sense of belonging is a strange thing. Most of us are born in a country, sometimes fight for it and either die in it or for it. But in my time I have found myself accepted by many different groups. There were the East India Company soldiers who all laid down their lives for me; I felt accepted in the Begum of Samru's army and was glad to see it escape Wellington's final attack at Assaye; I have even felt I belonged at one time amongst a band of Iroquois warriors. Compared to those experiences, it was not hard to feel an affinity for the French.

I had spoken the language continuously for the last few months and was even beginning to think in French. I had genuine friends among them now such as Lagarde and de Briqueville. They were defending their homeland and Hobhouse was right that it did seem reasonable to allow the French to choose for themselves who they wanted as their ruler. For all his avarice of other people's lands, it was obvious that Bonaparte was a far more capable ruler than fat old King Louis – which was precisely why the allies wanted him removed. And I say this as a man who has had a French musket ball through his innards and nearly died as a result.

I would have felt very differently if the French were invading England and there was the likelihood of the Imperial Guard marching up the drive to Berkeley Hall. But we were fighting in the Netherlands. Surrounded by more powerful neighbours, it was almost the traditional setting for continental wars. The southern part had until recently been part of France and I doubt that there has been fifty years of its history without some sort of invasion or disturbance.

Whatever Napoleon did, he could not attack Britain – the navy would see to that. Perhaps Grant was right when he claimed that I had gone native in the past when in enemy uniform, but I had spent too long in France to be indifferent to their fate. I had worked hard getting this army ready to campaign and as we approached Avesnes we saw a growing number of soldiers struggling through the muddy fields on either side of the road. The carriageway was kept free for wheeled vehicles and I confess that I felt a moment of pride when I spotted the artillery battery that I had helped pull together. This time, they had their pots of grease.

I had to remind myself that those guns I had helped gather could soon be firing shot at my countrymen. Men who had stood alongside me at Talavera, Busaco, Albuera and Badajoz and countless other places, back in the day when we had fought the men I now regarded as friends. Most of that army I had fought with then had been dispersed and Heymès was scornful of the new allied force. Many of the Prussians, he claimed, were half-trained militia who would not stand their ground. Meanwhile, amongst the so-called 'British' army, the majority of them had a first language that was not English. Many spoke German, others Dutch and a good number even spoke French. Some of those who had previously fought for France would still be wearing their French uniforms.

I too had studied the information received by the War Ministry about the allied forces and it made depressing reading. Of the forty thousand men under Wellington that were British, a good number of them were straight from the depots in England, and yet to smell gunpowder in earnest. Meanwhile, the loyalty and commitment of some of the foreign units was questionable at best. It was hard to argue against a crowing Heymès that if caught by surprise, the veteran French cockerels would tear through them as though they were chickens.

We arrived at Avesnes mid-afternoon, the last few miles crawling at a snail's pace through the crowded roads. It was a frontier fortress town that was packed with soldiery, with bivouacs of the Imperial Guard around the outskirts and parks of artillery on nearby fields. Even colonels like Heymès and I could not get room in the fortress itself, so we had to make do with crowded lodgings in town. Ney went to dine with the emperor and other senior generals while I shook off Heymès and went to get drunk. It was the best way to stop fretting about what I should and should not be doing.

Having got myself on the outside of two bottles of a rough red wine, things did indeed seem clearer. A drunken Flashy decided that he did not care if the French won the coming campaign or if the British and Prussians were beaten. It is strange how wine sometimes brings clarity of thought, for I saw that none of that mattered. What I did care about was getting back to England in one piece. I had finally achieved wealth and position with a loving wife and a son. I was damned if I was going to risk all of that in some death or glory charge across the lines. I would just keep my head down and let matters take their course. Then I would make my way to the Channel and never head south of Dover again.

I woke up next morning lying in a tent. My head was throbbing as though there were a steam pump in it. There were other regular rasping noises from nearby and something heavy was across my legs. I lay there for several minutes, unable to move or remember where the hell I was or how I had got there. Eventually, with a supreme effort, I managed to sit up. I had to shut my eyes for a moment to stop the tent spinning and to swallow back the bile that rose in my throat. God knows what I had been drinking the night before, but judging from the taste in my mouth, someone had brought a skunk from Canada and fermented it. Peering down I found an unconscious hussar lieutenant lying across my legs and two old soldiers sprawled beside me, snoring loudly enough to wake the dead. They both had the big bushy grey moustaches I had seen worn by soldiers of the Old Guard and one had his shirt open to reveal a colourful tattoo of an eagle raping a woman. I pushed the hussar off my shins; his head hit the ground with a thud but he did not wake up. Rolling over I crawled out of the tent on my hands and knees, gasping in pain as the bright sunlight outside found my eyes.

"Ah-ha, I wondered which one of you would wake up first," chuckled a voice nearby. Looking up I saw another moustachioed soldier sitting on a log near the entrance to the tent smoking a pipe. He was in his shirtsleeves so I could not see his rank, but he did not seem the slightest bit perturbed by a colonel crawling out of his tent.

"God, my head, I think I am dying."

"I am not surprised given what you were drinking last night." He laughed "After the wine you went on to some local firewater. You were properly raving then. Something about General Wellington fucking your wife and how he could go to hell."

I felt the bile rise in my throat again but realised that at least I had obviously had the sense to rave in French. "Is there any water?" I croaked.

The soldier passed me a canteen and I drank greedily. "What is happening?" I asked between gulps.

"You can relax. We are not marching until noon."

"Thank God." The thought of bouncing around in that carriage again was enough to make my guts churn.

"There are eggs if you want them and perhaps some pork left." The soldier gestured to a skillet that rested over a camp-fire.

"No thank you. Do you mind if I just sit here a bit?"

"They say you came in with Ney. Well if you are good enough for him, you are good enough for us. Stay there as long as you like." We sat companionably in silence for a few minutes and I gradually felt the sun warming my skin. My clothes were still damp from the rain the previous day. I was not surprised at the soldier's attitude to my rank; the Imperial Guard were an army within an army. Men would turn down commissions in line regiments to become a sergeant in the Guard and so they only treated their own officers with due deference. "I suppose you are too young to have fought here before," said the sergeant at length.

"Yes, I have only fought in Spain."

"Ah, I was here twenty years ago. We beat them then and we will do so again." He spoke with a calm matter-of-fact confidence. "It is proper killing country over there," he added pointing to the east. "Once you are over the river these wooded hills fall away and there is just a flat plain all the way to Brussels and beyond. That is where we fought before. We even had a balloon then to spot movements of the enemy. There must have been hundreds of battles there over the years. They say that's why the crops grow so tall, all the bodies that have been buried there.

"My father fought at Marburg, is that over there?"

"Marburg, no, that is much further to the east, about ten days' march for the Guard and at least two weeks for everybody else. Before my time, that. So your father was a soldier too?"

"For a while," I admitted. It was, in fact, his only battle and he had been fighting the French at the time but there was no need to mention that. "So are you sure we will win?" I asked.

The old soldier puffed his pipe for a moment. "I know we will win or I will not live to see us lose," he said simply. He tamped down his tobacco with a stick before continuing. "I put my faith in my emperor and my musket. And I know that when we advance nothing will stop us." It wasn't said boastfully, just a cold statement of fact, which made it all the more chilling.

I looked at that lined old face which had seen a lifetime of battles and charges. Even on the eve of the battles that would decide the future of his country, he just exuded a calm resolve. He saw me staring at him and smiled. Perhaps he sensed my natural cowardice or remembered the drinking of the night before, but he took out his pipe and reached forward and gripped me on the shoulder. "Drink won't give you courage, lad, you stick close to Ney and you will not go far wrong. We know what we are fighting for and what would happen if we lose. We will win, lad, don't you worry about that. Just do your duty by the emperor and all will be well."

I staggered back through that camp feeling strangely stirred, not in the way the old soldier had intended. For he had convinced me that the odds were in favour of the French. As I walked through the rows of tents and saw the stands of muskets in neat rows and men queuing to sharpen swords and bayonets, you could not fail to be impressed with the quiet professionalism. I had some vague recollection of the night before which involved some former prisoners of war swearing that they would take revenge for their years in captivity.

The previous invasion of France by the allies just a year ago and the rule of King Louis had shown clearly the consequences of defeat. None of them would want to see their country pillaged and humiliated again. So instead of courage, I felt despondency. Even if the allies were prepared for the attack, it would be a tough-fought contest. But with Grant as Wellington's eyes and ears, there was little chance of that. If caught unawares, the allies would be pushed apart and then their mostly inexperienced troops would be routed.

It turned out I was not the only one who was feeling depressed. For Ney had dined with the emperor and had still not been given a command. He had come back raging at Heymès that even traitors like General Bourmont, who had run out on him when he declared for the emperor, had been given brigades while he, a marshal of France was left idle. Ney was nowhere to be seen when I got back to the army's headquarters and so I fortified myself with a vegetable broth so thick you could stand your spoon up in it. As I ate I stared out into the castle courtyard where men were preparing to leave. It had started raining again, the dark clouds matching the grey stonework and my mood.

I had just finished my lunch when I caught a flash of red in the courtyard. There was Heymès riding in on, of all things, a pony and trap.

"What the devil are you doing on that?" I asked when I reached him.

"The carriage will be too wide for the country lanes and there are no spare horses anywhere. Everything is being used to carry men or supplies up to the front." The marshal looked similarly unimpressed when he saw his conveyance, but climbed aboard without comment. He seemed resigned to being a mere spectator to the coming contest, which was fine by me. I would much rather be with him brooding at the top of a hill, watching the action, than be dragged by him into the middle of it.

We joined the rest of the army following several paths leading north-east. There was barely room for two and our luggage in the trap. I had no wish to be jolted around again and so I led the pony by the bridle. The rain had increased now to a solid downpour and we were soon soaked through. We had to travel twelve miles to a small town called Beaumont near the border; the emperor did not want soldiers arriving there before late afternoon to reduce the likelihood of his army being spotted. Twelve miles on a normal summer's day would be a comfortable half day's walk. But when you have a hundred and twenty thousand men, horses and guns, ammunition wagons, limbers and all the other accoutrements of war travelling down narrow lanes in torrential rain, things are somewhat different. Infantry were ordered to keep off the roads and ranged several hundred yards in the fields on either side. Crops were trampled flat in the waterlogged ground as men searched for fresh earth where their feet would not sink down to their knees in the mud. Cavalry rode further out still and a sea of moving men and animals could be seen in all directions.

We followed down a lane in the middle of a line of guns. The cobbles slowly gave way to a mud track that was deeply rutted from previous vehicles. The cart was continually dropping in or climbing out of one of the furrows and I was glad I was not aboard. Ney sat their bare-headed, his plumed marshal's hat put away before it became a waterlogged mess that would have made him look ridiculous. But the braid on his uniform showed his rank and more than once soldiers trudging past would cheer him. They would point him out sometimes shouting 'There is the redhead,' which was his nickname in the army. He would smile and raise his arm in salute and if anything took some comfort from their recognition

Every time we reached the bottom of a valley the mud would get too thick for vehicles to move easily. The gunners would put down planks and push and strain at their pieces to get them through the ooze. As we followed them Ney and Heymès were forced to dismount and join me in pushing the trap across. Ney did not hesitate to put his shoulder to the cart and invariably several of the passing soldiers would see him and slide down into the road to help.

We reached Beaumont just before dark. The border was just a few miles further on and regiments were being directed to bivouac in woods or on slopes facing away from the enemy so that they would not be seen by British or Prussian patrols. Ney went to lodge in a house with Marshal Mortier, who commanded the Imperial Guard. The best that Heymès and I could manage was a loft above a stable, which we shared with a dozen other officers. We ate the last of the food that had been packed for us by Ney's cook and settled down to try and rest. I was cold and wet, so sleep did not come easily. Some of the others sharing the stables had passed around a flask of brandy, but after the previous night, I could not stand the idea of spirits. As it had finally stopped raining I got up and took a walk through the town. It was surprisingly light and then I realised that the sky had a strange pink glow. Gazing out over the hills I could see thousands of flickering lights from the army's camp-fires and these were reflecting on the low cloud. For all of the careful preparations, it was a clear sign to the allies that a huge force was nearby. Surely they could not miss that, some sentry must see it and report it.

I imagined messengers would at that moment be riding to Wellington and the Prussian commander to warn them of the attack. If the allies could combine in time they would have double the numbers of the French and twice as many guns. Napoleon would be forced to abandon his plan and a grateful Flashy could slide over the border and home.

I did not get a lot of sleep that night and I was not the only one. There was a mood of tense excitement amongst my fellow officers in the stable. The first regiments were due to start moving just after three in the morning and the emperor was to ride with the advance guard. One by one the officers slipped away from the company to join their men. Whispered calls of *'Bonne chance'* followed them down the loft ladder as they disappeared into the darkness. The rest of us lay there listening to the quiet tramp of men down the street outside, the jingle of harnesses and an occasional shouted order. More men slipped away until Heymès and I were the only ones left. Dawn light began to creep into the loft through a narrow slit in the wall and I went over to it to look outside. While the rain had stopped, the wet ground had created a low mist. I watched the columns of blue-coated men march north-east until they became shadows in the fog before disappearing entirely.

I stood watching this ghostlike army for ages as it reappeared on a rise of ground half a mile away before dissolving again like a spectre into the gloom. Then in the far distance I heard the first cannon fire. It sounded like a single battery of guns opening up on some obstacle and I could imagine the emperor cursing that the element of surprise had now gone. Well, I thought, if the allies had somehow been blind to the signs of a huge army just over the border, they would know about them now. It looked like it would be a race: Would the emperor be able to drive his enemies apart or could they combine in time? I heard footsteps behind me and sensed Heymès at my shoulder watching the men march away.

"Everything depends on them," he murmured half to himself. "If we fail then the Revolution and everyone who has fought and given their lives since, will have died in vain." I did not reply. Heymès was right but on the other hand, I wondered how many would have to die in the years of war that would inevitably follow if the French won.

We had our first stroke of luck that morning when we met Ney. As he had not been given a part to play in the attack, he had arranged for us to meet him at the leisurely hour of eight. We found him outside of

Marshal Mortier's quarters astride a fine charger and holding the reins of two others.

"Gifts from Mortier," he announced and then in a lower voice he added, "he is laid low with sciatica and cannot leave his bed."

"How unfortunate," sympathised Heymès as he swung up in the saddle.

"Unfortunate for him," agreed Ney as a smile played across his face. "But the emperor is now short of an experienced marshal." He wheeled his horse around while calling over his shoulder, "We should catch up with the army."

We had barely left the confines of the village when he reined up and gestured for us to do the same. "Listen!" he called and we sat there straining our ears. Then I heard it. More cannon fire, further away this time as either the wind or fog distorted the sound. But it was the steady crash of cannon, the sound of a full-scale engagement. "It has started!" he shouted and I don't think I had ever seen him look as happy. He was like a young boy with a new pony. "Come on!" he shouted, spurring his horse in the direction of the guns.

I knew that the first objective of the attack was to capture the city of Charleroi. It was fifteen miles away over hilly wooded country that was saturated from the recent rain. Charleroi was also the other side of the river Sambre, which was thirty yards wide at that point. There was a big stone bridge at Charleroi but according to the map Ney showed me there were two other bridges a few miles either side of it and the French planned to cross all of them so that they could outflank the allies in Charleroi if necessary. The city was defended by the Prussians and I wondered if they had mined the bridges so that they could be destroyed to stop any attack. When I mentioned this to Ney he just laughed.

"I doubt it," he scoffed. "They would not want to risk their destruction when they plan to use the bridges themselves to invade France."

We were glad of the horses now as they enabled us to leave the road and ride across the fields on either side. Most of the guns had been put on the road first to support the attack, but the narrow lanes were now jammed with ammunition and supply carts. They struggled up some of the wooded hills and often got bogged down in the valley bottoms. The River Sambre protected the left flank of the army and a few regiments peeled away from the main force to guard the few crossing points that led to the area garrisoned by the British, but there was no sound from that direction to indicate that the redcoats knew we were here. We continued in the direction of Charleroi. The mist was burning off and after all the rain of recent days, it promised to be hot and dry.

By mid-morning we saw our first prisoners, around fifty dejected Prussians sitting under guard beside the main road. A short while later the cannons stopped firing and then at noon we saw the reason why. Coming into view around a bend was the stone bridge leading into Charleroi. It was intact and full of French soldiers marching unopposed into the city.

The first French objective had been taken. Ney trotted forward beaming in delight, his decorations glinting in the bright sunlight. Even though we had taken no part in the attack, the soldiers nearby cheered him, often with cries 'Go the redhead!' as he went past. It had been a clever and well thought out attack, calculated to minimise French casualties. Bonaparte had waited for his two flanking columns to cross the bridges on either side of the town before he showed himself and some of his Imperial Guard on the approaches to the stone bridge leading into Charleroi. The Prussians had rushed to defend the bridge as a bottleneck to stop the French assault. They must have expected the French to storm the town but the soldiers in blue did no such thing. Instead, French artillery bombarded the exposed Prussians while the French, including the emperor, stayed in cover. The Prussians must have sent troops to guard the two bridges on either side of the town but they were ambushed by French forces that were now stealthily approaching the rear of the Prussian positions. Suddenly the Prussians inside the town realised that they were about to be encircled and fled. Bonaparte was offered the lunch that had been prepared for the Prussian commander.

The good people of Charleroi all spoke French and thought of themselves as French. They had been treated as second-class citizens by their new Dutch-speaking Netherlands government and so they welcomed the French as liberators rather than invaders. They offered food and wine to the soldiers as they passed, but the men had to eat whatever was offered on the move. Officers urged them on for while they had already done a day's march and captured a key border city, their enemy was in confusion and the emperor wanted to capitalise on their early success. Napoleon had already ridden out of Charleroi to view the pursuit of the enemy. There was the sound of distant sporadic fire as Prussian units desperately tried to extricate themselves from the unexpected French advance and regroup.

As the emperor had already left the city, its citizens concentrated their attention on Ney, the most senior and renowned of the officers they could see. Having been ignored and spurned for so many months, he clearly relished the recognition.

"We have the Prussians on the run already," he boasted to the people. "They will not stop running until they reach Berlin." There was cheering at that for the Prussians had not been popular in the town. Then the mayor insisted that we share some lunch with them. Whether it was part of the meal prepared for the Prussian commander I could not say, but it was served on abandoned regimental silver plates covered in Teutonic script and crests.

As Ney and the rest of us tucked into mutton and drank a chilled white wine, I did my best to appear to be enjoying the moment. Digestion was not helped by a large portrait of some starchy matron glaring down at us. We were told that this was the wife of one of the Prussian officers. From her look of scorn, it was as though she could see what we had done to her husband's army. One of the town officials borrowed a pistol and, to the delight of many, shot the picture. But as the tension in the canvas was relaxed she managed to look even angrier. I had some sympathy for the woman in the portrait. I had the feeling that if she had been here in person the Prussians might have been more vigilant to the possibility of attack.

I was astounded at how easy it had been. How had Grant and the others failed to notice an army of over a hundred and twenty thousand men marching up to the border? How had they missed the glowing sky from the camp-fires? Surely they had some spies and agents that they could rely on? The emperor had used his cunning to take the town easily and now he was on the plains beyond, he had more room to manoeuvre. He had the Prussians running like a disorganised rabble and he was determined to push them as far as he could.

At least a handful of the French were also running, though, for as we dined news came in that General Bourmont, the man who had abandoned Ney, had now also run out on his emperor. Bourmont and his entire staff had defected to the Prussians at the start of the attack. As an aside, I heard much later that the French general was not well received by the Prussians. Blucher, the Prussian commander, refused to see him. On being told that Bourmont was now an ally as he wore the white Bourbon cockade he replied scornfully, "A shit stays a shit whatever colour cockade he wears."

I could have made a run for the fast-receding allied lines myself, but I remembered my drunken resolution to keep my head down. To change sides halfway through a battle was the most dangerous thing. You were likely to be shot at by both sides, especially when one side is in headlong retreat and confusion. There must be, I assured myself, dozens of men now riding to Brussels with news of the attack. One more would not make a difference. I was also all too aware that if the allied rout continued and I was captured I could expect no mercy. Half the army had seen me riding up with Ney. While other captured British officers would be treated as honourable prisoners, all I could expect was a wall and a firing squad.

At least that was what I tried to tell myself. I knew I could provide a huge amount of detail on the French army and their plans, which would be invaluable to Wellington. But to return to the allied lines meant that I would also have to admit that I had been duped. My well-intentioned message containing the wrong dates of a French attack were one of the reasons that the British were not watching the border as closely as they should. We had been listening out for sounds of gunfire from the north, from British positions, and there had been none. If I was to return to the allies now I would be ruined and humiliated, Grant would see to that for certain. Far better to stay with the French and hope that they would be beaten in the end. Then I could claim to have played a part in their downfall.

The start of a new distant cannonade reminded us that it was time to get on the move again. Ney asked for the whereabouts of the emperor and was told he was on the summit of a hill on the outskirts of town. There he could watch his army pass by and try to make out the disposition of the Prussians. One of his aides told us that he had also taken the opportunity for a short mid-battle nap, as I suppose you can do when you have fought as many battles as Bonaparte. He was awake when we got to him, though, talking to a civilian wearing dust-covered clothes. The stranger's hard-ridden horse was being doused in water by a couple of cavalry troopers. There was a cluster of staff officers standing a few yards behind the emperor and Heymès and I headed to join them while Ney strode on to join Napoleon.

"Ah good day, Ney," Bonaparte called when he saw the marshal walking towards him. "I am very pleased to see you. Come, let me show you what is happening." With that he dismissed the civilian, who stepped back towards our group, while the emperor led Ney a few paces to stand at the edge of the bluff. I edged a bit further forward so that I could eavesdrop on their conversation. Napoleon was pointing out the cobbled road that led from Charleroi to Brussels. Even from where I was standing, I could see that columns of French troops were marching along this route to a town three miles off. The noise of the bombardment was coming from that direction and the town was wreathed in smoke. "That is Gossalie," said the emperor, raising his voice above the noise. "Some of the Prussians are making a stand there." He turned to Ney and smiled. "Would you do me a service, Marshal?"

"Of course, sire," Ney stiffened like a gun dog in front of game as he sensed the prospect of command and action.

"Take the first and second corps up the Brussels road to the crossroads at Quatre Bras, do you know it?"

203

"Yes sire, I campaigned here twenty years ago."

"Excellent. I will pursue the Prussians as far as I can while they are in disarray. Then once I have driven them off I will join you. With the Prussians out of the way, we can then march on Brussels."

Ney was grinning in delight for he had just been given a full third of the invasion force. It must have been far more than he was expecting. The other marshal in the campaign, the newly appointed Grouchy, only had a force of twenty thousand men and he was under the emperor's close supervision. Ney was being given an independent command. "It will be done, sire." Ney threw up a smart salute, his previous frustrations forgotten. I felt my stomach tighten as I realised that we would no longer be spectators in this mad affair. But then I heard something far worse from the group of officers beside me.

"Are you sure?" one of them was asking the civilian.

"I am certain. Wellington plans to go to a ball tonight in Brussels. All of the senior British officers will be there." I stared at the man aghast, unable to believe what I had just heard. For the last few hours I had been imagining riders hurtling across the countryside with news of our invasion and every British redcoat for miles around converging on our position. For all his faults, Wellington had always been an astute commander, energetic and quick to react to his opponent's moves. Now it seemed he and his officers had no intentions of leaving Brussels until tomorrow at the earliest. The day after tomorrow and the French would be in Brussels, while the isolated Prussians might well have been beaten.

"Have they not heard of our attack?" I asked incredulously.

The civilian looked irritated at the question. "Yes, as I have just said, they do not think it is the real attack." He turned to the others and chuckled. "From what I was told from one officer, this Lord Wellington is far more interested in conquering his new mistress than beating the emperor. She is the pregnant wife of another English lord." They all laughed at that, with one officer claiming that Wellington would still be in bed when we took the city. Meanwhile I stood there stricken, thinking that on the current showing he might well be right.

Napoleon's voice interrupted my thoughts. "Do you not approve of the distractions Brussels offers our enemies, Colonel?" I looked round to find Ney and the emperor staring at me. The laughter of the staff had interrupted their conversation. I must have stood out as the only one not laughing. The last thing I needed now was Napoleon paying me close attention, but he was more amused than curious.

"I was just thinking, sire, that it was a shame that there were no similar distractions in Spain."

"Indeed," agreed the emperor rubbing his hands together. "This day has gone better than I had hoped, but there is still much to do."

"We will take our leave, sire." Ney was now keen to get to his new command.

"Is Moreau on your staff?" Napoleon asked Ney and I felt my stomach tighten.

"Yes sire," replied Ney, "with Colonel Heymès."

The emperor nodded at Heymès but then smiled at me. "Keep an eye on Moreau, Marshal, I am sure I have met him before somewhere, but he pretends he cannot remember where."

Somehow I managed to smile back. "I assure you, sire, we have not met before this year." I saluted smartly. "But I look forward to seeing you again, in Brussels." I turned to go and was relieved to hear one of the other staff officers ask a question about pursuing the Prussians, which I hoped would take the emperor's mind off me.

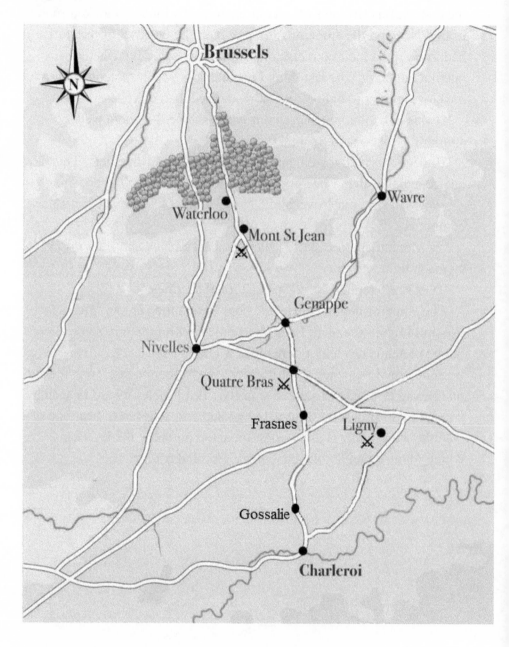

Chapter 27

"How many men do we have?" enquired Heymès as we hurried back to where our horses were tied up.

"The first and second corps each has twenty thousand men," replied Ney. "The emperor has also given me the light cavalry of the Guard, but he does not want me to overuse them. They must be fresh to guard our flanks on the march to Brussels. On top of those, tomorrow we should get General Kellermann's cuirassiers." The cuirassiers were armoured horsemen, named for their breastplate armour, who rode on heavy horses. They were another elite force, known for crashing through enemy formations of infantry and cavalry.

"How far is this place Quatre Bras?" I asked.

"Oh it must be another fifteen miles from here. There is nothing much there, just a few farms, but it is the place where the road north to Brussels meets another road from Nivelles in the west where there are British garrisons, and Ligny in the east where there is a Prussian force. If we hold it we can stop the British coming to the aid of the Prussians."

"Or perhaps we will stop the Prussians joining the British at their dance," cried Heymès gleefully. "It does not sound like we will have to concern ourselves with the British for a while."

"Maybe not," said Ney, "but first I have to find my men and let them know I am their commander." Ney was transformed by his meeting with Napoleon. Instead of resigning himself to being a mere spectator to the incredible events around him, he was now playing a part. In fact he was a principal actor in the performance. He was all military efficiency settling into a role he had done successfully for years. He found the general of the Guard light cavalry at the bottom of the hill and asked about the whereabouts of the rest of his command. Half of the second corps, under its commander General Reille, was in Gossalie; it was those troops we had seen from the hilltop. They had spearheaded the attack into Charleroi and the rest were scattered about the town and the bridges that had been crossed. The first corps, under General D'Erlon, was even further back. Some of them were still guarding the bridges across the Sambre on the road between Beaumont and Charleroi. Ney ordered the cavalry commander to send messengers back down the line of march to order his units to follow him to Gossalie, with D'Erlon's men to destroy the bridges before they left them. Then he led the remaining cavalry through the wooded hillside towards the sound of the guns.

It took half an hour to get to Gossalie, Ney riding out in front with Heymès and I on either side. Behind us trotted a column of nearly eight hundred cavalry troopers in their green uniforms and short bearskin helmets. For me, the whole venture was turning into a bad dream. Instead of watching from the rear as the invasion was blocked by alert, or even vaguely competent, allied troops, I had seen Prussians outmanoeuvred and routed, while the British refused to accept that the invasion had even started. More alarming was that the man to whom my fate was currently tied, had responsibility for the left wing of the entire attack. Any hope that he might command from a nice safe hilltop where he could oversee proceedings were dispelled as soon as we got to the small town that the Prussians were holding.

There were thousands of Prussians in Gossalie and a distant column of some nine to ten thousand more Prussians could be seen beyond them moving towards the east. The second corps commander, General Reille, clearly knew his business for he had already set up batteries on high ground which were shelling the defenders of the town. He had also organised two attack columns, each of some five thousand troops. They stood just out of range of the enemy, ready to advance when we arrived.

Ney and Reille greeted each other warmly and then the general briefed the marshal on his plan of attack. Ney rode up to the first attack column, who gave him a half-hearted cheer. It was still baking hot and the men were dripping with sweat under their woollen uniforms, their faces covered with the dust of the march. The poor devils had been awake since three in the morning, already marched more than twenty miles and had fought a battle to capture Charleroi. Heymès and I had ridden after the marshal and staring down at the vast mass of blue-coated soldiers, I thought he would struggle to raise enthusiasm to attack and capture a second town that day. If the distant column joined the defenders then the French would probably be outnumbered. But back then I did not know Ney and his extraordinary way of motivating his men.

He stood up in his stirrups so that as many as possible could see him and yelled, "I want to smell gun smoke again." There was another cheer at that but perhaps weaker than the first. Ney just grinned at them. "I know it is hot, but those of you who were with me in Russia will know that hot is better than cold." There was laughter at that as he reminded them of his earlier glories. "Now I will join your ranks and we will march together. You will show them some pepper with me, won't you?" There was a louder cheer of acclaim, but it was not universal. Ney was unconcerned and spurred his horse towards the front of the column. To my horror, Heymès set off to follow him. I cast desperately around for an excuse not to join them but Ney, to my immense relief, waved Heymès back. "I will do this alone," he called.

I watched in fascination as he rode along in front of the foremost rank of men. I wasn't the only one, as I saw hundreds of soldiers moving their heads to catch a glimpse of him between the shako helmets in front of them. He stopped in the middle and dismounted. As his men watched he plucked some anxious fellow out from the front to hold his horse and then took the man's place in the line

"The marshal is in the front rank." The whispering passed through the column like a wave and if it was possible these tired and dirt-covered men stood taller. Ney's sword glinted in the air above the rows of heads and the word 'Advance' could be heard, echoed by every sergeant down the line. The huge mass of men swung into motion and then a band I had not even noticed before struck up from the rear ranks of the formation. It was an old revolutionary song; I can only remember some of it:

The war trumpet signals the hour of the fight
Tremble enemies of France, kings drunk on blood and pride
The sovereign people come forth, tyrants go down to your grave

Then the chorus came and every single one of them was singing, some with tears mixing with the dust on their cheeks

The Republic is calling us
Let us know how to vanquish or how to perish
A Frenchman must live for her
For her, a Frenchman must die

As the singing grew louder you knew that somehow they had summoned some extra energy. Whether it was the presence of Ney in their front rank or the words of the song and the memories it summoned, who knew how it had happened. They probably did not know themselves but now they were nudging and grinning at each other as though fresh from a barracks to march in a review, rather than heading towards an entrenched enemy. I knew why they were grinning, for they knew with absolute certainty, as did I at that moment, that nothing on God's green earth was going to stop them.

I looked across at the second column, which was aimed at the western side of the town and had also started moving. They were singing too, although General Reille remained on his horse alongside the men so that he had a better view of the attack as it unfolded. The fresh confidence of the French must have been felt by the retreating Prussians in the town, small groups of them started to run northwards, seeking the safety of the larger column of Prussian troops marching beyond. Reille spotted the movement and released his men to the charge. With a guttural roar, Ney's column followed suit.

There were some crashing volleys from the defenders but they did not get time to reload before the French soldiers were swarming over barricades, climbing through windows and kicking down doors. In half an hour it was all over, although you can be sure I waited for all sound of shooting to cease before I advanced. There were twenty French dead on the approach to the town and a similar number of wounded. But I saw well over a hundred Prussian corpses in the streets and at least two hundred prisoners in the churchyard. Most of the Prussians had fled, with French bayonets just a few paces behind until they were north of the town. The Prussians in the column kept moving east, including a good portion of cavalry and that deterred the French from pursuing too far. Ney had captured the town and the road to Brussels lay open before him.

When I first rode into Gossalie I thought our casualties had been far higher: one side of the main street was almost carpeted with French soldiers lying in a state of exhaustion. Then I realised that they were all on the shaded side of the street and that there was a crowd of men around the one well, the water being drunk almost as soon as it was out of the pail. The euphoria of the recent conflict was wearing off and that last charge into the streets had sapped what little energy the men had left. It was just as well that the Prussian column we had seen had shown no appetite for a fight. They, and the survivors from the town, had just pulled meekly away to the east, trying to re-join the main Prussian body. We could hear gunfire from that direction and guessed that Napoleon's main force of the French army must be driving them on and trapping what it could.

I found Ney in the inn studying his map. In contrast to his men, he had found even more energy from the assault and was eagerly studying the next town along the Brussels road. It was Frasnes, another three miles away, with Quatre Bras another four miles beyond that.

"The men can't go much further, sir," Reille was cautioning. We will need to rest them here a while, make sure they get water and perhaps advance again in the cool of the evening. Some are low on ammunition and our supplies will probably not catch up with us until tomorrow."

Ney nodded in agreement. "I will take the cavalry and reconnoitre the route," he declared. "I doubt we will find much resistance if the British do not think this is the main attack." He looked at Reille. "Bivouac your men here but keep some ready to advance later if needed."

So it was that around six that evening, I found myself once more with Ney and Heymès at the head of a column of guard cavalry heading down the Brussels road. It was not as hot as it had been earlier that day, but it was still warm. We had around three and a half hours of daylight left and the countryside was flattening out, making it easier to travel. Grazing pasture was gradually replaced with fields of corn and

211

rye and, looking out at them, I remembered the words of the old
soldier in Beaumont, for the crops really were some of the tallest I had
seen. The wheat was as high as six feet and the rye taller still; you
could hide an army in one of the fields. From our high vantage point
on horseback we watched carefully for any flattened area or unusual
movement among the tops of the plants moving gently on the wind.

We needn't have bothered for we did not see a living soul between
Gossalie and Frasnes, but there, at last, we found the first outpost of
Wellington's army. They weren't British; they were green-jacketed
Dutch troops. Just a paltry few hundred of them with a couple of guns.
We watched them running about as soon as we appeared on the
horizon and then there were puffs of smoke as the cannon fired. But
we never saw the balls – they must have ploughed into the crops on
either side of the road. Ney sent half a dozen troopers back the way we
had come to get Reille to send up some infantry. They would be far
better at driving men out of buildings than men on horseback, and
anyway he had been ordered to preserve the Guard cavalry.

There was a wood beyond Frasnes to the right of the road and so we
turned our horses that way and ploughed a narrow path through the tall
crops. All the Dutchmen in the village could have seen was a row of
disembodied heads above the tops of the rye. They fired off their
cannon a few more times but again to no effect. Eventually we came
across a path running parallel to the road and turned north again
towards the trees beyond the town. As we crested a slope we saw that
the Dutch were pulling back, marching in a column down the road
towards Quatre Bras. There were clearly concerned that with us behind
them they could be cut off. Any hope that this indicated that a more
resilient force guarded the crossroads were dashed when we emerged
from the woods onto some high ground overlooking the junction.

From what Ney had told me, this was a key strategic point. The
Wellington I thought I knew would have had several thousand reliable
British veterans there to slow or stop a French advance. Unfortunately,
that Wellington had turned into a man who apparently preferred balls
and fornicating to sensible military precautions. Through my glass, I
could see no more than three to four thousand Dutch troops around the

crossing, although there could have been more hidden in a wood near the junction on the far side of the road. News of our arrival had preceded us. Officers on horseback could be seen galloping along the road between the crossing and the retreating force from Frasnes, while men were hurriedly being formed up into both columns and squares.

There were too many of them for our single regiment of cavalry to charge, but Ney sent a probing patrol down towards the green-coated troops to test their resolve. The nearest column of Dutch troops opened fire at an impossible range as the horseman approached, revealing their lack of experience.

"They cannot hope to defend the place," said Ney dismissively. "They will probably slip away during the night." I'll admit that at the time I thought he was right. Little did I realise that this insignificant junction would determine events far more than a bigger battle a few days later. We turned back and reached Frasnes at nine, just in time to see an exhausted advance guard from Reille arrive to occupy the place. Even on horseback and with a more leisurely start to the day I was tired too, having not slept much the night before. Ney chose to return to Gossalie in the daylight that remained, but along with most of the cavalry, I remained in Frasnes. It was clear the army would return here tomorrow and so it saved two trips. Sentries were set and I found a bed in a cottage and settled down for the night. It was my first time alone in what had been an incredible day. I still found things hard to believe: a French invasion had started, Dutch and Prussian forces were being driven back in headlong retreat and at that very moment instead of reacting, Wellington was dancing.

Map of Quatre Bras

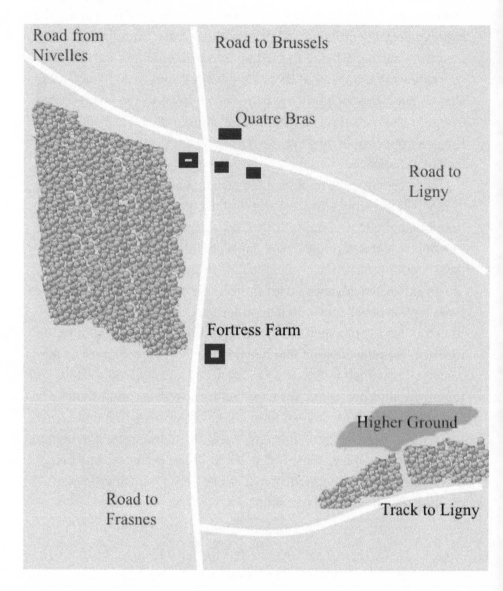

Just last week I heard some armchair general, who had never been closer to a battlefield than a painting in a gallery, loudly proclaim that Ney lost France for Napoleon at Quatre Bras. Well he did, but not for the reasons that the old duffer claimed. The man is not alone; many condemn Ney for not capturing the crossroads on the evening of the 15th or first thing on the 16th, as though his men had limitless energy and ammunition.

I would have liked to see some of his critics march thirty miles in heavy uniforms on a blistering hot day and fight two battles and then see how enthusiastic they were for a third. With the benefit of hindsight, I dare say Ney would have driven his men harder, risking losses from heatstroke and much higher casualties. But even if he had I suspect that the outcome of the day would not be much changed. For at last, very belatedly, Wellington was swinging into action. Little did we know it then, but at dawn that day thousands of men dressed in red were starting a march in our direction.

I had been woken by the clanging of metal, but when I gazed out of the cottage window it looked the perfect pastoral scene. The sun was rising in a cloudless sky that promised another hot day. Crops moved gently on the breeze for as far as the eye could see. Only the noisy farrier replacing some shoes on cavalry horses, gave an indication that anything unusual was happening. Downstairs I found that the village bread oven had been put to work with loaves and roast chicken to eat. I might have been one of the senior officers present, but there was little to do, for the regimental men knew their business. Disappointingly the Dutch had not taken the opportunity of night to slip away from the crossroads. In fact, early cavalry patrols indicated that they had been reinforced by another four thousand troops. But our horsemen had ranged beyond them some distance up the Brussels road and towards the British garrison at Nivelles and had seen no sign of further men heading in our direction.

The Dutch were seen as an irritation rather than a threat. Eight thousand poorly trained troops with no cavalry and few guns were not going to prove an obstacle for forty thousand French veterans. The commander of the advance guard put out a skirmish line close to the crossroads to keep the Dutch bottled up while our cavalry ranged at will to further intimidate them. Ney arrived shortly after I had finished breakfast. He was similarly unconcerned at the Dutch reinforcements. At Gossalie they were still waiting for supply wagons to catch up with the column, but once these had arrived Reille would bring the rest of his corps to Frasnes. D'Erlon's corps was behind Reille's but would also be up by mid-afternoon. Ney had received messages from Napoleon that indicated that he planned to use the right wing of the army to push the Prussians further, but there was no sound of any fighting to the east and we wondered if the sausage-eaters were continuing to pull back.

After meeting the local commanders, Ney took a cavalry patrol back to the vantage point we had been at the previous day; he wanted to see Quatre Bras again for himself. We stepped out of the woods onto the higher ground and studied the enemy disposition. Whoever was in charge of the Dutch was a fool. He had sent his men out in a long thin cordon more than a mile south of the crossroads in our direction. Our outposts had fallen back, realising that the thinner the enemy line was, the easier it would be to break when the main column arrived. The Dutch had more men in the wood on the far side of the Brussels road, which would be tougher to clear, but they had made no attempt to occupy the high ground we stood on, which dominated the area.

"We will place our main battery here," said Ney. "We can see anything that moves around Quatre Bras and we are close to the road should the British try to use it. He was just about to put his telescope away when a movement caught his eye on the road that led from Brussels. Coming down it were a group of horsemen, who reined in at the crossroads. Ney passed his glass to Heymès. "What do you make of that?" he asked. "One of them I think is wearing a blue coat. Doesn't Wellington often fight in a blue coat?" I stiffened at that and

216

strained my eyes to see, but at that distance I could barely make out the number of dark dots that were men, never mind the colours they were wearing. Ney's glass was much more powerful than my own and my fingers itched to get hold of it.

"It might be blue," agreed Heymès. "But British artillery officers wear blue too. It is much more likely to be one of their gunner officers. It could even be a Prussian searching for his army."

"May I look?" I tried to ask as casually as I could, but my heart was racing. If it was Wellington then that had to mean a British force was on its way. I took the offered glass and focussed it on the distant junction. A group of figures swam before the lens and I twisted the tubes for a clearer view. I could not make out his features, but there was a figure in a blue coat with a familiar erect pose in the saddle. The rest of the riders with him sat a respectable distance away and I was sure it was the British general. "No, it looks like an artillery officer to me," I told Ney. After a final look up the Brussels road for any sign of a dust cloud indicating marching men, I passed the telescope back. "Wellington is probably still in bed with his mistress after the ball last night," I suggested.

"You may be right," Ney grudgingly admitted, sounding almost disappointed. We sat and watched the newcomers as they stared out over the peaceful rolling hills. I thought that Wellington would soon reorganise the Dutch defences, but to my dismay, he saw nothing of any concern in the landscape; a few moments later, his party turned east and started to gallop down the road towards us in the direction of the Prussians. We turned our horses back into the trees as he must have passed within some five hundred yards of our position. There was no doubt then as to his identity, at least for me, while Heymès thought that the direction of travel was proof that the man was part of the Prussian force.

I sat there inwardly fuming. Of all the half-baked incompetence; they still had no idea that an attack was headed in this direction. Surely they would realise that the capture of Brussels would be a prime goal of any invasion. Even the most junior officer studying the map should see the significance of the Quatre Bras junction. I began to seriously wonder if Wellington was losing his wits. It was well known that syphilis could cause madness and given the way that Wellington had been ploughing his way through society women, it was quite possible he had caught a dose of the clap. When Ney and the others turned to go back to Frasnes, I hesitated and then announced that I would stay there and keep an eye on the Dutch position. I could not sit by and watch the allied army get destroyed without doing anything, but I had to find a way to warn them at no risk to myself.

Out in front of me was a field of rye, some if it seven feet tall. It covered a good number of acres but beyond that was a field of clover. That was just ankle-deep grazing for a few sheep. There were no animals there then – they must have been either eaten by the Dutch or taken by the farmer when he abandoned his land to the soldiers. Instead, there was a small Dutch outpost in the clover field, just half a dozen men, most of them lying with their coats off enjoying the sunshine. All I had to do was walk through the rye until I reached the clover field. I could shout a warning from there if necessary; they would not even be able to spot me among the crop.

I tied my horse to a tree and pushed my way into the tall stems. There was, I thought, little chance of me approaching with any degree of stealth with the noise of breaking stalks. The crop was not evenly cast; there were thick clumps and then patches with no plants at all. As I moved through the thinner parts for ease I kept the sun over my right shoulder to ensure I was moving north-west. It was a deceptive terrain to travel over as you could not get any bearings apart from the sun and without that it would be easy to lose your way. I became convinced that I was getting close to the edge of the field when in reality I was probably only halfway across and spent ages edging forward unnecessarily. But perhaps it was a good job I did as I nearly stepped on the boy before I saw him.

The tall crop was a paradise for those who wanted to shirk their duty as it provided an easy place to hide. The boy looked little older than sixteen – he had not started shaving yet. Possibly weary after a night-time march to get here, he had slipped away for a furtive nap. I found him lying on his side, half curled up with his musket and pack lying on the ground beside him. A lone sentry caught unawares, this was even better than I had hoped. I had a sword on my hip and a pistol in my pocket, but I picked up his musket and jabbed him with the barrel. He just muttered something in Dutch and turned over to resume his slumber. I remembered the masters at Rugby trying to wake boys in the dormitory and sometimes resorting to a bucket of water. The soldier's canteen lay beside him and so I picked that up as well. Having taken a couple of gulps to slake my own thirst, I tipped the rest over his head.

He came up then, all right, gasping and spluttering, talking vehemently in Dutch that was probably a curse on his comrades for their prank. Then he gave a small shriek of alarm as he dashed the water from his eyes and saw a French colonel standing before him, covering him with a familiar weapon.

"Keep quiet. Do you speak English?" I whispered hoarsely at him in that language.

"Ja, I am a Dutch soldier."

"Hopefully not a typical one," I muttered before continuing more urgently. "Listen carefully. There are forty thousand French troops marching towards this crossroads and they will be here within hours. You must get someone to tell General Wellington and tell him the message comes from Major Flashman." The boy looked singularly unconcerned at the news of this approaching onslaught and just stared at me blankly. I grounded the musket and shook him by the shoulder. "Do you understand what I am telling you?"

"Ja, I am a Dutch soldier."

Belatedly I realised that these were the only words of English he knew. I tried him with French and in desperation, Spanish, but with no success. He spoke to me in his own language, which contained lots of words from the back of the throat, but not one was familiar. I searched my pockets but you can never find a scrap of paper or stub of pencil when you need them. I remembered I had a pen, ink and paper in my saddlebag, but I was not going back for them. There was nothing for it but to press on with my prisoner and so, taking a glance at the sky to get my bearings, we pushed on through the long stems.

We emerged into the clover with the boy in front of me. I was holding him by the neck of his coat and shirt and had his musket under my arm. At first they did not notice me standing behind him but then the sergeant sprang to his feet shouting alarm to the others.

"Keep still," I shouted, covering them with the musket. "Do any of you speak English?"

The sergeant hesitated in the act of reaching for his own weapon. "Ja, yes…I come from Bruges, we have many English merchants there."

I felt relief wash over me. "Then listen carefully. I am an English spy with the French. There are forty thousand French soldiers led by Marshal Ney who will attack here in the next few hours. The French plan to march on Brussels, this is their main attack. You have to get a message to General Wellington, do you understand? Tell him it comes from Major Flashman, then he will believe you."

The sergeant gave me a cold, calculating look. "If you are an English spy why don't you tell the English general yourself?"

The honest answer was that from what I had seen so far, the poor devils did not have a cat in hell's chance of surviving the afternoon and I had no intention of dying with them. No, I thought, I would be far safer with the French for the time being. But it would not have been tactful to say so. Instead, I asked my own question. "Who commands here?"

"Prince William." A short answer that explained a lot. Prince William was the son of the new Dutch king. I knew from reports I had seen in Paris that the king had insisted his son be made second in command as a condition for adding his troops to the British force. By all accounts, the inexperienced prince thought he was a skilled tactician, at least the equal of Wellington. Davout had scoffed at the thought, although the way Wellington was behaving the prince might be right.

"General Wellington has asked me to remain with the French," I finally said in answer to the sergeant's question. "Now, will you pass on my message?"

"Yes, if you release Jan unharmed." The sergeant was watching me closely and I did not like the way his eyes flicked briefly towards the stand of nearby muskets as if measuring the distance to them. But I had little choice. I pushed the boy towards them and turned to go back the way I had come. Almost instantly there was a yell from the sergeant. While I don't know the Dutch for 'Take him prisoner' or 'Kill him', I am pretty sure I heard one of them. Out of the corner of my eye I saw the men rushing for their weapons, while I hurtled off into the crop like a startled hare. I ran straight for the first fifty yards, just going as fast as I could, holding the musket diagonally in front of me to smash the stems out of my way. Then I looked over my shoulder just in time to see a Dutch soldier emerge onto my trail. He gave a shout of triumph and charged towards me. I had no choice but to lower the musket and fire. I don't think I hit him but he threw himself to the ground, bellowing with rage as I darted off once more.

There was the sound of people crashing through the stems all about me, but this time I had the sense not to run in a straight line. At one point I think I crossed the path I had made on my way down to the field but I darted off that way again to make a new trail. Twisting left and right I ran on. I must have covered at least another hundred, possibly two hundred yards before I stopped again. My pursuers were further away but they were still coming on and calling out to each other, probably when they came across a trail in the crop.

This was turning into a deadly version of the game blind man's bluff. To succeed in that you had to use your ears as you could not see and I listened carefully to gauge their direction. At one point a man shouted and they all were quiet for a minute; I guessed that they were listening for the sound of me in the crops to follow. But I was making no noise at all. I silently edged behind a thick clump of rye and waited. The rustling came steadily closer, some to the left and some to the right – that side seemed slightly nearer. I crouched down behind my cover and hoped it was thick enough to conceal me. Then, squinting through the stems, I saw him. It was the sergeant. He was striding purposefully along, turning his head from side to side, but he was not looking down. He went past within a yard of me.

Well, if you betray Flashy you had better not show me your back. I silently got to my feet and hefted the musket into the air. I did not have room to swing it without making a noise and had intended to slam the brass-bound butt into the back of his skull. But as I launched forward he must have sensed I was there. He was fast and whirled around, but not quite quick enough. I adjusted my aim and hit him hard on the bridge of the nose. He staggered back, blood spurting down his nostrils and eyes watering. He gave a growl of anger. He had dropped his own musket but I saw his hand scrabbling at his back for where his bayonet was sheathed. Well, he was not going to get the chance. Never mind the fact that it is considered unseemly to hit a man when his back was turned, I am happy to hit them when they are blinded too, for already the heavy oak butt was swinging around in an arc. If the sergeant heard the stems snapping as it approached he did not have the sense to duck. The wood made a solid connection with his skull and, with a sigh, he crumpled to the ground.

His comrades had heard him shout and I could hear them crashing through the crop in my direction. It was time to run again and I took off, this time keeping the sun on my left. I sprinted away for a while and heard the shouts as they found the fallen man, but there was no sound of further pursuit.

Once I was sure I was not being followed, I took my time to push my way back up the slope. I felt I had done my duty: I had tried to pass on a warning, although it had probably not been wise to unsettle the brains of the one man who had understood my message. It was unlikely that he would be inclined to pass it on now. But even if he did, would this young Prince William have the wit to pass it on to Wellington? If I had surrendered, the fool would probably have ordered me to join his force. His desperate defence was doomed; anyone who had marched with the French could see that. To turn myself over would have meant certain death one way or another.

I emerged from the field near the trees that I had set off from. The sun and my watch confirmed it was midday. Apart from the very occasional crackle of musketry between skirmishers, it was eerily still, like the calm before a storm. Compared to the frenetic energy and pace

222

of the previous day, it seemed bizarre that half a day had been wasted with nothing being achieved. I craned my head but there was no noise of battle from the direction of Napoleon's force either. It seemed the whole army had outrun its supplies and were still waiting for them to catch up. If the allies had been prepared they could have used this opportunity to reverse most of the previous day's advance. I had no wish to go back to Frasnes. I would only have been sent back up the road to Gossalie to chivvy troops along in the heat of the day. Far better to settle back in the shade of a tree and rest.

I must have dozed for when I awoke there was a clatter of movement in the trees behind me and then just a few yards away I saw a French soldier high up in a tree calling out directions to another officer standing underneath with a map.

"It looks like three six-pounders, twenty yards to the right of the last building."

"What on earth is going on?" I asked.

"I am sorry to wake you, sir," the officer said, although the grin indicated that he was nothing of the sort. He was a captain, older than me, in his forties, but he wore the uniform of the Imperial Guard horse artillery. They were the elite gunners in an already elite formation, which meant that he could probably have been my rank in a line regiment and he knew it. "We are siting our batteries here," he said, gesturing to the high ground in front of the trees that gave a commanding view of the area. It was also an area that was then completely devoid of any soldiers or equipment.

"Where are your guns?"

"Back through the trees." Glancing through the foliage I could see a line of guns and supporting wagons waiting in the shade. "No point in showing the enemy where our guns are until we are ready," he continued. "Especially when they have been kind enough to put all of theirs out in the open."

"Is the attack starting, then?" I asked. I looked at my watch: it was half past one in the afternoon and there was still no sound of fighting from either our column or Napoleon's to the east.

"Soon," the captain confirmed as he studied the terrain ahead through a glass. "The roads are chaotic, every junction clogged with wagons. Our guns were given priority, of course, but even so, we struggled to get our ammunition carts through."

"But is Reille's corps now here?"

"Some of it. One division is in Frasnes and another can be seen coming up the road. The rest will get here as soon as they get more cartridges."

A division consisted of around five thousand men, including infantry and artillery. Cavalry had a division of its own. One division would be outnumbered by the Dutch defenders of Quatre Bras, although it would probably be enough to beat them. But I remembered that Ney was worried about more Dutchmen hiding in the wood on the other side of the junction. I suspected that he would wait for the second division before starting the assault. My duty was to return to Frasnes so that I could carry messages for him, but once I was down among the crops I would be able to see little. He also had cavalry troopers and Heymès for messages. I thought I could justify staying a little longer. I could see how the attack unfolded from my vantage point and then go and report.

Now, people can argue for hours over whether the British Guard regiments were better than the Imperial Guard, or if our heavy cavalry were more effective than the French cuirassier. But there is no debate about artillery, for the French was clearly better. Napoleon had started his career as an artillery officer and he never failed to make full use of his cannon. At Quatre Bras the Dutch and British artillery present stood no chance at all, for they were opposed by masters in their art.

The start of the attack was signalled by a growing crackle of musketry from the area north of Frasnes. A wave of French skirmishers was driving in the Dutch outposts who had been dozing complacently all morning. Soon groups of the green-coated Dutch troops could be seen running pell-mell down the road towards Quatre Bras, pursued by loose lines of the French infantry with cavalry squadrons protecting their flanks. The allied gunners started firing then and that was the moment the Imperial Guard horse artillery had been waiting for. While their opponents were distracted with other targets, the captain I had been speaking to had his battery set up and ready to fire within about three minutes with another set of six guns set up just as speedily beyond his. Every one of the men who led the gun teams was a grizzled veteran. I watched how the one nearest me weighed both the ball and the sack of powder in his hand before it was loaded. Then he felt the temperature of the bronze barrel of his gun and carefully adjusted his aim.

The guns fired within a few seconds of each other so that the fall of shot could be measured. I watched the allied battery just to the right of the buildings at the crossroads with my glass. A moment before they had been unaware of any enemy artillery and now balls were smashing all about them, some short, some over but a wheel went spinning away from an ammunition limber to show one hit. The next French salvo came quickly and was horribly accurate. One gun carriage was smashed to pieces; another gun lurched to one side as its wheel was shattered and men could be seen running for cover. The other enemy batteries visible fared no better. One tried to pull back and set up again on the far side of the crossroads but it did no good. Over the next half an hour they were all destroyed or driven out of effective range. In fact, allied artillery was to play no significant part in the battle for the rest of the day.

As the Guard cannon fell silent we, at last, heard the sound of distant gunnery to the east, the direction of Napoleon's men. Who was attacking who, we wondered, for if the Prussians had managed to combine their forces they outnumbered Napoleon's column by two to one. The result at Quatre Bras, though, did not seem in doubt as French columns were now advancing into view as well as more artillery, some twenty guns that would now be unopposed to support the attack. Some of the French were heading towards the wood on the far side of the junction while others were forming up to attack a farm in front of it that the Dutch were reinforcing as a bastion to their defence. Not that it was likely to do them much good; more French troops were advancing on my side of the Brussels road into the tall crops of rye to outflank the defenders. It seemed only a matter of minutes before the Dutch defenders would be driven out of Quatre Bras. Certainly things looked safe enough, I thought, for me to finally report to the marshal.

Finding Ney was no easy task, for as well as having no staff to speak of, he also had no headquarters. First of all I rode the track back to Frasnes, which stood on the outskirts of the battle area, but no one there knew where he was. A line regiment from Reille's corps, some five hundred men, waited there unsure where they were needed. Their colonel had already gone in search of Ney, while the men had broken ranks and were queuing by the well or sitting under some trees. I took some water myself as by then it was baking hot. I could feel my uniform sticking to me down my back. At least it seemed the battle would not last long and then I could retire back into the shade.

Having slaked my thirst I pointed my horse towards Quatre Bras and galloped off down the cobbled road. While not entirely comfortable with the prospect, there was little choice but to follow the sound of the guns and hope that the fighting was over by the time I got there. A few wounded men, some supported by comrades, were coming the other way and I saw a handful of corpses. Most of those were Dutch and I guessed that there were many more hidden by the tall rye and wheat growing on either side of the highway. A lieutenant I passed going back to Frasnes with a wounded arm told me that the marshal was leading the assault on the big farmhouse I had seen the Dutch preparing to defend. It was no more than a third of a mile in front of the junction. When I had last seen it, the building and surrounding yards had been packed with men wearing green. Well, if anyone thought I was going to get involved in a reckless storming of the farm against entrenched defenders they could think again and so I approached with caution. If the battle was still underway I could have hidden in the tall crops until it was over – the long grasses really were a shirker's delight.

But when I crested the last undulating slope before the farmhouse I saw that it was already in French hands. An artillery battery was being set up beside it to blast down the road at the scattering of buildings at the junction. There were plenty of Dutch dead around the farm but an officer there told me that many more had panicked and fled when they realised that the French were encircling it and they would be trapped. He also informed me that once the Dutch stronghold had been taken, the marshal had ridden on to lead the men clearing the wood on the western side of the Brussels road. A continuous crackle of musketry from that direction indicated that progress was being made there too and so I rode in that direction. I paused crossing the road and stared down at the crossroads – it was perfectly safe as the enemy still had no artillery that could reach me. I could see the distant Dutchmen running about, the French guns were battering the buildings; some were on fire with a plume of smoke rising into the air. I silently thanked my stars that I had stayed with the French, for Prince William's command was doomed. Then I set my horse towards the woods that ran virtually up to the Nivelles to Ligny road.

I had to leave my horse where the trees got too thick to ride through and found Ney half an hour later. At first I thought he had been wounded, but the blood was someone else's and he looked happier than a drunk in a distillery.

"We will have the place in a few minutes," he declared while wiping his bloodstained sword on his sash. "Then we will help crush the Prussians. Here, look at this." He fished in his pocket and brought out a crumpled note, which he passed to me. It was from Marshal Soult and it spelt the death knell for the allied army. The emperor had trapped the Prussians and 'caught them with their trousers down,' Napoleon's chief of staff boasted. They were already being attacked on two sides. Ney was ordered to take his force from Quatre Bras down the road to Ligny where he was to fall on the Prussian right rear flank. Such an encirclement, it was promised, would guarantee an overwhelming victory such that not a single enemy cannon would escape.

"That is excellent news, sir," I said passing the message back, while inwardly my heart lurched. For with the Prussians destroyed the entire French army could concentrate on the British and Dutch force and, based on recent events, that did not bode well. There was a burst of particularly heavy musket fire ahead and Ney's head snapped up like a glutton hearing the dinner bell.

"Come on, Moreau, let's not keep the emperor waiting." With that, he was pushing off through the trees towards the sound of battle, with me following somewhat reluctantly in his wake. We had barely covered twenty yards when there was the sound of distant cheering and shouting. A few moments later and the Dutch skirmishers in front of us were falling back and running through the trees. "Follow them!" shouted Ney. "Don't let them settle again." We broke into a run, the men around us yelling in triumph, but I remembered that the original cheering had come from our right. That was where the last of the Dutch were and from what I had seen they had little to celebrate. The mystery was solved as I reached the edge of the trees. For there, a line of French infantry stood, all staring across the Nivelles road and over the crops towards the road coming from Brussels. There we could see pieces of yellow and red cloth, hung from poles moving towards us.

I did not need a telescope to recognise the colours of British regiments when I saw them. The crops might have hidden the men, but not the flags that served as their rallying points, which were already unfurled as the soldiers were going straight into battle. I tried to count them, at least half a dozen regiments, perhaps five thousand men. It might give the allies a numerical advantage for now, but Ney had the remaining two divisions of Reille's corps joining the battle piecemeal, which would see the battle swing back to him, with D'Erlon's corps of another twenty thousand still on the road behind.

I thought Ney might have been dismayed for it would be difficult to march to his emperor's assistance now, but instead, he looked delighted.

"At last, a worthwhile enemy." He slapped me on the back, "Do you know Wellington, the emperor and I are all the same age?"

"No, I didn't," I replied, puzzled at the significance.

"We will leave the emperor to beat the Prussians and I will beat the British. There will be more of them coming, but we will deal with them as they arrive. They have no artillery or cavalry with them. Go and report to the emperor that we are now facing the whole British army here and that he will have to beat the Prussians without us."

Already the first British troops were reaching the crossroads. Green-jacketed riflemen were in the vanguard and they wheeled left in their half-run, half-march pace to line the southern edge of the Ligny road.

"What about the regiment at Frasnes? Where do you want those?" I had to shout above an increase in noise as French artillery batteries found new targets among the approaching troops.

"Send them to the right flank," Ney shouted in my ear. "The British are strengthening their left and I will leave men here to defend the woods." I ran back through the trees, glad to be getting away from the front line. A crackle of musketry steadily increased behind. I found my horse tied where I had left it at the edge of the forest near the recently captured farm. As I glanced back towards the junction I saw a flash of familiar red uniforms emerging from the Brussels road. I was damned if I was going to fight my own countrymen, but just as I was about to swing myself up into the saddle another colour caught my eye.

The green jackets of a newly arrived regiment of Dutch cavalry could also be seen at the crossroads. They were already attracting fire from our skirmishers and guns, but instead of giving them time to form up to make an attack, someone sent them charging up the road towards Frasnes in an unformed mass. They thundered along attracting a barrage of fire from French troops on both sides of the highway. Wounded troopers and horses fell away, often trampled on by those behind. I shrank back into the trees as they went past me. The cannon by the farm opposite had brought down at least a score of them at virtually point-blank range and the rest were running in panic with no room to rally or turn. Whoever was in command at the crossroads had just wasted their only cavalry, but for them, the situation was about to get even worse.

As the Dutch horsemen reached the end of the trees they found waiting for them a French cavalry regiment, properly formed up into line and perfectly placed to charge their flank. There was the briefest of mêlées before the Dutch were heading back the way they had come, and that was when I realised that the Dutch were still wearing the uniforms that they had worn in the French army. For mixed in amongst them and dressed almost identically were the French troopers. I dare say that some of the French soldiers lining the road fired on their countrymen before they realised that there were far more horsemen coming back down the road than went up.

But the confusion was far worse for the Anglo–Dutch troops at the crossroads. They did not realise that enemy cavalry was amongst them until it was too late. I watched through my glass as the column of British redcoats I had seen was scattered in all directions with sabres rising and falling over the stragglers. Then the French troopers turned to their right to ride along the Ligny road, getting behind the allied line of defence.

I hurried back to Frasnes to pass on the orders to the infantry colonel and another who had also arrived in the village with his regiment. They marched off down the road while I considered the prospect of riding to Napoleon with news of the British arrival. I had no wish to remind him of my presence again and besides, Ney's message meant that the emperor's carefully laid plans for a decisive victory would be thwarted. Generals never like to have their schemes undone and invariably take their frustration out on the unfortunate messenger. I needed someone to do the dirty work for me. Just then I spotted a flash of scarlet galloping along the road from Gossalie and I knew my problem was solved.

"Three more regiments should be here within half an hour," Heymès called as he reined in at the village square. "Where is the marshal?"

"I will tell him," I replied. "He wants you to ride to the emperor to inform him that we are now facing the whole British army at Quatre Bras and so we will not be able to assist him with the Prussians."

"Why are you not taking the message?" asked Heymès suspiciously.

"Oh," I tried to look embarrassed. "He is angry with me for not being at his side this morning. He thinks it is an honour I do not deserve."

As I expected, Heymès straightened in his saddle and looked pleased with himself. "It is certainly an honour to report to the

emperor. Make sure you tell the marshal about the reinforcements."
And with that the stuffed shirt wheeled his horse around to gallop the
four miles from Frasnes to Napoleon's headquarters.

I had no intention of going back into the fray. Instead, having
watered myself and my mount I walked the horse slowly up the hill to
the Imperial Guard artillery battery. From there, I thought, I would
have a much clearer idea of how the battle was going.

I am pretty sure that it was Prince William who was in charge of the
defence of Quatre Bras then, for even blindfolded and mounting one of
his society trollops at the same time, Wellington would not have made
such a hash of it. They were only saved from utter destruction by the
fact that Ney had no overall strategy either. As soon as a new regiment
came down the road from Frasnes he would just throw them into the
thickest part of the action.

There was no thought of building a reserve for a sudden push, or
turning a flank. He was like a small boy in a snowball fight, throwing
in ammunition as soon as it was made. To be fair he was often in the
thickest part of the fighting himself, but that meant that he was unable
to step back and view weaknesses in the enemy deployment to exploit.
Fortunately for the allies, this also meant that it was near impossible
and time consuming for messengers from Napoleon to find him too.

Now that they had British reinforcements, the Dutch troops made
an attempt to recapture the fortress-like farm I had been at in front of
the crossroads. They were bloodily repulsed. In the meantime, the
British started to advance across the fields from the Ligny road. It was
like the game of blind man's bluff I had 'played' with the Dutch patrol
earlier, but on a massive scale. From the higher ground of the French
battery I had a clearer view than those fighting and watched as the
crops were flattened in great swathes as regiments moved to and fro. I
watched one French regiment routed as it marched across a clover
field. We could see that another formation of troops was marching
through the tall rye towards them. As the last stems were trampled flat
a battalion of kilted Highlanders was revealed. They charged without a
moment's hesitation and the French troops, caught unawares, reeled
away and started to run back towards the French lines. The

Highlanders pursued them and the whole yelling mass tumbled from the clover field into a crop of wheat. The artillery was banging away, sending balls whipping through the men in kilts. But then the Highlanders were ambushed in their turn by a French regiment coming the other way and it was their turn to fall back. The cannon fell silent for a few moments as the men fought together, and that is when I heard the worst noise known to man. Looking back down the hill to the clover field the fight had started in, I saw a lone bagpiper torturing his instrument to make some wailing din that was presumably meant to rally his regiment.

"God I hate that noise." I turned to the artillery captain and asked, half in jest, "Why the hell couldn't you have killed him?"

The man laughed. "Let me see if I can oblige now." With that, he gestured to his nearest gun. The crew immediately began to lever the barrel round a few degrees and lower the screw controlling its elevation.

"You surely cannot hit a single man from here?" I felt a twinge of guilt at apparently ordering the execution of one of my countrymen. But then if you inflict that hideous racket on humanity you deserve what you get.

"We have hit a single horseman before, so let's see, shall we?" The grizzled old gunner nodded that he was ready and the captain gave the order to fire. Then we all took a few steps to one side, around the muzzle smoke, to get a clear view of the fall of shot. The gunner had missed, but to be fair to him the range was exactly right: the ball gouged a great lump of turf out of the ground just a yard to the right of the piper. To be equally fair to the Highlander, the bastard carried on playing without missing a note!

More French cavalry were arriving now and they allowed the three elements of the army to fight together in perfect unison. The presence of the horsemen forced the British regiments to form protective squares, a tight formation surrounded by bayonet points that the cavalry could not penetrate. But that made the men in red an easier target for French artillery and shot tore through the tightly packed ranks. The tall crops also provided perfect cover for French skirmishers, who closed in on the big lumbering formations like sharks on a whale. Inevitably the British started to fall back, they had no choice. Sometimes if they stayed too long in one place you could make out where they had stood from the lines of dead and injured that they left behind.

I knew some of those men and it was sickening to watch their destruction. I turned away and took the path back to Frasnes. As I emerged from the trees I saw marching down the road from Gossalie a huge column of men. It was D'Erlon's corps. Twenty thousand soldiers, who would turn a battle that was already slipping away from the British into a crushing defeat. Ney would have his victory over the British to match that of the emperor over the Prussians. Oh, I might be safer among the victorious French army, but I would be ruined when I finally returned home, as in due course I must. My well-intentioned message had left the allies woefully unprepared for the attack and there would be those like Grant who would take every opportunity to suggest that I had deliberately helped the French. Many of my army friends would view me with the same contempt or suspicion that I felt for Hobhouse when I saw him. And the most frustrating thing about it was that there seemed little I could do to put things right. But opportunity is a strange beast and in this case, it came in the form of a French general.

"Hold up, Colonel." I turned to see the officer galloping towards me along a track that came from the east, where the distant thunder of cannon indicated that the emperor's battle was still underway.

"How go things with the Prussians, sir?" I asked the general as he reined in beside me. He had a small escort of half a dozen dragoons, who fell in behind us.

"Very well. They have fallen into the emperor's trap and with luck, we will destroy them. Have you come from that high ground? Can you tell me how the marshal fares here?"

"Yes, I am on the marshal's staff. We are winning here too. The British and Dutch forces are being driven steadily back to the road."

"Excellent. Does this mean that the marshal's men will soon be able to march to aid the emperor in his victory?"

"It is hard to say, sir. With General D'Erlon's corps we should be able to take the crossroads, but more British keep arriving. The marshal would not want to show his flank to the enemy."

"So the marshal is not facing the entire British army now, then?" The general pounced on my answer and I remembered the exaggerated report that Ney had sent the emperor earlier. It was clear that the emperor did not believe it and had sent this general to check.

"No, not all of it. We have not seen any British cavalry yet. But if they were to arrive behind us while the marshal was marching his army to Ligny, they could cut us up badly."

"Quite so, quite so," the general smiled as though I was telling him exactly what he wanted to hear, which I thought was strange. I would have expected him to want to know that Ney could assist the emperor. "Would the marshal be able to contain the British without General D'Erlon's force, do you think?"

I gasped in surprise for I now realised what the general had been sent to consider. If Ney could not bring his whole force to help him, Napoleon was considering taking half of it back. More importantly to me, it meant that the British still had a chance.

"Good God," I breathed as the implications set in

The general saw my reaction and understandably misread it. He reached out to grip my arm. "I know you want to be loyal to your marshal and Ney will not want to lose his reserve. But we must consider the wider campaign. The emperor is already attacking the Prussians from the south and the east. If he can add an attack from the west we will have them virtually encircled. We can destroy the Prussian army and then we can turn our attention to the British. Ney will only have to hold the British here, not beat them. Wellington will have to pull back once the emperor has won or he will risk being outflanked. So tell me, Colonel, do you think Ney can hold the British here?"

I hesitated. Rarely do you have a moment in your life when so much hangs on what you will say. I could, I thought, save the British from being routed at Quatre Bras but would that only lead to a bigger calamity later on? On the other hand, I had known Wellington for too long now to underestimate him. He had at last woken up to the danger that faced him and I now had the chance to give him some time to concentrate his forces and organise their defence. "Yes, we can hold them here," I said quietly. "Our cavalry is pinning them down and our artillery destroys every one of their batteries as they try to set up."

"Good man," said the general. He reached into a pouch hanging from his saddle and extracted a sealed note. "Give this to the marshal; it explains what the emperor is doing. I will ride on and give D'Erlon his new orders." With that he spurred his horse forward and rode away. He had not even asked my name and I did not know his. I suspected that this was deliberate as he must have guessed that Ney would be furious when he found out what was happening.

I looked down at the note in my hand. Ney was unquestionably brave, but his courage was driven by a passion for glory. He had never struck me as a man who would make a cool assessment of the facts. He wore his heart on his sleeve and he had set his heart on victory over the British. It was his way of proving his worth to those who doubted his loyalty. If Ney knew what was happening he would do everything in his power to get D'Erlon and his men back. Perhaps that was why the general had not asked my name, for it gave me another course of action to consider. After a final moment of reflection, I tore the letter into tiny pieces. Like Ney's hopes of victory, they blew away in the wind.

"What do you mean they are not there?" Ney looked at Heymès as though he was mad or blind. "Twenty thousand men cannot just disappear."

Heymès twisted a corner of his jacket in agitation. I had stayed away again to make certain that I was not on hand when Ney called for reinforcements. In fact I had spent the rest of the afternoon with the Guard artillery. I had watched as more British troops arrived from Nivelles, pressing the French in the woods on that side of the battlefield. Twice British batteries had tried to set up to support them, but sharp bombardments from the accurate French guns had put them out of action.

Then I saw the familiar red jacket of Heymès galloping along the road to Frasnes and I guessed that Ney had decided to bring the gathering force of D'Erlon into the fray. I wanted to see what would happen next and found the marshal in the farm opposite the woods. I was just in time to watch as Heymès delivered the bad news.

"They told me in Frasnes that a general from the emperor arrived and ordered the entire first corps to march east to support the emperor's attack on the Prussians."

"What?" A look of mounting rage suffused Ney's features as he comprehended what he was being told. Then he dashed the earthenware cup he had been drinking from against the ground. "He will not steal my victory!" he roared above the sound of smashing shards of pottery. "Do you hear me? He will not steal my victory!" The man had lost control of himself and now he picked up his sword. For a brief moment I thought he would attack Heymès and, judging from the way the aide stepped smartly back, so did the man in the red jacket. Instead Ney brought the weapon down in a massive blow on the table top. He wrenched it free, leaving a deep gouge in the wood and raised it up again. "He will not..." thwack, "...steal my victory!"...thwack. Three deep grooves in the wooden table stood as testimony to the marshal's frustration as he lifted his head and roared his rage at the rafters. For a moment he was quiet and still as he recovered himself and then he lowered his head and, to my alarm, he looked at me.

"Moreau, you will ride after D'Erlon." He was speaking quietly now but with a barely restrained fury still boiling within him. "Tell him, no, order him, from his direct superior, to return here at once. Threaten him with a court martial, even a firing squad if he even thinks of disobeying."

"But the emperor…" Heymès almost squeaked the objection in terror but a glare from Ney made him stop.

"I will send you as a messenger to the emperor," growled Ney to Heymès. "You can go with that British colonel we took prisoner. He can prove that Wellington is now in command here and that the entire British army is either here or on its way to Quatre Bras." He glared at me. "Moreau, why are you still here? Go, man, and don't come back without D'Erlon."

"I am leaving now, Marshal," I said turning hurriedly to go. As I stepped into the yard and pulled the rough plank door shut after me I heard Ney's voice again. He was calling for General Kellermann and his cuirassiers, asking if they had also been stolen by the emperor. I made a show of galloping back up the road towards Frasnes, before turning off on a track that would take me east. But once I was out of sight of anyone around Ney's headquarters I slowed down to a walk. I estimated it was roughly an hour since D'Erlon's men had set off, which meant that they had probably covered three miles, taking them close to the battle at Ligny. If I took my time, with luck they would already be engaged in that conflict before I got there – which would make it near impossible for them to withdraw and return to Ney.

I heard the Guard artillery firing from in front of the woods to my left and on instinct turned my horse down the now well-travelled path towards them. It would not hurt to have one final look at the battle from that vantage point before I went on. It would waste some time but I could argue that it would enable me to paint an accurate picture of affairs for D'Erlon in the event that I did catch up with him.

"Ah, you are just in time," called my new friend the artillery captain. "Look." He pointed in the direction of the middle of the battlefield. I stared and could see that the British reinforcements in the far wood were now trying to push out. Three regiments were audaciously advancing in line, which was more than reckless with so many French cavalry roaming about. One was close to the edge of the woods but the other two were in the tall crops, steadily trampling the stems down as they moved in our direction. "No, not there," called the captain. "They are the mice. Look over there to see the eagles." I craned my head round and felt a surge of dread, for I had a horrible premonition of what was about to happen.

Coming down the road from Frasnes towards Quatre Bras was General Kellermann and his cuirassiers. In other circumstances sending some eight hundred horsemen against what must then have been over twenty thousand infantry would seem reckless. Well it *was* reckless, but Ney was desperate for a move that would force the allies back and these were not ordinary horsemen. All of their mounts were black to match the long horsehair plumes that flowed from their steel helmets, while their polished breast and back-plates gleamed in the late afternoon sun.

There were no bugle calls to warn their enemies of their approach and Kellermann launched them into the charge early, probably because he did not want his men to be deterred by the number of enemy that awaited them. The ground must have vibrated under the thundering hooves of those heavy horses and I saw the long straight blades glitter in the light as they were drawn. Reluctantly, with a feeling of dread, I turned my attention back to the mice.

The first to see them was the regiment near the edge of the forest. It collapsed into confusion, half the men trying to form square and the rest running for the shelter of the trees. It was not a time to be indecisive for in a moment the horsemen were up to them and cutting down the stragglers and those running between the lopsided square and the forest. The men in the square desperately tried to close up their gaps and straighten their ranks but they need not have bothered for the black horses were already veering to their right as other more vulnerable targets were seen. Hearing the screams and yells of the first regiment attacked, the second had some warning and threw itself into a tight square. It was not straight but it was effective, giving off a crackle of fire as the armoured riders swept on.

The third regiment was in a slight hollow. They could not have seen the horsemen until they were fifty yards off and to make matters worse they were inexperienced. They were, I discovered much later, the 69th, fresh from Lincolnshire, and this was the first action for nearly all of them. Some managed a stuttering volley but from the distance I stood, most of the line seemed frozen in shock at the vision of death charging towards them. Like eight hundred horsemen of the apocalypse, the cuirassiers rode straight through the line of red-coated men, which was torn apart. The big blades rose and fell as men died or fled into the crops. Then I saw one of the cuirassiers riding back with a flag, a British regimental colour, held aloft in triumph. The rest of the armoured men rode on, determined to ride through the centre of Quatre Bras itself, but the crash of volleys from better-formed squares nearer the road showed that they would have a tougher time now they had lost the element of surprise.

I turned away feeling sickened. I had never seen a regiment destroyed so quickly and comprehensively. As I watched the gunners near me preparing to shell the squares now the horsemen were out of the way, I realised that I was not as ambivalent about the outcome of this battle as I pretended. Deep down I was a redcoat and I could not stand around and watch them being annihilated. The armoured horsemen had been enough to break a regiment or two but there were not enough of them to break an army. To do that Ney needed D'Erlon and I was going to do everything I could to make sure he did not get him.

Chapter 31

Twenty thousand men leave a trail that is not hard to follow. As well as the flattened crops and wheel ruts, there were stragglers limping along with blistered and bloody feet and later, ammunition carts often carrying more injured men as well as cartridges. The noise of battle grew louder ahead. The forest that ran from the north of Frasnes and past the French artillery was still to my left and the sound of more fighting echoed through the trunks, although whether this came from Quatre Bras or Ligny it was hard to tell. Then I came across the first columns of men and saw to my surprise, that they were all standing still. I rode nearly a mile past the long line of the first corps and during that time they did not move an inch. When I finally got to the head of the formation I found a group of generals having a furious row.

"The emperor's orders are quite clear," one of them was yelling. "Look, you can see for yourself how an attack from here will trap them." I rode up and stared down the hill in the direction the man was pointing. The place I took to be Ligny was in the distance, although little of it could be seen through the skeins of smoke. But you could make out that there was no fighting on our side and that the French were attacking from our right and the far side.

"But Marshal Ney says he will be defeated unless we return at once," insisted another. I found out later that he was D'Erlon's chief of staff, who had been sent belatedly to ensure that the marshal was aware of their new orders. Ney had sent him straight back to insist on their return and this messenger had evidently overtaken me with the glad tidings. They were both looking at a third general, who kept glancing between them.

"The marshal must know of the emperor's plan," he offered, "and yet he still feels that his risk is the greater. It will not profit the emperor to win here and lose a third of his army to the British..."

"He won't lose a third!" exploded the first general. "The marshal is famous for a fighting retreat and he can do so again. Look man, we can destroy the Prussians! If we do that they cannot come at us again and then we can avenge any defeat that Ney suffers."

"Yes but Ney is my commanding officer and he is a man of great experience," said the third man, who I now took to be D'Erlon. "What if the British break through and attack the emperor's flank while he is still fighting the Prussians?" The man bit his lip and then looked up at the sky. "Although I suppose it will be getting dark by the time we get back to Frasnes and then on to Quatre Bras."

I snapped open my watch and suddenly realised that D'Erlon was right. It was getting on for eight, so dusk would be in an hour and a half. It would take at least another hour to get back to Frasnes – the men were tired, and they had been marching back and forth all day – then another half an hour to march up the road to Quatre Bras. There would then be no time to deploy these exhausted troops before nightfall.

Instead of just diverting twenty thousand Frenchmen towards the Prussians, I now saw the opportunity to keep them out of both battles entirely. It would take bluff and bluster to gammon these experienced men, but I had nothing to lose. I cleared my throat.

"Who the devil are you, sir?" asked the first general.

"My apologies, gentlemen." I threw up a respectful salute that took in all of them. "Marshal Ney has sent me to enquire how quickly the first corps will return. He fears that the British could break through his lines at any moment. Indeed, from the sound of fighting coming through the trees they may have already done so."

That put the Ligny debating society into a fine frenzy of squabbling. The general from Napoleon's headquarters was initially insistent that D'Erlon march at once for Ligny and fall on the rear of the Prussians. I left them to bicker amongst themselves for a while and then intervened and respectfully asked them all to stay silent for a moment and listen to the sounds coming through the trees. They did, reluctantly in the case of some, and sure enough you could still hear the distant banging of guns. It was not easy to pick up above the much louder sound of battle from Ligny, just a mile away, but it was definitely there.

"That could be coming from anywhere," insisted Napoleon's man. "It could be the noise of Ligny echoing back at us."

"With respect, sir," I offered, "I have heard the noise from the trees all the way on the ride from Quatre Bras, where it was much louder." I was lying; the noise was louder at the Ligny end, but I needed to paint a picture of Ney being in a precarious state, rather than just lacking the men to go on the offensive. "When I left," I continued, "the marshal was using a charge of Kellermann's cuirassiers as a desperate measure to keep the British infantry at bay. They had reinforcements pouring in down both the Brussels and Nivelles roads."

To my delight, Ney's other messenger also spoke up then. "Yes, I saw the marshal order Kellermann to charge the British. The general was not happy about sending his eight hundred men against the British army, but the marshal insisted."

"But the emperor's orders are paramount," insisted his man. "They must be obeyed."

"Enough," shouted D'Erlon, holding up his hand for silence. He considered for a moment and I found myself holding my breath as he made his decision. "If the British come through the forest and fall on the emperor's flank while his men are fighting the Prussians, they could turn the battle here. And if Ney is also beaten at Quatre Bras we could lose all of our gains and be driven back into France." He turned to Napoleon's man. "The emperor's orders are paramount but His Majesty does not have this information and I must act as I think he would want." D'Erlon paused and took a deep breath. He knew that the outcome of battles and the entire campaign could depend on what he said next. Some have dismissed him as a fool, but as I was to learn later, he wasn't that. He was cautious, perhaps too much so, and that was his downfall; but he was passionately committed to his emperor and desperate to see him succeed.

"I will leave a division here and some extra cavalry," he announced. "They will protect the emperor's flank from any British that emerge from the woods and give him time to react. The rest of the corps will return to Frasnes. If the British are driving Marshal Ney back through the town we will be able to fall on their flank and destroy them."

So it came to pass that twenty thousand men, who could have had a decisive impact on two battles, spent the afternoon marching back and forth between them without firing a shot. We can only wonder what would have happened in the following days if they had succeeded in helping the rout of the British force or completing the destruction of the Prussian one.

I woke that morning lying in a hedge on the outskirts of Frasnes. It had been a warm and humid night and while every building in the village was now full of men, I could probably have got some space at Ney's headquarters if I had wished. He had stayed in the largest house in the village with Prince Jerome Bonaparte, who commanded a corps under Ney that had arrived piecemeal during the battle. Doubtless Jerome had spent the evening listening to how his brother had stolen the marshal's victory. I had not wanted to join that unhappy gathering and so after reporting that D'Erlon's men were on their way back I had found a place where I could lie quietly with my thoughts.

Ney might not have had his victory, but with a steadfast defence he had not suffered much of a defeat either. Kellermann and his cuirassiers had brought terror to the British lines, but they had lost a quarter of their number in doing so. As the British squares closed up, the horsemen were shot at from all sides and in the end, they charged back towards French lines. Their flight did not end there. They went on past Frasnes and spread stories about a huge British army which caused many supply wagon drivers to flee for their lives.

As I had foreseen, by the time D'Erlon's men arrived, weary and footsore, it was dusk and too late for them to take part in the battle. There was no exposed British flank for them to attack. By nightfall, the British had pushed the French out of the fortress-like farm in front of the crossroads and the far forest, but the French still held the high ground that dominated the battlefield.

I had lain awake under that bush for half the night, considering what would happen next. The sound of distant cannon fire at Ligny had stopped at dusk. I wondered if the Prussians had been able to hold out after all, without D'Erlon's attack. If they had managed to resist Napoleon's forces and Wellington had stopped Ney, then there was still a chance that the allies could join together. With their larger combined army, they might beat the French yet.

It was not a peaceful night. Even though the sounds of battle had died away, they were replaced by the occasional scream of a wounded man in the now dark fields around Quatre Bras and the sporadic crackle of fire from the outposts. More disturbing were the odd single shots that rang out throughout the night. Some may have been nervous sentries, but others were soldiers ending their own or another person's suffering. Years before I had spent a night wounded on a battlefield expecting to die. I could easily imagine the horror and pain that would cause a man to end his existence while he lay alone in the darkness.

My melancholy mood was not improved by dawn, which brought with it a thick summer mist. I awoke under my hedge in the early morning chill, with my clothes damp from the dew and my muscles stiff. My stomach was also rumbling with hunger, but as I staggered to my feet, I noticed about a dozen field mushrooms growing under the bushes. I picked them and put them in my pocket. If I could commandeer some meat and eggs, they would make a handsome breakfast.

There was no point going near the battlefield – I would not be able to see anything and was just as likely to be shot by outpost sentries of either side if I loomed out of the mist. Instead, I walked down the road into Frasnes. My joints started to loosen and as I got closer I saw more soldiers emerge from their bivouacs until a whole army of ghost-like figures was moving through the fog.

I found Ney's headquarters but the good marshal was very sensibly still in bed. With no staff, he had no cook, but General Reille did. I was able to get a lump of bread – not quite the breakfast I had hoped for – although the smell from an oven promised more. However, I had barely wolfed down the last piece of crust when horses' hooves could be heard clattering on the cobbles.

"Victory!" the rider was shouting. "The emperor has had a famous victory!" I have never seen a crowd materialise so fast. Soon men were thronging about the horseman, who must have been sent off at the first glimmer of dawn's light. "The Prussians were driven from the field," the rider shouted in answer to a dozen different questions asked around him. The Imperial Guard had smashed through the centre of the Prussian formations and now the sausage-eaters were in headlong retreat, he announced. The emperor's men had blocked any move west to join the British and they had captured some guns that had been fleeing east back towards Prussia, but the man did not know where the Prussians had gone. "They are beaten," the rider assured us. "Their regiments are broken and scattered in all directions. Many ran away without their weapons. It will be weeks before they are ready to fight again. They may not stop running until they get back to Prussia," the man boasted before Heymès pushed his way through the crowd and insisted that the man follow him to report personally to the marshal. Looking up I saw Ney glowering from an upstairs window of his headquarters still in his nightshirt. If he was pleased with Napoleon's victory his face did not show it. But he could have just been annoyed that the messenger had announced his news to the army at large, before coming to inform him.

I wandered off feeling more despondent than before. With the French now occupying Ligny, I suspected that when the fog lifted it would show that the British had already withdrawn, giving up the ground that so much blood had been spilt for the previous day. They could not stay where they were with Ney able to attack their front and Napoleon ready to fall on their left flank, or even get behind them.

As the sky brightened the fog began to thin and Frasnes came more to life. As with the day before, the army took time to recover from a period of battle before it was ready to fight again. Horsemen were sent galloping down the road towards Gossalie in search of supply wagons, many of which had dispersed when Kellermann's horsemen had retreated. Having fired continuously for much of the previous day, the artillery, in particular, was short of ammunition; but many of Reille's corps who had fought from the beginning were also in need of supplies. Only D'Erlon's men had full ammunition pouches and they were the ones who now manned the outposts.

Soon carts were seen coming up the road. They were swiftly unloaded and refilled with the badly wounded, who were to be taken back to Charleroi. Many of the walking wounded did not wait for the transport. Instead, they set off by themselves, alone or in groups, helping each other, as they made their way back home. Alongside them trudged a straggling column of around a thousand prisoners –

mostly Dutch – but I saw a few redcoats mixed in with them. Some of those were also wounded, but there were no spare carts and so they struggled along with their comrades or were carried in makeshift stretchers. I have seen it a score of times and there are few sadder sights than wounded and beaten men being taken away to captivity.

Napoleon's great gamble had paid off. He had beaten the Prussians and driven them away. Isolated and outnumbered, the British would have little choice but to pull back to Antwerp for disembarkation to Britain, leaving their Dutch allies to their fate. The Austrians with their trump card of Napoleon's son would sue for a beneficial peace. That left the Russians, isolated and a long way from home. They might join up with the rump of a Prussian army, if Prussia could still afford to maintain an army in the field, but I did not fancy their chances.

So Napoleon would remain on the throne of France and while he protested he wanted peace, in the long run, a return to war would be certain. At least, I thought, my friends among the British army should get away, even if they would have to fight another day. It was a bleak prospect but things were about to get worse: a horseman came galloping down the road from our front line to announce that the British were still in Quatre Bras.

The man had to be wrong, it must be just a rear-guard, for if the British had stayed they would be trapped and destroyed. Ney was already sending the news to Napoleon as this was a capital chance for them to destroy two enemies in two days. I found my horse and rode out to the higher ground occupied by the Imperial Guard artillery. From there I would be able to see for myself.

The sun burned through the last of the mist as I galloped up the hill and into the trees: it promised to be another hot day. As I emerged from the forest behind the battery to stand amongst the guns, my hopes turned to dismay. There had been no mistake. The British army lay before me like an innocent lamb being stalked by wolves. They had a few guard outposts but most were at rest. Smoke from cooking fires rose into the air and hundreds of men could be seen out searching the battlefield, apparently without a care in the world. A few were helping wounded comrades back to the crossroads, but most were indulging in the time-honoured privilege of survivors: looting the dead.

"If the marshal wants to re-start the battle, he should know that we only have an hour's ammunition." I turned and it was my old friend the captain standing at my side.

"I am amazed that they are still here," I told him with feeling.

"They must believe that the Prussians are still at Ligny," said the captain. "Instead of pulling back they still have men arriving. Look, the road to Brussels is half jammed with their supply wagons." I pulled open my glass and could see the tops of wagons over the hedgerows, but also noticed hundreds of horses hobbled for grazing in a field of clover to the side of the road.

"Have their cavalry arrived?"

"Yes, they have also been pulling in all morning. There must be several thousand of them. They have more guns too, but we have marked where they are. They won't last long when we get started."

I dismounted and sat down on a nearby fallen tree trunk. Surely they were trying to reach the Prussians? They had to know soon that they were alone and exposed, surrounded by their enemy. There was nothing I could do to warn them for D'Erlon's men formed a solid picket guard in the fields. After men like General Bourmont had defected to the enemy earlier in the campaign, there would be no hesitation in shooting a senior officer suspected of doing the same. And even if I did manage to get past them I would just be ensnared when the French trap was sprung. For by then it was nine in the morning and I imagined that Napoleon would already be on the road with as many troops as he could muster. He only had some four miles to cover and then the British would be bottled up and at his mercy.

I sat and watched for some sign of alarm amongst the British and Dutch for most of the morning. The hands of my watch moved so slowly, they made snails look like greyhounds in comparison. Ten o'clock came and went but still the men around Quatre Bras were as oblivious to their fate as cattle in the slaughterhouse yard. Ammunition wagons for the French guns arrived and with them some news. Napoleon had refused to believe the first despatches from Ney. He thought Ney was exaggerating again about the size of the force in front of him and had sent his own general to confirm that the British were still there. That general had been and gone, galloping back to the emperor to assure him that Ney's report was accurate. Everyone now expected that the emperor would be marching on the crossroads with every man he could find. Napoleon's doubts had bought the British some time, not, however, that it seemed they had any intention of using it. Then finally, at around eleven, there was some sign of increased activity amongst the men in red.

I had a clear view of the Brussels road half a mile beyond the crossroads where it crested a shallow rise. All morning I had seen a trickle of walking wounded heading north but now the flow of men increased. Then carts parked along the road were being turned around and they too started heading north. Any doubts I had were allayed by the artillery captain.

"They are pulling out," he announced.

"Are you sure?" I asked, trying to keep the hope out of my voice.

"Yes, they are dismantling one of their batteries. Do you think the marshal will order us to attack?"

"I have no idea," I told him and I certainly was not going back to ask. But we had the chance to find out for ourselves half an hour later when Ney and several of his generals, including Prince Jerome, arrived at our vantage point. The marshal was still smarting from his stolen victory of the day before and just grunted an acknowledgement when the artillery captain reported that that the British were withdrawing. Jerome said something I did not catch and Ney retorted angrily, "Well if he had believed my despatches he would be here by now."

Jerome was pressing Ney to start another attack. "We can pin them down until the emperor gets here to destroy them," he insisted. The artillery captain piped up that they now had enough ammunition for at least three hours of bombardment, but Ney just brushed his suggestion aside.

"They outnumber us. We will wait until the emperor gets here before we start an attack," he announced while turning his horse away.

"But they are pulling back now," Jerome shouted after him. "If we attack without delay the emperor can rescue us if we are pushed back." I saw Ney's face at that moment; the marshal visibly winced at the thought of him being 'rescued' by the emperor. After his stolen victory the day before, that notion was just too much for his pride to accept. Muttering some profanity, he raked his heels hard into his horse and galloped away back through the trees, leaving his disappointed staff to follow on behind.

Ney's pride brought the British another hour, but then a large cloud of dust became visible in the east. It was noon by then, and stiflingly hot. There was little if any wind and the horizon was marred by a huge column of storm clouds that was coming our way. Everything seemed to portend a climactic clash.

Chapter 33

The British saw the dust cloud and their cavalry mounted up and formed three huge lines on the eastern side of the crossroads to cover their retreat. There must have been around seven thousand horsemen; heavy cavalry, lights, dragoons, hussars; you name it they were all there. The artillery captain cursed that they had no orders to fire, for it was a prime target. I kept my eye on the road; it was now thick with men and guns moving north and I suspected that yet more were moving west to Nivelles behind the far forest. The British outposts were pulling back and the French were moving in after them. I turned my glass to the east and saw that the long dust cloud now had a dark line at the bottom. From the glint of sunlight on metal, I guessed that these were thousands of French horsemen leading the emperor's advance.

It was a race and if either Ney or the emperor had shown any haste, it was a pursuit that the British should have lost. But while Ney sat indolent, the emperor also showed no hurry to close with the enemy. I heard later that he had been waiting for Ney to attack first. In the end, Napoleon sent his own horsemen forward. For a while it looked that the mounted British troops were willing to contest the field with them, but as the French came closer it became clear that the men in red were heavily outnumbered. So it was that the last British troops at Quatre Bras turned and, at the gallop, headed north over the fields.

The rest of Ney's force was already pushing forward to occupy the crossroads and I went with them. There was a nauseating sweet odour as we got closer. The cut-grass smell coming from the flattened crops was mixed with the stench of decay. Corpses were already bloating in the hot sun and many had been eviscerated by cannonball or sabre, with their guts spilling out and attracting swarms of flies. Near the fortress-like farm that had been fought over for much of the previous day, the bodies had been stacked in piles. A couple of trenches showed where grave-digging had been interrupted by the need to retreat.

At the crossroads there were plenty more signs that the British had left in a hurry; the place was littered with abandoned supplies. In the largest farmhouse I found a beef stew still cooking on the stove. Several infantrymen were already gathered around the bubbling pot and they glared angrily at this unfamiliar colonel intruding on their prize. My rumbling stomach reminded me that I had not eaten anything since a hunk of bread that morning. They were not my men and I doubted if they would easily obey an order to give me some of their captured food. But then I remembered something that might help.

"I have some mushrooms," I offered. "If you let me add them to the pot, can I share it with you? I am starving." They nodded their consent and so I went over to the pot and dropped in the field mushrooms I had found early that morning. Another man was stirring the pot with a wooden spoon and they disappeared into a rich sauce, which, from the smell, had been enhanced with wine too.

I settled down on a wooden bench in a corner of the room, glad of the shade on this hot day. It was strange, I thought, if I had come across these men during the battle and ordered them to advance, then they would probably have obeyed without question. But in all armies there were unwritten rules on the subject of captured bounty. Most soldiers dreamed of finding wealth in the aftermath of a battle and it was generally understood that what they found they kept. I remembered an arrogant young lieutenant in the British army in Spain. He had been foolish enough to confiscate a jewel he had seen one of his men find. Several officers warned him to return it, but he thought his rank would protect him. If I recall correctly his uncle was the regimental colonel. It was no great surprise when he was found shot and bayoneted to death after the next battle, particularly as he had been shot from behind. It paid to tread carefully when sharing any spoils of war.

The men I was with had lost one of their squad the previous day. Another had a bandaged arm, but was determined to continue the campaign. They were tough veterans who had more than a few battles between them. The wooden table in the room was marked with fresh bloodstains and seemed to have been used for amputations. There was a recent saw mark on one edge and they joked about how long the surgeon had sawed at a limb before he had realised he was cutting wood. The courtyard outside was filling up with people and several more put their heads around the door, but apart from one who was known to them, they were sent away. Then the self-appointed cook announced the food was ready. By then I was almost drooling with hunger and we all stood around the table as the big cauldron was carried to it. The men stood with plates and bowls from their packs and I was given a cracked pottery dish. Ten pairs of eyes watched the ladle dip in the stew and then as we licked our lips in anticipation, another voice called out from the door.

"Put that down, this building is to be used by the emperor!"

I turned in disbelief to find a stern-faced man glaring at us. He wore a uniform that was more gold braid than cloth and instead of a sword at his hip, he held a ceremonial staff.

"You cannot be serious," I protested. "We have not eaten all day. Surely you can wait a moment."

"You are to leave at once; the emperor will be here any minute." There was a growl of resentment from several of the men and they might have resisted yet had not one of them ducked their head to look out of the broken window.

"The emperor is riding into the courtyard," he whispered. At that the men reluctantly picked up their packs and then the cook went to lift up the cauldron too so that he could take it with him.

"Leave that," snapped the courtier. "You will have to find something else to eat." Feeling robbed and cheated, we stepped outside, blinking in the bright sunlight. A line of less gaudy courtiers was unloading a cart with chests carrying the imperial monogram. One was open with silver cutlery on show. I assumed that if anyone was now to eat our stew it would not be out of a cracked pottery bowl.

The emperor was on the far side of the courtyard and he looked furious. It was certainly not the moment to protest over a stolen dinner and I ducked into the thickest part of the crowd to keep out of his sight. I was just leaving the farm when I saw more horses pushing the other way. Marshal Ney had arrived.

"So you are finally here," Napoleon shouted at him as everyone else fell silent. "Twice I sent you message to attack this crossroads and yet you did nothing. You have let the British escape when we could have had them trapped."

Ney looked furious at this public reprimand. He took a deep breath to calm his temper before replying. "Perhaps if Your Majesty had believed my earlier despatch…"

"You have cost me France!" the emperor screamed at him. "Do you understand that? If the British get away unbeaten, then you will have cost me France."

"They will not get far," replied the marshal before wheeling his horse around and galloping from the farm. It was an extraordinary exchange. Looking back I think that Napoleon was remembering that he would probably need to beat a British army to force a change of government in London. Only that would stop the subsidies of gold that kept other allied armies in the field. But back then it looked as though he had every chance of getting that victory. The British army was strung out along at least two roads heading north towards Brussels. They were outnumbered and out-gunned, with many of their regiments having taken heavy casualties at Quatre Bras. Only an act of God could save them… and that is exactly what they got.

Ney had immediately organised his cavalry and horse artillery for the pursuit and now galloped off after the British, leaving the rest of his force to follow on behind. His mood was as black as the towering clouds that were gradually covering the sky. Being the sensible staff officer that I am, with no wish to bear the brunt of his anger, I chose to make myself scarce. I rode with some infantry officers near the back of the column, safely away from any risk of action. After an hour's march we heard what could have been the sound of cannonades, but they could also have been thunder. Certainly a storm was coming, for my horse nearly bolted after a particularly loud crash of thunder right above us. A sergeant just managed to grab its bridle in time and held on until the noise had passed.

"That sergeant is a good man," said the colonel of the regiment as I resumed my place alongside him. He looked up at the sky, "We will see rain in a minute, I think." He turned to one of his officers, "Get the men to fire off any loaded weapons. We don't want them clogged with wet powder." The words were barely out of his mouth before the first raindrops fell. Orders were shouted down the line and there was a roll of shots as muskets were discharged. I put my hand in my jacket pocket for my pistol, which I remembered loading as a precaution the day before. I quickly cocked it and fired it harmlessly into the fields. It was only then that I noticed some strange bright yellow staining on my hand.

"Good grief, look at that," I exclaimed rubbing at the marks. They would not come off and when I smelt my hand there was the distinctive odour of ink.

"How extraordinary," commented the colonel. "Is it a type of jaundice, do you think?"

"No, I feel fine, it does not hurt, but something seems to have stained my fingers." I put my hand back in my pocket and felt something lodged in the corner. Pulling it out I saw it was one of the mushrooms I had picked earlier, only this one was broken and bruised, with livid yellow marks where it had been damaged.

"I wouldn't eat that, sir." It was the sergeant who was now walking alongside my horse and gazing up at what I was holding. "They are poisonous," he added.

"Poisonous!" I exclaimed. "But they looked just like field mushrooms when I picked them. Dammit, I nearly ate a stew full of them."

"They won't kill you, sir. Some can eat them without harm, but most people will get a nasty ache in the guts for a day or so."

"Thank you, Sergeant, that is useful to know," I replied tossing the thing away. I thought back to my lucky escape from the effect of the mushroom and remembered the gaudy chamberlain. If there was any justice the arrogant bastard would have helped himself to a large bowlful and would now be suffering the consequences. Then another thought occurred. Could the emperor have eaten any of the stew? Surely he must have cooks with him to prepare his food. But then I remembered that he had galloped past about half an hour after I saw him in Quatre Bras, at the head of some of his Guard cavalry. He had been keen to join the pursuit and so perhaps he had eaten some food that was already prepared. I could vouch that it certainly smelt good enough.

Any further speculation was interrupted by the rain, which swiftly came down in torrents. It was like an Indian monsoon and within moments we were all soaked through to the skin. I had rarely known rain like it in Europe. We were marching on the fields to keep the roads clear for carts and soon the men were sinking down to their ankles in oozing mud. The pace of the march slowed to a crawl. At least at the rear of the column we were not expected to fight as well, although the rain would have soon put muskets and cannon out of action. I moved back to the easier road surface and wove the horse between the carts and guns advancing north. In the dips there were often small streams of water washing across the road, bringing mud and silt that the drivers had to push their vehicles through. On either side the soldiers trudged on, going increasingly further from the carriageway to seek ground that had not been churned up by the thousands of men and animals that had gone before. Others marched in bare feet; having tired of pulling their boots out of the mud, they now had them tied around their necks.

It was a miserable progression, but while they marched with their heads down against the wind and the rain, morale stayed surprisingly high. There were always volunteers to help push a cart out of the mud and I even passed one group defiantly singing.

"It must be worse for the British," called out one soldier who caught my eye.

"Why is that?" I asked.

"'Cos they know we are going to beat them when this rain stops," he replied grinning. I doubted that there was a man in the army right then who would disagree with him, and that included me. For even if it rained all day and the emperor's guts were now churning, I still would not have taken odds of a ten to one then on a British victory.

We stopped at a place called Genappe. Rumour had it that the British had formed a rear-guard on a ridge up ahead to cover their retreat to Brussels. Some officers were standing in a barn, gathered around a soggy map that they had spread out over the top of a barrel.

They showed me where the British line was forming, near a place called Mont St Jean. Knowing Wellington's partiality for fighting from ridges, I asked if there was a chance that he would make a stand there.

"He would be a fool if he did," said an opinionated major. "Look here, all the land on the western side of the road behind the British line is forest. It is woodland all the way to Brussels. There would be no way that he could organise a fighting retreat through the trees. If they are making a stand there they would have to win or that would be the end of them." He glanced around to ensure that we all looked impressed at his clarity of judgement. "No, you mark my words, tomorrow they will be on the march again, through this place." He pointed to the next town down the road. "What's it called? The map is smudged."

"Waterloo," replied another of the onlookers.

Map of Waterloo Battlefield

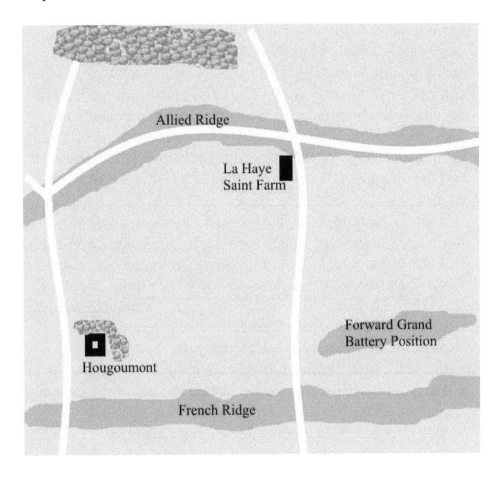

Allied Ridge

La Haye
Saint Farm

Forward Grand
Battery Position

Hougoumont

French Ridge

Chapter 34 – Sunday 18th June

In Shakespeare's *Henry V* he wrote that all those abed will count themselves ashamed that they missed the battle of Agincourt. In my time those that weren't there said much the same about Waterloo. But Shakespeare was a knave and a liar and I will offer odds that most of those at Agincourt would have taken the warm bed instead if it had been offered. I know I would have traded my place at Waterloo for the meanest cot and the forty thousand killed or wounded that day would have done the same. But the world might be a very different place now if I had.

It was the battle to end all battles and it ended an era. I doubt we will see its like again, I certainly hope not. As you will see, it was also, as Wellington claimed, a 'damn close thing'. There has been much debate about whether Wellington really won it or whether Napoleon threw away the chance of victory. For my money, a chap you almost certainly will not have heard of saved the allied line at the critical moment, but we will come to that presently.

Unlike the dawn of many battles I have fought, when I awoke in that barn in Genappe on the morning of the 18th, I was not expecting to fight at all. I was just grateful to have found a space that was relatively dry to sleep in. Most of Reille's corps had camped around Genappe and only a fortunate few had found a roof over their heads. I slept with the other officers in the upper hayloft of the barn, while the men were packed into the floor below. The door was constantly opening, creating a draught as others tried to find shelter and with so many wet men huddled together it soon became humid, not that anyone would have thought of going outside.

We had heard cannon fire the previous evening, which mixed in with the thunder. But as darkness fell, the only rumbles we heard were generated by the heavens rather than man. The tempest had continued throughout the night, with flashes of lightning and wind howling through cracks in the barn timbers, while the rain drummed on the roof. A superstitious man claimed that such a gale must foretell a great battle. He got quite carried away, comparing Napoleon to Moses freeing the Israelites from the Egyptians. If he thought he would awe his audience he was destined to be disappointed, for most had little time for religion. There were shouts of derision, until one voice called out from the darkness.

"No, no the lieutenant is right, it will be just like Moses." The man, who evidently knew what the British called the French, chuckled before adding, "In the morning the allies are going to get a plague of frogs!"

While we were cold, wet and hungry, there was no lack of confidence in that barn. We had heard that Marshal Grouchy and thirty thousand French had been sent off to pursue the beaten Prussians. Some thought that they would head east, back home to lick their wounds and recover, but a few thought that those still able to fight would try to rendezvous with the retreating British in Brussels. They would have to be quick as the city was only a day's march away. I could not see how Wellington could organise an effective defence with the French snapping at his heels all the way. Another unseen voice in the dark called out that he planned to spend the next night in a comfortable dry bed in Brussels. He thought he would share it with a pretty English girl seeking protection from his marauding countrymen. From the ribald comments that followed, many were thinking along similar lines. The man lying next to me offered to take me to the best brothel in the city as soon as it had been captured.

I lay there wondering how the British were feeling at that moment. They were on the retreat, camping on an exposed ridge in this same storm. With thirty thousand French off with Grouchy, I guessed that the armies were roughly the same size now, but the French had far more cannon and the best gunners to use them. The British still had some peninsular veterans, but I suspected not enough. At Quatre Bras I had seen the Dutch troops giving ground against French attacks, while some British regiments such as the one destroyed by Kellermann's cuirassiers, were woefully inexperienced. I reluctantly concluded that the next day the British would be beaten again, either on the ridge or in

261

Brussels. Colonel Moreau would have to serve a while longer before he could get home.

It stopped raining just before the men were ordered to stand to at dawn. The tightly packed bodies in the barn got to their feet and staggered out, their joints stiff and their clothes steaming. Once I got outside myself I realised how fortunate we had been, for all around men sat or stood shivering with the cold. Here and there fires burned, but they gave off more smoke than heat. We had orders to march at five, for the emperor wanted to be ready to fight at nine if the British were still there. With much grumbling about fighting on an empty stomach, the men fell into ranks and started to trudge north. We had only marched two miles when we were given orders to halt. The attack had been postponed and the men were allowed to cook and eat.

Within minutes fires were being built and animals butchered. There would not be time to cook large joints of meat and so most men had small lumps held in the flames on the end of ramrods. Often they had a shirt wrapped around the other end to stop their hand burning before the morsel was cooked, which served to help dry the shirt as well. Other bushes and trees that had not been ravaged for firewood were adorned with coats, shirts and other clothes, all flapping in a light wind as they dried.

I was not missing out on food this time and was soon gnawing down on some tough meat and some even tougher biscuits, but it was a most welcome feast. Gallopers were riding up and down the road with messages and from them we learned that the British were still on the ridge. The news that there was to be a battle rippled through the men. While they cheered at the prospect of driving off another would-be invader of France, I struggled to rid myself of a vision of routed redcoats being chased through the forest behind the ridge they had chosen to defend. I wanted desperately to believe that they stood a chance of holding out, but I could not see how.

I knew that nobody defended a ridge like Wellington; I had stood beside him at Talavera and seem him defeat a larger French force. But that had been with experienced, well-drilled troops. Here, half his army was at best unproven and at worst some had sympathies with the

French. Also for the first time in his career he was not facing a French general or marshal but the emperor. Napoleon's soldiers boasted that with him at their head they had conquered a continent; it was not tactful to remind them that they had lost it as well. But even I had to acknowledge that he had generally only lost battles when faced with overwhelming numbers, or in the case of Russia, an overwhelming winter.

This battle had been postponed until eleven that morning to allow time for the ground to dry out. The biggest advantage for the French was their cannon and on wet soft ground the guns would have dug themselves into the mud as they fired. As Marshal Ney's aide, I was once again long overdue at his side. So, having eaten my fill, I reluctantly climbed on my horse and rode north. I arrived at the battlefield at nine-thirty that morning. There was very little to set it apart from many of the gently sloping valleys I had passed through the previous day. You will have probably already seen maps or charts of it, but essentially there were two shallow, roughly parallel ridges. The British were behind the north one while the French formed up on the southern ridge. Through the middle, running north to south was the main Brussels to Charleroi road and just in front of the British ridge on that road was a farm called La Haye Sainte. As I looked from the French ridge, standing near the road I could see the roofs of some more buildings nearer the French line to my left. This turned out to be the château of Hougoumont. A few flattened tracks in the crops were the only sign that an army had passed this way at all as hardly any British soldiers or guns were visible on the far side. Napoleon stood with his generals by a table with maps laid out on it and they discussed the coming battle in between staring at landmarks with their telescopes.

I joined the group of staff officers standing behind them and learned that the British had garrisoned both the house and surrounding buildings at Hougoumont and the farm of La Haye Sainte, as bastions to break any advance. While we could not see the British line, French-speaking Dutch soldiers had deserted during the night and revealed that it extended a mile on either side of the road. We stood talking quietly as officers speculated when the main assault would start. Reille's men could be seen marching up the road behind me and I knew some units of the Imperial Guard were marching behind them, so I did not think it would be soon. Of more concern to me was making sure that I was out of the way when the battle did commence.

I had always promised myself that I would not fight my own countrymen but with a battle in the offing, this was going to require all my cunning. With the French likely to be victorious, I could not simply desert their army or hide. I would be missed and deserters faced arrest and imprisonment. I needed to keep my liberty to slip away later – surely I could find some nice safe courier duties for the marshal. I had managed it at Quatre Bras and I was sure I could do it again.

The emperor and his generals talked for ages and I had my first inkling that something was not right when Napoleon called for a chair and sat down. He winced with pain as he did so and clutched his stomach. I wondered if his waistcoat buttons were straining a little bit more than normal around the pot belly. Perhaps he had tried that stew after all.

My suspicion deepened a short while later when his white horse was summoned so that he could inspect his troops. The emperor walked gingerly to the stallion, whispering something to Ney as he did so. A nervous groom stood beside the mount with his hands ready to help boost the stout emperor into the saddle. Napoleon put out his foot and a moment later he was flying upwards with such speed that he nearly tumbled over the other side of his horse.

"You imbecile!" he roared at the unfortunate man, who stared aghast at his furious monarch. The horse trotted on a few paces as Napoleon adjusted himself in the saddle but just as his staff began to close in around him, the emperor had second thoughts. He wheeled his horse around and returned to the hapless groom.

"I am so sorry, Your Majesty…" the man began and fell to his knees, but the emperor smiled and waved him up again.

"Stand, my boy, and give me your hand." After the groom had shaken his hand I saw the emperor wince again and press his hand to his stomach before belching loudly. Ignoring this emission he continued quietly, "When you help a man my size, it must be done gently." With that, he turned again and, gritting his teeth, galloped forward to the waiting ranks of his army.

Despite the discomfort, the emperor rode nearly two miles, from his left wing to his right. It was in part a piece of showmanship to intimidate his enemies and I noticed a growing crowd of men appear on the British crest to watch. But there was no doubt about the effect his appearance had on his own men. They cheered and roared their acclaim, raising their hats on their bayonets and sword points and singing revolutionary songs as he rode away. Many of them might have spent the night soaking wet and shivering with cold in a field, but by then their clothes had dried in the wind and sporadic sunshine; most had brushed off the worst of the mud and they now stood tall, proud soldiers of France. They knew that one more victory over the very mixed force of British, German, Hanoverian, Nassau and Brunswick troops together with the French and Dutch-speaking Netherlanders, and they would stop any immediate threat of invasion to their homeland. Their families would be safe from the pillaging of foreign troops and the French 'Republic' would once again be secure. I just sat there feeling confused.

Patriotism is a funny thing. I have known many people who have given their lives to save some scrap of cloth representing their regiment or their country. Well, you can wipe your arse on any flag I have marched under and see what good it will do you. I had no wish to see the French king back on his throne and, if I was honest, I did not really give a fig about many of the assorted foreigners that were hiding beyond the opposite ridge. There were more than a few British soldiers I did not trouble about either; if a French skirmisher had put a ball through Colquhoun Grant's pompous head, I would have happily bought the man a drink. But there were some I did care about. I suspected that Campbell, my closest friend who I had served with in India, Spain and Canada might be over there. There would certainly be others like him, for whom I had gone to great lengths to hide the fact that I was terrified when we had fought together. Now, through a twist of fate, I found myself among their enemies, a force that was likely to destroy them.

The French certainly had the guns to do it. As I watched a huge 'grand battery' was being put together on a ridge to the right of the road. It was half a mile in front of the allied line and angled to cover the British left and centre. Even those troops well behind the ridge would be comfortably in range. But while I watched its formation, an artillery officer told me that once the attack was underway they planned to move the guns two hundred yards further forward, on another ridge, where they could provide even more devastating fire. There must have been nearly eighty guns in this huge battery, but there were many more scattered along the French line. I had already seen how well they would be served.

There was little I could do to change the course of events now and I resolved just to keep my head down and survive the day. Tomorrow could take care of itself. But then I discovered that I may already have made a difference to how the battle would be fought.

After his procession along the line of his soldiers, the emperor returned to his original vantage point. The ride did not seem to have done him any good. His face looked grey and the bouncing on his saddle had clearly shaken his guts further. As he dismounted he passed wind loudly, startling his horse, which skittered to one side until the unfortunate groom had it back under control. The emperor started to walk slowly back to his table and chair while the other senior generals who had ridden along behind him reined up nearby. One of them was Ney and he spotted me standing in the crowd.

"Colonel Moreau, where the devil have you been? I was expecting you to report to me yesterday." Like the swots at school, the other officers shrank back from me as I was reprimanded. I noticed Napoleon pause in his journey and glance across at me and I inwardly cursed Ney for once again bringing me to his attention.

"I am sorry, Marshal. My horse went lame and I could not get another one."

Ney gave a brief nod of satisfaction. "Well, I hope you have a sturdy mount today as I will have work for you."

At this, the emperor stopped and turned to face all of us. His eyes roved over the group and, perhaps it was my imagination, but they seemed to linger a fraction longer on my features compared to the rest. "Gentlemen," he spoke at last. "I have drawn up our battle plan, but as I am feeling a little indisposed, Marshal Ney will command the attack." He paused again before adding, "France is in your hands, but I know I can rely on you to do your duty."

For the first time I felt a flicker of hope for the allied cause. Only a flicker, mind, for the weight of advantage still lay overwhelmingly with the French. I could not think of a better defensive general than Wellington. On the other hand, at Quatre Bras I had seen first-hand that while Ney was undoubtedly brave, he had little strategic acumen. Ney was hot-headed and reactionary, while Wellington was cold and calculating.

I could not help but think back to those little mushrooms I had found the previous day. Were they the cause of the emperor's indisposition, and if so would they give the British general an advantage? The best I thought that the allies could hope for was an effective fighting withdrawal. Marshal Grouchy was supposed to be between the British and any remnant of the Prussian army still fit to fight, but perhaps they could re-join in Brussels after all. In fact, as I looked at the British ridge I began to wonder how many allied troops were actually still there. Perhaps even then most were pouring down the Brussels road.

Chapter 35

We found out that the British were still there soon enough for the attack finally started at eleven. A signal gun sounded and then five seconds later every single French cannon fired together. It was a trick the emperor liked to use to awe his enemies and I can tell you that even on the French side of the valley, it was pretty awe-inspiring. Lines of explosions and bursts of mud could be seen along the British ridge. In that first salvo I noticed that a British gun was disabled while the crew of two more were frantically pulling their weapon back down the far slope out of sight. Then as the guns reloaded I heard a new sound from my left: musketry. The French were attacking the château of Hougoumont. I watched as thousands of little blue-coated figures charged towards the trees and gardens that surrounded the buildings. The place lay in a dip in the ground and I could just make out some roof tops but even they were soon obscured by smoke as the guns fired again.

I had expected Ney to be good to his word of keeping us busy, but in fact, for the first two hours of the battle we did very little. The emperor sat nearby at his table surrounded by his staff officers. There was also a small group of Imperial Guard soldiers, who kept away a number of local civilians who had come to the battle to wish him well. He was still in pain and occasionally walked gingerly alone into a nearby farm building. One can only guess at the purpose, but I suspect he was using it as a latrine.

Ney, on the other hand, strolled up and down, apparently without a care in the world. This seemed strange for after a while it became apparent that the attack at Hougoumont was failing. To my dismay, I saw that there were plenty of British soldiers hidden behind the ridge, as a good number of them were pouring over its top and down a lane to reinforce the garrison at the château. While the lane was mostly hidden in a dip, it was clear that thousands of allied troops were moving, men dressed in red and green and even some artillery and cavalry to support the defence. Well, that disproved my theory that the British position was really a near empty rear-guard and I remember feeling quite depressed at the thought. I knew Wellington was no fool, so why on earth was he making a stand here? I became even more disheartened a few minutes later.

"Are we sending more men to support the attack at Hougoumont?" I asked Ney. He had kept glancing across in that direction and must have noticed the British reinforcements, but instead of showing any concern he was strangely satisfied with the outcome.

"Perhaps, but we have plenty of time."

"But isn't the attack failing?"

Ney looked at me and grinned. "Moreau, you should have more faith in the emperor and me. The attack has not even begun yet, but don't worry, when it does I will make sure you get to see it."

"I am sorry, sir, I don't understand."

Ney looked pleased with himself and was evidently keen to show off their cunning. He put his arm around my shoulders and guided me a few steps closer to the emperor and the high point of ground he stood on. Then he turned to face the British ridge. "We know the allied line is weak with lots of inexperienced men. If he hopes to keep them, Wellington must have put some of his best soldiers in that farm," he was pointing to La Haye Sainte, "and Hougoumont. Am I right?" he asked.

"Yes," I could only agree with his logic.

"By attacking the château we force him to send more of his best men to its defence, which will weaken his line further. Now we pound that weakened line with our guns. You must have been under artillery fire. Can you imagine how frightened inexperienced troops will be as balls from guns they cannot see, whip over the top of the crest and smash through the ranks they are standing in?"

I could easily imagine it. I had sat on my horse terrified at Talavera, as French cannonballs smashed all about me. Wellington had ordered his men to lie down then, which reduced casualties considerably and I wondered if he was doing the same now. It would save some, but the guns would still do terrible damage. "Then when their weakened line has been battered by our guns," Ney continued, "if they have not already broken, they will see this marching towards them." As he

269

spoke, he twisted me around so that I was staring over what had been my right shoulder. There before me, hidden from the allies by the southern ridge, several huge columns were being formed up. There must have been at least ten thousand men.

"Good God," I breathed for at that moment it seemed certain that the French would win. That certainty only hardened over time. The signal gun to start the battle had been fired at eleven. By one o'clock the British line had been under constant fire for two hours while battle still raged around Hougoumont, with yet more men sent for its defence. Having nothing to do, I counted the number of guns in the grand battery and calculated their rate of fire and estimated that some two thousand balls and shells an hour were being fired at the British line. That was just from the grand battery, which was about a third of the guns the French had. How on earth could anyone withstand such an onslaught? At Talavera I had only put up with it for a few minutes and I had been desperate to move.

There had been hardly any return fire from the British guns and a good number had been destroyed in the bombardment. Ney confidently announced that they must be short of ammunition and were saving their guns and fire. It was hard to see the British ridge now for the valley was full of cannon smoke that only drifted slowly in the light breeze. Then just after one o'clock came the moment I had been dreading. Ney scribbled a note and handed it to me.

"Take that to General D'Erlon," he ordered pointing at where the huge columns had formed. Then he slapped me on the back and added, "God I envy you, for it will be a wonderful sight to watch them run. But the emperor will expect me to stay here. Go on, man."

I tried to conjure a look of enthusiasm. "It will be a historic moment," I assured him and with regret I rather suspected it would be. As I swung up into the saddle another voice called out.

"Colonel Moreau." I turned and saw that the emperor had raised himself from his chair and was studying me closely. He stood silent for a moment and I felt the hair on the back of my neck prickle with alarm, but then he gestured down the slope towards the waiting columns. "Tell General D'Erlon that I know he will not let me down."

There was a smirk from several officers standing behind Napoleon, who evidently thought the emperor was reminding D'Erlon of his failure to support the Ligny attack two days ago. But I simply threw up a salute and replied, "Yes sire," before spurring my horse down the slope. The sooner I was away from those searching eyes the better.

As I galloped towards the waiting blocks of blue-coated soldiers I could not help but remember all the times I had seen French columns attack before. It had never ended well for the French, but this time I was destined to be among them. At Talavera and Busaco the French had outnumbered our forces and come on in huge columns. On both occasions thin lines of redcoats had met them and destroyed them with volley fire. While all the British muskets in a line could be brought to bear on a column, only the outer French ranks could fire, which gave the British the advantage. At Busaco the French had tried to counter this by having the outer edges of the column move forward like the wings of a bird. But the British line had curved around the column head so that the men in these wings had advanced into a devastating fire, which pushed them back.

Heaven knew what state the allied troops were in behind the opposite ridge after two hours of the heaviest bombardment I had ever seen. The ridge itself would have given some protection but the gunners had their balls and shells bouncing down the far side of it. Even if the men were lying down, hundreds if not thousands must have been killed.

As I got closer I saw that the columns were indeed huge. Despite the misleading name, the columns were always wider than they were deep. The front rank of these contained around a hundred and fifty men and there were another twenty-four rows of men behind the first.

If he was worried about the outcome of his attack D'Erlon did not show it. "Ah, Colonel, welcome, I remember you. Do you come again from Marshal Ney?"

I passed him Ney's note and gave him the emperor's message. "Do you think we will get over the ridge before they can get their line established?" I asked as it was the thought that was upper most in my mind.

"Ah, I see you have fought the British before as well." He grinned "Don't worry, it will not matter if they do have their line. In fact, this time, it might be better for us if they do." It was not an arrogant boast and I had already learned from my earlier encounter with him, that General D'Erlon was a very cautious man. But what he said made no sense. Why would these columns succeed against a British line when so many others had failed?

The puzzlement must have shown on my face as D'Erlon pointed to his men. "Look, instead of blocks of men, they are arranged by line. Each battalion makes up three lines. When we get close the battalions will slide out like drawers, some to the right and some to the left. The front rank and leading drawers will shield the ones behind and we will overlap any line they present. We will give them a taste of their own medicine." He looked pleased with himself and I am bound to say that at the time I thought it was an ingenious solution. I thought that the allied troops by then must be close to breaking point. Even if enough of them could be mustered into a line, they would not be expecting the French columns to spread out and threaten to wrap themselves around their flanks. It gave the French yet another advantage. It was strange: in any other battle I would have been horrified at the thought of marching with a French column; I had seen too many of them destroyed. But this time all of my experience told me that they were destined for success.

D'Erlon turned to address his troops. "Comrades," he shouted. "The emperor has placed the future of France in our hands. We will advance and we will conquer or die." Well it was a short speech but it was deuced effective. There was a massive roar of *Vive l'Empereur!* from ten thousand throats and then the drums rolled and the vast formation began to move forward.

From my perspective, conquer my old comrades or die was a rather bleak choice. However, as Ney's messenger, I at least had the additional option of loitering near the back and then returning to report on progress. I was glad that I would not have to stay and watch the allied soldiers being pursued from the field.

272

I waited for the first column to march past and then joined a group of officers riding in the middle of the second one. Other battalion officers rode along the flanks as though the formations had their own cavalry escorts. We veered to our right to start with, around the ridge crowned by the grand battery, which if anything had increased its rate of fire as the assault force started its march. As we drew level with the guns the noise became even louder and it was impossible to speak. But the officers alongside me grinned and gestured at each other, showing far more excitement than fear. We were already in a haze of gun smoke, but it got denser as we started to march down the gentle slope into the valley. At first the going was easy; the column in front of us had trampled a swathe through the crops and the flattened stems of wheat made a mat over the mud. I wondered if the allies had seen the huge formations of men descend the far ridge into the valley. Were they even now trying to work out where along their line we would emerge? Certainly, if they did not see them, they would hear them soon enough, for the regular beat of drums and shout of loyalty to the emperor was unmistakable.

We came to a halt on the valley floor. The front column had slowed down as it struggled through the heavily waterlogged ground. I saw several boots stuck in the mud; men were not able to stop and retrieve them when marching in the middle of a column. But all those who did still have their boots also had at least a pound of sticky clay attached to each one. With French shells and balls still screaming high over our heads towards the allied ridge, we re-organised ourselves for the attack. We were to assault the allied left, which meant marching to the right of the road. My column had the easiest time of it as we stayed still, while the one in front smashed through the crops until they were diagonally to our left while the column behind moved to their right. Eventually all three were in a diagonal line, and the order was given to advance again.

It was slower going now as each column had to smash its own way through the crops. Men slipped and splashed through pools of standing water and even the horses struggled as the weight of man and beast pushed their hooves deep into the mire. If the allied guns had been on the ridge and could see us they would have played merry havoc in our ranks, but we could barely see a hundred yards in the cloud of smoke and must have been invisible beyond that distance.

If the allies were shooting at other columns, I did not see the effect of their balls but surely they must know that an attack was coming. The blasted French drummers kept up their rattling beat and every minute or so they would finish with a flourish and thousands of men would roar out *Vive l'Empereur!* Then as we began to climb up the far slope, the allied slope, the firing from the French guns finally stopped. They did not want to risk hitting their own men. After two hours of cannonading, it was almost an eerie silence as we marched unseen through the mist. It wasn't that quiet, of course, there were still the drums and the sound of thousands of men breaking down crops and marching over them, but now my ears were picking up a new sound: English voices.

Sound travels further in fog or smoke and I distinctly heard a man shouting, 'Push it forward', and others yelling for men to 'Close up'. My mouth went dry as hearing my own language brought home to me what I was doing. How in the name of holy hell, I demanded of myself, had I ended up in a French column attacking British troops? Hearing those familiar commands reminded me of every other time I had seen a column attack a line and the bloody shambles of enemy troops that had resulted. Even a child understood that every musket in a line being able to fire, meant that it always beat the column.

Suddenly I had no faith at all in D'Erlon's scheme; instead, I had an awful premonition of being shot and some blood-spattered British redcoat plunging his bayonet in my chest. I felt trapped and stared around for a way out, but it was too late. I was in the middle of the second column, in a narrow strip of space between the battalion lines, with other French officers to my right. Staring to my left I saw that in their eagerness to close with the enemy, the ends of the ranks were pushing forward, closing the gap. I was entombed in the middle of the French attack whether I liked it or not and yes, 'entombed' was the word I thought of at the time. It damn nearly was my tomb too, for we were now emerging from the smoke.

I stared frantically around to get my bearings. The columns had spread out on the climb to give them room to extend their ranks. The left hand one was now ahead and close to the farm of La Haye Sainte, facing a furious fire from its defenders. But another column of French troops had advanced straight up the Brussels road and they had an escort of cuirassiers to guard their flank. Already I could see the British defenders in the farm garden pulling back into the buildings before they were overwhelmed. There was the sharper crack of rifles and in a sandpit across the road from the farm, green-jacketed soldiers were firing on the first column, trying to kill their officers, while swarms of French skirmishers were also pushing forward and threatening to encircle them.

Then on the far side of the farm, I saw a British regiment start to advance down the ridge to support the defence of the buildings. The farm was already wreathed in musket smoke but surely the colonel of that regiment could see the cuirassiers in front of them? In disbelief I watched as the British regiment came on and then wheeled to its left to fire on the French attackers. The ends of their ranks now pointed directly at the armoured horsemen. It was as though they were asking to be killed.

"Form square, you stupid bloody bastards," I found myself yelling as I watched them. But even if they had heard me it would have been too late, for the cuirassiers were charging. I realised with horror that I had shouted in English, but no one noticed, for at that moment there was a strange whirring noise, followed by terrible screams.

The whirring noise was once described to me as the angel of death's hum, and they were not far wrong. I had not heard it before, not like that, and I never want to hear it again. For it was the sound of canister shot whistling through the air, coming directly at you. Dozens of musket balls blasted from a cannon to create an arc of complete carnage with every shot. They came from the guns I had heard men shouting to be pushed forward. As we emerged from the smoke, some allied cannon changed their aim in our direction. Thank Christ there were only half a dozen of them on the ridge able to fire, for with the tightly packed blocks of men they could not miss.

275

I saw a corner of my column disappear as though a giant had swept an invisible scythe through their ranks. Men screamed, staggered and fell, but those behind did not falter and simply stepped over their comrades. Another cannon fired, this time into the centre of the column. One ball whirred right over my head like some lead hornet. Instinctively I ducked and looked round just in time to see the officer next to me plucked off his horse and hurled into the men marching behind us. The front ranks in the centre of the column were a patch of chaos; several men had been flailed apart by the storm of lead that had ripped through the air. I saw arms and legs, dismembered bodies and from some unseen soul, blood was spurting high in the air. A drummer was staggering along, one arm a bloody ruin, but incredibly, still sounding the beat of the march on his drum with his good limb. Two more cannon fired, and more men from our front line went down. I stared about me terrified, trapped in this mass of humanity, which despite this onslaught still marched to the beat of its drums.

A man shrieked beneath me as my horse must have trodden on him but I barely gave him a thought for my attention was focussed on the British gunners. They were desperately trying to reload their pieces, while in front of them French skirmishers swarmed up the slope to shoot them before they could succeed. I watched transfixed as a gunner shoved another load of canister into the cannon that had just moments before nearly killed me. A second artilleryman was stepping forward with a ramrod to press the charge home. While my voice was lost in the din of battle, I screamed at the skirmishers to kill him. The gunner fell away, hit, but I watched as another man picked up the rammer to try again. I yelled for his death too. I did not care anymore that these were British soldiers getting killed. I just wanted to live myself. There was another whir of balls and instinctively I ducked again, but this time the screams came from behind. When I looked again the second gunner was lying dead. I almost cried with relief as I saw those that were left hauling frantically to get their guns out of the way before they were captured.

I risked a glance to my left just in time to see a cuirassier wheel away with another British standard in his hand. The regiment that had marched to help the farm was destroyed, men fleeing in all directions like chickens from foxes. The farm itself was completely obscured by gun smoke but I could see the ground behind it and it was covered with allied soldiers running back up the hill in retreat. Commands were being shouted in the column ordering men to close up to fill the gaps in their ranks and then the battalions began to move outwards as the drawers opened. D'Erlon's plan was starting to work. We were only fifty yards away from the crest of the ridge, which was already occupied by French skirmishers, and from my higher vantage point on horseback I tried to glimpse what lay in front. What I saw filled me with both hope and despair.

Allied soldiers were running in all directions. They were shouting and yelling at each other; there was the sound of distant bugle calls and teams of horses pulling guns further back. To my left I saw that the cuirassiers – there were only three hundred of them – had gained the ridge top and regiments all around them were hurriedly forming square. There were some lines of allied troops but they were well behind the crest and starting to edge further back. I would have bet my pension on them not standing. They had cuirassiers loose to their right and more men than they could ever hope to beat spreading out in front of them. Some of them fired volleys as the head of the column crested the ridge, but the range was too long to do much damage. Their smoke just added to the fog that the battle was spreading over the British position.

More bugles called and the front ranks of the column began to scramble over the road that lay in a slight dip just beyond the ridge. The allied plateau was falling and with it any hope for an allied victory. The soldiers around me sensed it and set up a cheer. They now knew that they would be able to roll up the left flank of the allied army. There might be the odd pocket of resistance, but the rest would be pushed into the forest, to run for their lives to the coast.

"We have given the emperor his victory," shouted an officer near me. Then something caught his eye and he started to call out a warning. But as I heard that terrible whirring noise again, the words literally died in his throat. He saved my life, though, for that look of alarm was enough to trigger my poltroon's instinct to duck down beside my horse's neck.

Sadly though, my sturdy steed did not have the same cowardly tendency, for a canister ball smashed through its skull. I felt the impact as the animal's neck smashed into me. Then my chest and face were covered with its gore and, with blood in my eyes, I could not see. The horse went down as if a hangman had dropped the trap from under it. One moment I had been mounted and speculating on what the French victory would mean for me; the next I was blind, possibly wounded and sprawled on a dead horse as soldiers climbed around me. The fall had winded me and it took me a moment to be certain that none of the blood was mine. I was wiping it from my eyes as the noise of battle sounded all around; there was another whir of canister and the answering volleys from the spreading ranks and those wretched bugle calls. I tried to get to my feet but was knocked down again by a rank of men marching over me. Then a hand reached under my arm and pulled me to my feet.

"Come on, Colonel, we have gaps in our rank, we can make room." Men shuffled to one side and there I was marching in the ranks of the huge French column. The other mounted officers I had been with were either dead or further ahead for I could see nothing but a line of French soldiers' backs and their tall shako hats. All I could do was stumble along in my place in the line. Even then I had to stay alert as I discovered when the man to my right abruptly reached out and pulled me towards him and I just avoided stepping on a wounded man.

"Are we winning, sir?" the soldier asked as he gently pushed me back into my place in the line.

"We were when I could last see what was going on," I told him and heard the news getting repeated along the rank. You might think that marching surrounded by so much humanity would be comforting, but I found it unnerving not to know what was happening. All I had to go on were sounds and here were those bugles again and they were getting closer. Then realisation finally dawned and my blood froze.

I had not seen them when I was on horseback as the ground undulated and drifting gun smoke obscured my view, but the bugles were coming from up ahead. I knew that they were used by cavalry and unmistakably, they were sounding the charge.

Chapter 36

"Stop! Stop!" I shouted. "British cavalry are charging the front of the column. We need to get into square!"

"There is no room, sir," replied the man beside me, still marching, and I was pushed forward by the man behind when I tried to stop. Christ, King Canute stood more chance of stopping the tide than I did of halting this huge mass as just one voice in the middle. Then we heard the first screams coming from up ahead and the sound of metal hitting metal. There was a crackle of musketry, but I knew most of the front ranks had already fired at gunners and other obstacles and had not had chance to reload. Still I was being pushed forward, towards those swinging sabres and now I could see the weakness in D'Erlon's scheme. Battalions in solid blocks would form square easily as the officers sat in the middle of their command, but in this formation, each battalion was in a narrow strip and hemmed in by others. It was impossible for officers to hastily form them up to defend against cavalry. I looked along my line to the left. We had been edging in that direction as our 'drawer' extended to the left but two-thirds of the line was still in the column itself. I caught a fleeting glimpse of some men starting to run back and then I was squashed again in a great heaving mass of humanity.

I don't think my feet touched the ground for several seconds as I was jostled about. The men at the front of the column were pushing to go back, while those at the back, oblivious to what was happening, were still trying to advance. There were screams of agony and yells of terror from those being attacked, but I was powerless to do anything. I was just being tossed around like driftwood in a storm. As suddenly as it started, the pressure eased and men were turning and moving back. The man who had been in the rank in front of me was now in the line behind as we turned and he was shouting and pushing at me to run. But there was only room for a shuffling walk. Then we began to go faster, streaming back over the road, the noise of battle getting ever louder behind us.

If I had ever thought that there is no more terrifying sight than a cavalry charge coming towards me, well I was wrong. The most terrifying thing is *knowing* that a rampaging troop of murderous horsemen is hacking its way towards your back and *not* being able to see it. We were running now, still in a tightly packed mass as we streamed back down the allied ridge towards the French lines. My foot slipped on the leg of a man lying on the ground. I nearly stumbled but just managed to stay on my feet by grabbing at the man on my right. He was stumbling over the same corpse and, unbalanced, went down. He did not get a chance to regain his footing. As I was swept away in the throng, I heard his scream of panic as he was trampled in the stampede to escape.

I shook another man off who had tried to grab at me for support; I was not going to risk the same fate. It was every man for himself as we ran and I searched for some protection from the horsemen behind us. The rearmost French column had been given more warning of the horsemen's approach and had not yet deployed the 'drawers'. They managed to turn their ranks along the edge to form a rudimentary square and start edging back. They were firing their guns to keep both the horsemen away and other soldiers seeking the safety of their ranks. I knew there would be no shelter in that direction, for those men knew all too well that their survival rested on keeping their tight outer lines intact.

I kept running down the slope, but there was much less gun smoke to hide in now. The grand battery had not fired for some minutes and was halfway through moving to its new position on the forward ridge. At best only a light mist covered the lower ground. There was more space now; men were spreading out as they ran and for the first time I glimpsed some horsemen, British dragoons on black horses wheeling in from my left. Two of them were heading in my direction and I watched as the lead man gave a massive swing that must have broken the skull of a running Frenchman. I changed direction to get a larger group of soldiers between me and the dragoons and tried to sprint even harder, my lungs burning with the effort. I thought I had got away but then one of the riders saw me and gave a cry of triumph.

"Look, a colonel!" he yelled pointing his blood-stained sword in my direction.

I knew I could not outrun them. As other men streamed past I held up my hands and shouted. "No, I'm British, my name is Major Flashman."

"Huh, you lying knave!" cried the trooper as he spurred his horse towards me and raised his sabre in the air.

"I am a British spy," I insisted. "Take me to Wellington and he will confirm it." But the man just laughed. Many French, particularly if they had been prisoners of war, spoke excellent English. He evidently thought I was one of those and still he came on, giving his blade a practice swing to show me my fate.

I had no choice but to draw my own sword. I had to defend myself, but to try to kill them would confirm their suspicions and I still did not want to kill one of my own. I had dodged riders before and at the last minute I threw myself to one side and rolled away.

"I'm bloody British, you stupid bastards," I roared as I got up but the second trooper was almost on me and I just got my own blade up in time to block his blow. The force of it with the momentum of the horse knocked me down again and now both horsemen were circling in for the kill.

"No British spy marches in a French column. You are going to get what's coming to you," shouted the second man. As if things could not get any worse, over their shoulder I saw six more troopers charging in our direction. A fresh-faced ensign was at their head, who looked little older than my son. I stared around desperate for some refuge or help. Twenty yards away a score of Frenchmen had gathered into a group with their bayonets out like a hedgehog to keep the horsemen at bay, but I would never make it to them in time.

This was to be my fate, hacked to pieces by my own countrymen while mistaken for the enemy. If I thought there was one chance in a hundred of it working, I would have thrown my sword away and tried to surrender, but that would not serve here. The troopers had blood-spattered faces and uniforms; they had both been killing and had got a taste for it. They were laughing at me, rejoicing in their power over

282

their fellow man. I thought for a brief moment that perhaps I could make a final appeal to their boy commander, but it did not look like I would get the chance. My assailants were coming at the trot from opposite sides, both grinning wolfishly. Then a high-pitched voice called across to them.

"Twoopers, leave that wascal alone and fall in with me."

"But he is a colonel," shouted one of my attackers.

"And a lying bastard," added the other.

"Leave him," piped the cornet. "We are capturing their guns." The man in front of me reluctantly turned to follow his officer and I almost sagged to the ground with relief. It was a good job I didn't, for then I heard an ominous click from the man behind.

He had snatched up his carbine musket from the holster in his saddle, and having cocked the weapon he was in the act of putting it to his shoulder as I looked round. "I have never liked liars," he said grinning, and then he pulled the trigger. He was only ten yards away, virtually point-blank range. I saw the movement of the hammer on the gun and the puff of smoke from the priming pan. There was no time to move or even brace myself for the awful impact of the ball. Then… nothing… The main charge had not fired. It was literally just a flash in the pan. With a snarl of rage the trooper rode his horse straight for me, swinging the carbine in the air like a club while his officer yelled at him to fall in. I got the blade up in the air, holding it with both hands, but several pounds of brass-hilted oak was too much for the cheap steel. The sword snapped and I felt the butt crack into the back of my head. The last thing I heard was the triumphal yell of the trooper as the ground came up to hit me.

I don't remember how I joined the group of men who had formed the hedgehog of bayonets, but my next memory is being half held up amongst them. There were dozens of similar groupings of various sizes across the valley now. They were edging their way south, and all were staring in incredulity at the British horsemen. For instead of rounding up and capturing hundreds of French soldiers, a thousand British heavy cavalry had launched themselves across the valley to capture the French grand battery. I saw a couple of officers and even a bugler riding after them and calling for them to return, but they might as well have barked at the moon. The horsemen swarmed on, slowing down as they reached the boggy valley floor, but then forcing their tired horses up the other side.

God knows how they thought they would hold the guns against the entire French army, but the gunners were not waiting to find out. Most were streaming back to the safety of French regiments, several of which were forming square. Having checked that no more horsemen were in our vicinity, my group of soldiers broke and ran to join another, to make a larger formation. I was half dragged between two men and when we arrived a musket was pressed into my hand so that I could play my part.

"Those horsemen will be coming back in a minute," someone shouted, "so keep the sides straight." We were in a small square of perhaps a hundred men, with two ranks of a dozen on each side. By chance, I was pushed into the side that faced south and watched as the British cavalry captured the guns. They milled about shouting and waving their swords in the air as though they had won the battle all by themselves. They might have killed a few gunners and horses but I did not see one of them dismount to spike or disable a cannon. Then there was the sound of more bugles.

I don't know whether it was Ney or Napoleon, but the French counter attack was timed to perfection. They waited for the British heavy cavalry to complete their charge to the top of the ridge and then they launched thousands of their lighter, fresh lancers against them. The British troopers saw them coming before we did and with shouts of alarm they launched their tired beasts back down the slope towards us. But their horses were blown and could barely manage more than a trot, especially as they reached the boggy ground. Few of them got that far for the lancers in their green uniforms and brass helmets, with their nine-foot lances, swarmed over the crest after them, like ravening wolves after an old stag.

Cavalry hate being attacked by lancers as their swords offer little defence against the much longer steel-tipped lance. I remember one old trooper telling me that he had killed one by pushing aside the point and slashing as they swept past. He was either lucky or a liar, for as I had discovered years before, lancers do not hunt alone. Pay attention to just one and you will soon find a steel lance point plunged in your back. The lancers broke up into packs and started to hunt down their prey. It was a slaughter. A few of the dragoons managed to get off a shot with their carbines but I only saw one Frenchman get hit. As they reached the valley floor the British horsemen faced a new obstacle: dozens of formations of returning French troops like mine, in no mood to be merciful.

We were splashing our way through the muddy ooze at the bottom of the slope when six dragoons tried to get between us and another formation nearby. Two were wounded and slumped over their saddles and a third was walking, his exhausted mount still slipping in the mud. Every one of our group had nearly been killed by these horsemen and had lost comrades to them and now the call went up to halt and take aim. I had already looked and seen that they did not include the men who had attacked me. If the one who had tried to shoot me had been there, I will be honest and say that British or not, I would have tried to return the favour. But instead, as I cocked my weapon, I also swept the powder from the pan so it would not fire. Volleys crashed out from both my group and the one on the other side of the troopers. When the smoke had cleared, only the tired horse was still standing.

With lancers providing protection, thousands of us streamed back up the French ridge. We passed another group of British corpses and men went across to loot them. I was about to walk past when I noticed that one of them was the young cornet who had inadvertently saved me. His body had been pierced by at least four lances and in death he looked even younger than in life, although I guessed he had to be at least sixteen.

"You poor bastard," I muttered as I leaned over him. He had undoubtedly been brave, probably feeling that sense of immortality that young men do, but he had been woefully let down by his commanders. Infantry officers often claimed that the brains of the cavalry command lay in their horses rather than the riders. They were often titled young men who treated war like a hunt, chasing an enemy for miles away from a battle and leaving the poor bloody foot soldiers exposed to enemy attack. They had really surpassed themselves this time, though. Without the tools to disable the guns, their mad charge was always going to be futile and end in disaster. They could have saved themselves and secured thousands of prisoners, but instead, most of them now lay dead in the valley.

The boy's pockets had already been torn open by those searching for money but he still had his sword in his hand. It was not valuable, which was why it had been left, but it did have a 'Sheffield Steel' stamp on the blade. So I picked it up and gave it a few practice strokes. It was heavy but well balanced. I had bought the cheap French blade when I had first kitted myself out with my French uniform. Back then I had been sure that I would never have to use it so had spurned the suggestion of a better quality weapon. I was not going to make that mistake again. After a final cut through the air, I slid the new sword into my scabbard. It was not a perfect fit, but it would do.

By the time we passed the new forward position of the grand battery, the first guns were already firing again and most of the others would be doing so shortly. I remember staring back at the British ridge; it looked exactly as it had before. They had lost most of their heavy cavalry while the French had well over a thousand infantry killed or taken prisoner. But the British still held La Haye Sainte farm and both armies were exactly where they had started; with just a carpet of corpses in the valley to show that there had been a battle at all.

I might have re-armed myself but that did not mean I had any intention of participating further in this battle. I had never wanted to fight the British and I swore by all that was holy that I was not going to do so again. D'Erlon's attack on the allied position had started at around one-thirty in the afternoon and I know I was sitting back on the French ridge by three, as I remember checking my watch then. I had found a place to sit with other wounded men on the high ground where the grand battery had been originally sited. This, I decided, was where I would shirk my way through the rest of the battle.

You don't survive as many campaigns as I have without the ability to hole up out of the way sometimes and let others do some of the fighting. It helped that I was covered in blood and gore, which looked like it could have been mine. I took care to ease myself slowly onto the soft earth to give the impression of being injured like so many of those about me. Twice ambulance men came and offered to take me away on their well-sprung carts, but I nobly waved them away to those more in need. The last thing I needed was them cleaning me up and finding no wound at all. It wasn't all a sham, though, for my head still throbbed, a situation not helped by having the grand battery firing away in front.

I settled myself up against an ammunition box, accepted a flask of water and watched the battle as I might have spectated on a game of cricket. It was a shame that they did not have vendors selling food too as I was starving. The French guns were soon firing as strongly as ever. A few gun crews had been killed by the cavalry but they were replaced by new guns and crews from the Imperial Guard artillery and so I suspected that the fire was even more accurate. From their forward position they were also able to see further over the British ridge, particularly where it plateaued out on a stretch west of the road. The British troops there were horribly exposed to the fire and one by one the units I could see moved back. Between the noise of the cannon, there was a steady crackle of fire from the valley and before it refilled with smoke I could see French skirmishers moving between the unflattened crops as they harried the enemy, particularly around La Haye Sainte farm.

It seemed that Ney and Napoleon were content to pound the allies into submission with their vastly superior gunnery. There was no rush to order another major assault, although judging from the distant smoke, fighting was continuing around the château of Hougoumont. The reason for this apparent lethargy appeared on the north-eastern horizon nearly an hour after I began my period of repose. An artillery officer spotted them first and soon word spread around the ridge: 'Grouchy is coming'. I raised my own glass and sure enough, columns of troops could be seen marching to the battle. Whether Napoleon had recalled them or Grouchy had simply marched towards the sound of the guns like any good general, I did not know or care. But I did know that twenty-five thousand French infantry, five thousand cavalry and nearly a hundred guns arriving behind Wellington's left flank would spell the death knell of the allied army. The battle was effectively over, for as soon as he saw this new force approaching, Wellington would have to withdraw or he would be utterly destroyed.

In fact I felt so confident that the battle was over that I thought it was safe to show myself once more. After an hour in their vicinity with a headache, I was also keen to get further away from the guns. So I staggered to my feet and soon commandeered a captured British cavalry horse that was cropping grass by the side of the road. Having Grouchy's men fall on Wellington's flank was a masterstroke, I reflected as I trotted south along the cobbled highway. Perhaps the emperor had planned it as soon as he saw Wellington making a stand; it would fit his reputation as a master strategist. Wellington's defence had been doomed from the outset and I tried to feel sorry about that, but all I really felt was relief.

This dammed battle would soon be over and I convinced myself that this was the best outcome for the allies, well, the British at least. Instead of being ground down further by the steady bombardment, they would have to withdraw. The British would head to Antwerp and from there disembark to England. I doubted the emperor would pursue them hard for he wanted a peace and a new government in England. A humiliating withdrawal would serve his purpose, but a massacre would stiffen British resolve against him.

Chapter 37

There were at least fifty senior officers milling around the little farm that the emperor was using as his headquarters. Soult was there in his marshal's uniform stiff with braid, while around him were a riot of coloured uniforms of every description and probably enough ostrich feathers sewn into hats to re-plume an entire bird. A few yards in front of this gathering sat the emperor in his plain green artillery uniform, talking to a mud-spattered colonel. I realised that as well as his age, Napoleon had something else in common with his opponent: Wellington also dressed plainly, in a blue coat, for battle, so that he stood out amongst the peacocks of his staff. I pushed through the crowd of officers, searching for Ney, but he was not there. It was then that I heard the first whispered speculation amongst the staff that the approaching troops might not be Grouchy after all.

"I tell you, Donzelot thinks that they are Prussians and I have not seen any messengers arrive from Grouchy for hours," muttered an artillery major.

"But the Prussians will take days to recover after Ligny," insisted a cavalry officer. "They scattered in all directions. And anyway, Grouchy was ordered to stay between the emperor and the Prussians, to be his shield. To get past him there would have had to have been a battle and we would have heard it."

"Well we will know in a minute," announced the major, who nodded his head towards the emperor. "He is talking to General Bernard who has ridden out to see for himself."

I had been about to press on to find Ney, but at this I decided to linger a moment. In the very unlikely event that the new arrivals were Prussians, it would cast an entirely different light on things and it would be information that Ney would need to know.

Bernard, who had been leaning over the emperor's table and pointing out positions on the map, now straightened up and saluted his emperor. Without even a glance at the watching staff officers, he strode away towards where a cavalry trooper was holding the reigns of a dozen horses. The emperor sat for over a minute, staring at his map, and occasionally he would look up and survey a particular part of the field. An air of suspense grew in all of us watching, especially when he picked up his glass to focus on the growing columns of troops on the horizon. At length he gestured to a valet, who rushed forward and gripped an arm to help the emperor get to his feet. Napoleon winced in pain as he did so and slowly turned to face his staff. There was a hushed silence now and an almost imperceptible leaning forward, as in the public gallery of a courtroom when the verdict is about to be announced. Bonaparte watched us for a moment, his face expressionless. Then he forced a smile through the pain. "It is Grouchy," he announced.

There were shouts of delight and congratulation, for this meant that the battle was won and for the time being France was safe. I confess that I felt a sense of relief myself, for this also meant that the killing would stop and my old comrades would soon be marching, somewhat hurriedly, to Antwerp.

Napoleon held up his hand for silence and then pushed it back inside his waistcoat to massage his stomach. "Gentlemen, we do not need to wait for Grouchy to end this battle. We cannot have him thinking he has rescued his emperor." He smiled at his officers and they grinned and nudged each other in delight. Now any uncertainty had gone, their confidence had soared and most looked gleeful at the prospect of further action. That was not a reaction I shared, and I began to wonder if my 'recovery' from wounds had been premature. I needed to find an excuse to escape this gathering. "In a short while—" the emperor continued before being interrupted by a new mud-splattered courier, who reined his horse up hard from the direction of Hougoumont. Napoleon looked up, "Has the château fallen?"

"No sire," gasped the courier, who looked uncomfortably aware that he was now the focus of attention of both his emperor and almost the entire general staff. "Scouts on our left flank report that the allies are falling back. Thousands of them are retreating into the trees."

"They must have seen Grouchy," called a voice, which was the obvious conclusion. But if anything, Napoleon looked surprised at this development.

"You are sure that thousands of them are pulling back?" he queried.

"So the scouts report, sire," confirmed the messenger.

"Well then, I had better send new orders to Marshal Ney."

"I'll take them, sire." Like a fool I spoke up. Several officers there knew I was on Ney's staff and so they would have expected me to volunteer, but in that moment I actually thought it would take me away from danger. I could also take my sweet time delivering it to give the allies more time to escape. I was not going to help any *coup de grâce* on their collapsing line. Then I realised that I had no idea where to take the message. "Where is the marshal, sire? I have just come back from having my wounds treated." I gestured at my horse-blood stained clothes.

Napoleon gave me a look of genuine concern. "Ah, Colonel Moreau, I trust you are fit for the duty? The marshal is on our right with the cavalry." He gave me a look of close inspection before continuing. "Whatever you did to earn my attention before, if it was a wrong, you have righted it. The blood-stained ribbon on your Legion of Honour is far nobler than a pristine new one."

"Thank you, sire," I replied while unconsciously straightening the little white cross I wore on the ribbon around my neck. His eyes were boring into me as though he could see my thoughts. I knew I must be shifting awkwardly under his inspection, while I wished I had kept my damn trap shut.

"Did you have a moustache before?" he enquired and I felt the sweat break out on my brow. I had to distract him and close off this enquiry or he would remember where he had seen me and who I was with.

"No sire. But I had a brother who people say looked very like me. You may have met him, but he drowned at sea before he could mention it."

"Drowned at sea," the emperor repeated, his eyes closed and his brow frowned in concentration. "No, it wasn't a drowning."

The human mind is an awesome instrument, a tangled forest of memories, but sometimes it takes just a small spark of light to illuminate a whole panorama. I cursed myself for a purblind fool: why

291

had I mentioned drowning or anything nautical? I already knew that the emperor's memory was exceptional and now it was hard at work, burrowing away for that nugget he sought. When we had met at the Viennese embassy reception thirteen years before, we had talked about me being one of the few survivors of a naval battle. At that moment I knew exactly where his memory was going to take him and I was already edging back through the crowd as the emperor gave a cry of triumph.

"It was a ship wreck, he survived a ship wreck." The emperor still had his eyes closed but others were glaring curiously at me as I stepped away with Napoleon still considering my suggestion. "Where was it now?" he was musing. "No, not a French ship... Spanish, yes Spanish, one of their big ships in a battle with the British." I was pushing through the crowd now, for it could only be a second or two before he remembered I had been with Britain's spymaster. A hand tried to grab me but I shook it off, while another man cried out for me to stop. I was free of them and just turning to run for the horses when the emperor's voice called out, "Wickham, he was with Wickham!"

Half a dozen bounds and I had torn some reins from the hand of a startled trooper and swung up into the saddle. I glanced back; the emperor was standing there staring at me open-mouthed, as though his rational mind was struggling to believe what his memory was telling him. The rest just stared, either in anger at my rudeness or surprise. Probably none of them had the first clue who Wickham was. I did not wait for them to recover, but just pushed my heels back and galloped away.

"Arrest that man," the emperor roared after me. "He is a British spy!"

Chapter 38

The problem with a panic-stricken flight – and I should know as I have had more than a few in my inglorious career – is that you rarely know where you are going. My first thought had simply been to get away from the emperor. I had no further plan than that. When I looked over my shoulder again as I rode away, I saw an officer of his Imperial Guard running towards the horses and gesturing for some troopers to join him. I had to get away – and fast.

My mind raced through the available options: all were bleak. If I stayed in French-held territory I was bound to be arrested and, after an unpleasant interrogation, executed. Even if I managed to escape my pursuers, I would become the most wanted man in the empire within hours. If the emperor's people did not catch me, Fouché's would, and he would want me silenced too. On the other hand, if I rode for the allied lines, then the emperor would have every gun in the grand battery trying to blow me to pieces all the way across the valley. If by some miracle I survived that, then I still might be captured as Grouchy closed in on the allied rear. I was trapped. I glanced back again to see the Imperial Guard officer and four troopers coming after me, but only at the trot. The officer was pointing at me and laughing at something said by one of the cavalrymen. They knew they did not have to rush. They preferred to keep their horses fresh, for they could see as well as I that I had nowhere to go.

As I galloped on, I stared back at the allied ridge; I still preferred my chances on the allied side of the valley. There would be all manner of chaos to hide amongst during the retreat. If only I could find a way of getting across safely. Then I saw the French cavalry formed up ahead with Marshal Ney at their front and an idea began to grow.

The marshal had been studying Grouchy's men through his glass but put it down irritably when I reined in beside him. "Moreau, where the devil have you been? Oh…" He paused as he noticed my blood-stained chest. "Have you been wounded?"

"No, I am fine, sir." I gestured to the dark columns on the horizon that he had been watching. "The emperor has announced that they are

Grouchy and his men. He has also received reports from the left flank that the British are pulling back into the trees behind their line. Can I suggest, sir, that we send a squadron of cavalry to confirm the British are retreating? I would be honoured to lead it." It was, I thought, a masterstroke of a suggestion. The grand battery could hardly fire on a whole squadron of their own horsemen just to kill one man. Once I was up on that allied ridge I could escape my surprised comrades and ride for the trees to join the chaos of the British withdrawal.

"He has announced that those men are Grouchy's?" Ney queried. "Has he spoken to General Bernard?"

"Yes sir. That was how he found out it was Grouchy." I glanced back over my shoulder. My pursuers, sensing some mischief was now afoot, had increased their pace to a canter. In a minute they would be up to me. I turned back to Ney, who seemed lost in his thoughts, staring back to Grouchy's men and then along the ridge in the direction of the emperor's headquarters. I had no more time; I had to sting him into making a decision. "Sir," I whispered so only he could hear. "You don't want the emperor accusing you of letting the British escape a second time."

Ney's head snapped round at me and a look of indignation crossed his features. "How dare you…" he began. But then he must have mistaken the look of terror on my face for one of extreme concern. He had one final glance in the emperor's direction and took a deep breath. "We should finish this battle quickly," he announced. "We will do as you suggest, but with more horsemen."

At that very moment I heard a distant shout of, "Arrest that man," but it was too late, for already Ney was turning to the colonel of the nearest regiment of cuirassiers and ordering his men to advance in column into the valley. I did not hesitate to push my horse into the middle of their ranks, while shouting that the marshal had ordered me to join them. There were five hundred of the elite armoured horsemen in that first regiment. Some looked surprised at having a blood-spattered infantry colonel force his way amongst them, but reluctantly they made way. We were advancing at the trot – the more experienced French were not making the same mistake as the British cavalry; their horses would be fresh for that final charge up the slope. Unfortunately for me, that gave the Imperial Guard officer the chance to catch up. I risked a final look back. Amongst my steel-clad comrades, I stood out like a boil on a buttock, but equally, I was near impossible to reach unless the column stopped moving.

I saw the Guards officer pointing at me and shouting to Ney but he was paying no attention. Instead, he was having an altercation with the general commanding the cuirassiers, who was probably objecting to Ney giving them orders without informing him. With all the jingling of harnesses and continuing cannonade, I could not hear what was said, but Ney was losing his temper and pointing to the allied line. Then I was past them and out of sight, shielded in the armoured ranks. The mist of gun smoke began to close in around us as we descended into the valley and at last I began to relax a little.

Against the odds my plan had worked. I had escaped arrest, at least for now. But then I began to consider the price. A squadron of cuirassiers among a retreating enemy was bad enough, but a whole regiment could be devastating. I had seen the carnage a regiment of these elite cavalry had created during the earlier attack. I vividly remembered them carrying away at least one colour from a destroyed British regiment, not to mention the poor bastards they had caught in line at Quatre Bras.

We wheeled left once we were in the valley to ride along the hillside below the grand battery. The guns were firing shells across the allied ridge as fast as they ever had. They must have seen the horsemen and guessed where we were going. If there were any allied troops still on the ridge they were getting a pasting. The noise was deafening; you could feel the thuds as much in your chest as in your ears and any conversation was impossible.

Several of my new comrades were glancing at me suspiciously; perhaps some had heard the calls for my arrest. Certainly a man in the rank ahead was nudging the riders either side to point out that they now had a colonel riding behind. We crossed the road that ran through the middle of the battleground. Ney was planning to charge up the ridge on the British right as that was where the men had been seen fleeing. The sound of gunfire diminished slightly as we left the battery behind and the man next to me reached out and tugged on my sleeve.

"Is it right," he shouted, "that you told the marshal that the men on the horizon are Grouchy's command?"

"Yes," I admitted. "The emperor has just announced it."

The rider nodded and passed the confirmation along the line to his mates. Then he turned to me with another enquiry. "So why did that Imperial Guard officer want to arrest you?" I might have the uniform of a colonel but I had pushed my way through to ride among their ranks like a common trooper and they knew something was not right. I could have told him to mind his own business and was on the cusp of doing just that, when I noticed a crest on the saddle of the horse I had stolen. I grinned and pointed at it.

"I borrowed the wrong horse." The man looked and laughed. It was an imperial eagle; there was another on the saddle cloth, showing that the mount's original owner had been in the Guard. "I could not find my horse," I explained. "And the emperor wanted me to rush with the information to the marshal."

"Aye, they can be arrogant bastards sometimes," agreed the trooper. "They take what they want from others, but don't like it when someone does it to them." We rode in silence for a while. Well, when I say silence, there was still an artillery barrage behind firing shells and balls over us towards the enemy and a group of troopers behind me were singing a revolutionary song; but there was no conversation along my rank. The smoke was thinning now as we got further from the battery. While the steel breastplates were hard to spot in the mist, the black horses and horsehair plumes on the helmets of my comrades were not. Staring into the distance, I saw activity up ahead around the château of Hougoumont. The British gunners had seen our approach and as they were out in the valley, they were busy harnessing up and making a run for it. I did not doubt that British gunners on the ridge had spotted us too, but they would wait until we were closer before opening fire or they would be destroyed first by the grand battery.

I looked back over my left shoulder and was surprised to see another column of armoured horsemen coming up alongside. I pointed them out to the man I had been talking to.

"Are those men part of this regiment?"

He stared across and then grinned. "No," he replied simply and then he pointed to another officer riding out at their head. It was the man I had seen Ney arguing with earlier. "That is General Milhaud, commander of our corps. He must be bringing the rest of our cuirassiers."

"How many cuirassiers are there?" I asked with a growing sense of foreboding.

"We must have at least two thousand five hundred."

I repeated the number feeling slightly sick. I *might* have saved my own precious skin but in doing so I had virtually assured the destruction of the entire allied army. But then I stood up in my stirrups to see the rest of this force and discovered that the situation was even worse. The cuirassiers were coming in three columns but beyond them, I could see coming out of the gun smoke more horsemen, including hussars and lancers with their little pennon flags flapping at their lance points. Then, looking further down the French ridge I saw yet more horsemen coming to join the charge, thousands of them. Whether they had been ordered to join or just came of their own accord it was hard to say, for the dream of every cavalryman on earth is to find himself riding among broken infantry; when he can wield the power of life and death with virtual impunity.

I felt physically ill at the thought of what I had started. There must have been well over five thousand horsemen, of every description, preparing to charge the allied ridge. Nothing could withstand that. The allied army would be annihilated just because I was determined to live. I will be honest with you and say that there are not many things that I would not sacrifice to save myself. It is easy to be noble from a distance, but when the prospect of torture and a firing squad is very real, things are different, at least for me. But it was a heavy price. I tried to reassure myself that at least no one would know that I had started it and Ney or Bonaparte could have thought of it without my help, but it did not ease my conscience greatly.

"We should try to take as many prisoners as possible," I shouted at my riding companion. "It will help the emperor agree a peace with the allies."

"Then they'd better drop their weapons smartly," he laughed and loosened his sword in its scabbard. "My steel wants to taste blood today."

It took several minutes for the vast body of horsemen to form up. I watched as the allied gunners around Hougoumont made their escape, guns and caissons bouncing up in the air over ruts as they whipped their horses into the gallop. I thought that they would form up again behind the ridge, but heard later that they did not stop until they were halfway to Brussels. Some allied gunners did make their presence felt, though, for we were a target so large that they would struggle to miss. Most allied guns stayed behind the ridge firing over the crest, but one did show itself on top of the ridge and was soon under heavy fire from French guns.

A line was formed from roughly south of La Haye Sainte all the way to the edge of the trees around Hougoumont. This vast space was filled with rank after rank of horsemen. It was a riot of colour and uniforms; bugles were sounding, the occasional shell was exploding and horses and men were calling out in their excitement. I dare say none had been in a charge as big as this. I had certainly seen nothing this size before and I imagined that just over the ridge the allies were running pell-mell into the trees in panic to get out of its way. I just hoped that they had enough time, for at least it would be difficult for horsemen to pursue infantry into a forest. As soon as I got the chance I would be tearing off my uniform coat and doing my very best to disappear into the woodland too.

Then the bugles called the advance and the whole mass began to move forward. We went at the walk at first. My regiment, being the first to enter the valley was in the front rank at the extreme right of the formation. We were soon going through the boggy valley floor but many of the crops in this part of the field had not yet been trampled and it was not too heavy going, at least for the first few ranks of horses. There were more allied guns firing directly from the ridge now and I heard a horse scream a whinny of pain from further along the line as it was hit and shouts as other men moved around the flailing animal. Then men began to fire on us from La Haye Sainte farm. There were riflemen there, picking off horsemen at the end of the line. Those nearest edged their horses away, compacting us so that my legs often touched those of my companions on either side or their horses. Some claimed later that their horses were lifted off the field in the crush, but mine stayed grounded.

More guns fired from the allied ridge and while they must have done some damage, I did not see it. We were well up the far side now and bugles called and the pace increased again. The men on either side drew their long heavy swords and I tugged furiously on mine. It had got stuck in the scabbard and I nearly elbowed the rider next to me in the face as I finally got it free. I did not intend to use it, but had learned from long experience that it is always useful to have a weapon handy. The gunners ahead were running from their artillery pieces now. I had thought that they had been brave in putting up a desperate rear-guard action as it was certain that they would be ridden down on the other side of the ridge. We were less than a hundred yards from the crest and a new bugle call rang out, the unmistakable demand for the charge.

My mount sprang forward with the herd around us with little prompting from me. Swords were extended forward and men roared their challenges as with a final bound we cleared the road that ran along the ridge top and launched ourselves down the other side. As we crested the rise my eyes were set to the far horizon as that was where I expected to see the fleeing allied army. There were indeed men going into the woods, hundreds, possibly a thousand or two, but then my attention was taken by something far closer, as all hell broke loose.

Chapter 39

There have been a few times in my life when I have been really taken aback by an unexpected sight. A man-eating tiger appearing while I was taking a piss, a certain duke waiting for me in his daughter's boudoir with a horsewhip and a Spanish regiment running in terror from a horse's flatulence to name but a few. But nothing topped what greeted my eyes as my horse galloped over that ridge top. Instead of a broken army in defeat, the ground was covered by a patchwork of allied regiments, all formed up into square ready to receive cavalry.

I did not know whether to cry with relief that I was not responsible for the destruction of the allied army; shriek with terror at the thought of riding the gauntlet between their bayonet-bristling ranks; or put my heels back, my head down and pray as I galloped through. In the event, I suspect I did all three.

I was not the only one to be surprised, though, for there were shouts and yells from those around me. There was no thought of stopping the attack – we couldn't even if we wanted to, for there were ranks of horsemen sweeping up the slope behind us. We had to press on. As I glanced at the two nearest squares, however, they looked damn shaky. The front-facing ranks of both were trying to edge back, the expressions of the men horrified at the image of armoured death bearing down on them. The cuirassiers beat their metal chestplates with their sword hilts and roared their challenges to further intimidate the poor devils.

I knew it would only take one square to break to create carnage, for the frightened men would fight and claw their way into the intact squares around them and the armoured horsemen would follow through any gap created. Once cavalry were inside a square it was invariably doomed and so the process of running survivors breaking other squares would continue. The nearest square was Dutch and the whole formation was trying to march backwards out of the way. Men going forwards were faster than those retreating backwards and already gaps were opening up in the sides. Beyond them was a square of British troops where the men in the facing side were arching towards its centre and tussling with those trying to push them back forward. I found out later that some of those were the survivors of the Lincolnshire regiment who had been destroyed by cuirassiers two days earlier. So it was no wonder they were terrified at seeing the same cavalry charging towards them again.

It seemed only a matter of seconds before one or both of them would collapse into a huddle of frightened men and the troopers around me sensed it too. Then there were shouts of alarm and charging in on our right came a regiment of British cavalry. They hit the flank of my regiment and cuirassiers wheeled away to face this new threat, leaving the squares to the men coming up behind. The cuirassiers were heavier, armoured troopers but the British cavalry were on fresh, larger horses and within moments the air was ringing with the sound of steel on steel. I did not wait to see the outcome nor did I see if those two allied squares did break, although I heard conflicting accounts afterwards. Instead, as you would no doubt expect from your correspondent, I put my head down and made a run for it.

The allied squares had been arranged in a chequerboard formation to avoid them firing on each other, with plenty of space between the corners. I charged down the gap between the two wavering squares. I had no real sense of a plan, only to get away from the fighting. I wanted to get through the allied line and perhaps continue on to the forest as that would give me a head start in the rout when Grouchy and his men arrived on the scene. I would, of course, need to shed my French uniform along the way. At least a score of cuirassiers followed me as we galloped down the channel. A few muskets fired from either side but they did no damage; I could hear officers shouting at their men to hold their fire. They must have been able to see the huge numbers of horsemen coming over the top of the ridge behind us and were saving their volleys for when they could not miss.

There was a third square some two hundred yards ahead and they must have been less experienced, for swiftly the ranks disappeared behind a rolling ripple of flashes and gun smoke as some three hundred muskets shot their charges in our direction. The range was too long and I heard a couple of clangs as half-spent charges ricocheted off steel breastplates behind me. My mount stumbled a little and I saw that she had taken a ball in the shoulder, but it could not have been more than a flesh wound as she was still galloping as strongly as before. The long ranks in front of me were furiously reloading, but I would be past before they could fire again. The cuirassiers behind were yelling as we bore down on the men in front, but if they thought I was going to lead them to the square's destruction, well they were destined to be disappointed.

I was just judging whether turning left or right would take me past fewer squares, when more British cavalrymen came veering in from the right. They would soon be hopelessly outnumbered but before then they were determined to help defend the squares. They had been hidden by the musket smoke and I only just had time to get my sword up to parry a blow before some red-faced hussar was up alongside

"Take that, you blaggard!" he roared as he nearly broke my wrist when my blade blocked a huge swinging stroke

"Get off, you bloody fool, I am British," I yelled back at him through gritted teeth.

"What's that?" The man stared astonished at being spoken to in English and hesitated a moment before getting his blade up again. Instead of goggling at me, the poor fool should have been checking over his shoulder, for that was where the cuirassier who had been riding alongside me came up. His heavy blade was swinging long before the hussar could hope to recover and a moment later I was covered in a fresh spray of blood from the British trooper.

"Come on, Colonel, to the square," shouted my new armoured friend and he spurred his mount on towards the ranks that were still shoving ramrods down their weapons. The air was full of the noise of battle. Cuirassiers and British hussars were still shouting and clashing blades all around me, while now more volleys rang out from the squares as the French horsemen swarmed about them.

My erstwhile opponent was still sitting hunched in his saddle beside me, his sword dropped and a hand clasped over a deep wound in his side. He was staring at me as though still unable to comprehend what had happened. I had sworn to myself at the start of the day that I would not kill my countrymen, but I had left this one near defenceless. Staring about me I saw a gap open up in the melee and turned to ride through it. On impulse, I reached out and grabbed the bridle of the wounded British trooper and took him with me. A noble act of charity on my part? Perhaps, but I will be honest and say the fact he would serve as a shield against the nearest square, which, having now reloaded, was firing on all and sundry, also played a part in my thinking.

I rode through the gap to my left between the squares, releasing the hussar near the British troops where he would block the aim of those closest to me and then rode into the open space beyond. I looked around to get my bearings and saw that if anything I had jumped from the frying pan into the fire. It was a bloody nightmare. I was surrounded by danger and people trying to get me killed. On both my flanks were the sides of squares, loaded and ready to fire, although mercifully with their aim blocked or judging me too small a target. Further to my right, I saw more British cavalry, while to my left none other than Marshal Ney was leading the best part of a regiment of cuirassiers directly towards the space I was riding into. Ahead and still some distance off were two more squares of British infantry.

I swear to God that Ney was actually roaring with laughter as he went past. I think battle was a drug to him and while he had been robbed of an easy victory by the squares, he knew that if he could break just one, he would have a triumph that would be remembered for generations.

"Come on, Moreau," he shouted when he saw me. "Let's get at them." He angled his horse to ride alongside mine, which was the last thing I wanted. I had hoped to slip away to the back of the battle but now I had more cuirassiers coming up on my other side as we formed a phalanx aimed directly at the side of one of the largest squares.

"Come on, ride straight at them," yelled Ney, standing now in his stirrups and waving his sword above his head. His plumed hat had long gone, but his chest was adorned with decorations and gold braid. It was obvious he was a very senior officer in the front row and I knew that many of the muskets ahead would be aiming for the marshal. A lot would miss, which was very bad news for the poor fools like me riding alongside him. I was now properly hemmed in; we were riding knee to knee, with another rank of men directly behind. I could not turn or slow down; I was trapped in this charge until it smashed into the rows of men in red ahead.

My mind was half frozen in terror although I have a vague recollection of muttering the Lord's Prayer as my horse thundered along to what I was sure would be my death. Everyone knows that if a square stands steady it will defeat cavalry. Equally, anyone who knew him would also know that Marshal Ney does not lack courage to see a charge home.

You can sense when some squares are likely to break, as I had with the first two I saw on coming over the crest. I stared in vain for any sign that the one ahead would do the decent thing and fall apart, but it looked rock steady. Not a gun fired as we closed in. Two hundred yards, one hundred and fifty, one hundred, still the guns were silent with their bayonets glistening in the sunshine. We were at less than eighty yards away when I finally heard the shouts for the rear rank to fire above the drumming of the horse's hooves. *The bravest of the brave* stood in his stirrups again roaring a final challenge. In contrast, I crouched down against my horse's neck, wondering if its chestnut hide would be my last vision on earth.

I flinched with my eyes tight shut as I heard the crash of the volley. Then I felt its impact. My horse screamed and reared up as though it had been struck by a gate. I had been trapped by a fallen horse before and was already tugging my boots from the stirrups. My mount was foundering, its back legs collapsing, and I looked for space to roll away but the horses on both sides had been hit too and were already crashing to the ground in a welter of flailing hooves. In the end I had no choice as Ney fell against me and grabbed hold of my arm and we both tumbled into the gap between our falling horses.

"Christ on a stick," I swore with relief to find myself still alive and unhurt while I ducked the flailing hoof from my dying horse. Something soft had broken my fall and as it grunted with discomfort I realised that I was sprawled across a marshal of France. "Are you hit, sir?" I asked starting to get up.

"No, just winded... Get down, you fool." Ney reached up and pulled me back down towards him. He was just in time, for inches over my head went the steel-shod hooves of another horse as the second line of cuirassiers continued the attack. There was the crash of a further volley and a moment later a third rider crashed down beside us. He gave a groan as he landed on my horse's legs but two musket ball holes in his breastplate showed he was unlikely to get up again. I raised my head more gingerly now and saw that the next rank of cuirassiers was shearing off to the left. There was now an impenetrable pile of dead and wounded men and horses blocking their attack. I rolled off the marshal and gave a sigh of relief. Ney, though, was in no mood for resting.

"Come on, Moreau, we need to get some loose horses and renew the attack." He was already up on his feet, not even sparing a glance at the ranks of armed men behind him as he pointed to a cuirassier galloping past. "You there, grab that horse and bring it to me." With that he was off, waving an acknowledgement to my shout that I would be right with him.

Of course I did not move a muscle to go to his aid, for it had occurred to me that the inside of the robust British square might well be the safest place for Flashy. I would be safe from arrest by Napoleon and could warn them of Grouchy's army coming down on their flank. A square could retreat safely to the woods behind the allied position and then conduct a fighting withdrawal to disembark at Antwerp. The French would probably let most of them go and concentrate on taking Brussels and securing the rest of the country. The tricky bit would be getting inside the square without getting my head blown off by one side or the other.

For a while I stayed crouched down beside Ney's dead horse. Hundreds more French cavalry of every description galloped past the square and while they did not attempt another attack on my side of it, I heard charges going in against the other faces and the answering volleys. Shouted orders to reload after every attack confirmed that the square still stood. Across the slope the French cavalry washed around the other squares like waves against the rocks, and made as much progress in destroying them. Eventually, though, the horsemen began to give up, disappearing back over the crest like a receding tide.

Chapter 40

The battlefield grew eerily quiet. No guns were firing; men stood silently in their ranks waiting to see what would happen next and the only sound I heard was the pained gasping of a wounded cuirassier nearby. It was time to make my presence known. I tore off my French uniform coat. I had lost my shako helmet in the charge – for all I know it could have been shot off my head. My white shirt and trousers were blood stained but did not mark me out as a Frenchman. I gingerly put my head up above the flanks of the horse. The square was fifty yards off, its men standing at rest but vigilant and one immediately pointed me out to his comrades.

"Don't shoot," I shouted. "I am a British officer."

"I did not see any British cavalry amongst that lot, sir," called out a voice and several others added their agreement

"It will be another of those frogs claiming he is a royalist now he has been licked," shouted another.

"No, I am British," I repeated. "I am Major Thomas Flashman and General Wellington sent me to spy on the French. If you take me to him he will confirm it. I have urgent news for the general."

"A Major Flashman?" queried a plummy voice. "I happen to be familiar with most officers under the general's command and I certainly do not recall your unusual name."

I stood up. There was little point in hiding now that I had announced myself and I was fairly sure I would not be shot on sight. Arrested, perhaps, if I could not convince this blockhead of an officer who seemed to be taking charge of the situation, but not shot. "Then I can tell, sir," I started feeling an anger build in me, "that you did not serve at Assaye, Talavera, Busaco, Torres Vedras, Albuera and Badajoz; as the men who had fought in those campaigns would know me."

"I say," retorted the plummy voice indignantly. "I fought in Spain for two years." I could see the man now, a red-faced captain who had pushed his way into the rear rank to look at me. He was about to say something else but someone behind the ranks must have tugged on his sleeve for he turned irritably to the new arrival and asked, "What is it?"

"Beg pardon, sir," came a new voice, "but I am recognisant of this officer."

I knew of only one man who could mangle the English language in such a manner. "Sergeant Evans?" I asked.

"The very same, sir," replied a beaming Evans as he replaced another man in the rear rank. "He was my company captain at Albuera, sir," Evans explained to the plummy officer standing beside him. Then before the officer could object any further Evans added, "The colonel knows him well too, sir."

"Well in that case," said the officer huffily, "you can advance and join us, sir."

I stepped through the pile of dead men and horses which was all that was left of the earlier attack. As I walked up to the square I glanced down the ranks. They were not my old regiment, the Buffs, but my battalion had been largely destroyed at Albuera and the survivors distributed to other units. These men looked steady enough; some stared at me with curiosity while others were looking at the broken men and animals in front of them and doubtless wondering what loot lay just out of their reach. I turned and looked across the slope behind the British ridge. Smoke from volleys had drifted away and it was my first opportunity to take a leisurely view of the scene. There must have been at least a dozen infantry squares visible, perhaps twenty thousand men, scattered over an area of half a mile. The only cavalry I could see now were a few British survivors of the encounter with the French. I returned my attention to the captain. "If you have half the experience you claim, you should have some men out retrieving the wounded and arranging the dead into a rampart to help defend the square."

"But the cavalry have gone," objected the captain. He was going to say more but I held up my hand to silence him and then spoke to him slowly as though to a dim-witted child.

"The gentleman you saw me ride in with, the one with all the medals on his chest who was yelling like a lunatic, that was Marshal

Ney." There was a murmur along the ranks at this for Ney's fame had spread in the British army too. "While your men killed his horse," I continued, "Ney is unhurt. He is not going to give up after one charge, he will be back. So get those dead horses wedged on their backs with their legs up in the air, so that they make a greater obstacle to the next charge."

"Order the front rank forward, Sergeant," agreed the captain reluctantly. "But they are to return immediately should the French cavalry reappear." Evans went forward with the men and I remembered that I had more urgent business to conduct.

"Now, I really should meet your colonel and then report to Wellington." But before I could say more we were interrupted by an angry shout and another man was pulled away from the rear rank as a new officer appeared.

"What the deuce is going on? Cummings, who gave you permission to break ranks and— Good God is that you, Flashman? What the devil are you doing here?" It was Colborne, my old brigade commander at Albuera, but I barely recognised him. He was thirty-seven then, four years older than me, but he looked like there was a decade difference. His features were drawn and haggard, but they brightened into a grin when he realised who I was.

The plummy officer I now knew as Cummings answered for me, still with a note of indignation in his voice. "He charged in with the French, sir!"

"I don't doubt it," laughed Colborne, "he often did things his own way as I recall. What is that hanging around your neck?"

I reached up and felt the familiar white enamel cross. I had forgotten it was there but I was glad I had not lost it. "That," I said grinning, "is my Legion of Honour medal, awarded at the personal request of Napoleon."

Colborne roared with laughter again. "I remember you going behind their lines before Busaco, but you seem to have excelled yourself this time. I take it you have news for Wellington?"

"Yes, we should talk privately." I tried to keep my face neutral to avoid alarming those around us. Colborne nodded and then stepped forward out of the square and led me a score of paces on so that we could not be overheard. "There are columns of men coming from the east that will arrive behind the allied left flank," I told him.

"Yes, we have seen them," answered Colborne sounding unconcerned.

"It is Marshal Grouchy with thirty thousand men and a hundred guns," I whispered urgently. "Wellington has to pull the allied line back or it will be outflanked and trapped."

Instead of appearing alarmed at the news Colborne just smiled. "I don't know who told you that. Those men are at least forty thousand Prussians coming to our aid."

"No, they can't be. The Prussian army has been on the run since Ligny and I have just heard the emperor himself announce to his generals that the distant columns are Grouchy and his command."

Colborne put a hand on my shoulder and looked me firmly in the eye. "Wellington has told me that they are Prussians. I know that his liaison officers have been in contact with the Prussians since yesterday. So, Thomas, you know them both well. Who are you going to believe – Wellington or Napoleon?"

Well, that brought me up short and I took a moment to seriously consider the question. I knew that Wellington had misrepresented his ambitions when in India and I harboured dark suspicions that he had slept with my wife. He could be a haughty devil who often kept his cards close to his chest, but I could not see how describing a French force as Prussians would benefit him here. He was fighting a defensive battle, just looking to survive on the ridge. To mislead his army could only have disastrous consequences.

On the other hand, I thought about all the lies Napoleon had told when he had first landed in France. He had far fewer scruples and misleading his army would raise their morale for a final assault, so that the British would be beaten before the Prussians could intervene. Then other things fell into place too. Ney had asked if Napoleon had spoken to General Bernard when I told him that the distant force was Grouchy. He must have spoken to Bernard before the emperor and knew that Napoleon was lying. That was why he had launched the cavalry without infantry support. He knew that they had to win the battle without delay.

"Good God," I breathed as I realised the implications. For this was no longer just a battle of survival for the allies: if we could hold out until the Prussians arrived, the French could be beaten.

Chapter 41

It is impossible to adequately describe the horror, tension and indeed, at times, the absurdity of the next two and a half hours in a few paragraphs. For that is how long we waited for the next significant event in that momentous day. Two and a half hours is the time it would take you to walk six or seven miles. Now instead of walking all that while, imagine yourself packed with others tightly in a square and under bombardment by French artillery and attack by their cavalry. Often the guns were firing blind and so death was an entirely random affair. A man running alone with a message could be torn to pieces just as easily as a soldier in the front rank of a square. Sometimes an explosive shell would bury itself in soft earth and merely shower those standing nearby with mud. On the other hand, a Highlander regiment near us had seventeen men killed or injured by a single ball that slashed its way across a corner of their square.

This was the time when the allied army was almost destroyed. Not in a big attack, but whittled away in little groups, its flesh and its nerves frayed to breaking point. Previously during French bombardments, most of the men had been able to lie down and stay spread out in line. But that was impossible now with French horsemen just below the crest of the ridge. Not that we minded French cavalry any more, in fact men cheered their arrival and even goaded them to stay longer. For when the cuirassiers and others rode amongst us we knew that for a short while the guns would stop. And the cavalry did keep coming, five, six maybe seven times, I lost count; and each time the outcome was the same. They would charge, we would fire a volley and they would peel away, leaving a few dead and wounded. I remember seeing Ney again at one point; he was easily recognisable with his gold braid and red hair. He was on foot, presumably having lost another horse from under him, and beating an abandoned British cannon with his sword blade in frustration as another charge failed.

The final charges were almost a farce as by then we were running short of ammunition and so orders were given to fire only if the cavalry closed within thirty yards, point-blank range for a musket.

Weary horsemen had long since learned that to charge was invariably fatal and pointless. So thousands of French cavalry galloped in virtual silence around a dozen allied squares, searching in vain for a sign of weakness.

Colborne commanded the largest infantry battalion in the allied line. The 52nd regiment with over a thousand officers and men, formed a tempting target for horsemen and gunners alike. They had been in the reserve for the first part of the battle and so had missed the worst of the morning's bombardment, but they were getting more than their fair share now. Colborne had them divide up into two smaller squares, to match many of those around us. Then, like two giant red crabs, the squares moved slowly across the battlefield until they were behind the ridge above the château of Hougoumont. It had been a hazardous business, stopping for cavalry charges and moving around areas that French gunners favoured with shot.

Colborne had asked me if I still wanted to report to Wellington but I did not think that there was a lot of point. The news I thought I had was false and he might still be blaming me for my assurance that the French would not attack until July. What I really wanted to do was run for the distant woods, out of range of the French guns and beyond their cavalry charges, but I did not dare. My return to the British ranks had hardly been discrete and now Sergeant Evans was loudly regaling his comrades with some of my earlier exploits.

My absence would be noted and I would be ruined if it was discovered that I had abandoned the army without good cause. Colborne was also another of those brave and capable men who was deluded into thinking that I was cut from the same cloth. Like Cochrane and Campbell before him, he viewed me as a 'brother in arms' and as with the others, I took a perverse pride in having his respect. So while every fibre of my being was urging me to run, I forced myself to stand tall and act as cool as be-damned. Mind you, even I nearly lost my nerve when Colborne told me where we were going.

"Wellington wants us over on the forward slope of the ridge near the sunken road that leads down to the château. We are to protect the supply line to Hougoumont that runs down that track."

How I have kept my sanity in this kind of situation is beyond me. For I desperately wanted to shake him by the lapels and scream that this was madness and that in full view of the French guns we would all be cut to pieces. It would have done no good, of course, and cost me my hard won reputation. No, instead a gentleman is expected to remain unconcerned, whatever the danger. So I took a deep breath to steady myself, swatted away a couple of flies exploring the blood on my shirt and mentioned casually, "Their guns will give us a hot time of it."

"Yes, it is likely to be vexing," agreed Colborne with a monumental level of understatement. "But we must keep the line open."

If there had been anything left in my guts for my nerves to churn I would have been making butter as we came over the top of the allied ridge. My mouth was dry and I had my hands clenched together to stop them shaking. The grand battery was just half a mile away and I imagined every single gun adjusting its aim in our direction, with Napoleon offering a hatful of gold to anyone who could blow my head off.

It was my first view of Hougoumont, such as you could see it through the trees and smoke. The fighting had been continuous there since eleven that morning and it looked like several of the buildings were on fire. Between us and the château, more cuirassiers milled about at the valley bottom along with some French skirmishers. One of the 52nd's squares went to the left and stopped next to a swathe of tall rye that had not yet been flattened during the course of the battle. It would obscure their exact position from the guns but it would not stop a shell. The other square veered right towards the sunken road. There was a slight rise in the ground that gave it some protection and so I chose to join that one.

I have already described the carnage that results from artillery shelling infantry forced to remain in square and so I shall not dwell too long on it here. It had been a gruesome affair when I had watched it at

314

Quatre Bras with the gunners, but at the receiving end, it was infinitely worse. In the event, only a few guns switched their aim to us but it was enough. There was a constant rumble of gunfire and so you could not tell when guns were firing at you. Instead, with no warning at all, a man standing near you would just be plucked away by an unseen hand and smashed to bloody ruin. It was the randomness of it that left you twitching in barely concealed terror. Most of the guns were still firing on the troops over the ridge, so things were no safer there either. Only the wounded, who were carried away to a ditch by the sunken road, had any degree of safety.

One advantage of being on the forward slope was that we had a good view of the French attack on La Haye Sainte. Even someone as stubborn as Ney had finally realised that the cavalry charges were unlikely to succeed and so he had switched his attention to the farm. That was why most of the French guns had remained focussed on the British centre, around La Haye Sainte, rather than on the only British troops they could see. We watched the huge attack columns form up on the French side of the valley and march across up the British slope. The farm itself lay in a dip a quarter of a mile away so we could not see it, but we heard the increase in musketry and then distant cheers. No French were seen running back into the valley and as French guns were moved forward towards the farm, our suspicions were confirmed that it had fallen. Napoleon's men now had a strong bastion right in front of the centre of the British line.

Our only hope now was the swift arrival of the Prussians, but there was no sign of the lazy sausage-eating bastards.

"I don't understand it," I told Colborne as we scanned the eastern horizon in vain for any sign of our allies. "It was just after three this afternoon when I saw columns of troops coming over the horizon. They should have been here ages ago."

Colborne looked at his watch. "It is just after six. Perhaps Grouchy did catch up with them or Napoleon sent some other troops to block their approach."

"Or they stopped for lunch," I offered, "or simply ran away after the pasting they got the other day. Some of their volunteer regiments would not have relished marching to the sound of the guns a second time."

"No, no I can't believe that," insisted Colborne. "They will come." He paused as he considered the alternative and added quietly, "They have to, or we are done for."

Well, that is just the kind of comforting reassurance from a commanding officer you don't need. I have slid out on some pretty desperate last stands in my time and if anyone thinks that they are getting Flashy fighting to the last man, well they are in for a disappointment. It was obvious that the British could not hold out for much longer now. Even as we watched, more French skirmishers were pushing forward up towards La Haye Sainte. The battle had already been raging for seven hours and there were still at least another three hours of daylight. Without help we could not survive that long and when the line finally broke it would be every man for himself.

I had no intention of waiting that long. By then the roads and tracks would be jammed with men, guns and horses trying to escape, with harrying French cavalry adding to the panic. I planned to get a head start as I had more to fear than most from recapture by the French. We were on the British right, which meant the western end of the line. I would need to travel west to reach the coast and so I began to study the terrain, looking for the best escape routes that would give me cover from the pursuing French. All I needed was some pretext I could use to run out on my comrades with a degree of respectability. After all, a few of them would escape and others would be returned as prisoners; I could not have them blackening my name.

Some eager missionary told me in Africa a while back that if a devout Christian seeks, the Good Lord will provide. Well, I was seeking then and he did indeed deliver the goods, although probably not in a way that the pious little Bible-thumper would have approved of. Dammit, even I would have preferred almost any other way.

A few moments before, Sergeant Evans had called out to a young ensign as a cannon ball rolled over the turf beside him. The lad had been putting his boot out to stop it, but Evans and I had both seen people lose their foot doing that. Such balls carry with them considerable force. Then as a messenger rode up with a note for Colborne there was another thud of a ball pitching close to the square. There had been so many that I no longer flinched. Men in the front ranks opposite the impact threw themselves out of the way, but the snapping sound of bones and yells of pain from behind me revealed that some had been less fortunate. I turned to see two men writhing on their backs, each with one leg a bloody ruin. One of them was Evans; he had been standing behind the first man hit and so had not seen the flight of the ball.

I rushed over to my old comrade. "Evans, are you all right? No, of course you are not, but don't worry we will get you sorted."

"Bit more than a scratch this time sir." Evans spoke calmly, gazing down at what was left of his limb in dazed disbelief. It was bleeding heavily and another soldier quickly passed a cord around his thigh as a tourniquet. I looked around for something to tighten the loop. There was nothing suitable on the ground but then I remembered the ramrod in my pistol.

"Here, use this," I said passing it to the soldier, who immediately started to twist the string. Evans gasped in pain as it bit into his flesh but at least it would stem the bleeding. I gazed down at my old friend, initially with compassion but then, guiltily, another thought occurred. This was the perfect opportunity to help me slip away from the army.

I turned back to Colborne. "If you don't mind I will stay with Evans for a while when he is taken down to the ditch with the other wounded. You may recall he looked after me when I was wounded at Albuera – I would just like to make sure he is comfortable."

"Yes of course," replied Colborne looking up from the note that had just been delivered to him. "But don't be too long, Flashman," he called waving the paper. "We have just been ordered to withdraw back over the ridge.

"No, I will come as soon as I can," I agreed realising that it would now be even easier to slip away. Once his wound was dressed as best as it could be in the circumstances, Evans was laid on his blanket and four soldiers, one at each corner, helped to carry him down to the ditch by the sunken road. I went with them and inwardly sighed with relief as we started down the reverse slope which gave us protection from the French bombardment. As I looked over my shoulder, Colborne had started moving his squares back up towards the crest of the allied ridge.

There were already at least twenty broken bodies lying by the side of the track to Hougoumont. Some were missing arms or legs; there were two with head wounds and others appeared to have been hit in the chest with musket balls or shell splinters. At least three were dead already and for several it looked like only a matter of time. A corporal, whose arm now ended at the elbow, was moving about getting water into a canteen from the small stream running at the bottom of the ditch and passing it to those that wanted it. The rest of them lay still, with just the odd gasp or whimper of pain to show that they were alive.

They lay Evans down at the end of the row and I sat down beside him. I noticed that his leg was still bleeding a little, but he had screamed with agony when they had tightened the tourniquet at the end and I did not have the heart to twist it any more. I just had to hope that the bleed would stop if he lay still.

"Would you like some water, sir?" The corporal had come up the little line and gestured at the blood from my earlier horse and the hussar, which was splashed all over my shirt. "Is it a bad wound, sir?" he added.

"What? No, no, it is nothing. I am just here to look after Evans." I took the flask, though, and offered it to the sergeant, who drank greedily. The man's eyes had glazed over and he seemed to be struggling to comprehend what had happened to him. In the past I had always been at a loss as to how to comfort the wounded, but it had got easier after I had experienced similar circumstances myself.

"I think that they have done for me this time, sir," he whispered hoarsely as the corporal scurried off to another man. "I am precipitate, sir."

I took some comfort he was well enough to indulge his bizarre lexicon and pulled my shirt open so that he could see the huge star-shaped exit wound I had received from the musket ball at Albuera. "Nonsense, man. You saw me survive this. If I can live after a hole

318

through my chest, you can get over losing a leg. You must have seen other men survive after losing a leg, there is no reason you cannot do the same." I squeezed his shoulder in encouragement. I knew from my own experience that the thing he wanted most at this moment, perhaps even more than a surgeon, was hope.

Evans did not look that reassured. "I have seen some live with one leg," he admitted, "and I have pitied them. For most it would have been better if they had died. What life can they have like that begging for coins? I have been a soldier all my life; I do not know any other trade to make a living."

I laughed at that and he looked at me in surprise. "Don't you worry about that," I told him. "If we get out of here I will give you a job."

"You can't, sir, I know you had to watch the coin when we were together before."

"Ah but since then my fortunes have changed." I smiled at him and for a moment I pictured in my mind Louisa, little Thomas, Berkeley House and the rolling, peaceful fields around my new home. "I'm married now, well, I was before too, but now I am properly married, a man of property and I am going to need a new steward. A one-legged one would suit me perfectly."

"Really, sir?" You could see that Evans desperately wanted to believe me, but he probably remembered when I had told people what they had wanted to hear in the past.

"I swear it. I have a beautiful house in Leicestershire and you will be its steward." I watched the tension ease out of his body and a tear began to well in his eye. I got up; he was a tough man and would not want me to see him cry. "Oh and don't think it is charity," I called back over my shoulder as I began to walk up the bank. "All those country bastards want to talk about is calves, crops and who has got the fattest pig. Having you there for a sensible conversation will be the only thing that will keep me sane."

319

Chapter 42

I was feeling quite pleased with myself as I got to the top of the slope. Doing an old friend a good turn is almost as enjoyable as dishing revenge to an old enemy. Of course, the way things were looking, Evans would have to survive a spell as a prisoner of war first, but at least he would have something to live for.

I wanted to take a last look out across the battlefield before I made a run for it, just in case the long-overdue Prussians had finally arrived. Corpses marked where the 52nd's squares had stood, but the living had disappeared over the ridge. French troops were still streaming up towards the farm of La Haye Sainte and the distant French batteries were continuing their bombardment. It was hard to see in the distance through the smoke but no French troops were moving to their right to meet a new Prussian threat on the eastern end of the allied line. I was just about to duck down again and make my way back towards the road when a movement to my right caught my eye. The château of Hougoumont was surrounded by smoke from French cannon, burning buildings and the continued fighting, but as I watched a huge dark shape was moving. A gust of wind suddenly revealed the front of a new French column that was aimed at the allied line halfway between where I stood and the farm. I crouched lower as I watched with a growing sense of unease. Normally such columns had their flanks guarded by cavalry and sure enough a few moments later a regiment of cuirassiers appeared – heading directly towards me.

I spun round and ran back towards the ditch. If the French broke through, and there was every chance that they would, then the cuirassiers would slaughter or capture anyone running between the allied line and the forest behind. There was no time for me to reach the safety of the trees; I just had to find somewhere else safe to hide until nightfall. It was only as I ran towards the pitiful line of broken bodies that the solution occurred.

"Cuirassiers are coming," I called out to the corporal. "Drop that flask and lie down, they won't kill wounded men."

"Are you sure?" croaked Evans. "Their Polish lancers weren't that choosey."

"Well we cannot fight them or outrun them," I replied while pulling a blood-soaked bandage off one of the corpses. "We might get robbed but I don't believe we will be murdered." I lay down beside Evans and draped the bloody cloth across my chest. He was deathly pale and some of his muscles had started to tremble. There was no doubt the cuirassiers would see he was badly injured, but if they found out I wasn't wounded at all then at the very least they would give me something that would require a surgeon. But I could not think of another way of surviving. While I still had it, I snatched a quick glance at my watch. It was seven o'clock, the sky was clouding over and it would start getting dark in a couple of hours. Surely I could hang on that long and then I could make my escape.

You can read about the attack of Bachelu and Foy's divisions on the British line in many accounts of Waterloo, but not in mine. The reason is simple: I saw absolutely none of it while I lay in that ditch. I heard every gun the British had left open fire on the approaching mass of men and could guess that the French batteries were doing their utmost to destroy those guns. I listened to the crackle of musketry and distant shouts and cheers but it was impossible to make out what was happening above the sounds of the cannon. The only people I actually saw were half a dozen cuirassiers who rode to the edge of our slope and looked down on the line of broken and in my case, shamming, men. Through half-closed eyes, I saw their commander stare at us for a moment and then slowly shake his head before turning his horse away. We continued to lie still – you never knew when someone else might ride to the edge of the slope. I could feel Evans still trembling beside me and whispered some words of comfort. He grunted a reply and slowly as the sound of battle began to diminish his shaking ceased.

While the noise of firing from the allied ridge gradually died away, the French batteries continued to fire, indicating that there was still an allied presence. The only explanation I could think of was that the French attack had been beaten back and so at length, I cautiously sat up. I felt we had laid there for an eternity but when I looked again at my watch it was just seven forty-five.

"I think we have beaten them back," I told Evans as I got to my feet. "I will just go and look over the slope again." I ran forward, keeping low. The allied crest was as empty as before but now there were hundreds more French dead and wounded on the approach to it. God alone knew how, but the giant column had been stopped. I turned to look down into the shallow valley between the armies; the cuirassiers were back there and showing no sign of moving. There was still no sign of any Prussians. It was time to leave. I ran back to Evans, to tell him I would send on help if I found any. Then I stopped, feeling as though I had just been punched in the face. Evans was dead, his lifeless face staring up at the sky, and only then did I remember that he had not responded when I had run forward.

We will never know, but I think it was the shock that killed him. I had seen men go like that in the past, it did not seem to matter how strong or tough they were. I have even had a man die from it right next to me before. That was in India after Assaye. Like Evans he appeared to be recovering. He had eaten, drunk and made jokes before sleeping beside me. But in the morning a cavalry trooper and I found him dead between us.

I reached down and closed his lifeless eyes. He would have made a good steward, but there was no time for sentimentality. There was an evening chill in the air and my white, though bloodstained, shirt would stand out in the darkness. Looking along the line I saw one of the dead men in the row had been a captain and his officer's coat was hanging from a branch in the hedge.

"Sergeant Evans is dead," I told the corporal. "If you don't mind I will borrow this coat and see if I can get you some help."

"Captain Edmonds has no further use for it," agreed the corporal staring sadly down at his officer. "Good luck to you, sir." By instinct the corporal started to raise his arm in salute, before remembering that part of the limb was missing.

I climbed over the bank and onto the road that led from the château of Hougoumont and up over the British ridge. There were ditches and hedges on both sides and the track was littered with the detritus of war. There were broken weapons, a smashed ammunition limber and three dead horses, one of which had been ridden over by a cart and half crushed. But there was not a soldier to be seen. I grinned in delight: my escape might be smoother than I thought.

Just fifty yards up the path I came to a crossroads. The track to the right was the one that ran along the length of the British ridge, a route that would take me straight back to the battle. To go straight on would take me north to the woods, but I thought that there would be a lot of people who might interfere with my escape that way. The left hand path went north-west, away from the battle and towards more woods and ultimately the coast. It was signposted to a village called Mirbebraine. I turned left.

It was the logical choice and any charitable person would agree that I had been sorely used that day and well overdue for a stroke of good fortune. But the fates had not finished with me yet and had more surprises in store. The first of these called out to me five minutes later as I walked past a cattle barn near the road.

"You, sir, where are you going?" I cursed myself for not suspecting that guards would be posted to stop deserters and wished I had brought the bloody bandage to support my disguise.

I looked up to see a pair of British dragoons nudging their horses out from behind the barn, their short carbine muskets drawn but resting easily on the crupper of their saddles. Beyond them were some more troopers and around a dozen men sitting dejectedly against the barn wall who had evidently tried to make the same mistake I had. Well, I was an officer and practiced dissembler, I was still confident I could talk my way out.

"Ah, thank goodness you are here," I replied giving them my best weary smile. "I am Captain Edmonds of the 52nd." I gestured at the insignia on my coat which confirmed both my rank and regiment and reminded my interrogators that I outranked them. "I was with some wounded men just a hundred yards down the road to Hougoumont," I told them. "Now we have beaten off that column, I was told that I could get some carts to take them to the surgeons from this Mirbebraine place."

"I don't know about that, sir," replied a trooper woodenly. But I noted the 'sir' as he glanced back at the barn for guidance from his own officer.

"Well, what about those men?" says I pointing at the deserters. "Surely they can carry the wounded. I can take you right to them – it will only take a moment." The trick to a good lie is not to give your opponent too long to consider it and to stick as closely to the truth as possible. I would have got away with that one, rescued the wounded men and still found a way to slip away, had it not been for an appalling mischance.

"Arrest that man," called out a new voice. "His name is not Edmonds, he is a notorious French spy called Flashman."

I whirled round staring in shock as the dragoon officer rode his horse out from the shadow of the barn. There staring at me was a face that I had last seen looking at me from inside a brandy barrel in Brest: it was Colquhoun Grant.

"You?" was all I managed to say as I tried to comprehend what had just happened.

"Yes, me," sneered Grant with an expression that was a mixture of rage and delight. "You have no idea how long I have waited for this moment."

"Now look," I started. "I had no idea that they were not going to take the barrel you were in as well."

"Do you think I did not look at the lid after they had gone!" He was almost shrieking at me now with flecks of spittle flying from his mouth like a madman. "There was no mark on it. You betrayed me and left me for the French. You are a liar, a cheat, a seducer, a betrayer of every noble cause and now you have sunk as low as to sell your own country to the enemy."

"You bloody fool," I interrupted. "I sent that message in good faith having heard it directly from the lips of the emperor. And we both know that I was not the only one to send it."

"What do you mean?" demanded Grant, now on his guard.

"Fouché has been writing to Wellington, betraying the emperor's plans, and he sent the same message, which arrived just before mine."

"How could you possibly know that?"

"Because Fouché himself told me."

"Huh, I might have known you would be in league with that snake," cried Grant triumphantly.

"I met him because the courier you gave me was compromised. In fact everything about you is compromised. Virtually all of the agents you have near the border actually work for Fouché and feed you what he wants. He even has an agent working in your office to control what you see."

"That's not true!" Grant objected like a petulant child.

"Then how did Napoleon march over a hundred and twenty thousand men right up to the border without you even noticing. For Christ's sake, you could see their camp-fires from twenty miles away and still you did nothing."

"You could have sent another message warning of the attack," he insisted.

I became aware that the troopers were watching and listening to our exchange with a look of astonishment. Grant's demeanour was a mixture of rage and frustration. The unexpected arrival of the whole French army must have been a major blow to his reputation as an intelligence officer. That might also explain the reason he was out here on outpost duty instead of with Wellington.

"Why do you think Napoleon changed the date of the attack?" I asked, continuing my robust defence. "He rightly suspected Fouché was betraying him and so only moved things forward at the last minute when it was too late for either Fouché or I to send any kind of warning."

Grant looked up and saw his men watching him. They might have been just simple cavalry troopers, but they were no fools. It was obvious that their commander and I had history and that I was no ordinary infantry captain. Grant sensed their interest and tried to regain control of the encounter. "Well you are still under arrest," he snapped and then he turned to his sergeant. "Tie his hands and then give me the other end of the rope."

"On what charge?" I demanded.

"Desertion and masquerading as another officer," announced the pompous fool. "For all I know you could have killed the owner of that uniform and might still be working for the emperor. Perhaps he has sent you forward to spy on our retreat."

"Don't be ridiculous." I immediately dismissed the idea of telling him that Bonaparte wanted me arrested, for he would have been tempted to hand me over to the French. "You know full well why I don't have my own British uniform," I protested as the sergeant tied my hands. "This coat is the wrong rank and probably has the man's name sewn in it somewhere. I just thought it would be simpler to use it if stopped."

"Rubbish," Grant snapped taking the end of the rope and then wheeling his horse back in the direction of the British line. He yanked hard on my tether, nearly causing me to fall over as I half ran to keep up. "We will see what Colonel Colborne has to say about 'Captain Edmonds'," Grant announced.

"By all means," I agreed. It was taking me back to the battle I had been trying to avoid, but at least Colborne would help me get off this ridiculous charge. Then I would have to find a new way of sliding out.

As though he could read my mind Grant leaned down and hissed so that only I could hear. "I know you, Flashman, always trying to talk your way out of trouble with one lie after another. I have never trusted you and I never will." He gave a vicious laugh. "Do you know that there is a merchant following the army with four large empty barrels that he plans to fill with teeth? He has told soldiers that he will pay for any healthy teeth that they take from the dead so that he can use them to make false dentures back in England. I am sure with the right inducement he would be happy to take yours while you are alive." He sneered, "You would not find it quite so easy to talk your way out of trouble then."

"You're mad," I told him. There was no way he would get away with that without having his reputation ruined, but as I looked up at him there did seem a glint of insanity in those eyes. It was clear he hated me with a passion and, as I ran my tongue over my teeth, I had to wonder just how far he would go.

Chapter 43

As we got close to the crossroads I nodded towards the track to Hougoumont and called out, "You will find the wounded men I was with, including the body of Captain Edmonds, a hundred yards down there on the left." The sergeant must have looked to Grant for assent and then he and another trooper spurred their horses and galloped on ahead and turned down the track. By the time I had been half dragged and stumbled to the junction the sergeant was just pushing his horse back into the road from the ditch at the side.

"He is right, sir," he shouted. "There are wounded men here; Captain Edmond's had his legs shot off by cannon from the look of him."

Grant gave a growl of rage by way of reply and yanked hard on my leash as he kicked his horse on up the slope towards the British line. I heard the sergeant organising a cart for the wounded men and then we were over the crest. It was my first view of the ground behind the British ridge since I had marched off it in one of Colborne's squares. The transformation was an awful spectacle. Before the ground had been covered with a patchwork of British and allied squares. There had been dead and wounded aplenty then, but nothing as to how it was when I beheld it again now.

The ground was carpeted with the dead – in some places you could see where the squares had stood under bombardment from the lines of corpses still at right angles. Then closer to the ridge top was a new tidemark of bodies where lines of troops must have stood to destroy the column I had seen approaching with the cuirassiers. There was an eerie silence too, for not a single British gun at this end of the ridge was firing. The reason was not hard to spot: every gun I could see on the ridge crest had been either abandoned or disabled. The only firing seemed to be coming from the centre of the allied line, but as I stared into the distance I realised that they were French guns rather than our own. Their soldiers, pushing up from La Haye Sainte farm, had created a huge gap in the allied defences.

I must have stopped to gape at the transformation for the next thing I knew I was tugged off my feet and lay sprawled in the mud. That was when I really lost my temper. "For God's sake, cut me loose, you bloody idiot. Where the devil do you think I can escape too?"

"Knowing you," snarled Grant, "back to your friends on the other side of the valley."

I got on my hands and knees and looked up into a row of curious faces. The 52nd regiment were on the extreme right of the line, their nearest ranks just twenty yards away. Several looked on in astonishment as a British colonel dragged a captain wearing their uniform through the mud.

Then, over the heads of the soldiers, I saw two other figures on horseback. They had been studying the valley but now looked over their shoulders at this unexpected interruption. The familiar figure in the plain blue coat stared at me with an icy disdain before returning to his inspection of the enemy. But thankfully Colborne wheeled his horse around in my direction.

"Colonel Grant, what on earth are you doing, sir?" he shouted as he approached.

Grant gave me a look of triumph before replying. "I found this man masquerading as one of your officers. I have reason to believe that he is in league with the enemy and so he is under arrest."

Colborne reined his horse in beside us and spoke in a low urgent tone that the men standing nearby could not hear. "Have you lost your mind, sir? We are facing an attack from the Imperial Guard, fighting for our very survival and you think this is a time to undermine the morale of my men by literally dragging one of their officers through the mud?"

"But he is not one of your officers, he is a—" insisted Grant, but he got no further.

"I know very well who Major Flashman is," Colborne hissed at him with barely suppressed fury. "I have had the honour of serving with him in Spain and Portugal and know him to be a brave and resourceful officer. He has also been attached to my regiment since the middle of this afternoon. Now I would be most obliged if you would cut him free so that he can return to his duties." They might both have been colonels but Colborne had the seniority.

Grant looked up in mute appeal to the man in the blue coat, but he still had his back to us and showed no intention of intervening. "I can tell you, sir," Grant whispered to Colborne, "that this officer is not who he seems." And with that he threw down the end of the rope attached to my wrists and spurred his horse away.

"I do believe the man has gone quite mad," I said getting to my feet and holding out my bound hands to one of Grant's troopers who was approaching with a clasp knife. "But your tale of the Imperial Guard seems to have put him to flight."

"That was no tale," murmured Colborne quietly as my bonds were released. "A French cavalryman rode over a short while ago to tell us that the emperor is personally to lead the Imperial Guard against us."

"But he can't," I gasped looking about me. "Or at least we cannot possibly hope to stop them. Why, there is hardly anyone left." The largest contingent of men I could see was the 52nd. Being on the end of the ridge and perhaps the time spent on the facing slope had spared them from much of the bombardment. They still had well over eight hundred men left. The British Guards regiment was next along the line with barely five hundred men, but beyond them were a series of regiments that had been battered into near non-existence. Some were little more than company strength, with around a hundred men left still standing. Many of those had pulled well back from the ridge to escape the fire from the French in the centre.

"You had better speak to Wellington," said Colborne, gesturing at the man in the blue coat. I walked across the still soft turf, aware of the curious stares of the soldiers about me, many of whom had heard Grant's outburst. I had last seen the duke when he was the ambassador in Paris. Since then I suspected that he had seduced my wife, while I had unintentionally misled him regarding the timing of the French attack. It was not an encounter that I relished.

"Ah, Flashman." Wellington looked down from his saddle at me as I approached. He looked tired and drawn. His calm and measured demeanour during a battle was one of his hallmarks, but the tension of the day must have been pushing him to breaking point. He gestured at the slope up which I had been dragged. "I had forgotten how you like to make an entrance." He grinned and held out his hand. As he did so he looked me in the eye and I sensed that there was an unspoken agreement between us, that if I shook his hand we would both let things in the past rest. This was certainly not the time to stand on my dignity and so I shook his paw with a sense of relief.

"Colborne tells me that they are to launch the Imperial Guard against us." I glanced along the ridge to the east; there was still no sign of reinforcements. "If the Prussians are coming, they seem to have left it too late."

"The Prussians are here. They have started their own attack behind the French right flank at a place called Plancenoit. Over there, beyond the French batteries." Wellington pointed in their direction. "Another Prussian division is to join our left flank, but it will be touch and go if they arrive before the Guard attack."

"But surely," I protested, "you are not thinking of trying to defend this ridge against the Imperial Guard. You have hardly any men left and some that *are* here look unsteady. I have seen the Guard; they will not stop for anything."

"The 52nd will stand firm," interrupted Colborne but Wellington waved us both to silence.

"It is too late to retreat," he said wearily. "I have called in the last of our reserves, so we must trust to the Prussians to arrive in time." He tried to force a smile. "Anyway, we have all seen British lines beat French columns in the past. Who is to say that it will not happen again?" Wellington tried to look us both in the eye, but he could not hold our gaze. We all knew that this was no fresh British line of redcoats and it was certainly no ordinary column.

We stared silently into the valley for a while, no one sure what to say. Even the French guns had quietened as though they sensed that there were fewer targets now over the ridge. Only the guns in the centre of the allied line kept up any rate of fire.

"I doubt the emperor will lead the attack in person." I spoke up to end the silence and even managed a weak grin. "Because I have poisoned him."

"You have done what?" asked Wellington astonished.

"Poisoned him," I repeated as casually as I could, as though I did such things every day. "Not fatally, but he has a terrible ache in the guts that has forced him to leave Marshal Ney to manage most of the battle."

"How in God's name did you manage that?" asked Colborne.

"I put poisonous mushrooms in his stew yesterday," I told them. There was no need to reveal that it was by accident. After I had been fooled over the date of the attack I needed to rebuild my reputation.

"Well I never…" started Wellington before roaring with laughter. "You never cease to surprise me, Flashman," he said at last. "I had thought that the French attacks had lacked a certain imperial flair – that explains it." But then he turned serious and glanced over his shoulder to check we were not being overheard. "But gentlemen, you must keep that information to yourselves. Whether we win or lose here today, it will not be to our benefit to have it known that the emperor was incapacitated." He turned back to me. "Is there anything else that we need to know?"

"Napoleon told his men that the Prussians seen on the horizon were Grouchy's men. The soldiers that attack us will be expecting French reinforcements to arrive on their right and not fresh enemies; that is if the Prussians do arrive in time."

Wellington was about to reply when there were shouts of alarm behind us. I twisted around and for a moment I thought that the 'imperial flair' had caught us out after all. For there, marching towards us from our rear, was what appeared to be a column of blue-coated French infantry. As troops hurriedly turned to face them and muskets swung up into the firing position, a British cavalry officer galloped forward shouting, "Don't shoot, they are Dutch."

"General Chassé's men," murmured Wellington quietly. He turned to Colborne. "Keep your eye on Chassé. He fought for the French against us in Spain. I doubt his troops are reliable, that is why I have kept them in reserve until now. Many are French-speaking Dutch who would probably welcome the chance to change sides."

Just what we need at this moment of crisis, I thought: an ally that is as likely to stick a bayonet in your back as fight alongside you. But aloud I said, "They march smartly enough," for they were coming on in a determined manner and I noticed bringing some horse artillery with them.

"Oh yes," agreed Wellington sardonically. "General Chassé is famous for his bayonet charges. It is just that until now they have been directed against men dressed in red." The new arrivals gradually formed up behind the Guards regiment and the miscellany of regimental survivors forming a line to their left. This included over a hundred survivors of the Lincolnshire regiment that I had now seen charged twice by cuirassier. Most of these had formed up well back from the crest of the ridge and the Dutch made their own line of four ranks behind them. There were over three thousand of these blue-coated reinforcements, more than the rest of the allied defenders on this end of the ridge put together. I was glad that they were not behind the 52nd, as if they did change sides the defenders would be trapped between them and the Imperial Guard.

Already I was gazing longingly at the road back to Mirbebraine. I cursed Grant: if it had not been for him I would have been safely into the forest by now. Instead, I was stuck back on the allied ridge awaiting an attack by probably the best infantry in the world. Wellington rode off along the crest to encourage his men. Every few minutes he could be seen scanning the eastern horizon and then staring at his watch, clearly hoping that the Prussians or nightfall would arrive before another enemy attack.

He was to be disappointed, for if anything the evening got a little brighter as the clouds started to break up and shafts of evening sunlight illuminated patches of the valley. One of these areas was where the French ridge crossed the road that ran through the middle of the battlefield. There, just after eight, we got our first glimpse of the Imperial Guard. The forward units came over the far crest already formed up into hollow squares, to protect themselves from any cavalry. For most regiments to move in square was a slow and ungainly process, the lines wavering as they crossed rough terrain and obstacles. But watching as they came down the slope, their lines remained ruler straight. I knew by instinct that the first three squares to appear were regiments of the Old Guard. You could almost sense their pride and determination from a mile away as they started their descent into the valley. Any lingering doubt was dispelled by the single rider on a white horse who rode alongside them.

"Is that the emperor?" asked Colborne.

"Yes," I replied, "and those men beside him are the toughest veterans you are ever likely to meet." Beyond those first squares came more regiments, but marching in column rather than square. They were, I guessed, regiments of the Middle and Young Guard. Batteries of horse artillery were being driven between each column. To my alarm, they were veering off the road and heading in our direction.

All of the French artillery had stopped now, even the French skirmishers held their fire, while any British guns still able to fire were waiting for the enemy to get closer. The silence across the battlefield made the hair on the back of my neck stand up. It was a moment of suspense before the final act in a play. For I guessed that everyone who looked at the scene knew that, one way or another, the immediate future of the new French empire was about to be resolved. Even the chatter in the ranks behind me died away. The lines of the 52nd were some yards back from the crest, but while they could not see into the valley, even they sensed something significant was happening. Looking over my shoulder I saw them nudge each other and lick their lips nervously as they steeled themselves for whatever came at them next.

Then a band struck up from somewhere in the French formation and thousands of voices burst into the same song I had heard at Gossalie days before. It was becoming more like a review than the closing stage of a battle and it sent shivers down my spine.

"What are they singing?" asked Colborne.

"It is an old revolutionary song," I told him. "It is about liberating countries from tyrants and despots and washing the streets with the blood of freedom."

"A cheery ditty, then," laughed Colborne. "Perhaps I should start the lads up with a chorus of that song about the pig herder's daughter to balance things out. Hello, what's this? Are they stopping?"

The squares of the Old Guard had indeed come to a halt on the valley floor, just before the incline up to La Haye Sainte farm. Napoleon rode his horse between them, acknowledging their cheers as the remaining columns approached. There was a hatless marshal with red hair at the head of the following columns, who I was sure was Ney. He led them past the Old Guard and then started to re-organise them to form two new huge columns. All the while the soldiers were singing and the band playing as though they were on the parade ground. It was a piece of theatre designed to awe their enemies, and I can say that it worked for me. Each new column must have contained at least 2,500 men, but to my immense relief, they were angled to attack closer to the centre of the allied line.

"I pity the poor devils that are going to face them," I muttered to Colborne as we both looked along the line at the troops that would have that dubious honour. The leading French column was aimed at the rag-tag survivors of various regiments I had seen earlier. They were being pushed and shoved together into rough ranks. They looked more nervous than a virgin bride on her wedding night. They did not know the men around them, they probably did not trust the suspiciously French-looking troops and bayonets behind them and while they could not see the Imperial Guard forming up in their direction, they could certainly hear them.

"That is what is left of Halkett's brigade," murmured Colborne. "They have been in the thick of it all day." But then he gestured to the second large column that seemed to be aimed at the line between us and Halkett's men. "They should attack the position held by the British Guards Brigade. It will be our Guards against theirs."

We both sat there silently considering the odds. All the tenets of war had shown that a well-drilled line firing volleys of musketry can defeat a column of infantry. We had seen it happen many times before, relentless disciplined fire forcing the French ranks to a standstill and then a headlong retreat. There may only be some six hundred men left in total from the four regiments in Halkett's Brigade, but that might be enough if they could maintain their order. On the other hand, these were no ordinary French infantry. They were the Imperial Guard, men who claimed that they had never been stopped. The emperor saved them to deliver the death blow in a battle, as he had at Ligny just two days before. I would not have given a farthing for a guinea that Halkett's men would stand at that moment. I suspect that Colborne was of the same mind for he suddenly swore and exclaimed, "Where are those damned Prussians?" Wherever they were, it was too late, for at that moment a signal gun fired and the attack began.

Chapter 44

Within a few seconds, every gun in the French batteries renewed their bombardment of the allied ridge, concentrating their fire on the ground that the Imperial Guard was to cross. Even though the guns had been firing for most of the day, the contrast with the earlier silence made this shelling seem even more devastating. There is something terrible about being fired on and not being able to hit back. The crash of shell and ball around the ridge reminded all of the horrors of the earlier fire. The British troops to our left were already lying down to reduce the likelihood of being hit, while Colborne yelled in my ear above the din to stay where I was while he ran back to his own men. I took the opportunity to crouch down too although few shells were coming in my direction.

While the three hollow squares of the Old Guard remained in the valley, the two giant columns of the Young and Middle Guard had already started their march up the slope. The one nearer the road was leading and, riding a horse in front of the foremost ranks, was Ney. He was virtually daring the British gunners to shoot him down, although from what I could see, precious few British gunners had ammunition or serviceable guns to take up the challenge.

On the Imperial Guard came, like an unstoppable machine it followed Ney steadily up the slope. While the sound of cannon almost drowned it out, you could just hear the beat of the drums marking time. As they got closer at least one British gun did open fire and I saw a swathe of their front rank go down to a burst of canister. Two mounted officers fell but Ney was unhurt and in a moment the ranks had closed up as though the wounded men had not existed. The column did not come alone; there were Imperial Guard horse artillery teams on either side and they swiftly opened a counter fire on any British gun that showed itself. Behind the first column, the second was now also moving and beyond that, just about any Frenchman left alive in the valley was on the march towards the allied line.

The moment of decision was fast approaching. I stared at Halkett's men to my left: some were lying down like the 52nd behind me, but others were on their feet and already edging back. They must have been close enough to hear the roars of *Vive l'Empereur!* from the men approaching and I knew first-hand how that could chill the blood. British cavalry were trying to drive Halkett's men back into position while behind them the Dutch soldiers silently watched and waited. I glanced to my right: the road to Mirbebraine was still clear, but I knew that it would quickly fill with panicking men once the line broke. Crowds of terrified British soldiers would attract French cavalry like bees to honey. There was broken scrub and bushes between the road and the forest and I decided that I would go there. With just an hour or two until nightfall I could hide out and pass as a French or English officer in the dark as circumstances required. Then I could get either a horse or into the woods.

There was no thought then that the allied line could withstand this final onslaught. Ney led his men steadily up the hill, a hundred yards to the crest, then fifty, and all the while the men that were supposed to force him back down the slope were edging back themselves. He must have expected a fusillade from a line of redcoats as he crested the summit, but instead the plateau was empty. The faltering line of Halkett's brigade was at least a hundred yards back and the marshal must have been sure of victory then. I saw him wave his sword in the air and urge his men forward and they gave a roar of victory as they swept on.

Instead of disciplined crashing volleys by company, there was an extended ripple of fire across the whole of Halkett's line. The men disappeared behind a bank of their own musket smoke but from my vantage point I could see that more than a few were not staying to reload. Rather than remain and continue the fight, they were trying to escape through the horsemen behind them. A volley from the front ranks of the Imperial Guard encouraged them on their way and then Ney released his men in a wild charge to clear the plateau once and for all.

That's it, then, I thought, for even if the British Guards could stop the second column they could not do so with the first column attacking their rear. It had been like watching a prize-fighter take on a child, with an entirely predictable outcome. It was time to go. I was up and edging my way west when I heard the cannon fire. For a moment I thought that they were French guns, but then I remembered the two batteries of horse artillery that I had seen the Dutch troops bring with them. The question now was: Who were they firing at?

The whole area was obscured by smoke; I could see the Imperial Guard pushing forward into the maelstrom. They were shouting and yelling but other unseen voices were screaming and then the cannon roared again. I remembered all too well from D'Erlon's attack the devastating effect of canister shot at short range into the packed ranks of a French column, but I still could not see what was happening. I ran back, springing over the prone figures behind me to get a better view. Then I saw the Dutchmen. They had angled their cannon to fire across the space in front of their long line of four ranks. The Imperial Guard were charging into this killing zone and as the twelve guns spat out their lethal cones of death I guessed that they were taking a terrible punishment. Still they came on, though. I saw their bearskins moving forward above the smoke and then the musket volleys began.

General Chassé had drilled his men well. They fired by rank and by company so that there was a continuous stream of lead pouring into the men ahead of them. The smoke from their discharges now completely obscured my view of both the Dutch and the French. Then the Dutch cannons crashed again and I saw a man emerge from the smoke and run back towards the crest. He was wearing a bearskin of the Imperial Guard. Then came two more, then six and now a score of the guard were running back to the ridge, some having lost their weapons. Incredible as it seemed, the unbeaten Imperial Guard was retreating. I heard new orders shouted among the Dutch soldiers, and the volley firing stopped. I did not need to understand the language to guess that General Chassé, known as

General Bayonet to friends and foe alike, was about to live up to his reputation. There was a roar as his men launched their charge and then hundreds of the Imperial Guard could be seen streaming back out of the smoke.

"My God, did you see that?" I shouted at Colborne. He didn't reply, instead he stared over my shoulder as though he had just seen a ghost. I whirled round. I was twenty yards back from the edge of the British ridge then and just in time to see a line of waving black objects appear at its crest: Bearskins of the Imperial Guard. The second column was arriving on the scene.

At first glance, it looked as though only Wellington, mounted on his chestnut charger, was there to receive them. Then he was shouting something and waving his arm and as though from the bowels of the earth, long ranks of redcoats stood up in front of him from where they had been lying on the flattened crops. The first volleys crashed out. The British Guards were well drilled but their line was just two ranks deep. I knew that the five hundred men in it were outnumbered five to one by those in the column before them.

The Imperial Guard, wearing their grey greatcoats, were still coming and at any moment would return fire and start to whittle down the line of defenders. There were no more reserve regiments behind the British Guards should they fail, Chassé's men were still engaged with the first column. The 52nd, my new regiment, were the only sizeable force not fighting, but we were away to one side. I gave a silent prayer of thanks that for once I was in the right place.

"I will check on the right-hand companies," I shouted to Colborne, gesturing at those that were the furthest from the fighting. Once there I planned to keep on going but instead of trying to stop me Colborne grinned and slapped me on the back.

"Good thinking, Flashman, they will have the furthest to go." I stared at him in amazement. What the devil was the man talking about? Still, he hadn't stopped me from running away, positively encouraged it in fact, and so I hurried along the line.

"The line will advance," roared Colborne above the din of battle and abruptly the whole formation I was walking along started moving forward. Did Colborne think that there was a third column coming, I wondered? I tried to remember if he had still been at the ridge crest with me when the Imperial Guard had been forming up. Yes, that must be it. The bloody fool was attacking a phantom enemy. There would be a few French skirmishers coming up the ridge, but our appearance would soon put paid to them and make it safer for me to slide out. Still, I can't say I was pleased when I noticed a line of British cavalry following our advance, much as they had with Halkett's men, presumably to deter anyone from going backwards.

Then we were at the crest and I thought we would stop once Colborne had seen that no other attackers were coming. I could not stomach the thought of going into that accursed valley again. The French guns had stopped once the Imperial Guard had reached the top of the allied ridge to avoid hitting their own side, but if we were to show ourselves, we would get their full force. But Colborne was not stopping. Over the top we went and I glanced once more at the grim-faced cavalrymen that dogged our tracks. I still had no idea where we were going but then Colborne was shouting and waving and the line nearest him started to wheel to its left. It was only then that I realised what he intended. He was taking the 52nd to attack the flank of the Imperial Guard column so that it was assailed on two sides. That was why my end of the line had the furthest to travel. I looked up aghast for it meant that as we turned I would be furthest into the valley, probably surrounded by the enemy.

God knows what my expression looked like to Colborne, but he was waving and grinning at me as he urged the men round. The renewed thunder of fire from the grand battery made shouting impossible, but Colborne pointed to an ensign running towards me down the line.

I ducked as a shell from the French guns showered me with dirt. They were firing high to avoid hitting their own column, which meant that end of the 52nd nearest the enemy was hardly hit at all. But my end, the place I had thought would be safer, was now under a ferocious bombardment.

"Run, you lazy bastards," I shouted at the men in front of me and they shambled into a faster step.

"Keep the line straight," called out a sergeant but I cut him off.

"Never mind that, run or we will be a straight line of corpses." The men in front of me grinned at their sergeant getting reprimanded and broke into a jog. "Come on, boys," I yelled at the others, "the sooner we are closer to the column the sooner they cannot shell us."

A cannonball thudded into the turf, where I had been standing just a few seconds before. I decided that it was time to break my golden rule. I pushed my way through the line and, waving my sword in the air, I sprinted out ahead of them. The men cheered and ran after me, enjoying that rarest of sights: Flashy leading from the front.

With the sergeant desperately yelling to keep them in some semblance of a line, my end of the 52nd ran pell-mell across the slope. We were set to bend around the back of the column; if you are going to attack the Imperial Guard, then shooting them from behind must surely be the safest way. Already one or two were nervously staring over their shoulders and I did not doubt that the rear rank would soon turn and face us. I was just judging that I might be wise to resume my traditional position behind the men, when someone tugged on my sleeve.

"Mr Colborne's respects, sir," shouted the ensign I had seen earlier. He took a moment to gather his breath from sprinting after me. "But you are to pay particular attention to any horse artillery that might try to establish themselves on our flank."

There was a grim inevitability to the sight that greeted me as I looked over my shoulder. After the day I had experienced, I was pleasantly surprised that there were only three guns bouncing behind teams of horses as they charged up the slope towards us. They would want to get close to avoid hitting their own men and were already no more than three hundred yards away. We had to attack them before they could get set up or we would be torn apart.

"My company," I roared. "Down the hill and attack those guns."

The noise was deafening now. The French grand battery was still firing, while as I issued the order the first volleys were fired from the 52nd at the end of the line closest to the Imperial Guard. If any had heard my command, they ignored it. The sergeant was some distance off, still chivvying the men to try and keep the line straight. Another glance down the hill showed that the gun teams were already wheeling the horses round to point the cannon in our direction. There was no time to waste. I grabbed at the nearest man; he stared at me wild-eyed, whether with fear or the exhilaration of battle it was hard to say.

"Down there, man," I pointed at the gun teams. "We need to attack those guns or we will be done for." He shook my arm off and for a moment I thought he would run on but as he stared down the slope the sense of what I was saying became obvious. He turned and shouted at his nearest mates and together they started down the hill. I ran after the rest of my command and saw the ensign was still at my elbow. "Get the men to attack those guns," I shouted at him, pointing further up the line. I grabbed another man and used the flat of my sword to stop a third. I merely now had to point to what was already a dozen men running down the hill for them to understand. The ensign had grabbed another half dozen and as I watched the teams of horses being unhitched I realised that we had no more time.

As a boy, I had run two hundred yards in half a minute and I would have to be even faster now. The gun crews could see men turning towards them and went through the motions of loading their guns with polished efficiency. Pounding down the hill I watched as men with powder charges rushed to the muzzles, swiftly followed by men holding rammers to push the charges home. I was still a hundred a fifty yards away when I saw them bringing the metal cans of musket balls, the canister shot itself.

I knew then that we weren't going to make it, but there was no cover to hide behind. To stop meant certain death and so I ran on hoping for some kind of miracle. Then I saw the officer in charge of the half battery – it was none other than the captain I had spent the

343

best part of the day with at Quatre Bras. I remembered all too well how deadly accurate his men were. He was busy overseeing the aiming of the guns, they were being angled so that the cone of fire would hit us and not the column of the Imperial Guard.

As the canister was pushed in the barrels we were still over a hundred yards off, but if the men did not shoot now they would be swept away before they reached the guns.

"Fire," I yelled at the men around me, "aim for the gunners."

Half a dozen of them fired wildly while still running and the shots could have gone anywhere. I could have wept at the waste when my life was at stake. The rest, however, either dropped to a kneeling position or stood, but at least they were taking more careful aim. I ran to one side to keep out of their line of fire, cursing that I had not thought to pick up a musket myself from the ridge top. A crackle of shots rang out and two of the men with ramrods fell along with another gunner beyond.

The artillery captain rushed forward to the nearest gun and picked up the fallen rammer himself. He was raising it to the muzzle when in desperation to delay him I shouted in French, "Don't shoot, it is me, we are working for the emperor."

He looked over his shoulder at hearing his native tongue and as he caught sight of me he hesitated. He must have recognised me for I saw his mouth open in surprise and then there was the crack from the musket of one of my kneeling men and the captain fell back against his gun before toppling to the ground.

"Aim for the third gun," I shouted, for the uninjured man on that was just withdrawing the rammer and then it would be ready to fire. But when I looked across at the men, they were either still charging towards the guns or trying desperately to reload. We were too late; men around the cannon were springing back to escape its recoil and, throwing myself to the ground, I shouted at the men to get down too.

Once again there was that awful whistling sound, I pressed myself into the soft earth and felt something tug at my right boot. Miraculously I was unhurt, but screaming from nearby indicated that others were not as fortunate. Then I heard more shouting ahead of me and, gingerly raising my head, I saw that many of the men who had run on had somehow escaped the hail of shot. A bloody smear in front of the gun showed that one man must have been torn apart by the lead balls, but as the gun was angled to avoid the column it missed all those charging from that direction.

I was up in a moment. There was a desperate fight now around the guns, as redcoats stabbed with bayonets while the French gunners swung their rammers and tools to hold them off. More muskets fired and then the gunners were falling back, running for cover among the approaching skirmishers. There were still two guns almost ready to fire and I knew just what to do with them.

"Quick, you men," I was gasping for breath after my run. "Pick up those rammers and push those charges home." Realising my intentions, grinning redcoats ran to do my bidding, while others put their shoulders to the wheels of the cannon and slowly started to turn them.

After a few grunts of exertion, the barrels were facing the rear of the huge column. It was a vast target that would be impossible to miss and I knew all too well the devastation the guns would cause. But so did the skirmishers, who were charging up the hill to stop us. There was a clang as a musket ball hit one of the guns and a soldier swore loudly as a ball struck his arm. Others were reloading or kneeling to aim down the slope at our new assailants. I glanced over my shoulder to see that the rest of the 52nd were now firing their volleys into the second Imperial Guard column. A cloud of gun smoke at its head indicated that it was still contesting the ground with the British Guards to its front. At any moment one side or another would break and then it would all be over. There was not a second to lose.

Checking the breeches of the guns I saw that the quills of priming powder had already been inserted. All I needed was a piece of slow match to fire them. I found that beside a French gunner who was clutching a bayonet wound to the belly. As I bent to pick it up the man standing next to me screamed and fell clutching his leg. The French skirmishers were closing in fast.

"Stand back!" I yelled and touched the match to the priming tube of the first gun. The cannon crashed back and a plume of smoke obscured my view of the column. I remember a splinter flying from one of the wooden wheels as it was hit by a skirmisher's ball and then I was over to the next gun. I touched the glowing match to the tube. There was a slight 'ffft' noise as the quill of finely ground powder took the flame to the charge and then the second gun roared out.

Something struck me then, to this day I am not sure what; a spent ball, probably, but I found myself lying on the ground with a stinging pain in my shoulder. There was no blood but I did not have the energy to get back up. I remember lying there, suddenly feeling exhausted. As I think anyone with an ounce of humanity would agree, I had suffered a trying few days and I simply could not summon the strength to do more. You have done all you could, I thought and if it was not enough, well, I was done for.

I lay there and watched as more of the 52nd ran down the hill to protect the cannon. As the smoke cleared I saw two huge swathes of dead and wounded men at the back of the column where the canister had struck them. Men were screaming and for those in the centre of this mass of men, it must have sounded as though their front, left and rear were being assailed simultaneously. I remembered all too well what it was like to be in the middle of a column like that, unable to see what was going on. Perhaps they knew that the first column had already been defeated and they could only imagine what was being inflicted on their own outer ranks. Then there was a cheer from the ridge and I guessed that the British Guards were preparing to go in with the bayonets.

This was the critical moment: one side or the other had to break now. I watched the column for any sign of retreat but it did not seem to be moving. Then someone dragged me clear as the men who had run down the slope with me set about reloading the cannon with more canister shot. Perhaps the sight of that was the final straw for those at the rear of the column, for in the blink of an eye where men had been pushing forward, they were now starting to step back. A few seconds later and where they had been edging back, they were now running. Then, as though the floodgates had been opened, hundreds of the Imperial Guard were streaming back down the slope like the earlier column before them.

For the French, it was a shocking sight. This was the unbeaten Imperial Guard, sent to deliver the deathblow to a battered and diminished enemy. Instead of bringing them victory it was retreating, no running, back across the valley. On top of this, across the battlefield, I could see more soldiers in dark uniforms: The Prussians had finally arrived. The French on the eastern side of the road were swiftly discovering that instead of joining with Grouchy's reinforcements, they were facing a new wave of fresh and unexpected enemies. Napoleon's deception would have hit their morale hard and on top of the retreat of the Imperial Guard, it was too much. Everywhere I looked the French were starting to retreat.

The volley firing stopped, orders were shouted and then I watched as the 52nd fixed bayonets and was released into the valley to drive the enemy from the field. The men around the guns followed suite; victory and loot were there for the taking.

I rolled to one side and crawled over to the nearest gun to sit with my back resting against the wheel. I had no inclination to move further and certainly no wish to complete the defeat of the French. I watched as Wellington signalled a general advance and the pitifully small number of allied soldiers left started to appear on the ridge and move forward.

If they thought that they were to have an easy time of it they were to be mistaken, for fresh volleys crashed out from the valley floor and I saw the squares of the Old Guard were covering the French retreat. They were now the only organised resistance left as French guns, infantry and cavalry all started to stream towards the road back to France. Instead of following, the Old Guard spread their squares out to cover each other and seemed to dare the allies to take them on. I watched as a cavalry regiment charged one square, only for the veterans to shoot them with contemptuous ease at virtually point-blank range. Half the troopers were left dead and dying at their feet. Grey-moustachioed men stepped out of the ranks to casually despatch the wounded before more horsemen could return. Infantry regiments began to trade volleys with them and what little artillery the allies had left was brought forward to blast canister at them, but still the Old Guard showed little sign of retreating.

I was glad that my view was obscured by the growing skeins of musket smoke that surrounded their squares. I remembered many of them, such as the man who had been given the bearskin and promised to show it glory or his death. I wondered if he still lived as they seemed determined to die where they stood. Quite why Napoleon had kept these granite-hard men in the valley was beyond me. But I was bloody glad he had as they would have broken the British line for certain. The defenders would have been spread too thinly to resist them.

I sat there for ages watching the final act in this drama. Beaten French soldiers streamed back towards the road to Charleroi and France beyond. Their empire had been vanquished and Napoleon's great gamble had failed. Hobhouse's tree of liberty had been well and truly felled and while I did not give a fig about that, I struggled to celebrate the return of the fat king and his courtiers.

It was dusk and when all the French army that could get away had done so, only then did the Old Guard squares slowly start to pull back. They left a mound of dead and injured in their wake; at least one square had been battered into a triangle. But still their muskets rippled fire at anyone who got within range. I didn't see it, but I heard that they made a final stand at the top of the French ridge and then those that were left slipped away into the night.

I sat there with nowhere to go and nothing to do other than simply celebrate my survival of that extraordinary day. There were shouts for help from the wounded and occasional single shots. Dark figures were moving across the battlefield alone or in small groups but whether they were offering aid or simply robbing the dead and the wounded it was hard to say. As the first star appeared in the sky, my thoughts were interrupted by a gargling sound close at hand. I turned to see, lying on his side between the guns, the artillery captain. He must have been unconscious and it would have been better for him if he had stayed that way, for the ground around him was covered in blood that also soaked his clothes. He was dying for certain and with the last of his energy he was reaching out across the blood-covered grass as though grasping for something.

He had been a good professional soldier and I did not feel proud about deceiving him, even if his death had helped tip the balance of the battle. I got to my feet and only then noticed that the heel of my right boot had been torn off in that final burst of canister as I had pressed myself into the ground. I felt slightly sick when I realised how close the ball must have come to the top of my skull. A fraction of an inch lower and I would have been dead or dying like the poor bastard scrabbling near my feet.

Suddenly nations and sides did not matter compared to common humanity and I dropped down again and gripped the man's hand. He made another gargling noise as he tried to speak and his eyes stared at me but with little recognition.

"It is all right," I told him in French. "You are not alone."

His mouth opened and more blood gushed out before he took another noisy breath. "Did we win?" he gasped.

I stared about me at the scene of devastation and shattered dreams with the last of the fighting on the far horizon. He was going to die anyway so what did it matter. "Yes, we won," I told him in his own language.

His grip tightened as he exerted the very last of his strength and I heard his voice rasp "*Vive l'E...*" before his breath died away in a rattle.

Epilogue

Lobsters are vicious creatures. I do not mean British redcoats, who are sometimes called lobsters, no I am talking of the crustaceans. I remember thinking that on the harbour wall at Boulogne as I waited to board one of the troop ships that would take me home. From the cliff top on my way into the town I had already seen the shore of England, as a smudge on the horizon. Perhaps because it was so close I felt the pang of homesickness all the sharper. I had been ten months in France and had not seen Louisa and my son for five of them. I yearned to be safe back in Leicestershire. Having learned my lesson from this adventure, I was determined never to leave it again, even if it meant a lifetime talking about two-headed calves. Bolougne was packed, of course, full of soldiers just as eager to get home and recount their own tales of our famous victory.

Oh, I was pleased we had won but I could not share their pleasure in quite the same way. I had too many friends on both sides of the battle to celebrate. In the days after the conflict I had been part of the force that had escorted Louis XVIII back to his waiting subjects. Neither party seemed pleased with the arrangement, the king waving somewhat nervously from his carriage at a sullen populace. At Charleroi, where I vividly remembered the genuine welcome for Napoleon, the people had been forced at bayonet point to line the king's route and any cheers were at best desultory.

Now I just wanted to be alone, which on a crowded troopship was not going to be easy. But I had my own cabin, well, it was more of a canvas-sided pen, but it had a cot, a table and a chair that doubled as a commode to save officers going to the heads in rough weather. I had decided that I would eat by myself that night, which was why I was standing by a Boulogne fishmonger as he opened a wooden trunk half filled with water and some twenty lobsters. As they sensed the change in light all of the creatures jostled about and put their claws up in the air to defend themselves.

"See they are fresh. Careful sir, they could break a finger if they catch you." I had reached down to grab one, but the little tartar had

350

moved faster than I expected. "I'll get him for you, sir," offered the shopkeeper grabbing it deftly down the body just out of reach of the pincers. "Would you like me to kill it or will you take it fresh?"

"Fresh please. Do you have a box I can take it in?" I already had some good wine in my luggage, which was loaded aboard, and I could get the galley to boil the creature. Fresh lobster with some melted butter would be a nice treat and something I could arrange without difficulty to enjoy alone. Soon I was striding up the gangplank with a box of wet straw containing a lobster in one hand and a small pot of butter in the other.

Colborne had arranged a berth for me on the troopship being used by the 52nd. We stood together on its deck as the ropes were cast off and the tide started to pull it out into the harbour as the sails were unfurled.

"I trust you will join us for dinner, Flashman," Colborne said, gripping my shoulder. "It might be our last together for some time."

"If you don't mind, I would rather not. I am not really in the mood for celebrations and I don't want to dampen your party. I will just eat in my cabin."

"If you are sure," said Colborne grinning. "But you may change your mind when you know who is in the cabin next to yours. I have had to give Grant a berth home too, but I doubt he will want to join us either."

The thought of spending an evening just the other side of a canvas screen from Grant was too much to bear and so I agreed to join the officers for their final dinner of the campaign. We had just got settled and the first bottles were passing when the door was pulled back and Grant stood in the threshold. He gazed around the table. A look of irritation crossed his face as he saw me. I thought he would turn away again, but Colborne was up and welcoming him to the gathering.

"Please, Colonel, join us," he cried steering Grant to a place at the opposite end of the table from me. "I wanted us all to be together on our final night." With that he winked at me and I realised that the cunning bastard had probably tricked Grant into attending in much the same way as he had me.

The talk around the table was inevitably about that great final battle and much of it was centred on the efforts of the 52nd to subdue the last defence of the Old Guard. Everyone has probably heard the story of their reply when called upon to surrender. "The Guard dies, it does not surrender," was the response; often attributed to Cambronne although he had been captured by then.

Colborne turned to me and asked, "You know them, Flash, why do you think they did it?" Heads turned curiously in my direction. Many had seen me charging them with Marshal Ney. They knew I had a better understanding of the French than most, but few knew what I had been doing on the French side of the valley.

"Those were the veterans who had built the French empire," I told them. "They had never been defeated in battle and you know how close that final attack was to a success. "If the emperor had committed the Old Guard too it might have made all the difference."

"Nonsense," interrupted Grant. "The Prussians would still have helped us win the battle."

"The Prussians were not on the ridge then," pointed out Colborne. "If they had broken our line… well, it doesn't bear thinking about. There would have been a general advance by the French through the gap and God knows what state we would be in when the Prussians got there. They would probably have been just in time to cover our retreat."

"But why didn't the Old Guard just surrender when we had them beat? asked another officer called Jennings. "The other columns of the Imperial Guard retreated. There was nothing that the Old Guard could have done then, they could see that the battle was lost."

"That is the point I am trying to make," I said. "They stood because they knew the battle was lost. You have to understand what these men had been through. Many of them had been with Napoleon from the start. They were drilled to perfection, but it was not the discipline that ensured that they were unbeaten, it was their pride. They were their emperor's most trusted troops and they would never let him down."

"Well they certainly knew how to fight at Plancenoit," said an officer I did not know. "They say that two battalions of the Old Guard defeated fourteen Prussian battalions when they retook the town."

"But at the end," persisted Colborne, "when they were the last French soldiers standing on the battlefield, well there was no dishonour in surrendering then."

I thought back to those huge men weeping as they re-joined the ranks on our march to Paris and was at a loss to know how to explain it. As I paused Grant interjected again.

"Our Guards regiments are just as brave but I am sure that they would not behave as foolishly."

"Our Guards regiments have not been disbanded," I told them. "Their men have not had to watch the empire they built torn apart by their enemies. They have not lost the status of honoured guardians of the empire and had to find whatever work they could. I watched those hard men cry with joy as they saw their empire reborn. I think that they stood there defiant because they would have rather died as members of the Old Guard with their comrades, than lived on in a whipped France under a hated king."

There was silence after that for a few moments as most around the table reflected on what I had said. Then Grant sneered, "Well I still think that they were fools. As I have said before, Flashman, when you spend too long in a French uniform you tend to go native."

Several shifted uncomfortably around the table at that and Colborne muttered, "I think Major Flashman has proved his value to this army many times over." But at that moment I did not care what any of them thought. I had taken my fill of armies and wars and diplomacy.

"If you will excuse me, gentlemen, I need the jakes." I got up and walked around the table and was on my way to the heads when I remembered the commode in my cabin. Now I was moving the swell of the sea under the ship became more apparent and so I staggered to this nearer convenience. There was a curtain doorway and I pushed it back. The lantern in the passage provided enough light in the cabin through the canvas screens to make out the chair. Soon I had lifted the cover off the seat and was sitting comfortably listening to my piss splash into the chamberpot underneath.

God I hated Grant. The arrogant, opinionated little swine had no idea what he was doing and had risen entirely on the efforts of others. Surely, I reflected, Wellington could not be that blind to his faults. My musing was interrupted by a strange rustling nearby. It was that wretched lobster, which must have heard my noise. Well, I thought, I would have it for breakfast. But then as I put the lid back on the seat of the commode, I had a much better idea.

A few minutes later and I was walking back into the wardroom with a bottle in each hand. "Friends," I called out to still their conversation. "It occurs to me that this will probably be my last night in uniform and I could not think of a better bunch of fellows to spend it with. Here are a couple of bottles I have been saving for a special occasion and I would be honoured if you would share them with me."

There were cheers at that and general back-slapping. We had spent too long around that table in serious conversation, much of it depressingly gloomy. We all knew that many regiments would be reduced or disbanded now the war was over and several around the table were likely to be dismissed from the army or languish on half pay. There was a general feeling that it was time to celebrate and lighten the mood. I said a 'general' feeling but it was not absolute. Grant glared disapprovingly from his side of the table, as though he were a Calvinist minister and I had just suggested a bacchanalian orgy on the Sabbath. He had barely drunk anything all night and had a glass of what I suspected was watered-down wine before him. I was not the only one who noticed, though.

"Come now, Grant," called out Colborne. "We have won a war and beaten the most feared soldier in Europe, surely that deserves celebrating?"

He still looked stuffy and uncomfortable, but I knew just the angle to take. "Why, Colonel Grant is understandably suspicious as I will own that we have both used each other poorly in the past. But for my part, I would like to apologise. As I leave the army I do not want any bad feelings." And here I looked him squarely in the eye. "So what do you say, old fellow, will you share a drink with me?"

Of course, after an invitation like that, he had no choice. He smiled agreement, no doubt through gritted teeth, and warily watched as his old glass was swept away and a fresh, well-filled one put in its place. Oh, he knew me well enough and he must have suspected that my good humour was fishier than a mackerel gutter's apron. But while the others were calling out what a bluff sound fellow I was and how it had been an honour to serve alongside me, well he could hardly disagree without appearing mean-spirited. So once all glasses were charged young Jennings raised his and proposed a toast, "To the final victory." Glasses were drained and then refilled before Colborne offered 'Mrs Mulligan', who, it transpired, was some fearsome army wife who had once chased off two French infantrymen while armed with just a ladle. More stories and laughter followed while I settled down to watch and wait. One by one, officers got up to go to the jakes but Grant stayed put. Jennings went twice and I was beginning to give up hope when at last Grant staggered to his feet.

"If you will excuse me," he said primly before making his way to the door. I pictured him staggering his way down the passage. If anything the sea was even rougher now and he would probably be reaching for the wooden beams for support. There was not a chance someone as punctilious as Grant would be seen using the heads with the common seamen. No, he would go to his cabin and, like me, make out the layout of the little room from the light shining through the curtained doorway and canvas walls.

I reached forward and topped up my glass as I imagined him unbuttoning and lifting the lid of the commode to sit down. Would he spot my waiting friend before he lowered his wedding tackle well within the reach of those vicious pincers? I held my breath for a moment as I lifted my glass and then an ear-piercing shriek came from forward. It was a howl of animal agony that you could never imitate and it sent my brother officers running down the passage to investigate.

I did not need to hasten after them, I knew what they would find. It is true what they say: revenge is a dish best served cold. Grant had planned to sell me out when we were last in Paris together and then he kept quiet about my existence so my father and others thought me dead. I could just imagine how much he had enjoyed landing me in the soup when I was in Paris this time, not to mention the threat to my teeth. Well if you cross Flashy you had better watch your back… and your vitals too, for I will get even one way or another.

In their rush to leave the cabin no one noticed that I had stayed seated, and as the last officer left I raised my glass and smiled. Now, what was that toast of Jennings? Ah yes, "To the final victory!"

Historical Notes

As always, I am indebted to a range of sources for confirming the information detailed in Flashman's memoirs. These include *Waterloo* by Tim Clayton, *Marshal Ney* by A H Atteridge and *Napoleon and the Hundred Days* by Stephen Coote. These, in turn, reference a huge range of source material including hundreds of first-hand accounts, Wellington's despatches, Fouché's memoirs and other documents such as Napoleon's proclamations. So it is that most of the events and even some of the dialogue in Flashman's account is authenticated by others who were present at the time, the main exception being actions principally involving Flashman himself.

These references confirm not just the major incidents but the more trivial ones too, such as the last minute changes to the carpet in the Tuileries Palace and Napoleon being given too much help to mount his horse on the morning of Waterloo. But as well as being aligned with known historical facts, Flashman's extraordinary account also goes a long way to answering many of the questions that have puzzled historians for generations, such as why Ney changed sides, why Wellington was so sure that the initial French attack was only a diversion, whether Napoleon was ill on the day of the battle and how that extraordinary cavalry charge started. It also solves one of the great disputes that was bitterly argued between several generals after the battles. Soult and others were insistent that a message had been sent to Ney explaining the emperor's intentions for D'Erlon's men at Quatre Bras, but those around Ney were equally adamant he did not receive it.

I am pleased to say that Flashman also gives full credit to General Chassé's command in the outcome of Waterloo, something that was often omitted from contemporary British accounts that did not want to embarrass the regiments who fell back. It was often claimed that Halkett's brigade somehow 're-formed' while being charged and then fought off the first column of the Imperial Guard. Some may well have re-joined the battle, but it is clear that they could not have done so alone. Chassé complained bitterly that his men's efforts were not recognised in despatches while accounts from them, and survivors of the Imperial Guard, confirm that it was Chassé and his brave Dutch (and Belgian – although Belgium did not exist at that time) men that saved the allied line at this critical point. One can only wonder what would have happened if Napoleon had committed the three squares of the Old Guard left in the valley as well.

Finally, in the interests of public health, I should also point out that the yellow staining mushroom mentioned by Flashman exists and grows in French hedgerows in the summer, particularly during damp weather. *Agaricus Xanthodermus* can, in fact, be found across Europe and North America and does resemble a field mushroom. If you are in doubt which kind you have picked, you should cut them in half. If there is a yellow stain near the bottom of the stem, it should not be eaten.

Louis XVIII

Louis XVIII was the brother of Louis XVI, who was executed on the guillotine during the Revolution. He spent many years in exile before being given the throne of France on Napoleon's abdication in 1814. He was, as Flashman describes, grotesquely obese, far too big to mount a horse, never mind lead an army. His return was accompanied by many royalists who expected to have their lands and privileges restored. Louis XVIII was in a near impossible position as he had to balance the demands of loyal courtiers who had been in exile with him for over twenty years with the need to win over post-revolutionary France, which had culturally and economically moved on from the reign of his brother. On top of that, his treasury was empty after years of war, forcing him to go back on promises to abolish various taxes and pay Napoleon a pension.

The Duc d'Orleans was considered by some an alternative monarch, but the overthrow of a legitimate crowned head of state was unlikely to have been supported by royal families ruling the allied powers. Louis was restored after the Waterloo campaign and continued to rule France until his death in 1824. The Duc d'Orleans finally became king in 1830 and ruled until 1848 when he was overthrown and a second republic created – with its president Louis Napoleon

Bonaparte, nephew of the man beaten at Waterloo and later to become Emperor Napoleon III.

The One Hundred Days

Napoleon Bonaparte's second period of rule in France, lasting just one hundred days, is one of the most fascinating events in history. The emperor of the French had been forced to abdicate in April 1814, his soldiers defeated, betrayed by some of his generals and with parts of the country in open revolt. He had feared being lynched by his own people on his journey to Elba and yet less than a year later he was able to reconquer the country without firing a shot.

While most books on Waterloo concentrate on just the battle, Flashman's account goes into some detail on the changing circumstances in France that helped facilitate the emperor's return. His landing with just a few hundred men was viewed with scorn by royalists but they greatly underestimated Bonaparte's appeal to the army. He had made them masters of Europe while the royal princes generally viewed the soldiery with contempt. Napoleon capitalised on their complacency with rapid marches, bluster and bravado. Many sources both of this period of his rule and earlier, also confirm that Napoleon did indeed also have an exceptional memory for faces. Encounters with old soldiers, as described by Flashman, were one of the things that greatly endeared him to his men.

He was not universally popular and many questioned whether he could withstand a renewed war with the allies. But he did represent the recent pride and glory of France, while the alternative was to turn the clock back to pre-revolutionary royalist days. His return raised expectations across the political spectrum from the fervent revolutionary Jacobins to the Bonapartists, while many tried to keep their options open in case he was defeated. As Flashman shows, Napoleon was as much a politician as he was a general and not beyond telling lies to achieve his goals in either role.

He was much criticised for appointing Marshal Davout as his minister of war. Davout was the only marshal who had refused to join the Bourbons and was unquestionably loyal. He was an accomplished and skilful general and his presence instead of any of the marshals that Napoleon did take to Waterloo, may well have changed the outcome. However with Ney, Soult or Grouchy in charge at the War Ministry, there would probably not have been an army at all. Davout oversaw a Herculean effort to organise a massive increase to the French army and have them all equipped and ready in a very short amount of time. His commitment to his emperor meant that he was also the best man to leave in charge in the capital with the likes of Fouché on the prowl.

Fouché

Joseph Fouché, Duc d'Otranto was an extraordinary political schemer and plotter, whose remarkable career is well described by Flashman. He was Minister of Police from 1799 to 1810, accumulating an immense amount of information that he used to exert considerable influence. This made him too valuable for Napoleon to ignore on his return to power; indeed, he does seem to have defused a revolt in the west of the country as described by Flashman. In his memoirs, Fouché asserted that he was in communication with Wellington during the 'hundred days' of Napoleon's second period of rule. While this boast was initially dismissed as a malicious lie, evidence has been found that supports this claim.

After Napoleon's defeat at Waterloo, Fouché formed a provisional government. The emperor returned to Paris where Fouché encouraged him to flee to the United States. He even organised two French frigates to rendezvous with Napoleon on the French coast to convey him on his escape. However, in a typically duplicitous manner, Fouché was also sending messages to the allies to inform them of the emperor's escape plans and precisely where he could be found. Ultimately, Napoleon surrendered to a British naval vessel and spent his final days as a prisoner on the island of St Helena.

As a reward for his apparent support of the royalist cause, Fouché was restored to his post as Minister of Police under the rule of Louis XVIII. During that time he enthusiastically pursued and prosecuted a number of his former Bonapartist colleagues during a period known as the *White Terror*. But many royalists could not stomach the thought of this notorious regicide in government and he was dismissed in 1816. After a lifetime of treachery and intrigue, he died peacefully in his bed in 1820, aged 61.

Ney

Marshal Michel Ney's career is much as described by Flashman. He was unquestionably a courageous commander; the stories of his rescue of de Briqueville and bringing back the French rear-guard from Russia are all confirmed. But he was also notoriously hot-headed and few would describe him as a great strategic thinker. He has been roundly condemned by many as being responsible for the failure of the Waterloo campaign. In particular, he has been blamed for not capturing Quatre Bras late on the 15th or early on the 16th of June, but this seems unfair. On the morning of the 16th, both Napoleon and Ney needed to allow their troops to recover from the previous day's march and fighting. Even if he had captured the crossroads early on, it was unlikely that he would have been able to disengage from a growing British attack to go to the emperor's assistance at Ligny.

However, his decision to recall General D'Erlon did have disastrous consequences for the campaign. If D'Erlon had carried out the emperor's instructions then the Prussian army would have been comprehensively destroyed and in no position to come to Wellington's aid two days later. Additionally, if Ney had launched an attack on the British during the morning of the 17th at Quatre Bras he could have kept Wellington and his men pinned down until Napoleon arrived. Outnumbered and attacked on two sides with no prospect then of Prussian support, the British would almost certainly have been beaten.

There has also been much speculation on who ordered the massive cavalry charge at Waterloo and why it was not supported by infantry – which would have made the venture far more successful. The consensus seems to be that the charge was ordered by Ney, following reports that the British were in retreat. As Flashman suggests, the timing of Napoleon's announcement that the troops on the horizon were Grouchy, may also have had some bearing on Ney's need for an early resolution to the battle.

In the final stages of the encounter, Ney demonstrated almost suicidal courage, having five horses shot from under him during the day, but he remained unscathed. After Waterloo, he fled back to France and was encouraged to go into exile. Instead, he went into hiding and became one of the most wanted Bonapartist figures after the return of the Bourbon government. They could not forgive him his failure to arrest the emperor and eventually he was betrayed and brought to trial. The result was a forgone conclusion and he was sentenced to death by firing squad in December 1815.

Colquhoun Grant
Colquhoun Grant will be familiar to readers of *Flashman in the Peninsula* and *Flashman's Escape*. He had come to Wellington's attention as one of his 'exploring officers', essentially a uniformed scout behind enemy lines. In this role, assisted by a Spanish guide called León, he had been particularly effective. However, once he had been captured and León summarily executed, his decisions became somewhat more questionable. In particular, he gave a promise not to escape to a French general when Wellington was organising partisans to rescue him. Then when he was set free close to the French/Spanish border, instead of heading back to Spain, he decided to continue on to Paris.

He was appointed by Wellington as his Head of Intelligence for the Waterloo campaign. But as Flashman describes, he was singularly ineffective, allowing a huge French army to approach the border undetected. He did command some cavalry during the battle and maps show him stationed near Hougoumont.

His reputation struggled to recover from his failings at Waterloo but eventually he was given a regimental command in the first Anglo–Burmese War in 1821. He fell ill in the Far East and while he returned home his health never fully recovered. He was invalided out of the army in 1829 and died while taking the waters at Aachen the same year.

Thank you for reading this book and I hoped you enjoyed it. If so I would be grateful for any positive reviews on websites that you use to choose books. As there is no major publisher promoting this book, any recommendations to friends and family that you think would enjoy it would also be appreciated.

There is now a Thomas Flashman Books Facebook page and the www.robertbrightwell.com website to keep you updated on future books in the series. They also include portraits, pictures and further information on characters and events featured in the books.

Also by this author

Flashman and the Seawolf
This first book in the Thomas Flashman series covers his adventures with Thomas Cochrane, one of the most extraordinary naval commanders of all time.

From the brothels and gambling dens of London, through political intrigues and espionage, the action moves to the Mediterranean and the real life character of Thomas Cochrane. This book covers the start of Cochrane's career including the most astounding single ship action of the Napoleonic war.

Thomas Flashman provides a unique insight as danger stalks him like a persistent bailiff through a series of adventures that prove history really is stranger than fiction.

Flashman and the Cobra

This book takes Thomas to territory familiar to readers of his nephew's adventures, India, during the second Mahratta war. It also includes an illuminating visit to Paris during the Peace of Amiens in 1802.

As you might expect Flashman is embroiled in treachery and scandal from the outset and, despite his very best endeavours, is often in the thick of the action. He intrigues with generals, warlords, fearless warriors, nomadic bandit tribes, highland soldiers and not least a four-foot-tall former nautch dancer, who led the only Mahratta troops to leave the battlefield of Assaye in good order.

Flashman gives an illuminating account with a unique perspective. It details feats of incredible courage (not his, obviously) reckless folly and sheer good luck that were to change the future of India and the career of a general who would later win a war in Europe.

Flashman in the Peninsula

While many people have written books and novels on the Peninsular War, Flashman's memoirs offer a unique perspective. They include new accounts of famous battles, but also incredible incidents and characters almost forgotten by history. Flashman is revealed as the catalyst to one of the greatest royal scandals of the nineteenth century which disgraced a prince and ultimately produced one of our greatest novelists. In Spain and Portugal he witnesses catastrophic incompetence and incredible courage in equal measure. He is present at an extraordinary action where a small group of men stopped the army of a French marshal in its tracks. His flatulent horse may well have routed a Spanish regiment, while his cowardice and poltroonery certainly saved the British army from a French trap.

Accompanied by Lord Byron's dog, Flashman faces death from Polish lancers and a vengeful Spanish midget, not to mention finding time to perform a blasphemous act with the famous Maid of Zaragoza. This is an account made more astonishing as the key facts are confirmed by various historical sources.

Flashman's Escape

This book covers the second half of Thomas Flashman's experiences in the Peninsular War and follows on from *Flashman in the Peninsula*.

Having lost his role as a staff officer, Flashman finds himself commanding a company in an infantry battalion. In between cuckolding his soldiers and annoying his superiors, he finds himself at the heart of the two bloodiest actions of the war. With drama and disaster in equal measure, he provides a first-hand account of not only the horror of battle but also the bloody aftermath.

Hopes for a quieter life backfire horribly when he is sent behind enemy lines to help recover an important British prisoner, who also happens to be a hated rival. His adventures take him the length of Spain and all the way to Paris on one of the most audacious wartime journeys ever undertaken. With the future of the French empire briefly placed in his quaking hands, Flashman dodges lovers, angry fathers, conspirators and ministers of state in a desperate effort to keep his cowardly carcass in one piece. It is a historical roller-coaster ride that brings together various extraordinary events, while also giving a disturbing insight into the creation of a French literary classic!

Flashman and Madison's War

This book finds Thomas, a British army officer, landing on the shores of the United States at the worst possible moment – just when the United States has declared war with Britain! Having already endured enough with his earlier adventures, he desperately wants to go home but finds himself drawn inexorably into this new conflict. He is soon dodging musket balls, arrows and tomahawks as he desperately tries to keep his scalp intact and on his head.

It is an extraordinary tale of an almost forgotten war, with inspiring leaders, incompetent commanders, a future American president, terrifying warriors (and their equally intimidating women), brave sailors, trigger-happy madams and a girl in a wet dress who could have brought a city to a standstill. Flashman plays a central role and reveals that he was responsible for the disgrace of one British general, the capture of another and for one of the biggest debacles in British military history.

Due to be published Autumn 2017:

Flashman and the Emperor

This seventh instalment in the memoirs of the Georgian rogue Thomas Flashman reveals that, despite his suffering through the Napoleonic Wars, he did not get to enjoy a quiet retirement. Indeed, middle age finds him acting just as disgracefully as in his youth, as old friends pull him unwittingly back into the fray.

He re-joins his former comrade in arms, Thomas Cochrane, in what was intended to be a peaceful and profitable sojourn in South America. Instead, he finds himself enjoying drug fuelled orgies in Rio, trying his hand at silver smuggling and escaping earthquakes in Chile, before being reluctantly shanghaied into the Brazilian Navy.

Sailing with Cochrane again, he joins the admiral in what must be one of the most extraordinary periods of his already legendary career. With a crew more interested in fighting each other than the enemy, they use Cochrane's courage, Flashman's cunning and an outrageous bluff to carve out nothing less than an empire which will stand the test of time.